More praise for <u>BLACKOUT</u>
and the "King of the aviation thriller."*

"Brilliantly hair-raising . . . nonstop action."

—*Publishers Weekly*

"Pounce on John J. Nance's terrific aviation drama. *Blackout* [is] terrifying."

—*New York Post*

"Nance keeps the tension high. His hand for crackling intensity remains peerless."

—*Kirkus Reviews*

THE LAST HOSTAGE

"A thrilling ride . . . [Will] keep even the most experienced thriller addicts strapped into their seat for the whole flight."

—*People*

"Nance . . . knows how to keep his readers turning the pages."

—*Booklist*

"Slam-bang special effects . . . right up to its startling . . . climax."

—*Kirkus Reviews*

MEDUSA'S CHILD

"So compelling it's tough to look away."   —*People*

"A high-flying thriller . . . Nance delivers plenty of punch."

—*The Orange County Register*

"Gripping."   —*The Indianapolis Star*

"Fast-paced and exciting."   —*Detroit Free Press*

"The nonstop ride of your life."   —*Rocky Mountain News*

"Nance puts the thrill back in 'thriller'."

—*Statesman Journal* (Salem, OR)

"Will leave readers breathless."   —*Montgomery Advertiser*

Hold on tight for more praise . . .

PANDORA'S CLOCK

blackout

JOHN J. NANCE

JOVE BOOKS, NEW YORK

This is a work of fiction. Names, characters, places and incidents are either the product of the author's imagination or are used fictitiously, and any resemblance to actual persons, living or dead, business establishments, events or locales is entirely coincidental.

BLACKOUT

A Jove Book / published by arrangement with
the author

PRINTING HISTORY
G. P. Putnam's Sons edition / February 2000
Jove edition / February 2001

All rights reserved.
Copyright © 2000 by John Nance.
This book, or parts thereof, may not be reproduced
in any form without permission.
For information address: The Berkley Publishing Group,
a division of Penguin Putnam Inc.,
375 Hudson Street, New York, New York 10014.

The Penguin Putnam Inc. World Wide Web site address is
http://www.penguinputnam.com

ISBN: 0-515-13012-5

A JOVE BOOK®
Jove Books are published by The Berkley Publishing Group,
a division of Penguin Putnam Inc.,
375 Hudson Street, New York, New York 10014.
JOVE and the "J" design
are trademarks belonging to Penguin Putnam Inc.

PRINTED IN THE UNITED STATES OF AMERICA

10 9 8 7 6 5 4 3 2 1

Acknowledgments

The history of this work would fill a book in itself, and there are far too many people across the miles to thank, including a cadre of law enforcement, legal, aviation, and communications compatriots arrayed over a half-dozen continents.

Some specific thank-you's, however, are appropriate.

First, my great appreciation to my editor at Putnam, David Highfill, and to my publisher, Leslie Gelbman, for all their help and enthusiasm, and to my agents, George and Olga Wieser of the Wieser and Wieser Agency in New York.

Thanks also to Dr. Gary Cowart of Seattle, now an outstanding dentist and fellow author, but thirty years ago a Marine stationed near Da Nang, Vietnam. Gary helped immensely in checking and refining my personal memories of Vietnam in getting the terrain, flora, and fauna right. And thanks also to Dr. Cowart's brother, Randy, who added insight to a delightful afternoon of maps and memories.

My specific thanks as well to retired FBI Agent Larry Montague, who once again lent his expertise to make sure Kat Bronsky's world squares with the real thing.

There are some folks I've got to thank anonymously for obvious reasons: the individual inside the U.S. State Department who helped with a myriad of information from Vietnam to the way a Secretary of State uses communications; the unnamed source who helped with the capabilities of the National Reconnaissance Office; and a supervisor at Hong

Kong Approach who sidestepped the normal political worries late one night to talk to me.

And thanks as well to the uncounted Kat Bronskys out there who are truly Kat's prototype: capable, professional, dedicated women who refuse to surrender their femininity or their sense of humor in the face of the indefensible career barriers raised by the clueless among my gender.

John J. Nance
University Place, WA
October 15, 1999

To my mother,
Texas poet Peggy Zuleika Lynch,
whose dynamic creativity and
love of life lights the way

Author's Note

Chapters in this novel list the local time and, after a slash, the Zulu time. In the aviation world, Z time, or Zulu time, refers to Universal Time—formerly known as Greenwich Mean Time.

In winter, when Daylight Saving Time is not in use, the East Coast of the United States is five hours earlier than Zulu time; for example, 4:00 P.M. in Washington, D.C., is 2100Z, and 3:00 A.M. is 0800Z. The time in London in winter is the same as Zulu time, and Germany is an hour later (Zulu plus one hour). Hong Kong is eight hours later than Zulu. Vietnam is seven hours later.

Prologue

Karen Briant suppressed a smile as she watched Jim Olson struggle. His athletic body was stretched to its six-foot limit, his jeans just inches from her face as he stood on tiptoe and yanked again at the door of the overhead compartment. It opened at last, and she heard him unzip his carry-on bag and rummage around. He grunted with satisfaction and reclosed the bag before looking down at her.

"Good. I feel better now," he said, snapping the compartment shut.

"And what, exactly," she began as he slid back into the window seat, "were you afraid you'd forgotten, Sir?" She ruffled her shoulder-length auburn hair and looked at him with mock suspicion. "Not another self-indulgent gift from Victoria's Secret, I hope?" Another bikini would be too much. She was already feeling overexposed in the revealing sundress that he'd bought for her.

He smirked and shook his head in response as he scanned the right wing of the huge three-engine Boeing/McDonnell-Douglas MD-11 jetliner, noting the towering cumulus clouds in the distance. He turned back to her sparkling green eyes, his laugh coming easily. It was a feature of him she particularly treasured.

"Not important, young lady," he said, tuning out a routine PA announcement.

"Sure it's important!" Karen coaxed. "When I agree to spend a week in the Canary Islands with a man, I want to make sure he's got the right stuff."

"How do you mean, 'right stuff'?" Jim asked, raising his eyebrows.

"Well, you're a pilot, and pilots are supposed to pack the right stuff, right?"

"I'm an airline pilot, not Chuck Yeager."

"Maybe that's not the 'stuff' I'm talking about. You obviously have something in that bag up there you were worried about leaving."

"And now I'm not," Jim said, suppressing the urge to give her the engagement ring now as he rode the small wave of relief that he hadn't left it back in Houston.

No, he cautioned himself. *It all depends on this week together.*

He had to be sure.

She squeezed his hand and chuckled as Jim looked out the window, mentally calculating the distance to the line of 60,000-foot-high cumulonimbus clouds towering over the Gulf of Mexico to the north of the jetliner's course. He wondered what the pilots were seeing on radar. The small but vicious hurricane north of that line was threatening New Orleans, but they should slip safely to the south of it—according to his check of the weather map a few hours ago.

Relax, for crying out loud! Jim told himself. *This isn't even your airline! Besides, we're on vacation. They can handle it just fine without me.*

He squeezed Karen's hand in return, breathing in the soft hint of her perfume and letting a warm tingle of anticipation wash over him.

This was going to be a wonderful week.

KEY WEST NAVAL AIR STATION, FLORIDA
11:43 A.M. LOCAL/1643 ZULU

Retired Chief Master Sergeant Rafe Jones looked up from the complex instruments of the mobile test van he operated under civilian contract for the Air Force. He squinted through his sunglasses, trying to focus on the aging F-106 fighter/interceptor as it sat at the far end of the runway, its image undulating in the heat, waiting for his remote control team to start the takeoff.

Rafe took a deep breath, savoring the signature aroma of the Gulf of Mexico wafting in on a hint of fresh salt air, the heat a balmy pleasure. He double-checked the data link between the mobile control van and the aircraft, satisfied it was steady on all channels. His mouth was dry again, and not for want of water. This was the part that always unnerved him: launching a full-sized pilotless airplane over a populated area with nothing to keep it safe but a data stream of radioed commands. Sometimes the F-106 target drones his team operated carried a live Air Force safety pilot, but today only a dummy crammed full of sensors occupied the cockpit.

He glanced at Randy and Bill, the flight techs who controlled the jet.

"Rafe, what's the holding fix again?" Randy asked on the interphone.

"Fluffy intersection, about thirty miles south," Rafe answered, mentally picturing the specially created MOA—Military Operations Area.

"Isn't that awful close to Uncle Fidel's turf?"

"We know nothing," Rafe said, smiling. "We have no reason to confirm or deny our intention to irritate Havana."

"Yeah, right," Randy replied. "Wink, wink, nudge, nudge, say no more."

The tower controller cleared the F-106 team for departure. Rafe nodded to his team and watched Bill push the throttle to full power in preparation for brake release.

ABOARD SEAAIR 122, IN FLIGHT,
230 MILES SOUTH OF TAMPA
12:01 P.M. LOCAL/1701 ZULU

The staccato pulse of lightning from the angry clouds to the north flickered through the left-hand windows of the MD-11, riveting Karen's attention and stiffening her back. Jim could feel her left hand tighten on the armrest as she turned to look.

"We're a safe distance to the south," he reassured her, momentarily puzzled by an incongruous flash of lightning from the right side of the cabin. The MD-11 suddenly rolled sharply to the left. The bank reversed itself as quickly, and the nose came up.

Obviously he punched off the autopilot and the bird was out of trim, he thought. Jim glanced at Karen, feeling uneasy.

"Must be a buildup just ahead, Honey," he said, forcing a smile. "The flight crew was probably debating which way to go around it and changed their minds. We'd all like to be smoother on the controls."

The bank angle was past thirty degrees now, which was the normal maximum for a jetliner.

But why is it increasing?

The nose pitched up as if they were climbing, but more power would be needed to climb, and the whine of the engines hadn't increased. Another sudden roll, this time to the left, and the nose was coming down.

Jim felt himself get lighter as the flight controls were pushed forward up in the cockpit. He felt a cold chill up his spine as he tried to recall what normal maneuvers would cause such gyrations.

There were none. It wasn't normal.

Jim glanced toward the right wing, puzzled by the complete absence of clouds in that direction. There had been lightning out there.

"Jim?" Karen began, her voice tight. She sat forward in her seat, aware of the increasing slipstream as the nose continued to drop and the airspeed built.

There were voices around them now, acknowledging the shared concern, a communal rumble accompanied by alarmed glances. The MD-11 steepened its left bank, the nose dropping more, the speed rising, the huge jetliner turning sharply toward the thunderstorm to the north.

"Jim, what's he doing up there?" Karen asked, her face ashen, her hand now squeezing the blood out of his. His answer stalled in the back of his mind as he fumbled for his seat belt. "Stay here. I'm going to the cockpit."

She said nothing, letting his hand slide reluctantly from hers as he rose from the seat and pulled away, glancing back for a second, noting how beautiful she was.

The MD-11's roll had reversed back to the right. The nose was coming back up slightly, but the control movements had become jerky and excessive, as if the pilots were fighting the aircraft. Jim moved forward quickly, his eyes on the cockpit door some eighty feet away, aware that his intervention in another airline's affairs would be unwelcome. He could see two flight attendants ahead of him, their eyes betraying concern, their professional smiles trying to mask it.

The growing asymmetrical G-force was pulling him off balance, pushing him into the row of seats to the right. Jim fought to stand upright, but the cabin was heeling over like a yacht about to capsize in a gale, the MD-11's right turn obviously uncoordinated, as someone's foot pushed the left rudder pedal.

What the hell? Jim thought. There were gasps of fear around him as he struggled to keep moving forward. Something was very wrong, but it couldn't be loss of control. The flight controls were operating but being jerked in crazy directions.

He moved with urgency, supporting his weight on the seat backs, his hands brushing the heads of startled passengers. In the galley ahead he could hear plates and utensils sliding and clattering, some spilling from the service carts as a wide-eyed young blonde in a flight attendant's uniform spotted him.

"Sir!" Her hand shot out, the palm extended. "SIR! Take your seat immediately and fasten your seat belt!" She moved into the aisle to block him.

"I'm a pilot!" he said, regretting the lame response.

"I don't care, Sir . . ." she began, stopping in midsentence as the gravity went fully to zero and she floated up before his eyes toward the ceiling.

Ahead of Jim, two dozen shafts of sunlight stabbed

across the first-class cabin from each window and moved vertically from low to high as the aircraft rolled to the right. He grabbed the bulkhead and propelled himself past the flight attendant like an astronaut, his peripheral vision picking up the ocean's surface through the windows.

We're inverted! The potentially fatal fact was merely a benchmark in an impossibly bizarre sequence. His entire being focused on the cockpit door less than thirty feet ahead. The door would be locked. He had to get there, get in, and stop whatever was happening!

The huge MD-11 was still rolling, coming back right side up as gravity once again claimed the occupants of the cabin, and people and service carts and flight attendants crashed to the floor. Ahead of him half the overhead compartments had popped open, spilling their contents into the air, pummeling the passengers below.

An elderly woman had floated up from her seat during the zero-G maneuver, then crashed painfully to the floor. Her body was blocking the aisle ahead as Jim tried to step over her and tripped. The G-forces increased as the scream of the high-speed airflow outside rose, forcing the nose up as they continued to roll, undoubtedly hurtling now toward the surface of the Gulf of Mexico.

Jim's hands clawed for a seat back, raking across a man's head in the process. There were sharp cries of fear from all around him. Once more he pulled with all his might, launching himself through the air and slamming into the back of the cockpit door with a painful thud. He pulled frantically at it and found it locked, as expected.

Time had dilated, seconds moving past like minutes, the feeling of running from a horror and getting nowhere overwhelming him. There was no way to tell if they were upside down or right side up, but they were diving, with only seconds left.

Jim braced his feet against the doorjamb and pulled.

It wouldn't budge.

He pulled again, harder, but the lock was too strong.

The airspeed increased. They couldn't be more than 10,000 feet above the surface. The whine of the slipstream was deafening. A mental snapshot of his bride-to-be alone in the cabin behind him drove him on. He tightened his grip on the door handle, willed himself beyond the limits, and heaved backward, feeling an explosion of pain in his hands as the rising, screaming sound of nearly supersonic flight washed out all other sensations.

The door broke open and he forced himself into the cockpit in time to see the windscreen fill with the sight of white caps and blue water as the MD-11 traversed the last few yards to the surface in the space of his last heartbeat.

chapter

1

FBI Special Agent Katherine Bronsky yelped as she fell backward across the far edge of the king-size bed and rolled out of sight behind it, landing on her hip with an unceremonious thud.

Wonderful! she thought. *Another bruise the size of Cleveland.*

"Kat? *KAT?*"

The male voice coming from the speaker of her notebook computer wafted over the bed to compete with the vibrant roar of downtown Hong Kong's living wave of sound, which cascaded through the partially open balcony doors.

Kat lifted herself to a sitting position and peeked over the bed as she blew a wayward strand of hair away from her eyes, feeling like a klutz.

Now that was embarrassing! Thank goodness he can't see me.

Assistant Deputy Director Jake Rhoades's puzzled expression was clearly visible on her computer screen as he made a futile effort to see her from his end in Washington. There was a tiny camera built into the lid of her laptop computer, but she'd draped a pair of panties over it while dressing. The new secure video capability was fun, but there were limits to what she wanted Washington to see.

"I guess in the interest of full disclosure I should admit that the thud you heard was me hitting the floor. I tripped," she explained in a loud voice, leaving out the fact that she'd tangled her feet in her own panty hose and all but hog-tied herself. "Sorry to interrupt what you were saying. You were in the process of warning me not to embarrass the Bureau, but you hadn't said why."

He ignored the reference. "You sure everything's okay there? I still can't see you. My screen is just showing a gauzy white."

"I don't *want* you to see me." Kat laughed as she began hopping again on one foot across the plush rug toward the desk, trying once more to pull on the other leg of her panty hose as she glanced at the clock on the bedside table. "I'm not decent."

There was a pause and a wicked chuckle from Washington. "Well . . . now that you mention it . . . there *are* those in the Bureau who would agree with you, Kat."

She finished adjusting the panty hose as she shook her head in mock disgust, glad he couldn't see the gesture. "I meant, Sir, that I'm not appropriately attired to appear on your computer screen in front of my brother agents, some of whom may not be gender-blind."

"Ah. Then I'm technically glad you didn't, since I wouldn't want to be accused of sexual enjoyment."

"That's *harassment,* Jake. You wouldn't want to be accused of sexual *harassment.*"

"That too. Look, let's get back to the Cuban crash, okay?"

Kat moved behind the desk to look at herself in the full-length mirror, listening carefully to what he was saying but substantially pleased by what she saw. Fifteen pounds lighter in the last six months, with a firm stomach at last, was something to be proud of. Solid evidence of the self-discipline she expected of herself.

"I thought that MD-eleven was an American airliner," she

said, glancing at her handwritten notes while adjusting her bra and straightening a cascade of shoulder-length chestnut-brown hair. Jake Rhoades was an important official at FBI headquarters, while she was assigned to the D.C. field office, reporting to him on special assignments. Nevertheless, Jake was easy to talk to, and their relationship, while appropriately professional, was cordial. She could kid him without fear.

There was a mumbled reply from the Beltway and she glanced back at the screen to see if the signal was breaking up.

"I'm sorry, Jake. Say again, please."

"I said I probably ought to just give you a synopsis of the situation."

"Good idea," she replied, glancing at her watch and diverting her gaze toward the couch, where she'd laid out two blouses. She had to appear downstairs in thirty minutes, looking perfectly professional and perfectly feminine at the same time. The expensive charcoal-gray suit she'd bought especially for the speech was ready. But which blouse sent the right message?

"Okay," Jake continued. "You already know the basic fact situation, right?"

She walked quickly to the couch, holding her chin in her right hand as she looked at the two blouses and nodded unseen toward the computer screen. "I believe so," she said, smoothing the frilly one, aware that it still bore the scent of her favorite perfume. "An American MD-eleven crashed with no survivors a mile inside Cuban waters for unknown reasons, killing three hundred twenty-six, and the President ordered a naval blockade of the recovery area, which triggered a hysterical reaction from Castro, which in turn has triggered hysterical speculation that Cuba somehow shot it down for penetrating Cuban airspace, which would be bizarre given all the commercial air traffic flying daily over Cuba. The cockpit voice recorder and flight data recorder were missing for three weeks, then mysteriously showed up, pinging their little hearts out underwater, and the National Transportation Safety Board seriously suspects that someone recovered them earlier and tampered with the CVR tape since the last three minutes are gone, even though the aircraft never lost power." She straightened and glanced at the screen. "Is that about right?"

Jake's eyebrows had risen. "I'm impressed, Kat. You listen well."

She picked up the plain white blouse and held it at arm's length. It was spartan and uninteresting, but in keeping with the seriousness of a major address on airline terrorism. "Did I miss anything?" she asked.

"Not really, except we're sure Cuba has a small submarine, and there is some evidence that they could have snatched those black boxes and altered them to hide whatever really happened. And you know that the Bureau and the NTSB are working hand in hand on this, which means *we* get more than our share of media pressure."

"Don't worry. I won't talk to the media."

"Well, you may not have a choice. A major conference on air terrorism with you as the closing speaker is a magnet for media types looking for a quote. I'm not saying don't talk to them. What I'm saying is, don't speculate! The nuts are coming out of the woodwork with every conceivable conspiracy theory, trying to tie it in with Swissair, EgyptAir, TWA 800, and God knows what else. Before long, they'll have this connected to the *Challenger* accident and the loss of the *Titanic*."

"Such is the nature of conspiracy theorists," Kat replied, studying the extreme fatigue showing in Jake's eyes. He was only forty-six, but he looked a decade older.

"True. Look, Kat, the President and his people are pressing the hell out of NTSB, and us, to find a theory that doesn't include Cuba, conspiracies, space aliens, or terrorists. The Bureau isn't going to give in to that pressure, of course, nor is the NTSB, but I've gotta tell you, it's becoming excruciating. All I'm saying is, whatever you do, don't fan the flames by pointing in one direction or another."

"So, if they ask me whether this *could* have been an act of terrorism . . . ?"

"Then say we have insufficient information to point in

any direction. Tell them that massive mechanical failure is just as possible as anything else. The NTSB's favorite phrase, I'm told, is that it's too early to rule anything in or anything out."

"Got it."

"I mean it, Kat. Be *really* careful. One slip with the media and your name goes up in lights. Again."

"And . . . you're saying that this would be bad, right?"

"Kat!"

She suppressed a chuckle. "I'm kidding, Boss. But what if it *is* Cuba?"

"Then after the inevitable invasion force lands, you can apply for a position as the Bureau's legal attaché in Havana. I almost pity Fidel if he's responsible for this."

"What's the chance this is terrorism, Jake? The real word, not the party line."

There was an ominous silence from the other end, broken at last by a sigh.

"If this is an act of terrorism—not a mechanical malfunction, and not something the Cubans did—then we're in deep trouble. We haven't got a clue how they did it, although a missile is a distinct possibility. That's why I doubt . . ."

There was the sound of a telephone ringing in the background.

"Kat, can you hold a second?"

"You bet," she replied, looking at her watch again, her mind focused on the mystery of the MD-11 crash and the frustrating lack of evidence. Her eyes drifted back to the couch.

The frilly one. I enjoy looking feminine. If the boys have a problem with that, so be it! She snatched the blouse from the couch and began putting it on, smiling to herself, remembering the compliments and the glances she always got when she wore it. She buttoned it and removed her dark gray skirt from the hanger, pulling it on and adjusting it to let the hem fall just above her knees, wondering how much longer Jake would be. A touch-up with the hair spray and a quick review of the script and she'd be ready.

Jake's voice returned. "You there, Kat?"

She began moving toward the computer as she finished fastening the skirt. "Right here, Jake."

"I've got to go. Break a leg."

Kat reached out and snapped the panties off the tiny camera, smiling broadly. "Thank you for your support, Sir! I'll report back tomorrow."

"Ah, may a senior officer be permitted to tell a subordinate agent that her appearance is, ah, in keeping with the highest traditions of the Bureau?"

She smiled and cocked her head slightly. "He certainly may."

"Then please be so advised."

She saluted smartly. "Yes, Sir. Highest traditions. I take it that's a reference to J. Edgar's alternate dress code?" She laughed, noting his momentary confusion, her blue eyes sparkling at the compliment. Jake was married and moral, but very male.

"Ah, I meant . . ."

"I know what you meant, Jake," she said, "and I appreciate it very much."

Kat disconnected and closed the screen as her eyes darted again to the time. *Twenty minutes!*

She finished touching up her makeup to fit the harsh lights of the ballroom twenty floors below. Makeup, hair, earrings, the dark-gray pumps, and the suit coat. Then a quick run-through of the script.

Men have it so easy! she thought. *Shirt, tie, pants, coat, and out the door.*

The exotic aroma of sandalwood filled her consciousness again, and she stood for a moment with her eyes closed to breathe deeply. The cabinetry was made from it. Sandalwood and teak were set off by the fresh arrangement of fragrant tropical flowers sent to each speaker, along with a tray of fruit and cheese and champagne. A Bach concerto was playing softly in the background, adding a touch of panache.

She picked up a piece of aged Brie and sipped a wineglass of mineral water, trying not to look at the digital clock that nagged her from the bedside table. There was an incredible sunset of deep reds and oranges gathering beyond the balcony like a living palette, filling the harbor with reflected color. It was too much to ignore—like the sunsets her father used to point out at unexpected times and places, even in the middle of an angry lecture once when she was eight.

Or was it nine?

She smiled at the memory of how he could be so firm and forbidding one second—the epitome of untethered authority—and a wide-eyed, wondering disciple of nature's beauty the next. An iron-hard senior FBI agent with the soul of a poet.

She leaned over to the bedside controls to raise the volume of the concerto playing on the built-in audio system. The lyricism of Vivaldi had heralded her entry into the room two days ago, heightening the feeling of unbridled elegance with each sunrise and sunset in the exotic port whose very name evoked images of intrigue.

Kat slid the door open and stepped onto the balcony, hugging herself absently as she drank in the exotic beauty before her.

Here I am, Dad, a full-fledged FBI agent on assignment in paradise! she thought, the small wave of pride and delight metered by the reality that she could no longer pick up the phone and share moments like this with him.

Her smile faded as she studied the glow to the west.

I miss you, Daddy. But I'm making it.

chapter
2

Kat Bronsky stood behind the ornate rosewood podium in the cavernous auditorium and mentally counted to five, milking the dramatic pause. The audience was virtually silent now, hanging on her words and waiting, all 1,600 of them, their minds whirling with the graphic images she'd painted of the well-known international hijacking that had terminated in New York.

"Eighteen hours we held off a final assault with the SWAT teams," she continued, speaking the words with deliberate care, giving the various translators working in carrels behind the curtain time to do their job.

"Eighteen hours of continuous demands, continuous threats, countered by the only humane weapon we ever really have: the fine art of negotiator delay. But in that eighteenth hour . . ."

Again she paused, relishing the sight of the huge chandeliers above the audience and memorizing all of it—even the slight aroma of cigarette smoke supposedly banned from the hall. They all knew the conclusion, but they were caught up in the art of her storytelling.

". . . suddenly the left forward door of the seven-forty-seven opened, and instead of a firestorm and dead bodies, three weary, defeated hijackers emerged, hands in the air, leaving two hundred eighty-seven passengers alive and uninjured and free to go home to their families. That, you see, is the point. We're human. Even the worst among us. Not every hostage situation can be ended this successfully, of course, but the reactions of even the most hysterical and maniacal humans can be manipulated to some degree for the greater good, if we refuse to be stampeded. Thank you very much!"

Kat stepped back slightly and nodded to the audience, wondering what to expect. The conference had been fruitful, but she was the last act and most of the delegates were tired and ready to leave. Yet they were getting to their feet, clapping heartily for her. Some of the Asian delegates even bowed in her direction.

Good grief, a standing ovation! The noise was sustained and tumultuous. Kat was stunned. She was losing the effort to control her broad smile.

The host of the conference materialized beside her as the applause subsided, announcing that they had ten minutes for questions. A hand went up too far back to make out the owner and someone with a portable microphone moved toward the man.

Kat fielded questions about the AirBridge 737 hijacking that had made her famous in the Bureau, then answered several about tactics. Glowing with success and trying to hide it, she almost missed the name and position of the last questioner.

"Robert MacCabe, Agent Bronsky, from the *Washington Post*. We're all aware of the MD-eleven crash just inside Cuban waters several months ago. So far, no cause has been clearly indicated and Cuba claims they're not responsible. What is the likelihood that the flight was brought down not by the Cubans, but by an act of terrorism? And, if there is a possibility, what weapon could have been used?"

Robert MacCabe? she thought, trying not to look startled. *Jake was right! What's one of the* Post's *star investigative reporters doing in Hong Kong?*

Kat cleared her throat. "Are you asking for my personal opinion, Mr. MacCabe, or the Bureau's official reaction?"

"I'll take whatever I can get," he quipped, sending a ripple of laughter through the hall. "Please just give us your best assessment on cause."

"I can't speak for the Bureau on an active investigation," she replied with a forced smile, wishing he'd sit down and stop deflating the bubble of goodwill now threatening to drain away from the auditorium. "As you know, the FBI is deeply involved, which means it's out of bounds for me to talk about. Are there any other questions?" Kat asked, looking pointedly away from MacCabe.

"Yes," Robert MacCabe said into the microphone.

Kat's eyes shifted back to him.

"We're here," he continued, "for one of the most important conferences on terrorist hijackings in history, and *you're* here, Agent Bronsky, because, as a hostage negotiator, you're one of the FBI's experts in an area that has caused the FBI to project itself into worldwide involvement against airborne terrorist acts."

"And your question, Mr. MacCabe?" Kat interjected.

"I'm coming to it. On top of that, your excellent speech shows there probably isn't a delegate in this room who knows more about the subject than you. Yet, even though it didn't involve hostages, you want us to believe that you're not aware of the details of the Cuban crash investigation as a potential terrorist act?"

A murmur of voices rippled across the audience as the translation was finished.

"Oh, I'm *very* aware of the details, Mr. MacCabe, but I'm also well aware that our time is up." Somewhere overhead a jet was passing, and she found herself concentrating on the subtle vibrations coursing through the hall.

"I'm wondering," MacCabe went on, "why no one seems to be openly talking about the possibility that a terrorist act is involved? The FBI certainly wasn't slow to come to that conclusion with the TWA crash off Long Island in 1996."

"And we were dead wrong, weren't we!" Kat snapped, cautioning herself too late to keep irritation out of her voice. "Look. This isn't the appropriate forum for your questions, Sir. And we're out of time. Thank you again," she said to the audience, nodding as she stepped away from the podium. She let her eyes roam around the hall, aware that the spell her speech had cast had been broken.

Damn him! she thought, as the host moved to the podium to thank her once again before closing the conference.

Kat was engulfed at the foot of the stage by delegates wanting to talk, offering business cards and congratulations for a good speech.

So the damage wasn't total! she told herself, but the smoldering desire to find Robert MacCabe and snap his head off was leading her to short responses and a continuous push toward the exit. With her purse slung over her shoulder and a leather folder held tightly against her chest, she paused for a second outside the door, her eyes sweeping left and right before coming to rest on a figure almost directly in front of her.

Robert MacCabe was waiting ten feet away. His large hazel eyes watched her as he leaned uneasily against a huge concrete post with both hands shoved into the pockets of his suit coat. A case that probably held a computer was at his feet.

Kat strode the few feet to him with her jaw set, ignoring the mingling aromas of rich coffee from an espresso cart and suppressing her desire for some.

"So, Mr. MacCabe, to what do I owe the honor of that attack? That little sabotage-the-speaker routine?"

He smiled nervously, a disarming, toothy, Kennedy-esque smile, his tanned face framed by a full and slightly tousled head of dark hair. *Five foot ten, late thirties, and probably an Ivy Leaguer,* Kat decided. He was very young to have won a Pulitzer, but a lot better-looking in person than in the newspaper picture she remembered.

Robert MacCabe straightened up and took his hands from his pockets, raising them in a gesture of capitulation. "Agent Bronsky, honestly, I wasn't trying to sabotage you."

She fixed him with a steely glare. "That's pretty hard to believe!"

He stared back, his eyes penetrating hers with equal intensity. "Look . . ." he began.

"No, *you* look, Mr. MacCabe! What I want to know is precisely what . . ."

She paused as he put his index finger to his lips and inclined his head toward several delegates standing nearby, talking in a cloud of cigarette smoke. The gesture instantly irritated her. She lowered her voice to just above a whisper, angry with herself for having lost control and ignoring the pleasant hint of a woody aftershave.

"I want to know what you were trying to accomplish in there, needling me about that MD-eleven crash and terrorism."

"We have to talk," he said simply.

Kat straightened up, her eyebrows raised. "I was under the impression that we were doing precisely that. Talk about what?"

His eyes had shifted to another group of delegates talking in the distance, audible above the background din of distant traffic and closer voices, and he continued to watch them as he answered. "About that crash. About the reason for my questions in there." He wasn't smiling now, she noticed.

Kat shook her head in disgust. "Sorry to disappoint you, but you are *not* going to trick me into a statement!"

Robert MacCabe's hand was up in a "stop" gesture. "No! I'm trying to *give* you something, not get an interview. I remember you from the Colorado hijacking. I've been following you."

Kat tried not to look stunned. "You *followed* me here?"

His eyes snapped back to hers. "No, I mean I've followed your career. I was assigned to cover this convention for the *Post.* That's why *I'm* here."

Kat stood in silence for a few moments, trying to read his expression. He shook his head and rolled his eyes before filling the silence. "Look, I'm sorry, I'm afraid I'm not making myself clear. I bored into you back there because I had to know if you were the right one to talk to." MacCabe looked around quickly. "And you are. Can we, maybe, go somewhere private?"

"Why?" Kat asked, aware that one of the delegates was waiting patiently at a respectful distance to talk with her. She smiled at the man and gestured "just a moment" before turning back to MacCabe.

"Because . . ." He stopped and sighed, shaking his head as he momentarily dropped his gaze to the floor, licked his lips, and struggled with a decision. Once again he glanced around, taking inventory of the man waiting and various stragglers nearby before nodding and leaning toward her.

"Okay. Look. Something's happened. I've ended up as the recipient of some very frightening information . . . maybe I should say allegations. From a very, very reliable source. I wasn't sure what to make of them at the time, but now . . ."

"Allegations about what?" A second delegate was waiting for her, she noticed.

"The MD-eleven crash and what might have caused it."

"I told you in there, Mr. MacCabe, I am not on that investigation."

His hand was up again. "Hear me out. Please! Something happened this morning that I don't want to talk about here, something that makes me think the information I was given is dead-on correct." He waited for a response, smiling nervously while running a free hand through his hair.

She sighed and shook her head. "So, why come to me? I'm not on duty here in Hong Kong. Well, I am, but only as a delegate."

"You're FBI, Agent Bronsky. Even when you're taking a shower or sleeping, you're FBI. I remember you said those words yourself in an interview after the Colorado hijacking.

I'm coming to you because you know a lot about international terrorism. And I'm asking you to listen because I've changed my reservation and am flying back to Los Angeles in a few hours, around midnight, and it frankly scares me to death that I'm the only one who knows what I now think I know."

Kat could see genuine worry in his eyes. "So," she began, "this information is something you picked up here in Hong Kong?"

"No. Back in D.C. But I *really* don't want to discuss it here, okay?"

"You said you're leaving around midnight. Is that on Meridian Airlines?" Kat asked, her voice still cool, her thinking cautious.

"Yes," he replied.

"Then we're on the same flight."

A look of surprise crossed his face. "Really? Tell you what. I'm staying in a hotel down the street and I have to go check out and get my stuff. Let me get a cab and come by here to pick you up early, say in about forty-five minutes. If you'll let my newspaper buy you dinner, I'll lay this all out for you."

Kat shook her head no, then shot another "please wait" smile at the gathering fan club ten feet away. There were four men now waiting for her.

"Please!" Robert MacCabe added, keeping his voice low.

"I've got a better idea, Mr. MacCabe. Let's just talk on the plane."

"No. Please! I hate to make this sound like cloak-and-dagger stuff, but what I have to tell you is too sensitive to throw around on a crowded airplane." He reached out and carefully touched her arm. "Look. I'm not kidding. This may be very serious and I don't know whom else to talk to."

Kat studied him carefully for a few seconds, wondering what sort of ploy could possibly spawn such a request.

None, she decided. She sighed and nodded.

"All right, Mr. MacCabe. Forty-five minutes. As much

as I hate to admit it, you've tweaked my curiosity."

"Great!" he said, turning to go.

She watched him walk off, reminding herself suddenly that people were waiting to talk to her.

chapter

3

Robert MacCabe folded the international edition of *USA Today* and put it in a side pocket of his computer case. He glanced at his watch, his mind far away as the hotel elevator opened on thirty-two. Forty-five minutes had been ambitious, he concluded. He'd have to hurry to pick up Katherine Bronsky on time.

He shot through the elevator doors and almost collided with a large man in his path. "Sorry," Robert mumbled, as he turned down the long hallway, belatedly aware that he hadn't heard the elevator doors close. He was thirty feet down the hall when a sudden compulsion to look back overwhelmed him. He stopped and turned.

The dark, heavyset man was still there, a lit cigarette in his hand. Watching. One hand held the elevator door as the other clutched a plastic shopping bag with a Mercedes-Benz logo emblazoned on it.

The man made eye contact for no more than a moment before turning without a word and stepping out of sight into the elevator, letting the doors shut behind him.

Strange, Robert thought, reminding himself that, although he was considerably short of being a celebrity, his face had become public when he'd won the Pulitzer.

He stepped around a service cart in the middle of the hallway and nodded to the maid as he fished out his card key, wondering almost in passing why the door would swing inward before he'd turned the handle.

What the . . . ? He stood in confusion for a few seconds. He'd checked the door when he left, hadn't he? He was always careful about such things.

Of course. The housekeeper! She must have just opened it.

Robert looked around, but the housekeeper and her cart were gone, which was curious. He turned back with a growing feeling of unease and pushed the door open. He moved inside slowly, flipped on the light switch, and came to a sudden halt.

Everything was in shambles. Drawers had been pulled and dumped. The contents of his bag were everywhere. The seams of his gray suit had been ripped open. His computer disks were spread over the bed, several of them bent and destroyed.

Good Lord.

The scene in the bathroom was no better. The room reeked of his cologne; the remains of the green bottle lay strewn on the bathroom floor.

He placed the small computer briefcase on the edge of the bed and moved to check the closets before slamming the door to the hallway and bolting it. His heart was pounding, apprehension driving his blood pressure through the roof.

As the door clicked closed, the phone rang, causing him to jump. He moved to it immediately and lifted the receiver, but there was only an open line—followed by a deliberate hang-up. He replaced the receiver and the phone rang again almost instantly.

Once more he answered. Once more someone listened without a word for nearly fifteen seconds before deliberately breaking the connection.

The chill that had crept up his back when he walked in returned as a virtual ice storm of apprehension, as if someone were watching him with malevolent intent. Whoever had searched his possessions knew he was back in his room.

There was no time to call security. Robert yanked his upended roll-on bag back to the bed and began piling his possessions inside as fast as he could. What if someone knocked? There was no other way out. He was on the thirty-second floor.

The telephone began ringing again, each repetition a malignant presence.

The gray suit was a total loss and he decided to leave it. He dumped his shaver into the mound of clothes in his bag and struggled to close the fabric top, working the zippers and kneeling on the bag to compact it, succeeding at last. The room was too warm suddenly, and he found himself perspiring, whether more from effort and apprehension than atmospheric conditions, he couldn't tell.

The telephone continued to ring as he rushed to the door and pressed his eye to the peephole to survey the distorted version of the hallway on the other side.

It was empty.

He threw open the door and entered the hall, carrying his roll-on in one hand and his computer case in the other, feeling like a panicked child leaving a haunted house. The elevators were a hundred feet distant, and he broke into a run, the roll-on bag banging painfully against his shins along the way. He could still hear the telephone ringing in room 3205.

He reached the elevators and jabbed at the DOWN button. The rancid aroma of cigarette smoke still hung in the air as his eyes took in the furniture of the elevator lobby: a small table, two end chairs, a potted plant, and a plastic shopping bag someone had left propped against the wall.

A bag with a Mercedes logo.

Blind panic washed over Robert as he recalled the bag in the hand of the heavyset man at the elevator ten minutes ago. The man had obviously come back, or never left. *Probably the one who trashed my room,* Robert concluded. He recalled the brief, cold moment of eye contact, and the man's hesitation at the elevator door suddenly made sense.

There was no sign of the elevator, but there was an emergency stairway a dozen yards back and Robert dashed in that direction, throwing open the door and hefting his bags through the opening to race down the staircase, relieved to hear the heavy fire door slam shut above him.

He stopped on the twenty-ninth-floor landing, out of breath, wondering if it would be safe to try for the elevator again. The air in the stairwell was musty, with a disorienting hint of garlic mixed with the dust of a seldom-used enclosure. *But this is better than walking down twenty-nine flights with these bags.*

He reached for the doorknob to the hallway and found it locked. He tried it again several times, but it wouldn't budge.

There was a sound from somewhere above. A fire door being opened, followed by the footfall of heavy shoes on the landing.

Once more the feeling of unfocused panic welled up in his stomach, this wave more sustained and unyielding. He struggled blindly with the locked door, his face plastered against the little wire-mesh-embedded glass window as he rattled it and struggled. But it was immovable, and the hallway beyond was empty.

The footsteps above began moving down the stairs with an ominous, confident, unhurried gait. Whoever it was knew there was no way out for the quarry.

Robert dashed as quietly as he could down another flight to the twenty-eighth floor, finding that door locked as well. As he turned, a small sign caught his attention, warning that there were no exits from the stairwell except on the ground floor.

He plastered his back against the door and tried to think. *Calm down, dammit! How do I know whoever's coming is a threat?*

His trashed hotel room and the ringing phone answered the question.

Once more he lifted the bags and ran on the balls of his

feet down the stairway as fast as he could go. The footsteps from above sped up suddenly.

Robert's heart was pounding, his mind focused only on escape, his feet slipping every few steps as he tried to accelerate the descent. He scrambled around the landing of the twenty-second floor, calculating his leap to the next set of steps, when the fire door flew open and knocked him off his feet. His roll-on bag flew out of control into the wall with a loud crash that reverberated in the concrete shaft.

"Oh! So sorry!" A feminine voice reached him through the fog of panic. Two young girls, probably fifteen, were standing in the doorway, holding the door open and wondering what to do for the wild-eyed man they'd decked with the door.

Robert picked himself up quickly, grabbed the roll-on, and dashed past the startled girls into the safety of the hallway to head for the elevator. He heard the girls reenter the hallway behind him and let the door close.

"You all right, Mister?" one of them asked, some thirty feet behind him, as he moved to the elevator and jabbed at the DOWN button.

"Yeah, I'm okay," he shouted. "But don't let anyone else in through that door."

"I . . . not understand," one of them said.

The bell chimed above the elevator. The elevator doors would be opening in a second, and whoever was chasing him in the stairwell would be approaching the hallway door, which was now locked.

He turned toward the girls again. "Don't let anyone out of that stairwell, okay? Do not open that door. No one's supposed to come through there." Their blank stare and startled expression told him it was a losing battle.

The elevator doors were sliding open, the car blessedly empty, and he launched himself inside before repeatedly punching LOBBY and DOOR CLOSE.

The doors remained motionless.

The unmistakable sound of the fire door being opened reached his ears. A male voice was drowning out the girls' startled reply.

Finally the elevator doors began to close, but there were heavy footsteps now running in his direction. The doors moved in slow motion, now halfway closed. Robert tucked himself into a forward corner to stay out of sight just as the footsteps reached a crescendo and a male hand thrust into the remaining crack, grabbing the door and struggling to reopen it. The doors kept closing relentlessly, and the hand was withdrawn.

The elevator began its descent, the soft noise drowned out by the pounding in Robert MacCabe's head. He quickly secured the computer case on top of the roll-on bag and extended the handle. If he could lose his expression of panic and move into the lobby like a normal guest, maybe he could meld into the crowd and find a taxi.

The lobby! He'll radio down and have someone waiting!

He punched MEZZANINE just in time, stopping the elevator one floor above the lobby level, and stepped out as soon as the doors opened. The lobby was visible from the upper railing of the balcony, and he moved quickly toward it, surveying the crowd and spotting two dark-suited men leaping onto the escalator and taking the moving steps two at a time, both of them holding walkie-talkies.

Another surge of adrenaline coursed through his system, propelling him down the nearest hallway, through a pair of double doors, and into a large service bay behind the convention and ballroom areas. He could hear employees on both sides of the large hall talking, but no one was paying any attention to him as he ran the length of the hallway and down two flights through another set of doors into the steam-filled hotel laundry, racing past startled employees to a small stairway on the far wall. There were several angry shouts, but no one moved to stop him.

Robert yanked open the door and stepped into a dark, wet alleyway behind the hotel. He slammed the heavy metal fire door behind him, feeling deliverance in its reverberation.

The alley ran to an adjacent street, and he raced the entire length, moving into the flowing crowd and blending with it before realizing that it was carrying him back toward the main hotel entrance.

A surge of guests spilled from the interior of the hotel through the main entrance doors, tangling with the city crowd as they moved onto waiting buses, each of them happily chatting with friends, and each of them carrying a familiar shopping bag.

He looked more closely at one of the bags, recognition coming as a shock. There were hundreds of them, each emblazoned with a Mercedes-Benz emblem.

Robert MacCabe stopped in his tracks, shaking his head. The Mercedes bag he had seen on the thirty-second floor could have belonged to anyone. They were all over the hotel. He'd panicked for nothing.

But what about the pursuer in the stairwell? Hadn't he come through a locked stairway door . . .

Good grief! Of course! Robert thought, wincing. *He had a key because he was hotel security! I probably set off an alarm when I opened the stairwell door.*

He felt like an idiot as he took a deep breath and began walking calmly toward the main doors, adrenaline making his legs wobbly. Obviously no one had been chasing him. He'd allowed his imagination to get the best of him, building on what had probably been a simple burglary unconnected with terrorism or Cuban crashes or potentially overheard conversations with FBI agents.

I'd sure make a lousy spy! Robert thought. *Jumping out of my skin every time the phone rings.*

The aromas of Hong Kong began to awaken his other senses, the pungent smell of various seafoods and the essence of fresh garbage mixing with a delicious smell from a steakhouse grill. The street was glistening with moisture from a passing shower, the lights reflecting from the surface of the street in a kaleidoscope of colors.

He looked at the hotel entrance and checked his watch. He'd have to hurry to report the burglary and check out by phone. There was barely enough time to get a cab.

The hotel driveway where the taxis were waiting was

incredibly crowded, and Robert had to push into an incoming group of conventioneers, several of whom seemed to be pushing back—one on his left and one on his right—pressing in on both sides and herding him away from the main entrance door as he struggled to hold on to his bag and computer case.

It was no use. Their rudeness was ridiculous, and Robert stopped suddenly to let the two men go ahead. But both of them stopped, too, and at the same moment he felt something hard and metallic poke into his right rib cage.

"That's a gun barrel," the man on the right said quietly.

"What . . . what do you want?" Robert managed.

"Keep walking. Keep looking straight ahead."

Robert tried to twist away, but firm hands clamped down on his arms as his hand was ripped from the handle of his bag. The voice was in his ear again. "I have a silencer, Mr. MacCabe."

American accent, Robert concluded, the thought scaring him even more.

"It's aimed very accurately at your backbone. One more try to wiggle away and you'll hear a small pop as a nine-millimeter bullet bores in and efficiently severs your spine, and we'll simply disappear. Or you can cooperate and keep your legs."

"Okay, okay. I'm walking. Who are you?"

The barrel was thrust harder into his side. Robert winced with pain. "Shut up," the voice said.

"Look, I don't . . ."

"I SAID SHUT UP!" It was more an intense snarl right in his ear than a shout, but the effect was the same.

Looking ahead, Robert could see a dark sedan waiting at the curb and the heavyset man from the thirty-second-floor elevator emerging from the passenger side to open the rear door, his face devoid of expression.

"Where are the bags?" the man by the car asked.

"Got 'em," the gunman replied. The man on Robert's left released his arms as the one with the gun pushed him toward the backseat.

Robert felt time distend. Whoever they were, if he got in the car he was dead. Of that he was sure. He had less than a few seconds to act, and no idea what to do.

The gun barrel was withdrawn from his right side as one of the men started around to the other side of the car. The burly one climbed into the passenger seat, leaving only the gunman between Robert and a slim chance of escape.

Robert turned to his right to look at the gunman, a sudden move that startled the man and caused the barrel to rise again.

"You did get my computer, didn't you?" Robert asked.

The man smiled an evil smile, not caring that his face was fully visible. It was obvious he didn't expect the reporter to live long enough to identify him, a confirmation of Robert MacCabe's death sentence.

"How good of you to ask, Mr. MacCabe. That's precisely what we were looking for, as a matter of fact. Pity you didn't leave it in your room." He held up the computer case with his left hand as he let the aim of the pistol in his right hand drop toward the pavement, its barrel clearly visible to Robert.

There was no silencer.

The energy behind the sudden kick of Robert MacCabe's right leg encompassed every ounce of his will to live. His aim was perfect; the toe of his size-eleven shoe catching the gunman squarely in the crotch and literally lifting him into the air. A piercing cry of pain punctuated the air, followed by the roar of the gun firing wildly as it left the injured man's flailing right hand. The crowd cringed and turned in his direction to see what was happening.

The force of his kick propelled Robert backward against the car, but he lunged forward instantly, diving to catch his computer case as it fell from the gunman's hand. Robert grabbed the computer in midair and fell to the pavement, rolling once before leaping up and regaining his feet. He ran for his life, literally, past the hotel entrance and across the crowded street beyond, ignoring the commotion in his wake. The screech of brakes and honk of horns accompanied his frantic, broken field run as he darted left and then right. He spotted what looked like an alley a hundred feet away, dodged between and behind everyone he passed, and skidded around the corner through a loose stack of cardboard boxes into the middle of a bazaar full of startled people.

He could hear running footsteps and shouts behind him, but he had the advantage of surprise, if only for a few seconds—along with the horrid certainty that his paranoia had been justified. Someone really *was* out to kill him for what they thought he knew.

A jungle of handcarts and tables full of wares were spread like an obstacle course in front of each of the tiny shops that opened into the street. A cacophony of music from Asian rap to the Beatles filled the street as he wove back and forth, his computer case flapping alongside. He darted beneath colorful awnings and through myriad aromas of food and smoke as he eyed first one entryway, then another, trying to decide which might have a rear exit.

Toward the end of the second block he shoved too hard past an angered merchant, and the man caught him by the sleeve to yell at him in Mandarin. Robert twisted away, apologizing in English. He looked back at the crowd and tried to spot his pursuers. He knew they would be following him, or even waiting for him on the other end.

He had to disappear, and quickly.

A small shop full of exotic fabrics appeared on his right and he hunched down behind a row of wares to dash through the entrance. He ran straight for the back, bursting through beaded curtains into the presence of a surprised man and woman hunched over their evening meal.

The man came to his feet, his eyes wide, his chopsticks held out like a weapon.

"Quick!" Robert said, gasping for breath. "I'm sorry to bother you, but I need a back way out of here."

"What?"

"A back door. Do you have a back door?"

"Why?" the old man asked with suspicion, chopsticks at the ready.

"Because I'm being chased. Not by the police or the army. But by someone who's trying to kill me, okay?"

"She come now?"

"What?"

"Chase you?"

"Yes!" Robert said, confused.

The old man brightened and nodded. "I understand. Come this way!"

He pushed through another beaded curtain to a small door, which he opened, stood aside to let Robert pass, then caught his arm, speaking urgently in his ear, his breath reeking with garlic. "Two blocks that way, go into shopping mall, down one level. Buy ticket for movie, go inside, then slip out back exit near screen. You come up on street two blocks away. Big secret. Never fails."

Robert paused and looked at the man quizzically. "This . . . happens a lot?"

The man shook his head. "No, no, no. But when my wife chase *me,* that how I get away!" He grinned, showing a mouth of imperfect teeth. "She like to chase me down the street, yelling and carrying on. Family tradition. All our friends laugh."

"You're kidding?"

"No, no, no. Just a game, but when that woman get angry, she scary."

"Women," Robert said with a smile.

The old man nodded with the same wide, toothy grin. "Women."

The movie theater was fairly new, and Robert tried to blend into the crowd as he pushed through the turnstiles, then moved quickly through the exit the old man had described. There was a long underground hallway leading to steps and, as promised, an exit to the street above.

Robert opened the door to find a taxi sitting at the curb in front of him. He yanked open the taxi's rear door and dove in, giving the address of Katherine Bronsky's hotel as he hunched down out of sight.

"Only the hotel?" the driver asked, calculating whether this strange intruder was worth the small fare.

"No. Then to dinner, then to the airport. Big fare, big tip, no more questions."

The driver nodded and gunned the car down the street.

chapter

4

Kat Bronsky stood under the covered drive of the hotel, breathing exhaust fumes, and looked at her watch in disgust. It was time to give up.

That's it. I've been stood up.

Until MacCabe had appeared in the equation, she hadn't planned to wear the same clothes back to L.A., nor to check out early. But now she was without a room, her luggage sitting on the drive beside her. She could carry her bags back in and go eat at one of the hotel's restaurants, or she could take a cab by herself to the new airport, which sounded like the better idea.

When MacCabe shows up on that flight, he's going to get an earful.

Kat caught the eye of the gaudily uniformed doorman and indicated the need for a taxi. He whistled one into the breezeway with practiced flair and opened the door, motioning the bellman to load her two bags. She had one leg in the backseat when another taxi squealed to a halt behind them. The rear door flew open to disgorge the prodigal journalist, his eyes wild as he rushed up to her.

"I . . . ah, I'm sorry . . . I'm late. Something happened."

"Apparently," she said, getting out of the cab and approaching him with her hands on her hips. He was out of breath, which seemed strange for a man riding in a cab. "Forty-five minutes, you said," Kat reminded him.

"I can explain, but not here." He was looking behind him as he turned back to her. "We really need to get the hell out of here."

They transferred her bags to his taxi and she joined him in the backseat, barely getting the door closed before the driver shot off into traffic again.

"So, where are we going for dinner?"

"Ah . . . first, we're going to an overlook of the harbor that I know," he said.

She shook her head. "I don't go to overlooks with strange journalists on the first date. Not even on a beautiful evening like this do I watch submarine races."

He twisted completely around in the seat to search the traffic behind them, oblivious to her attempt at humor. "I think we're okay," he said quietly. "I don't see anyone back there."

She reached out and grabbed his arm to get his attention. "Earth to Robert MacCabe! What's going on here? Why are you so spooked?"

He licked his lips and looked around again before sitting back in the seat and relating the events of the previous hour, finishing as they pulled into the overlook.

"Good Lord!" she managed. "What, exactly, did they want?"

"They didn't say, but there's nothing else I've been exposed to but the . . . information I was mentioning."

Kat nodded. "Okay. We're here. Now tell me the whole story."

Robert leaned forward and winced. "Oh, jeez! They got my suitcase."

"Anything important in it?"

He shook his head. "The computer's all I care about." Robert slapped several bills in the driver's hand and asked him to turn his engine off and wait. "If someone comes up to you, you're just enjoying the night. No passengers, okay?"

"Okay."

Kat followed Robert MacCabe off the pathway to a grove of trees. The twinkling lights of the city formed a glowing carpet beyond, set off by a freshening breeze that carried the unmistakable aromas of a busy harbor metropolis.

"In here," he said, motioning her behind one of the tall shrubs into a small glade brightly illuminated by the reflected glow of the city lights. "You want to sit on the grass?" he asked.

"In this suit?" She laughed, motioning to a concrete bench and inspecting it closely before sitting down. "This will do. I think it's clean."

He sat down beside her and put his arm on the back of the bench in order to face her. His face was drawn and serious as he waited for the noise of a newly airborne 747 to pass, its lights winking as it climbed past them at what appeared to be a sedate speed.

"Agent Bronsky, I think—"

"Wait," she said, holding up a finger. "Call me Kat, okay? 'Agent Bronsky' sounds too much like my dad."

"Oh?"

"My father was career FBI, too," she explained. "An assistant deputy director when he died. Sorry to interrupt."

He shrugged. "Kat, what I didn't want to say within earshot of anyone else is this: I think evidence exists that the crash of that SeaAir MD-eleven in Cuban waters was a terrorist act."

She nodded solemnly. "You think evidence exists? That's a strange way to put it. What evidence?"

"I don't know yet," he said.

She cocked her head and raised her eyebrows. "You don't *know*?"

"I need to explain that."

Kat nodded slowly. "You certainly do. What, for instance, makes you think SeaAir was a terrorist act as opposed to a mechanical failure or a Cuban missile?"

"Because my life has been threatened within the past hour, Kat, possibly for talking to you, and definitely because of something that happened in D.C. several days ago. I think our intelligence community is scared to death over something they can't control and are trying to suppress."

She raised her hand. "Okay, whoa. Let's start at the beginning. You said someone had given you information. Is that the evidence you're talking about?"

"No. And yes. That was Walter Carnegie of the FAA, an old friend of mine. We go back twenty years to when he joined the Defense Intelligence Agency as a terrorist analyst and I was a cub reporter in the Beltway. Wally racked up fifteen years at DIA and then CIA before moving to the Federal Aviation Administration to try to give them a better, more intelligent ability to sort out terrorist threats."

"But what did he give you?"

"Nothing," Robert said. "It's what he told me."

"What did he tell you?"

"A month after the SeaAir crash near Cuba he called me one afternoon, scared silly, from a pay phone. He told me he'd stumbled into something related to the SeaAir accident that had him very, very upset and worried."

"Did he tell you what it was?"

"No details or supporting facts, but he said he'd been asking questions about SeaAir that were apparently upsetting someone, because his life had just been threatened by a couple of goons in a Metro station. At first he thought they were Company operatives—CIA. But by the time he called me, he wasn't sure. He told me that nothing like that had ever happened to him before."

"But, Robert, what the heck did he have? What was he probing? How was he involved? You say he was asking questions . . ."

"On behalf of the FAA, in his official antiterrorist role. Wally said that when he went to our intelligence community, he found them totally spooked over SeaAir."

"You said that."

"Let me finish. He said they're spooked and totally uncooperative because they think the crash is the first major act of a new, sophisticated terrorist group about whom CIA and DIA know nothing. They know nothing and don't want to admit it."

"What else?"

"Wally also said the airline industry is pushing the President to flat-out tell the public that SeaAir was *not* a terrorist act. Is FBI getting the same pressure?"

Caution led her to sidestep the question. "Go on about Carnegie."

"Wally said he had hard evidence, and he was scared. He wouldn't give me any more details. He wanted a deep-throat meeting, and we set a place and time. He was desperate to tell what he'd found. Time, he said, was running out."

"Meaning what?"

"I wish I knew. I asked him if he could get me a copy and he said he had the file all locked up. He repeated that twice."

"'Locked up'?" she asked.

"Yeah." Robert held up his hand to stop her from continuing.

"Well, is Wally a credible guy?"

"Completely, though he did sometimes see the shadow of conspiracies that weren't really there."

"So, he didn't tell you what the evidence was, or what he had, and he didn't give you anything directly. Did he tell you what he thought this so-called new terrorist group wants? It makes no sense to blow an airplane out of the sky if you're not trying to accomplish something. Even hijackers have a goal."

"I don't know. As I say, he never showed for the rendezvous. I couldn't reach him by phone or with messages the rest of that day or the next. I even dropped by his house. He wasn't there. A day later I had to leave for Hong Kong on this trip."

"Have you tried to call him from here?" Kat asked, noting the pained look on his face as he nodded.

"Kat, Walter Carnegie is dead."

She crossed her arms and looked at him for a moment. "How?"

"Suicide, so his secretary told me."

"And you don't believe it."

He was shaking his head. "The pope would be a better candidate for suicide."

"Did he leave you anything in writing?" she asked. "Of course there's no way to know yet. You haven't been back."

"That was just this morning. I've been trying to assemble the pieces in my mind ever since. Why would someone murder Wally unless they wanted to suppress or reclaim whatever information he had? He said the crash was terrorist-caused, and the group was new and powerful and unknown. Three days later he's dead. That's too coincidental for me, even *before* I have a chance to start asking questions."

Kat was chewing on an index finger, recalling the afternoon conversation with Jake Rhoades. He'd used the word "spooked" to describe the administration's attitude. But MacCabe was still a dangerous ace reporter for a major paper . . .

She turned to him suddenly. "On deep, deep, permanent, unbreakable, blood-oath background, okay?" she said, as she tracked another jumbo jet climbing past them with a throaty whine that even a private pilot like her could not resist watching.

He nodded, his eyebrows raised. "Of course. Absolutely deep background and unattributable. You know something?"

Kat shook her head. "Probably not, other than the fact that he was right about the administration wanting a cause other than Cuba or terrorists."

"That much was accurate, then."

"But we don't even have a viable theory, let alone knowledge of a specific terrorist group who might have wanted to shoot down that MD-eleven, and we don't know what this so-called evidence is." She slapped at a mosquito, the only one she'd seen.

"But you are getting administration pressure not to label it terrorism?"

"I didn't say that, Robert. Not officially. In fact, I didn't say anything," she said slowly. "Truth is, we're not even having this conversation, and come to think of it, I'm not even here."

"Okay, okay. But, Kat, none of that really helps with this mystery. My friend's dead and I know in my heart he was murdered, especially now that *I've* been attacked. If those guys back at the hotel had pushed me into that backseat, I'd probably be dead by now, too." He shifted around to face her more squarely. "You disagree? You think I'm paranoid?"

She shook her head. "Just because you're paranoid, the old saying goes, doesn't mean they're *not* out to get you. No," she sighed, her words coming in a quieter tone. "From what you just told me, they could easily have intended to kill you. The psychology is right. A professional doing a kidnapping who doesn't mind showing his face is not expecting to have to deal with a witness in the future."

Robert MacCabe swallowed hard. "Oh, Lord. I just realized that if they knew where to find me, they know what flight I'm on tonight. They could be waiting at the airport." He turned to her. "You could be in danger, too."

She got to her feet and began pacing back and forth in front of the bench. "This is nuts, Robert! What you've told me is all you have, right?"

He nodded.

"Well, other than speculation on Carnegie's death and the attempted abduction, all we've got is general speculation based on his statements," she said, turning to look at the harbor lights through the trees. "I'm sorry, but that's not even enough to launch an investigation of whether an investigation needs to be launched."

"I don't understand."

She whirled back around. "Look, we don't know for sure that Walter Carnegie had anything but a theory in regard to the SeaAir crash. You said yourself he tended to be spring-loaded to the conspiracy position. And at least as of this moment, standing here with me in Hong Kong, you can't even be certain he was murdered."

"So who were those guys who ripped my room apart and tried to kill me?"

"I don't know, and *you* don't know. Do you have enemies?"

"Probably a lot, including the phone company back in Virginia. But no one's ever come after me before."

Kat resumed pacing, smoothing her hair against a gust of

wind. "If there's a new terrorist group, and if they found Carnegie had talked to you, and if they know Carnegie had evidence or information they didn't want released, then they should also be sophisticated enough to know that you two never got together, which means you couldn't have received any damning information. That, in turn, means they shouldn't be worried about you." She turned to look at him for a few seconds of uncomfortable silence. "You *don't* have any information, do you?"

"Not a clue! No letters, no calls, no disks."

"Then why *would* they chase you all the way to Hong Kong?"

"Maybe they know he sent me something, and I don't know it yet because I never received it. One of those goons said they'd been searching for my computer. Maybe he expected to find what he was looking for on my hard drive."

She nodded, deep in thought, her eyes on the brightly lighted cityscape. "That could mean a disk, or they suspect you downloaded something by modem." She turned to him. "But you did save your computer, right? You got it back before they had a chance to look at it?"

"Yeah. It's safe back there in the—" He gestured toward the parking lot.

"Taxi." Kat finished his sentence as he came off the bench, both of them breaking into a run back to where they'd left the taxi.

The cab was still there, the lights out, the engine stopped, but they could see the driver slumped over in the left front window, barely illuminated by the streetlamp.

"Oh my God!" Kat exclaimed as they approached the driver's side, keeping an active lookout for anyone else around. She reached out and touched the cabbie's arm, fully expecting to see blood.

Instead, the man yelped in fright as he jumped awake.

"Excuse me!" Kat said. "You were leaning over and I thought you were hurt."

"Sorry! I only fall asleep."

Kat stood looking at the city. She took a deep breath before turning back to the driver. "Another five minutes, okay?"

"Okay."

"Robert, you want to bring your computer?"

He reached in and retrieved the case, then followed her a dozen yards away to the edge of the viewpoint, surprised to see her unfolding the antenna on a satellite phone. She pulled a business card from her purse and looked up at him.

"I met the security chief of the Chek Lap Kok Hong Kong Airport today," she explained. "Let me see what I can do about your security worry."

Several minutes of relayed calls led to the chief himself. The conversation was swift and she thanked him and disconnected.

"We'll meet a security team several miles from the terminal and they'll take us right to the aircraft. If anyone's lying in wait, he won't have a chance to spot either of us. Mr. Li was nice enough to say he'd arrange for immigration and customs clearance on board for us, and they're beefing up security on this flight."

Robert sighed in relief. "Wonderful. Thank you."

"Hey. I'm aboard, too. Now, are you booked straight to D.C. out of L.A.?"

"Yes," he said.

Kat nibbled her lower lip before speaking. "I was going to spend a day lying unconscious on Newport Beach, but now I'm going to go back with you. I'm not sure we've got anything, but we'll take it to my boss, if you agree."

"I agree," Robert said.

The two of them fell silent for a few moments as Kat watched another jetliner climb away from the airport into the night. A rumble of thunder had accompanied their exchange for the past few minutes, and flashes of lightning both to the east and the west continued to flicker in the distance. A line of thunderstorms was obviously moving in from the west, crackling with lightning as it drifted closer. The wind was beginning to pick up as well, though the temperature was balmy.

"Kat, I've been shot at in Bosnia, Somalia, and Riyadh, but always because I was a reporter they didn't want there. Any reporter would have drawn the same attention. But I've never been personally targeted before, and it isn't comfortable."

She nodded. "I can imagine."

"So what's your best guess?" he asked.

"You mean, who's been chasing you and who may have killed Carnegie? Or my guess about whether terrorists brought down the SeaAir MD-eleven in the first place?"

"Both."

She paused, chewing her lip again, sorting out the logic. "Well, *someone's* apparently worried about what Carnegie may have found, and their tactics are not CIA or DIA, to say the least. That means there *could* be, in theory, I suppose, some dark and dirty new group out there that wants you cashiered. If so, they've got to be private and well-organized and probably not Middle Eastern or religious in origin. I don't know, Robert. Carnegie could have been right about some new, very sophisticated group looking to accomplish some strange, new, unknown goal that they haven't announced to the rest of us."

"In my experience, that would surely terrify the Company."

She nodded. "But a formal, embarrassed cover-up back home?" she said, shaking her head slowly. "I don't know." A distant flash of lightning caught her attention.

"Maybe," Robert said, "it's a case of 'we can't control it, so we're all going to pretend it doesn't exist.'"

"That," Kat replied, "sounds like a conspiracy theory, Robert. As a rule, I don't believe in such things."

"Nor do I. Most groups, no matter how focused and intense, can't even make a group decision on where to go for lunch. The way I look at things, Oswald was a solo act, and the only aliens here are from Guadalajara."

"But . . ." she prompted.

"But, well . . . I can understand why the airline industry doesn't want the SeaAir crash to be a terrorist act. If Wally was right and there's a new mad-dog group out there with money, sophistication, and a cause, they won't stop with SeaAir. They'll keep on killing airliners until they have our undivided attention."

Kat was shaking her head as she looked at him. "My God, Robert. Can you imagine the impact on the bottom line of the airline industry if the whole country could hear what you just said?"

CHEK LAP KOK/HONG KONG
INTERNATIONAL AIRPORT
NOVEMBER 13—DAY TWO
12:15 A.M. LOCAL/1615 ZULU

The security car braked to a halt beneath the tail of Meridian Flight 5. Kat got out and glanced up, oblivious to the smell of jet fuel, and wholly unprepared for the monstrous, looming bulk of the Boeing 747-400 that was poised to fly her and nearly three hundred others across a quarter of the planet's surface to Los Angeles by way of Honolulu.

"Good Lord!" she managed, as Robert MacCabe joined her, bag in hand.

"Can I at least quote you on that?" he asked, craning his neck as well.

"This thing is incredible!" she added, momentarily forgetting the two officers who had picked them up at the appointed rendezvous. "I've flown on seven-forty-sevens for years, but I've never seen one from ground level."

"I know. We're always walking in through a jetway twenty feet above ground. Passengers never really understand how huge they are, or how heavy. We'll take off tonight weighing over three quarters of a million pounds."

The officers guided them into the back of a large catering truck parked by the right, front door of the aircraft. It raised itself on huge hydraulic arms thirty-four feet to the main floor level where lead flight attendant Britta Franz was waiting for them. A tall, well-proportioned blond with a pronounced German accent and twenty years as an American citizen, Britta exuded authority. The Chinese customs official who had been waiting with her hurried through the formalities of a passport check before bowing and leaving.

"Now that you're entirely legal," Britta said, "let me escort you both to the upper deck first-class cabin."

Robert looked at his ticket, then at Britta. "Ah, I think we're in coach."

She smiled. "Not anymore. We upgraded both of you, if you don't mind."

"Absolutely, we don't mind!" Kat replied quickly, with a broad smile.

They had barely settled into the luxurious seats when Britta reappeared, wearing a deadly serious expression. There were two Chinese police officers behind her. "I'm . . . sorry to bother you, Ms. Bronsky, but these officers insisted on . . ."

"Katherine Bronsky?" one of the policemen asked in a lightly accented voice.

Kat could sense Robert stiffen beside her as she studied their eyes. Both were in their twenties, immaculately groomed, and humorless.

"I'm Special Agent Katherine Bronsky of the American Federal Bureau of Investigation. What can I do for you?"

"You must come with us, please."

"I mustn't miss this flight." She looked at Britta. "How much time do I have?"

Britta frowned. "Less than five minutes."

"You must come, please," one of the officers said. "Bring your bags."

"Look, the airport security chief brought us aboard," Kat began, but the closer of the two was shaking his head.

"He is from a different agency," the officer replied. He gestured toward the stairs at the back of the cabin. "Please."

"What are you? What agency?"

"Hong Kong Police," he said.

Kat unsnapped the seat belt and stood. "One second, please. Wait for me back there."

Both of them bowed and retreated to the top of the upper deck stairs as Kat turned quietly to Robert. "I don't know what the heck this is all about, Robert, but I'll find out and be on the next flight. I'll probably be only twelve hours behind you into D.C."

"I'm going to wait for you in L.A.," he said suddenly.

She looked at him for a second, thinking it over. "Okay."

"There . . . may be more to tell you."

Kat watched him scribble something on a business card. He finished and handed it to her. "My nationwide beeper number. When you arrive at LAX, beep me with a phone number and stand by. I won't be far away. I'm going to lie low in the L.A. area and wait for you."

"Keep out of sight." She extended her hand for a correct handshake. Instead, Robert held it gently and squeezed, leaving her slightly off balance.

The 747's forward door closed behind her as Kat followed the two policemen into the jetway, surprised to find her suitcase waiting for her. She picked it up, fighting rising anger at being yanked from the flight for some stupid bureaucratic reason. Someone higher up had obviously been angered by the security chief's actions, but it was strange that MacCabe had been allowed to stay. Obviously professional courtesy didn't extend to the FBI this week in Hong Kong.

Kat extended the bag's handle and rolled it behind her as she reluctantly followed the two men up the jetway, looking forward to chewing out whoever had screwed up her plans.

At the top of the jetway Kat stopped and put her hands on her hips, leaving both policemen unsure what to do. "Precisely where are you taking me, and why?"

One of the men motioned down the concourse. "This way, please."

She shook her head. "Not until you tell me where we're going."

"We must bring you to our commander's office."

"Why?" She saw total confusion cross their faces. She

sighed and grabbed the handle of her bag again. "Never mind. Lead the way."

Less than 200 yards down the concourse, they opened a door and ushered her into a small office populated by several other uniforms and an important-looking man in a business suit who was holding out a telephone receiver.

"Please," he said. The room reeked of cigarettes, but she tuned that out and took the phone, expecting a higher Chinese official on the other end.

"This is Agent Katherine Bronsky of the United States Federal Bureau of Investigation," she began, as officially as she could manage. "Who is this?"

There was a familiar chuckle on the other end, which smoothly transitioned to a more official voice. "This is Deputy Director Jacob Rhoades, also of the United States Federal Bureau of Investigation."

"Jake? What on earth?"

"Sorry, Kat. Change of plans."

She rolled her eyes before turning her attention fully to Jake. "I was about to snarl at these folks for pulling me off. What's up?"

"You know we've got a consulate there?"

"Of course."

"Well, they need you. Specifically, they need an FBI agent to deal with a security matter. We were going to send someone next week, but they were insistent."

"A . . . security matter?"

"I don't know the details, but there's supposed to be a car waiting curbside to take you there, put you up for the night, and get you on the first flight out in the morning after you deal with whatever's bugging them."

"Is this usual, Jake?"

"The State Department moves in mysterious ways. Please help us on this."

"Well, of course. My flight's probably pushing back as we speak."

"Just one night."

"Yeah, but they'd upgraded me to first class. Tomorrow I'll get steerage." She stopped herself from mentioning anything about Robert MacCabe on an unsecured line.

"I hear the speech was a real hit. Congratulations."

"News travels fast."

"Heck, Kat. We're the FBI. We're supposed to know everything."

"Oh. I didn't know that." She chuckled, pleased by his words of praise.

The driver from the U.S. Consulate was waiting, as promised. Kat let him carry her bag as she followed him through the sparkling new airport terminal to the exit. She wondered if the men who had tried to shanghai Robert MacCabe were watching and knew she had been with him.

The whole thing seemed surreal. Had MacCabe not been someone of substance—someone whose reputation she already knew—her diagnosis would be raving paranoia. *But wait a minute. What, exactly, DO I know about Robert MacCabe?*

The thought was cut short by the sight of two Asian men standing to one side of the exit from the secure area, both wearing dark suits, both watching her. Kat kept her eyes straight ahead as she passed, straining to see with her peripheral vision what they were doing, certain their eyes were tracking her.

A hundred feet away, she stopped and looked over her shoulder at the men, who quickly averted their eyes just as the two young women they had apparently been waiting for emerged from the secure area, waving and smiling. Seconds later, laughing and talking, the two couples walked past Kat without a single glance.

She snorted softly to herself and shook her head. *Real good instincts, Kat. MacCabe's paranoia is rubbing off.*

She turned to the driver and gestured him on, wishing she were still on the 747 next to MacCabe in first class.

chapter

6

First Officer Dan Wade hesitated by the forward main-deck galley and glanced back, trying to maintain contact with the eye candy moving up the stairway, an attractive young woman wearing a black leather miniskirt slit partially up the back, tantalizingly matched by the seams on her dark stockings. He tried to turn away before Britta could catch him looking, but it was too late.

"Danny! Get your eyes off my passengers!" she kidded, as he tried to look innocent.

"I was just worried she might be cold in that dress she's almost wearing."

"Yeah, sure, President Carter."

"What?" Dan asked, not comprehending the reference.

"You remember: 'Ah had lust in mah heart'? You're in lust. A girl can tell."

"More accurately, a mother superior," Dan mumbled.

"I heard that!" Britta shot back.

The station manager had handed a sheaf of flight papers through the door before closing it, and Bill Jenkins, the only male flight attendant, handed them in turn to the copilot. Jenkins, round-faced, balding, and good-natured, was a thirty-year veteran putting triplets through college. He frowned at the papers. "How's the weather doing, Dan? It was looking ugly out there a while ago."

The copilot nodded, arcing a thumb toward the ceiling. "In an hour this place will be roiling with thunderstorms, so we need to get the flock out of here."

"In the vernacular, of course."

"Of course." Dan smiled back.

"You fellows up there on the bridge do realize," Bill Jenkins continued, "that we've got a bigwig trade delegation aboard tonight, including some big-city mayors?"

"We heard. Captain Cavanaugh and I were trying to calculate how much lift the additional hot air could give us."

Jenkins laughed as he pointed toward first class. "We lose an engine, let me know, and I'll ask them to make speeches." He winked at one of the female flight attendants, who winked back as she watched the copilot climb the stairs. Dan was in his early fifties, newly divorced and on the prowl.

On the flight deck some fifty feet above ground level, Captain Pete Cavanaugh toggled the Engine Start switch for the right outboard engine. The driver of the tug four stories below slowed the 747-400's backward movement from the gate. Dan Wade, in the right seat of the two-pilot cockpit, checked the engine gauges and radioed the ground controller for taxi clearance before looking at Cavanaugh with a grin.

"You're *sure* you're awake enough for this?"

"Oh, give it a rest, Dan!" Pete said with mock disgust. "I wasn't sleeping the *entire* layover."

"Worst antisocial act of hibernation I've ever witnessed," Dan said, shaking his head sadly. "I couldn't even get you out of the room for dinner yesterday."

"I love thirty-six-hour layovers, okay? No yards to mow, no phones to answer, no grandkids or cats to wake me up at seven A.M., and no copilots to give me a hard time. My only job is to rest. So, how about that Before Taxi checklist?"

"Roger. How *about* that Before Taxi check?"

Pete grimaced. "Ten thousand comedians are starving in Los Angeles . . ."

"And I'm trying to be funny. Okay. Stand by for the checklist," Dan replied. The entire southern sky lit up in a massive display of lightning. "By the way, we do have our taxi clearance when the tug lets us go, which I hope is soon, because I'd sure like to beam out of here before that weather arrives."

"Beam out?" Pete rolled his eyes. "Lord, please deliver us from Trekkies."

The click of the public-address system echoed softly through the cabin as Britta swung onto the stairway to descend to the lower deck. Pete Cavanaugh's voice filled the cabin. He sounded and looked the part of the seasoned captain, she thought. Deep, calm, steady, and reassuring. The senior captain stood over six foot two, thin as a rail, his perpetually smiling face crowned with a mane of silver hair, carefully cropped in Julius Caesar–style. Britta smiled to herself. She considered Pete unflappable in the air. A wing could come off and he'd probably order coffee on the way down.

Dan, on the other hand, was more excitable and kinetic. Funny and friendly and slightly overweight, his inadvertent trademark—and the bane of his existence—was his thick, somewhat wavy dark hair and his incessant attempts to keep it under control. No matter how hard he tried to contain it under his pilot's hat, a lock or two always seemed to escape and curl up somewhere around the hat band, giving him a slightly avant-garde appearance. Women seemed to love his slightly disheveled lost-puppy manner. When Dan Wade, at five foot nine, and Pete Cavanaugh flew together, the Mutt and Jeff contrast caused heads to turn.

Britta reached the bottom step just as Pete finished his greeting. Ten hours of flight time ahead to Honolulu, he'd said, with routine weather on a routine flight. The passengers were settling into the sumptuous environs of the main first-class section as she moved through it. Coats and shoes had already come off and the personal TVs installed at each seat were in use now that the usual life-vest-and-evacuation demonstrations had been done. The aroma of leather filled the air.

"Did you get a blanket, Sir?" Britta asked a distinguished-looking man in the first row; he smiled and nodded. She moved aft, her eyes scanning the passengers for fastened seat belts and any looks of discontent.

A well-dressed black woman with dreadlocks and an infectious smile looked up and beamed at Britta. The woman was busily plumping up several pillows beyond their normal capacity.

Britta glanced toward the rear of the cavernous aircraft, judging whether she had time to walk the entire cabin. *I'll make the time,* she decided.

Alice, Jaime, and Claire, all old friends, were buttoning up the forward galley as Britta moved through business class and into coach, letting her eyes range over the passengers. She noted the forty-five-person tour group headed back to the States after a ten-day excursion of China, most of them tired but smiling. The tour director caught her eye and waved from across the cabin.

Somewhere to the rear, Britta heard the squawk of a shortwave radio. She moved on down the aisle, spotting a teenage boy with the red-and-white-striped badge of an unaccompanied minor clipped to his shirt. He was trying to plug in an earphone to silence the speaker of a handheld scanner.

"I'm sorry, Sir, you'll have to put that away now," Britta told him gently, unprepared for his response.

The boy yanked the earpiece from his ear and glowered at her. "This can't hurt the instruments," he said.

She knelt beside him. "The rules on this airplane require us to have all radios, even this one, turned off until we're in flight. Okay?"

"It's an aviation scanner, okay? Buzz off!" the boy snapped, stuffing the earpiece back in his ear.

Britta felt the 747 turn to the left. The final announcement for takeoff would come any second. She reached up and caught the wire, yanking it back out of his ear.

"OW-W! That hurt!"

Britta metered her voice to a low growl of authority. Her slight German accent intensified the intimidating effect.

"You turn the radio off now, or you'll permanently lose it."

The boy glared at her, but the possibility that she could carry out the threat forced him to snap off the switch. "Okay. Jeez."

"What's your name, young man?"

"Steve Delaney."

"You need to learn some manners, Steven Delaney."

He started to speak, but she held up a finger, and he thought better of it.

Britta stood and left the boy sulking. She turned toward the rear galley at the exact moment the captain jammed on the brakes, throwing her into the aisle. She pulled herself up immediately and took inventory, brushing her skirt, smoothing her hair, and trying to smile at the shaken people around her. All the passengers had been seated safely, but two of the other flight attendants had also been thrown to the floor, and she could see Bill Jenkins in the distance standing up and dusting himself off near the forward galley. The sound of cascading items hitting the floor in the rear galley had reached her ears, and she walked back quickly to check on the mess. Pete Cavanaugh's voice returned to the PA.

Folks, sorry about that sudden stop. Another aircraft illicitly cut in front of us on the taxiway here, and I had no choice.

In the cockpit of Meridian Flight 5, Pete Cavanaugh was shaking his head as Dan Wade pressed the Transmit button. "Hong Kong Ground, Meridian Five. We had to panic stop for a business jet that pulled in front of us. Where did he come from?"

An American-accented voice cut in before the ground controller could reply. "Sorry about that, Meridian. We thought you were going to hold for us."

"Who is this?" Dan asked.

"Global Express Two-Two-Zulu."

"Thanks a lot, Two-Two-Zulu! We had the right of way here, and we weren't even aware you were on the air patch."

"Well, no harm done."

"Tell that to our passengers and flight attendants!" Dan snapped, noting Pete's right hand raised to calm him down.

"Enough, Dan!" Pete said.

"Meridian Five, caution please for the emergency departure ahead of you," the tower controller said.

"Who is he?" Dan replied on the radio, anger still audible in his voice.

"We're an air ambulance medivac flight, Meridian," the Global Express pilot interrupted. "Again, we're sorry."

Dan shook his head. "That'd be a great thing to happen to you in your last six months before retirement, Pete. Crush a forty-million-dollar bizzjet with a hundred-seventy-five-million-dollar Boeing."

Pete chuckled. "You're right. That's not how I'd like to be remembered. Dan, check with our folks downstairs and make sure everyone came through that okay."

Dan was reaching for the intercom handset as the chime rang with Britta on the other end.

"No one's hurt, but would you two please not do that again real soon?"

"Sorry. I know we've got white-knucklers aboard."

"Always!" Britta added. "I know the passengers are spooked when I can't hear your PAs over the clicking of the rosary beads."

Dan laughed. "Yours or the passengers?"

"Mine. And I'm not even Catholic."

Britta replaced the intercom handset and rolled her eyes at her aft galley crew as they picked up the last of the spilled items. Pete's voice was on the PA again.

Well, folks, again I apologize for that brief brake test. They work, by the way. We have a red-faced air ambulance pilot to thank for that, but I figured if we didn't stop, I'd have to explain to someone why we'd compacted him down to the size of a roller skate. It was a bit like a minnow challenging a whale.

We're at the end of the runway now and ready to go, and . . . the tower's telling us to hold a few minutes for clearance. So, while I'd like the flight attendants to take their seats for departure, understand we may be sitting here up to four minutes or so. Good to have you with us tonight. We'll be talking to you briefly after departure.

Pete sighed as he looked at the approaching storm now showing up on the 747's radar as a line of angry red splotches fifteen miles out. "I hate it when they hold up our takeoff clearance."

"Probably for that air ambulance," Dan said. "Probably going in the same direction. That's a U.S. call sign he's using."

"I'm astounded," Pete replied, studying the approaching thunderheads in the distance, "that anyone would be using something as ritzy and expensive as a forty-million-dollar Bombardier Global Express for an air ambulance. That's the six-thousand-mile-range rival to the Boeing Business Jet and the Gulfstream Five. Looks a little like the Canadair Challenger. Same manufacturer, in fact."

"Here comes our takeoff clearance, Pete," Dan said, holding his earpiece with one hand and copying the clearance with the other before reading it back to the controller. He nodded to the captain as he changed to the tower frequency.

"Hong Kong Tower, Meridian Five, ready to go."

The slightly accented voice issued the takeoff clearance. Pete pushed up the throttles and guided the 375-ton aircraft onto the runway. Dan ran through the last items on the checklist and clicked on the landing lights.

"All ahead full, Danny. Steady as she goes."

Dan shook his head, pretending disgust.

"'All ahead full'? Jeez, you Navy guys! The proper terminology, Captain, Sir, is 'Power set, N1 checked, autothrottles engaged.'"

There was another burst of lightning to the southwest as the huge aircraft began moving forward, the airspeed indicators coming to life as both pilots let their eyes scan around the cockpit, verifying all was normal.

"Airspeed alive both sides, eighty knots," Dan called.

"Roger," Pete replied, his eyes roving over the instruments once more before returning to the runway, which seemed to be moving lethargically beneath the nose as the 747 approached flying speed.

"Vee one, and rotate."

Pete Cavanaugh pulled back gently on the yoke, lifting the 747's nose into the air, increasing the wing's angle of attack until lift exceeded weight and the big bird rose gracefully from the concrete. The slight shudder of the sixteen wheels of the main landing gear extending on their struts could be felt rather than heard in the cockpit.

"Positive rate, gear up," Pete commanded.

Dan reached for the gear handle, speaking the requisite words—"Roger, gear up"—as he raised the handle to the Up position.

This was the crystalline moment Dan loved so well, the moment of transition between ground and air, when the laws of aerodynamics took over the job of physical support of the jet. He'd become a pilot for this very moment: the feel of mighty engines and the roar of the slipstream, all converging on the reality of sustained flight on an invisible highway of air. Flying was a thrill in even a single-engine airplane, but to levitate a leviathan—a metallic eggshell longer than a football field and heavier than a house—was a magic he could never quite comprehend. Every liftoff was a philosophical wonder that left a broad smile on his face.

The gear lights went out in sequence, indicating all the wheels were up and locked. Dan glanced to the right as he moved the gear handle to the Off position, drinking in the twinkling lights of ground-bound civilization as they dropped away and the 747 soared over the water, steadily gaining altitude into the night.

chapter

7

Kat Bronsky paused on the front entrance to the American Consulate compound, smelling flowers, watching the flashes of lightning from the approaching storm, and wondering why she was so distracted. She smiled at the consular officer waiting for her in the doorway and went inside, making a mental note to phone customs in Honolulu before going to bed to arrange special handling for Robert MacCabe.

She wondered if the 747 was airborne yet. She could imagine herself comfortably seated in the first-class seat next to Robert MacCabe, and not just for professional reasons. There was a basic attraction there, although his plight was what primarily concerned her. She had a proprietary interest in what he thought he knew, but it would also be nice to get to know him better. Despite a bad initial impression, MacCabe seemed like a truly nice guy.

That's a dangerous conclusion, she reminded herself. *At least bad boys are as advertised. The nice guys can always fool you.*

A consular officer had waited up to greet her. They would

arrange a 7 A.M. meeting for her on what was a criminal matter involving a staff officer. With luck, she could make a noon departure to L.A.

She thanked him and followed an aide to the guest house, the thought of a soft bed and six hours of sleep a luxury.

ABOARD MERIDIAN 5,
ON TAKEOFF FROM CHEK LAP KOK/
HONG KONG INTERNATIONAL AIRPORT

"Quite a sight, huh?"

Robert MacCabe turned his head away from the windows to the source of the voice: a well-dressed man in his late thirties, sitting in the opposite row.

Robert managed a smile, slightly irritated at the forced engagement. "Yes."

"A good view of Kowloon should be coming up on your side as we turn east."

Robert nodded and looked left again.

"You one of our regular customers?" the man asked.

Once again Robert took his gaze away from the window and looked over at the speaker. "I beg your pardon?"

"One of our regulars? You look very familiar."

Robert smiled thinly and shook his head. "No. First time on this airline."

A seat belt clanked open as the man leaned over with his hand extended.

"I'm Rick Barnes, CEO of Meridian Airlines. And you are?"

"Really enjoying this view," Robert said, trying to hide his displeasure at the interruption. The beauty the man had heralded was sliding past unseen on the left as Robert reluctantly shook Rick Barnes's hand. "MacCabe. Robert MacCabe."

"Who're you with, Robert?"

"The *Washington Post*."

"Really? Well, I think we've met before somewhere. You look exceedingly familiar. Good to have you with us."

Robert nodded as he looked left, feeling Barnes's eyes on the back of his neck.

"Were you in Hong Kong to cover the trade delegation aboard tonight?" Barnes asked.

Robert sighed and looked over, smiling thinly. "Let's talk a bit later, if you don't mind, Mr. Barnes. I'd like to take this all in."

"Oh, sure!" Rick Barnes said, waving Robert back to the window. The young airline president got to his feet and walked back toward the galley, nodding to the couple in the second row of seats.

Dr. Graham Tash nodded back as he squeezed his wife's arm and spoke softly in her ear. "Great safety example. We're hardly off and he's running down the aisle."

"You recognize him, Honey?" Susan Tash asked.

"Should I?"

"One of the founders of the Costclub warehouse stores. Made about a billion dollars by age thirty and doesn't really know what to do with it."

"So he bought an airline?"

"Bought into it, more precisely," she said. "*Forbes* magazine had an article on him. He put himself on the board and made himself CEO, even though he knows virtually nothing about aviation. Meridian is his new toy."

"I'm not envious," Graham said. "I have my toy." He squeezed her hand again and felt her pull away slightly, feigning offense.

"Surely you're not referring to your new wife as a *toy*, Doctor!"

He looked hurt. "Well, wait a minute. Let me check. You're incredibly beautiful, perfectly proportioned, sexy beyond Bardot and Monroe, brilliant beyond comprehension, and sexually insatiable. Yep! Definitely my favorite toy."

She swatted his shoulder, trying to look insulted, but her smile betrayed her.

He smiled back. "Does this mean you *won't* meet me in the bathroom in five minutes for meaningless sex?"

"Sh-h-h! Behave yourself!" she whispered. "You're a professional."

"Look, seriously, this trip was a wonderful idea, Honey."

"I thought you'd like Hong Kong."

"What I like is being with you. Anywhere. I haven't been happier in decades. Who knew? My own nurse. Right there in the OR all the time. Scrubbed and everything."

"Yes, isn't it romantic?" she said, smiling. "I can tell people we flirted over an appendectomy, got serious during a bowel resection, and fell in love in the middle of open-heart surgery."

He leaned over to kiss her as the 747 rolled sharply to the right, shoving everyone on the upper deck to one side.

"Who in the hell was that?" Dan Wade asked, as Pete Cavanaugh brought the Boeing back to wings-level and punched the Transmit button. "Hong Kong Departure, Meridian Five. Another aircraft just passed from left to right across our flight path, very close, almost a near hit. We'd estimate we missed him only by a quarter mile."

"Roger, Meridian, there is no known traffic ahead of you."

"Did you have any a minute ago?" Dan pressed.

"No, Sir. There was no . . ." There was a pause and another controller's voice came on frequency, presumably a supervisor.

"Meridian Five. Stand by."

Thirty seconds went by before the supervisor's voice returned. "We were apparently getting an intermittent raw radar return in that vicinity a minute ago, Meridian, but our computer did not consider it valid traffic, so we did not call it out to you. We have only an inbound DC-ten and an outbound Global Express out there."

HONG KONG DEPARTURE CONTROL,
CHEK LAP KOK/HONG KONG
INTERNATIONAL AIRPORT

The controller was pulling on the sleeve of his supervisor. "Two-Two-Zulu has disappeared, Sir. The Global Express."

The supervisor looked at the controller he'd superseded. "Where was he?"

The controller ran his finger over the glass of the computer-generated radarscope to a spot several miles in front of Meridian Five. "Here. The data block started coasting, then just dropped out."

The supervisor took a deep breath. A missing airplane in Chinese airspace translated to an instant political problem, especially since mainland China had taken over. Officially, the aircraft couldn't be missing unless it had crashed.

"Did you see the altitude going down?"

The controller shook his head. "No, Sir. It was stable until he blinked out."

"How about a basic radar return? Did you see anything after he disappeared?

The controller shook his head as he pointed to another spot on the screen. "There's that other target. No transponder signal. Just a raw radar image."

The supervisor looked at the shadowy target the controllers called a "skin paint," the echo of the radar beam off a flying metal object, unenhanced by the electronic information usually provided by an aircraft's transponder.

The controller moved his finger just below the intermittent target, which was to the right of Meridian this time. He toggled a switch to enhance the raw signal, and it flared more brightly, clearly moving laterally toward the 747.

The supervisor pushed the Transmit button. "Meridian Five, Hong Kong. We have that intermittent target again to your three o'clock position, altitude unknown."

Aboard Meridian 5, Dan's face was pressed to the side window. "I see nothing over here, Pete!"

Pete shook his head. "You suppose the Chinese Air Force is out here playing games?" Pete triggered the radio with his Transmit button. "If this is some sort of military game, Hong Kong, tell them to stop. It's a violation of civil rules."

The supervisor's voice was back in an instant. "We know of no explanation, Meridian. We are also missing a business jet who was ahead of you. Have you had any contact with Global Express Two-Two-Zulu?"

Dan and Pete exchanged glances.

"This is weird. What do you suppose happened to them?" Dan said to Pete, just as the supervisor's voice came back, intense and rapid.

"Meridian, we've lost that target. We are informing our military authorities."

"Dan, look up the numbers for our Air Force base in Taiwan, just in case."

The copilot reached for his bag and pulled out the appropriate manual, flipping to the right page. He was in the process of glancing up from the manual at the same instant the world seemed to explode in an incredible burst of hideously bright light that saturated the cockpit, stabbing his eyes and thrusting him back in the seat with unbelievable pain. An unearthly, agonized scream erupted from the left seat and the 747 shuddered into some sort of shock wave.

Dan's eyes were on fire. His eyelids slammed shut, the pain all but unbearable, an endless field of white where his vision should have been.

"Pete! Are you okay?" Dan called.

There was another guttural screech from the left seat, and Dan reached out to touch the captain. He felt Pete Cavanaugh's body slump to the left.

"Pete? Pete! Speak to me!"

Dan felt for the control yoke in front of the captain. Pete's hands weren't on it.

"Pete? For God's sake, answer me!"

There was no sound from the left seat.

The supervisor in Hong Kong Control was in his ear, asking what they had seen. Dan wanted to answer, but his mind was in complete confusion, his eyes two burning coals of intense pain, his captain unresponsive—and the 747 obviously wobbling around, out of the control of either pilot.

Autopilot!

Dan reached to the upper console and punched the square push button that engaged the autopilot, and felt the giant machine begin to right itself.

My God, what's going on here? No depressurization. Windshield's intact.

The autoflight system had been set for climb at Mach .74 before Pete disconnected, he recalled. He needed to reengage the autothrottles, too. But should they climb? Maybe not.

Declare an emergency . . . got to go back . . . may need to dump fuel, we're heavy.

Dan snapped on the autothrottles and selected the Altitude Hold button, praying he'd gotten the right one. He could hear the throttles adjusting themselves as he fumbled for the Transmit button.

"Hong Kong, has there been a nuclear detonation somewhere ahead? Something . . . something exploded up here!"

"Say again, Meridian."

"Something exploded just in front of us! I think we're hit. There're only two of us on the flight deck, and the captain is not responding. I'm on autopilot, but this is the first officer and my eyes have been badly hurt. I can't see. I need your help."

The voice from below sounded almost as shaken as his own. "Ah—Meridian, this is Hong Kong. You are heading now zero-eight-two degrees, and you appear level at one-two thousand feet, ground speed three hundred forty knots. Say your intentions?"

"Hell, Hong Kong, I don't know. I'm, ah . . . let me calm down up here and try . . . try to figure out what I've got, okay? Stay with me. Give me a turn if necessary to stay in your radio range." Dan realized he was almost hyperventilating with fear and pain. He forced himself to slow his breathing rate, willing the searing pain to the back of his consciousness as he tried to deal with the crisis.

"We'll need to come back, I'm sure of that. Ah . . . declare us . . . I mean, I'm declaring an emergency right now."

"Roger, Meridian. We have your emergency declaration. Be advised Hong Kong is now under a severe thunderstorm watch, and rain is beginning. There is more weather to the east. We can keep you clear in the meantime, but for now, please maintain present heading. Were you hit by lightning, Meridian?"

Maybe that's it, Dan thought. *No. It couldn't be. Lightning isn't that bright.*

"Meridian, a question, please. Are there relief pilots aboard your aircraft?"

The stabbing pain behind each eye was getting worse, blanking out even his thoughts as Dan struggled to stay engaged and rise above the pain.

"No, Hong Kong. This is a two-man crew."

Have to get someone up here! he told himself, fumbling with his left hand at the back of the pedestal for the interphone. He couldn't find the right buttons at first, but finally pushed All Call and listened to the majority of the flight attendants come on the line from various sections of the aircraft.

"Britta, are you there somewhere?"

"Right here. Is this *Dan*? You sound strange."

"Please . . . get up here right now! We have an emergency. I need you—WAIT! First, make a PA, ask for any other pilots on board, even . . . even if it scares everyone."

"It's scaring me, but I'm on the way."

Britta Franz felt her stomach contracting into a singularity as she punched the PA button on the same handset and put it back to her mouth, trying to sound calm.

> *Ladies and gentlemen, this is the lead flight attendant. Please listen carefully. Our flight crew is requesting that anyone aboard who is a licensed pilot, please identify yourself by ringing your Call button.*

There was silence amid the wide-eyed looks she was getting from the cabin passengers on the left side, the only ones who could see the apprehension on her face.

Bill Jenkins materialized at her side, waiting silently as she tried again.

*Again, folks, please. If anyone on this aircraft is a
licensed pilot, regardless of what you fly, please ring
your Call button immediately. I . . . do not know the
reason for the pilots making this request, folks, but
please comply. Anyone?*

Bill leaned toward her. "Britta, I'll keep trying. You'd better get up there."

She gave the handset to him without a word and raced
toward the staircase, breaking into a run at the top of the
stairs with the cockpit key in hand. She found the door
unlocked.

Britta instinctively shut the door behind her, letting her
eyes adjust to the subdued light. She could see Pete in the
captain's seat, but something was wrong. He was slumped to
the left with his head lolled back.

"Dan?" Britta said. "What's going on?"

"Check Pete! Check him. Now!"

Britta's mouth felt dry as she turned to the captain. A stab
of fear ran through her mind as she realized his eyes were
open. She reached for his neck and felt for the carotid artery
as she would before administering CPR, but there was no
pulse. She moved his head, and it rolled lifelessly to the
other side.

"Oh my God, Dan! He's not breathing! I can't find a
pulse!"

"Can you get him out of the seat and do CPR?" Dan
asked.

She turned to the copilot, wondering why he was flying
with his head down. "Danny, what's wrong?"

"I can't see, Britta. Something exploded in front of us."

"Oh my God!"

"The plane's on autopilot. Help Pete! Don't worry about
me for now."

"You can't *see*?"

"Britta! Help Pete!"

She nodded, breathing rapidly. "Okay. Ah, I'll need help."

She dashed to the cockpit door and flung it open, her eyes

falling on the very person she was hoping to see. Memorizing the names of her first-class passengers had always been a matter of pride for her, and now it was a godsend.

"Dr. Tash!"

The physician and his wife had been watching the cockpit door since she ran inside. His eyes locked on hers as he came out of the seat.

"Right here."

"I need help! The captain's injured and not breathing."

Britta stepped aside to let the doctor rush in. Robert Mac-Cabe followed. "Can I help?" MacCabe asked.

"Probably," Britta replied.

The doctor was leaning over the captain, his eyes wide with surprise as he ran the same basic checks for pulse and breath. "How do I get this seat back?" he asked.

"It's electric. The buttons are on the forward left edge," Dan replied.

Robert moved forward and joined Graham Tash in maneuvering the captain's deadweight out of the seat, pulling Pete as gently as they could through the cockpit door and into the forward aisle, where Susan Tash was waiting.

"What do we have, Graham?"

"Start CPR, Susan. His airway's clear. Breathe first. Miss?" Graham said to Britta. "I need the aircraft emergency medical kit."

She nodded and immediately disappeared back into the cockpit, emerging with the large white metal box. Graham began opening it.

"How can I help?" Robert asked the doctor.

"Check on the copilot for me."

Several of the occupants of the first-class cabin were on their feet, standing by their seats and watching, unsure what to do. Britta looked up and held up her hand. "Stay calm, folks! We'll explain in a minute. The other pilot is at the controls." She knelt alongside Pete and looked at the doctor. "How bad is it?"

He shook his head. "I don't know yet." He popped a stethoscope into place and began probing for a heartbeat while Susan finished the first round of breathing.

There was none.

"Is that a crash cart?" Susan asked.

"Not completely," Graham replied, "but we've got a defibrillator."

Robert MacCabe reentered the cockpit and moved to the copilot's side.

"Who's there?" Dan asked, sensing his presence. The question confused Robert. The light in the cockpit was not that dim.

"Ah, Robert MacCabe. Are you okay?"

"No."

"What—what happened up here?" Robert could see that the copilot's eyes were squinted closed; his head was down, his face bloodless and contorted in pain.

Dan shook his head. "Something exploded in front of us. The light was unbelievable. I think I've temporarily lost my vision to flash blindness."

Robert felt his heart accelerating. He told himself this couldn't be happening.

"What's wrong with the captain?" the copilot was asking.

"You say . . . your eyes—"

"I CAN'T SEE! Okay? Are you a doctor?"

"No, but there's one working on the other pilot."

"Then tell me about the captain."

Robert felt his head swimming. He glanced back toward the door at the rear of the cockpit. "He's . . . we're giving CPR. He's not breathing."

Robert heard an agonized noise from the occupant of the right seat. The man was breathing rapidly, obviously in deep pain. "Let me get the doctor up here."

Robert turned to go but Dan stopped him. "Hey! Are you a pilot?"

"No."

"Any aviation experience?"

"I'm sorry, no."

"Okay. If they find another pilot, get him up here immediately."

Robert left the cockpit with his stomach in a knot and his mind in complete confusion. What could have exploded? A missile? Maybe that was it. What was the political situation? Suddenly he couldn't recall, but the possibility they were under attack by China flitted through his mind.

What else could flash-blind a pilot? he wondered, the answer coming with nightmarish implications. *Oh my Lord, a nuclear blast could do it.* But why hadn't there been a shock wave? Wouldn't that have torn them apart? *Maybe not,* he thought, *if the explosion was several hundred miles away, or the detonation was small. But we could all be doomed from radiation exposure.*

Robert was standing just outside the cockpit door. "Ah, the copilot . . . says he can't see, Doctor. He needs you up there."

Graham Tash looked up and caught Robert's eye. "Just a second."

Robert nodded and disappeared back into the cockpit as Graham looked at his wife. "Okay. CLEAR!"

"Clear!" she echoed.

Pete's body convulsed once. Graham threw the paddles down and jabbed the stethoscope in his ears as he leaned over the chest.

He straightened up and shook his head. "Keep going!"

Susan Tash began pumping again immediately as Graham scrambled to his feet and raced into the cockpit. Robert stepped aside and the physician introduced himself.

"Let me look at your eyes!" Graham ordered.

Dan lifted his head toward the doctor's voice. "It hurts so bad, I don't know if I can open them."

Graham leaned down, positioning his thumbs to open the left eye. "Try to relax the eyelid if you can."

"I'll try. OW-W! The light! That's horrible!"

Graham let the eyelid close. "I'm sorry. I'll try to find some painkiller for you as soon as I can. I've got to get back to the captain."

"How bad are my eyes?"

"I don't know. Not like the captain. You've been flash-blinded by something, but the damage is internal."

He moved toward the cockpit door, but the deadly urgency in Dan's voice stopped him.

"How long to recover?" Dan asked. "For flash blindness, I mean?"

Graham Tash shrugged. "I don't know. Up to a few days, maybe. Best guess."

"Doctor," the copilot began. "With the fuel we're carrying, we don't have days. We have, at best, about eight hours."

ABOARD MERIDIAN 5, IN FLIGHT,
WEST OF HONG KONG
NOVEMBER 13—DAY TWO
1:15 A.M. LOCAL/1715 ZULU

Rick Barnes had been slow to get out of his first-class seat when he saw the captain dragged out of the cockpit. The CEO of Meridian Airlines finally overcame his shock and forced himself to put down his Bloody Mary and stand up to offer help to the female passenger in the yellow dress who was giving CPR. He prayed she wouldn't take him up on the offer—since he'd never taken a CPR class.

Britta had been assisting Susan. She looked up now and smiled. "Thanks, Mr. Barnes. If you'll help, I need to check on the cockpit."

Rick knelt and watched the captain for signs of life, trying to appear unruffled.

"Okay," Susan Tash said, "you can spell me on this next cycle. Two . . . three . . . four . . . five . . ." She was pumping Pete Cavanaugh's chest and counting. She transitioned back to his mouth and motioned Rick Barnes into position over the captain's chest, holding up a finger for him to wait.

"Now," she said as she straightened up.

"What do I do?" Rick asked.

Susan looked at him like he'd lost his mind. "You don't know CPR?"

"It's been a long time since I had the training," he lied, but she'd already swept him aside to resume the chest-pumping and counting. "Two . . . three . . . get the flight attendant . . . four . . . five . . . back here . . . or get another . . . six . . . ready to take over for me."

Rick got to his feet as Susan transferred back to the captain's mouth. He was marginally aware of a male voice on the PA, asking for pilots again. Why? Wasn't one enough? They were still flying, so obviously there was at least one pilot left.

"Would you please go!" Susan snapped.

"Yeah. Sorry." Rick walked quickly to the stairway leading to the main deck as a male flight attendant hit the top step and froze, recognizing the CEO.

"Mr. Barnes. Are you a pilot?"

Rick snorted and shook his head as if insulted. "No. But I need one of you flight attendants to take over the CPR for that lady in yellow up there."

Bill Jenkins spotted the captain on the floor. He pushed past Rick Barnes none too subtly and ran to Susan Tash's side. "I'm Bill Jenkins, one of the flight attendants. What *happened* to him?"

She shook her head. "Some sort of explosion. We've lost him, Bill."

Bill Jenkins looked at the cockpit as Britta came out. He was wholly unprepared for the quick briefing she gave him.

"Did you find any pilots down there?" Britta asked her stunned coworker.

Bill shook his head. "I repeated the announcement three times and in Mandarin as well. No one."

Britta rubbed her head. "There's got to be someone. Try again. Ask for anyone with any aeronautical training, licensed or unlicensed, current or not."

Bill stepped carefully past Pete Cavanaugh's body to find the PA as Britta knelt to help Susan. Graham Tash had returned as well and was picking up the defibrillator paddles.

• • •

On the main deck below, a murmur of worried voices blended with the background noise of the engines and slipstream. The passengers looked at one another with startled expressions and tried to discern what might be happening.

Bill Jenkins's voice cut through the noise, triggering complete silence as everyone strained to hear a reassurance that all was well.

Instead they heard another plea for *anyone* with aeronautical training to ring the Call button, a request urgent and frightening enough to bring several passengers to their feet, looking around in shock, unsure what to do.

Those who stood were pounced upon immediately by flight attendants. "Are you trained as a pilot, Sir?" "Can you fly, Ma'am?" "Are you responding to the PA?" were questions fired at high speed with high hopes, but only one had the right answer.

"Excuse me," a tall, distinguished man asked, "some chap asked for anyone with any aeronautical training to come forth and I do have a bit."

Another call chime rang in the coach, and Alice Naccarato responded.

"Hey, Miss?" a voice called out.

Alice stopped and turned, looking past a teenage boy to an ashen-faced man in a window seat.

"Yes, Sir?"

"Not him. Me," the teenager said.

Ah, yes. Alice thought. *The kid Britta warned me about.*

"I'm Steve Delaney, and I know I'm just an unaccompanied minor, but I know about flying and you need a pilot, right?"

"You're a pilot, Steve?"

"I can handle it."

"But *are* you a licensed pilot?"

"No, but . . ."

"Have you ever flown a real plane this size?"

"No."

"Have you ever flown a real plane of *any* size, Steve?"

"No."

Alice smiled thinly. The last thing Dan needed in the cockpit was some adolescent amateur with an attitude.

"Steve, I appreciate your responding, but we just had an experienced pilot come forward, and I think we'd better go with him."

"Yeah, I know the routine."

"I'm sorry," Alice sighed, and stood. The boy scowled and looked away.

In the cockpit the interphone call chime caused Dan to reach too rapidly for the handset, lacerating his knuckles before he could pull it out of the cradle.

"Cockpit."

"Dan? This is Bill. I've found an older guy with Korean-vintage flight experience down here."

"Good. An Air Force type?"

"British, actually. Not military aviation, though. Korean War–vintage. He says he took civilian flying lessons back then. His name's Sampson."

Dan snorted to himself. *Just my luck!* "Thanks. Send Mr. Sampson up."

In seat 28G, Julia Mason had already decided to do more than sit and worry. After all, over the previous month, the forty-five members of her tour group had come to expect her to have all the answers. Well into her sixties, she took pride in being firmly in charge and refusing to accept head-patting answers from crew members.

Julia rose quickly from her aisle seat and strode to the middle galley, finding one of the younger flight attendants, a brunette with beautiful dark eyes and a perfect olive complexion, who gave Julia a briefing she wished she hadn't asked for: The captain was dead, something had exploded in front of them, and the copilot was flying.

"My Lord, that's awful. But shouldn't that copilot be telling us something on the public address system?" Julia asked, trying to recover her composure.

"Ma'am, all I know is what I just told you." The flight

attendant's response was gentle but firm, triggering Julia's instincts to bore in.

"What's your name, Dear?"

"Nancy," the flight attendant replied, her eyes focused on the other passengers.

"Now, Nancy, surely we're going back?"

"I honestly don't know."

"Well, that's simply not good enough, is it? Won't you get on that interphone and find out? See, I've got forty-five people expecting *me* to know. What do I tell them?" Julia realized her voice was shaking.

Nancy shook her head. "Ma'am, as soon as we know anything, you'll know it. Please go back and sit down now."

"Absolutely not. Not until I have some information to give to my people."

"Ma'am—"

"My name is Julia, Nancy."

"Julia, look, I'm . . . I'm worried too, because—"

"Bottom line, Nancy, is you're a crew member and supposed to be in charge. Now. What can we expect to happen next?"

The flight attendant shrugged and pursed her lips, tears betraying the tension. She fought for control, but it was a losing battle. "I . . . I don't know, but . . . I . . ." She flailed the air with her right hand as she struggled for composure. "Frankly, I'm scared, and I would appreciate . . . very much . . . your leaving me alone right now."

Julia felt her resolve evaporate as she looked at the young woman, forty years her junior, feeling the same apprehension that they were in uncharted territory. Julia moved forward to enfold the young woman in a motherly embrace.

"Meridian Five, what is your status?" the voice boomed over the cockpit speakers, startling Robert MacCabe, who was standing behind the center console and gripping the captain's empty seat as he surveyed the technological jungle of dials and gauges and lights on the forward panel.

Dan Wade took a ragged breath and punched his Transmit

button, talking into the tiny boom microphone he wore. His voice emerged strained and low.

"We're . . . ah . . . stable right now, Hong Kong, but we're trying to find someone aboard with pilot experience . . . because I'm . . . not in good shape."

"Sorry to ask, Sir, but can you repeat what happened?"

Dan sighed. "I don't know, Hong Kong. Something exploded just in front of us. It shook the whole airplane, flash-blinded my eyes, and somehow triggered a heart attack or . . . or something in the captain. I don't know what it was. I've never even heard of anything that bright and painful, other than a nuclear fireball, which is what I said earlier, but I guess it couldn't have been. Ah . . . but Hong Kong, the explosion happened just after that unidentified aircraft crossed our path."

There was a pause from the controller, followed by a sin-gular response that triggered a chill down Dan's back. "Meridian, we're missing Global Express Two-Two-Zulu. Is it possible you collided with him?"

Dan swallowed hard, trying to envision the 747 essen-tially ramming the smaller jet. How could that happen with-out even depressurizing the cabin? But somehow it must have. It was the only logical explanation, short of some attack.

"Either someone shot a missile at us that exploded in front, or we hit him. If he's missing, then I'm sure we hit him. But if we're not damaged . . ."

"Meridian, are you able to land the airplane, Sir?"

Dan tried to gauge what consequences there might be for speaking the grim truth on an open radio channel. If they couldn't find another pilot, he would have one option only: use the autoflight system to let the airplane land itself, a maneuver that would require setting up the autopi-lot and autothrottles perfectly, and standing by to hand-fly a missed approach literally in the blind if anything went wrong.

There was no reason to sugarcoat it, he decided. He couldn't even open his eyelids, let alone see anything. For now he was a blind man.

"Hong Kong," Dan began in a constrained, almost hoarse voice, "I'm the only pilot left up here, and I cannot see to fly. But . . . ah . . . our autopilot is working, and I'm going to get us down with that."

"Roger, Meridian."

Dr. Graham Tash reentered the cockpit, brushing Dan's arm.

"Who's there?" Dan asked.

"It's the doctor, Dan."

"How's Pete?"

The physician cleared his throat. "Dan, I'm sorry, but he's gone."

"Oh, God! How? How could that happen?"

Graham put his hand on the copilot's shoulder. "I don't know. Probably a coronary. Maybe a stroke."

Dan took a ragged breath and swallowed. "Pete only had six months before retirement. He . . . was going to take his wife around the world."

"We did everything we could. We could never get a heart-beat."

Dan was shaking his head. "He's got a huge family. Kids, grandkids." He was quiet for a few seconds before taking a sharp breath and wincing from the effort. "Doc, do you guys carry little black bags anymore?"

"Not really. But there's an emergency medical kit aboard."

"I . . . ah . . . need something for the pain. Not enough to run the risk of knocking me out, but to get the edge off. I'm . . . having trouble handling the pain and thinking."

"I have it right here," Graham said. "I'm only going to give you a small amount, for the same reasons you indicated, Dan."

"Could you please hurry?"

Graham ripped open an alcohol swab with his teeth as he struggled to unbutton the copilot's left cuff and pull his sleeve up, swabbing the target area. He drew the appropriate amount of anesthetic into the syringe and injected it into Dan's vein. "You should feel that almost instantly."

There was a sigh and a nod from the copilot as a wide-eyed Bill Jenkins came through the door with someone in tow.

"Dan? I've brought Mr. Geoffrey Sampson."

The copilot nodded. "There's no time for courtesies, Mr. Sampson. Please get in the captain's seat—the left seat, and fasten the seat belt."

"Very well," the man said in a classic Oxford accent, climbing into the seat.

"Mr. Sampson?" Dan began as soon as he heard the belt snap to.

"Geoffrey, if you please," he said.

"Yeah. Geoffrey. Look, I'm going to need your assistance flying this aircraft."

"Oh, dear. That could be a difficulty, then, Captain. I've had frightfully little experience."

"My name's Dan."

"Of course. Dan, I had flight lessons in small single-engine airplanes during the fifties, but that's a world away from this cockpit."

"You know the basics? Airspeed, altitude, heading, attitude?"

"Most of them, yes."

Once again Dan had to remind himself to slow his breathing. He was getting light-headed—or was that the effect of the morphine?

"Geoffrey. Take . . . ah." Dan stopped and shook his head to clear it. A wave of pain rewarded the effort. He heard himself whimper, a sound he was determined not to repeat, and swallowed hard against a cotton mouth.

"Okay . . . Geoff . . . take a good and careful look at every major switch and everything on the display screens and see how much looks familiar."

"Okay."

"We're . . . going to . . . have to let the autopilot land the airplane back in Hong Kong, since I can't see."

"I must be misunderstanding this—are you telling me that you're unable to see *anything*?"

"That's the problem."

"Oh my!"

"Were you instrument-rated?"

"No. And I most certainly can't fly this machine! I—I—"

Robert clamped a reassuring hand on Sampson's right shoulder as Dan held up his left hand to interrupt the Englishman. "Hold it, Geoffrey. *You're* not going to fly. The airplane will fly itself. You're just going to be my eyes, reading the basic instruments and watching to make sure the autopilot doesn't disconnect. Okay?"

"Very well. I can try, but I must have you understand I am not able to fly an airplane like this."

"Understood. Robert, are you still here?"

"Yes, Dan."

"And Doc?"

"Right here, Dan."

Dan took another ragged breath. "Okay. All of you watch this panel." He pointed to the push buttons on the forward glare shield that engaged or disengaged the autopilot. "As long as this button is lit, the airplane is flying itself. If that snaps off, we have to get it on again. Now. See the radar display, Geoffrey?" He pointed to the screen, and the man acknowledged.

"Do you . . . just a second."

Once again Dan's head went down into his hands, his body shuddering. The three men in the cockpit watched in alarm. After nearly thirty seconds the copilot sat up again.

"Sorry. Okay. Do you see any big red areas in front of us? Those would be storm cells we don't want to get into."

"Not in front of us," Sampson replied. "There is a big red area to the left. Let me read the range. Yes. About sixty miles."

"Good! Keep watching that, too."

Dan leaned forward and gingerly touched his eyelids, feeling the swelling. He was dizzy, in pain, nauseated, tired, and scared, but the plan was becoming clearer. *I can do this. She's a new bird, the equipment works, and Hong Kong's got a long runway. I can make this happen!*

He pulled himself back to an upright position. "Is Britta up here?"

"No, Dan. This is Graham Tash."

Dan nodded, trying to swallow again. "Okay . . . ah . . . stand by." He triggered the Transmit button. "Hong Kong Approach, Meridian Five. I'm going to need vectors to—no. I'm going to need more time to prepare for landing. Is this course okay?"

"Roger, Meridian. Please turn left or right now to a heading of two-eight-zero degrees. We show you still level at one-two thousand feet."

"Okay. Coming left to a heading of two-eight-zero." Dan inclined his head toward the left seat. "Geoffrey? Can you see the little window I'm pointing to here on the forward panel?"

"Yes, Dan."

"What does it say?"

"It says oh, eight, oh."

"Zero-eight-zero, right?"

"Correct."

"Look straight ahead of you at the compass rose on what we—what we call the HSI, on the video screen." Dan sighed deeply.

"Very well."

"What heading is under the lubber line, that little line at the top of the case?"

"I believe it's the same, Dan. We're heading zero-eight-zero, as you call it."

"Okay. Great." He was almost panting again. *Got to keep the breathing slow! Pain's eased up some, so I ought to be able to make it. Take it easy.* "Geoffrey, that little window I was pointing to is the heading that we're asking the autopilot to fly. Use the little knob beneath it now—we call that the heading selector—and turn it counterclockwise until it says two-eight-zero, okay?"

"Understood, Dan. I'm moving it."

The 747 began a left bank, and Dan could feel the roll begin. There would be frequencies to set up for the instrument landing system approach, and they would have to descend carefully to 3,000 feet while he made sure a half-dozen other items were correctly positioned, but with a little help, they could do it.

For the first time in several minutes, he began to feel hope.

chapter

9

Lucy Haggar, the newly elected mayor of Austin, Texas, released her seat belt and got to her feet, brushing back her impressive mane of silver hair before walking to the galley where Claire Brown and Alice Naccarato were standing in tense silence. Still trim and attractive in her late fifties, Lucy was used to being in control.

She pulled back the privacy curtain and stuck her head in the galley. "Girls, excuse me, but I need to ask a question."

"Yes, Ma'am," Claire replied, turning to face her.

"What in hell is going on here? And don't fib to me, now. Flight crews don't beg for passengers who can fly unless there's one granddaddy of a problem. Are the pilots dead?"

She meant the question as a joke, but Claire, a young red-head, took a deep breath and nodded. "One of them is."

Lucy felt her eyebrows flutter up involuntarily and her stomach leap to her throat. All the progress she'd made over the years in suppressing her fear of flying evaporated in the space of a heartbeat.

"You're kidding. Oh Lord, you're *not* kidding?"

Claire motioned her inside. "You're . . . Mayor Haggar, correct?"

Lucy nodded. "Yes."

"Mayor, we don't know much yet either, except that something exploded in front of our aircraft and the captain's dead."

"But you have a copilot, right? Tell me he's okay!"

Claire pursed her lips and hesitated a moment too long.

"Oh my God! The copilot's hurt, too, isn't he?"

The flight attendant nodded.

"How bad?"

"I honestly don't know."

"Oh Lord," Lucy said, "I came back here to ask you to tell someone upstairs to *please* get on the PA and talk to us! I was only scared then. Now I'm terrified!"

The sound of the PA system clicking on precluded a reply. They could hear a man clear his throat before his strained voice began speaking.

Folks . . . this is your copilot, First Officer Dan Wade. I'm going to speak very frankly, and I expect you to remain calm and collected. Something of an unknown nature exploded in front of this aircraft a few minutes ago. It's possible we hit another aircraft and he exploded. It's also possible someone shot a missile at us that. . . detonated just in front of the cockpit.

The PA clicked off for a few seconds, and then on again.

Sorry. Whatever exploded was so bright, it somehow triggered a deadly physical reaction in the captain, and I'm very, very sorry to report to you that Captain Pete Cavanaugh has died . . . which is why we asked for any pilots to come forward.

Again the PA clicked off, then on. More scraping noises and a heavy sigh before Dan Wade's voice resumed, echoing through an absolutely silent cabin. Over 200 passengers looked toward the overhead speakers as if they could see into the cockpit.

Ah, folks, I'm . . . ah . . . the only remaining pilot, which normally would not be a problem, but that explosion of light has injured me, too, and blinded me, at least temporarily. But . . . our airplane is undamaged, and this beautiful new Boeing seven-forty-seven is fully capable of automated landings. All I have to do is set things up, and I'm doing that now. No, I can't see a damn thing. Yes, I'm in some pain, and I know I sound a bit strange. But I know this cockpit, and I've got several folks with me helping to be my eyes. Is this serious? Of course. Are our chances good? They're excellent. I'm not going to give you some happy nonsense about there being no risk, but we should be okay. Anyway . . . a few prayers are in order. When we stop, we'll be stopping on the runway to be towed in, since I can't see to taxi safely. Okay. That's it. I'm sorry to be short and brutal.

It was a full twenty seconds before Lucy Haggar and the two flight attendants with her could exhale.

"Okay," Lucy began. "I asked for straight talk, I got straight talk. Now I think I need a straight bourbon. Maybe the whole damn bottle."

"I can get that for you," Claire replied, but Lucy had her hand up, her head cocked, and a strange smile on her face.

"I'm only kidding, Honey. Nightmares are best handled sober. But later I'm gonna close a few bars in Kowloon before I take the train back to Austin."

She turned and headed back to her seat as Bill Jenkins began a translation of the announcement in Mandarin Chinese.

The Autopilot Disconnect Warning coursed through Dan Wade's consciousness like an electric shock, causing him to jump at the same instant the huge 747 lurched downward.

"Gad!" He grabbed the control yoke, turning his head toward the captain's seat. His left hand was already on the control panel along the top of the glareshield, feeling for the square button, which he punched again to reconnect the autopilot while holding the control yoke as steady as he could.

The feel of the panel was reassuringly familiar, and for a split second, he almost forgot his eyesight was gone. But reality came back in a tidal wave of fear. He felt the bandage and the salve that Dr. Tash had slapped on his eyes minutes before. Fear was eating at him, distracting him from the task of trying to land. Despite his reassuring words on the PA, a safe landing was anything but certain; that reality was clouding his judgment, pushing him to rush the landing to get it over with.

It seemed far too hot in the cockpit to Dan, but there was no time to fumble for the temperature control. He was thirsty, too.

"What's my altitude, Geoffrey?" Dan asked the unseen passenger to his left.

"I'm—I'm looking," Geoffrey replied, his cultured voice cracking in fear. "I believe it says . . . yes, it says we're at just under twelve thousand."

"Good. Please verify that the altimeter is steady."

Another pause.

"It's steady."

"Geoffrey, did you push that sideways button on the control yoke?"

"Yes. I am most terribly sorry. I was just trying to get familiar with things."

"That's the Autopilot Disconnect button. I'll ask you to punch that when we get on the ground, but *only* on my command, okay?"

"Certainly."

Bringing him to the cockpit was probably a mistake, Dan thought. A few hours of instruction in light airplanes forty years ago was pretty thin preparation for being thrown into a space capsule. But what other choice did he have?

"First rule, Geoffrey," Dan added, holding his left index finger in the air, his voice shaking slightly, "is never push, turn, punch, twist, or alter anything up here unless you know precisely what you're doing, or I tell you to. We desperately need the autopilot to stay connected."

"I understand. I apologize."

Dan was sweating profusely, his breath coming in spurts, his hands shaking.

"How're you doing?" Graham Tash asked evenly. It was mostly rhetorical. He could see how the copilot was doing. The copilot was in pain and struggling and scared to death, like every one of his passengers.

There was a derisive sound from Dan as he started to shake his head, then winced. "How am I doing? I'm sorry, Doc. I'm just . . . I'm just . . . trying to cope, ah, with all this, okay? We're flying level on autopilot, we've got plenty of fuel—in fact, too much—and I'm just about ready to get this beast to land itself."

"Did the shot help?"

"It took the edge off, but it feels like someone's stabbing burning knives in my face and my eyes. I've . . . I've never felt pain like this, but I can't let you knock me out with too much painkiller."

Dan turned his bandaged face toward the British passenger in the captain's chair. "Ah . . . Geoffrey?"

"Yes, Dan."

"We need to go over the plan again." Dan rubbed his forehead above the bandage before continuing. "I'll, ah, tell you each step I need to take, and if—if you'll read me whatever I'm pointing to, I'll . . ." He stopped and grimaced as a wave of pain engulfed him; then, with great effort, he continued. "In other words, when Hong Kong Approach gives me a turn toward the localizer—that's the radio beam that leads us to the runway—I'll put my hand on the heading selector I showed you a few minutes ago . . . *here*." Dan held his finger on the glareshield panel and moaned. He took a deep breath and readjusted himself in the seat.

"Okay. This . . . ah, is the heading selector. What heading is it dialed to?"

"Two-eight-zero, Dan."

"Good."

Geoffrey Sampson watched with great concern as the copilot hung his head and moaned again.

"Are you all right, Dan?" Robert MacCabe asked. Robert

reached over to grab the copilot's shoulder and shake him gently. "Dan?"

The copilot nodded, his head still down. He took a ragged breath. "I'm . . . fine. No. That's a damned lie. I'm *not* fine. I'm in pain, but I'm going to *be* fine. I'm just trying to deal with it. Geoffrey, after the heading, I'll . . . dial in a lower altitude, *here*." Dan reached over with obvious effort to touch the altitude selection knob.

"Very well," Geoffrey Sampson replied.

Dan pointed to the airspeed dial, his words coming with substantial effort. "Then I'll slow us down . . . with this one and . . . arm the approach mode. That's where I'll need precise readings from you to make sure I'm hitting the right buttons."

"I understand, Dan. And then the airplane will land itself, correct?"

There was a pause from the right seat. "As . . . ah . . . as long as I set it up right, it will get us down safely. I have to dial in the right radio frequency and . . . extend the flaps and gear . . . but the autopilot should do the job. The thing you'll need to do is . . . hit the Autopilot Disconnect button when I tell you to . . . the one you accidentally punched."

"I understand," Geoffrey responded.

Dan slumped over again, his hand furiously rubbing his forehead.

Robert had been sitting in the jump seat immediately behind the captain's chair. The doctor stood behind the copilot's seat, keeping a worried eye on his patient. Robert got up suddenly and took Graham's arm, guiding him to the rear of the cockpit for a whispered conference.

"I'm not a physician, Doctor, but I don't know if he's going to make it without a reduction in that pain. Have you been watching his reactions?"

Graham nodded, his face grim. "He has to disconnect every few minutes in order to hold on. But he doesn't want any more painkiller, and, in truth, much more would leave us without a pilot."

"Try asking him again, okay?"

Graham nodded, moving to the copilot as Robert slid back into the jump seat.

"Dan?" Graham asked. "This is the doctor. You hanging in there?" Graham put his hand on the copilot's right shoulder.

There was no answer.

"Dan, this is Doctor Tash. Can you hear me?"

Dan nodded. "Yeah, yeah, Doc. I'm here. I'm . . . just hurting very badly."

"Look, maybe you need a very small booster shot."

"No. NO! Look . . . I'm sorry, but I've got to tough this out. Now . . . I need to go over with Geoffrey . . . what to do if . . . if, God forbid, we have to pull up and go around."

Robert glanced at the worried eyes of the physician. Graham swallowed in a shared gesture of apprehension, then leaned over toward the jump seat to whisper in Robert's ear.

"Would you keep an eye on him? I want to go talk to my wife."

Robert nodded. "You bet."

Graham moved to the cockpit door but stopped and looked back. It was like looking at a surreal scene through a thick lens, he thought. A terrifying dream, laced with the background hum of electronics and the sound of the slipstream, all of it leaving him momentarily dizzy and disoriented.

The man in the left seat—Sampson—had been just an ordinary passenger like him less than an hour ago. But in the blink of an eye, everything had changed, and now their lives depended on an automatic system and a blind pilot.

Maybe it would work. The agony of not knowing was weakening his knees.

Through the windscreen Graham saw a wall of puffy cumulus clouds looming dead ahead, illuminated by the landing lights, the impending impact inevitable, if harmless. The onrushing certainty of the collision with the cloud would be a chilling dress rehearsal for what might lie ahead in Hong Kong within the hour if the copilot lost control. He found himself feeling detached, wondering what the impact would feel like if the cloud were solid. They were racing toward it at over three hundred knots. There would be no pain and no time to scream. Not even time enough to tell Susan how much he loved her.

The thought of his beautiful new wife caused him to turn back toward the upper first-class cabin, where they had the aisle and window seats in the third row. He'd navigated through two failed marriages to find Susan, though she'd been there all along, working for ten years as scrub nurse on his surgical team—someone he always admired, and sometimes lusted after, but never knew. "You always knew me, though," she was fond of saying, "just not in the biblical sense."

He opened the cockpit door now, catching her eye and reveling in the warmth of her smile. He tried to smile in return, but the paralyzing fear that they could lose the exhilarating new life they'd found was too overwhelming.

Susan was terrified, too, but she could hide it better. She had helped move the captain's body to a small crew bunk behind the cockpit, then returned to her seat to wait for him. How she could even force a smile amazed him.

Graham covered the twenty feet to where she sat, ignoring the haunted expressions on the faces of the other passengers. He sat down beside her, taking her hand.

"How bad, Honey?" she asked quietly, inclining her head toward the cockpit.

"If all the equipment works right, no problem."

chapter

10

In the business-class section of the main deck, Dr. Diane Chadwick glanced at her watch again, aware she was putting off the inevitable. The idea that a serious in-flight crisis was a perfect moment for observational research had felt like a cruel joke when it first ricocheted through her mind. She was too busy trying to control her own fear to worry about anyone else's. There were limits to what a behavioral psychologist could be expected to do, weren't there?

But this is my field! she reminded herself, slowly prying her fingers from around the armrests of her seat. She had written papers about the reactions of airline passengers and crews in a crisis, and here she was in the middle of an unscheduled laboratory experiment. *How is this going to look back at NASA Ames if I survive this and have to admit I just sat here like a catatonic moron?*

There was a steno pad in her large purse. She had to use every ounce of willpower to reach down and retrieve it, along with a pen.

Four rows of business class stretched in front of her, and then another eight rows of first class extended to the nose of the 747. She was trying to discern what was going on by looking at the backs of the heads ahead of her, and that would no longer do.

Okay. Up. Now! Diane unsnapped her seat belt and tried to smile at her seatmate, a quiet Asian gentleman who was gnawing his fingertip and paying no attention to her. She smoothed her cropped auburn hair and adjusted her glasses before walking all the way forward, then all the way to the rear, making mental notes that she would transfer to paper later.

Two of the flight attendants looked up as Diane passed, but they didn't interfere. It was an advantage, she thought, knowing how to dress innocuously. She enjoyed those occasions when she could put on "girl clothes" outside the academic arena and really feel feminine, but for some reason, even on her own time—such as flying to and from the terrorist conference in Hong Kong—"academic mousy" was the style with which she felt most comfortable.

Diane reached the small forward closet in the first-class cabin and turned, forcing herself to remain calm as she strolled back. The first five rows were a mixture of men and women—a political delegation, she had heard. One woman was standing and talking to a wide-eyed man, but most were sitting with their seat belts on, hands clasped together, or talking quietly with a seatmate in a picture of tightly controlled fear. Eyes were cast in Diane's direction only as long as it took to conclude that she wasn't the bearer of news, good or bad.

In the galley behind first class, the two flight attendants she'd passed had been joined by a third. They were talking quietly to one another as they worked to keep the liquor flowing. There were a few brief smiles and a nervous joke they tried to keep her from hearing. An older, male flight attendant joined them as she passed, placing both hands on the shoulders of two of the three women and saying reassuring things.

A father figure, or so he's trying to be, she concluded. *Probably decades on the job. I'll want to find out.*

The calm atmosphere in coach class was a surprise.

Everywhere she looked, people stood talking earnestly to one another, gesturing forward and to the ceiling, and engaging any flight attendant who happened by. The atmosphere wasn't panicked, but it was serious and concerned, and she knew from her studies that passengers were capable of turning ugly if they felt they weren't being told the truth.

On her left, in the twenty-third row, a young woman sat weeping. She was trying to hide it, and her male seatmate, with a look of disgust, tried to signal that he was wholly unaffected by the situation and not subject to the emotional instability of the "weaker" sex.

She's reaching out to him and he's rejecting her.

In the third coach cabin a gray-haired woman brushed past Diane officiously and leaned down to talk to first one row of passengers, then another. Diane moved closer to hear the woman's message, a broad interpretation of the announcement the pilot had already made.

"He's just being the usual conservative pilot, dear. These airplanes don't really even need pilots except to program their fancy computers, so this shouldn't be a problem, okay? Relax. We'll get another night in Hong Kong out of this, free."

Several rows to the rear a teenage boy sat in a window seat, wearing the first truly angry expression Diane had noticed. He had the candy-striped badge of an unaccompanied minor on his shirt, and was holding a small headset connected to an electronic device in his hand.

Diane reached the rear galley and took a deep breath. She'd start talking to selected passengers now, such as the young couple holding hands tightly enough to cut off circulation, and the obese man playing solitaire while maniacally munching potato chips. The range of human emotions being displayed was awesome.

Her own fright forgotten, she paused next to the rear galley to make notes.

In the cockpit, Robert MacCabe was watching Dan Wade carefully. The quick breathing, the sweating in the cold cockpit, and the clipped speech told a tale of incredible stress—not to mention pain. So far Dan was handling it, but how long he could hang on was a deep concern. Although the copilot appeared to be in his early forties and in good health generally, Robert found himself praying that Dan had a very strong heart.

There was movement suddenly at the cockpit door, and Rick Barnes stepped inside, shutting the door behind him. He spotted Robert and nodded to him, then pointed to Geoffrey Sampson with a mouthed "who?" Robert introduced them and Barnes extended his hand to Geoffrey Sampson.

"Glad to meet you. I'm the CEO of the airline. Thanks for helping."

"I assure you, Mr. Barnes, my efforts are pure, enlightened self-interest."

Rick turned to look at the man in the right seat, the sight of the bandage around his eyes sending a chill up his back. "Ah, Dan? Rick Barnes."

There was a long sigh from the copilot. "Yes, Mr. Barnes?"

Rick hesitated, feeling unsure what to say. "Ah, I just . . . wanted to—"

"Come up here and take over? Lord, I wish you could."

Rick laughed nervously. "God no, I'm not trying to take over. Just . . . get us on the ground safely, Dan. I have no idea how bad this is with your eyes, but we'll stop at nothing to get you the best doctors in the world."

A crack about the recent reduction in pilot medical benefits crossed Dan's mind, but he rejected it. This wasn't the time. Barnes was as scared as everyone else.

"I appreciate the support, Mr. Barnes, but you need to go sit down now."

Rick Barnes nodded. "You're right. I'm just outside if you need—I don't know, if you need the airline chief to yell at someone on the ground, I guess."

He turned and left as Britta entered with a small bottle of water, which she placed in Dan's hand. "How are you doing, Danny?"

"Okay, I guess. I just wish you had pilot experience, like Karen Black."

"Who?" Britta shot back, a puzzled expression crossing her face.

"It was . . . a movie, Britta. Never mind. It doesn't matter."

"Oh! God! You mean that awful film. *Airport Seventy-something.*" Britta let a few seconds of silence pass before speaking again, her eyes ranging over the cockpit, her voice a shade softer. "Dan, I need to know our status, and precisely what you want me to do."

The copilot moved his head to the left as if to look at her, then stopped. "We're probably about ten minutes away from starting the approach, Britta. I want everyone strapped in. Put them in a brace position. Brief them all on the emergency exits. And there's something else that's really important."

"Yes?"

"You, Britta, are going to have to make the determination of when and how to evacuate. If . . . things don't go well, and you don't hear from me, make sure we've stopped, then get them out of there. Okay?"

"You're going to do fine, Dan. We'll make it."

The copilot took a deep, ragged breath. "I'll do my best, but we've got to get on the ground while I'm still functioning."

Britta began massaging his shoulder as she looked forward through the windscreen, trying to discern anything familiar. There were very few ground lights visible in the darkness. Just the hint of a town somewhere to one side and the glint of distant lightning on the ocean's surface to the left; the staccato flashes illuminated huge clouds on both sides in a visual melange worthy of van Gogh.

Britta looked back down at Dan and leaned over to kiss him lightly on the cheek. "I mean it, Danny. You'll do fine." She straightened up. "Who do you want here in the cockpit?" she asked. "Mr. MacCabe is here. Should he stay?"

"I can't believe you remembered my name," Robert said.

"Britta," Dan replied, "you need to be in the cabin. Stay upstairs, but sit in the cabin. Mr. Sampson sits where he is, in the left seat. Mr. MacCabe, if you don't mind, sit where you are in the jump seat. Britta, if you should find another pilot hiding somewhere, get him up here."

"You bet, Dan," Britta replied.

"And please keep Rick Barnes out of my cockpit. He's not much of an inspiration." Dan paused and rubbed his head again, breathing rapidly, before continuing. "What I really need is Leslie Nielsen standing in the back, reminding me every few seconds that everyone's depending on me." He tried to smile, turning his head carefully to face forward again.

Good! Britta thought. *If his sense of humor is still alive, we'll make it.*

"I just want you to know we *are* all depending on you, Danny!" she said, echoing Nielsen's repeated line from *Airplane!,* the movie that had become an icon to airline crews.

The overhead speakers tuned to Hong Kong Approach came alive again. "Meridian Five, how many miles out from the airport would you like to start the ILS approach to Chek Lap Kok?"

Dan held up his right hand for silence.

"Hong Kong, I need a lot of room to make sure we're . . . lined up. Can you . . . see me on radar . . . far enough out to give me a . . . fifty-mile turn on the localizer?"

"Our weather radar is painting a line of severe thunderstorms forty miles to the west, Sir, moving east at ten knots. We'd like to keep you clear of those."

"Okay, Hong Kong. A thirty-mile turn to the inbound course, then, I guess."

"We can do that, Meridian," the controller replied. "Call me when you're ready, Sir. Meanwhile, turn left now to a heading of one-eight-zero degrees.

Britta Franz descended the stairs to the main cabin deck and motioned Bill Jenkins, Claire Brown, Alice Naccarato, Nancy Costanza, and four other flight attendants to the middle galley for a quick briefing. She tried to sound as upbeat as possible.

"Okay, this is what we train for. The public thinks we're glorified cocktail waitresses and waiters here just to serve drinks, but this is when we shine as professionals. I'm in command in the absence of Dan giving any orders. You know the protocol. If I say evacuate on the PA, do it. Under no circumstances do you pop those doors and slides until we are stopped, and do not make an independent decision unless you're certain that I physically can't order the evacuation. Understood?"

They all nodded.

"We're going to make it, team. Dan's hurt, but he's a pro, and he'll get us down safely."

Britta returned rapidly to the upper deck to secure the galley, unaware that someone was following her up the stairs and calling her, the unfamiliar voice not registering.

"'Scuse me! I said, excuse me!"

Britta turned to find herself face to face with the owner of the voice.

"I was trying to catch you below," the woman said. "You the head mama?"

"I beg your pardon?" Britta replied, her eyebrows rising slightly at the woman's phraseology.

"Head mama, Darlin', as in chief flight attendant and whip-cracker."

"I am the head flight attendant, if that's what you mean." Britta instantly regretted her tone. She had puffed herself up in reaction to the woman and knew she sounded haughty.

"That's exactly what I mean, Honey." The woman smiled brightly, glancing around at Graham and Susan Tash. "Look, you'd probably forgive my linguistic vernacular if you knew I was black, which I was until just after takeoff, when I got the color scared out of me with people asking for replacement pilots and all."

Britta closed her eyes and shook her head as if to restart the entire encounter. "I'm sorry. *Who* are you again?"

The woman stuck out her hand with a smile, and Britta shook it somewhat tenuously. "I'm Dallas Nielson, from seat Two-A downstairs. I'm one of your first-class passengers, okay? I'm really not some peon who crawled up out of the baggage compartment. Don't let these dreadlocks fool you." She tossed her head.

"I'm sorry, I didn't mean to imply . . ."

Dallas Nielson held a palm up in a stop gesture. "It's okay, Honey, I'm just so damn nervous I'm chattering at Warp Seven. That's a *Star Trek* term."

"Yes, I know *Star Trek,* but—" Britta began.

The huge smile again as Dallas Nielson continued. "Good. *Good!* See, we've got something in common, other than being trapped in a giant pilotless airliner."

Nancy Costanza had come up the stairs and moved in behind Dallas to motion for Britta's attention. Britta looked at her with no intention to snap, but did so anyway. "*What,* Nancy?"

The young flight attendant stepped back as if she'd been slapped. "Britta, I'm sorry, but I need your help. There's a tour director down there . . ."

Britta shook her head in self-disgust. "No, *I'm* sorry. There was no reason to bark at you, Nancy. Give me a couple of minutes, please."

Britta turned back to Dallas Nielson, still trying to discern the thrust of the conversation. "Ms. Nielson, are you by any chance a licensed pilot?"

"*Me*? Good grief, no! I'm dangerous enough driving."

"Then I'm really not sure why we're having this discussion, or what I can do for you, and I don't have much time. I've got to get the cabin prepared for landing."

"Britta, was it?"

"Yes."

"Okay, Britta, I've just got one question, but it's a doozy. How in hell is a blind pilot going to land this monster? I've been sitting down there trying to stay quiet like a good girl, but I've gotta know."

"Oh." Britta glanced over her shoulder at the cockpit, then looked back. "We have an automatic flight system that can literally fly the aircraft to the runway and even stop it. Now, would you please take your seat?"

Dallas was already nodding. "I didn't ask that right. I *know* this airplane is automated. I heard the pilot. Autopilot, autothrottles, autobrakes. But how's he going to set them up if he can't see them? Anyone up there helping? Come on, girl. You don't have to give me the usual airline crap. I'm not licensed to fly airplanes like this, but I know a lot about them, so maybe I should go up there and volunteer to help. Whaddaya think? Good idea?"

Britta shook her head no. "This would not be a good time, Ms. Nielson. Not unless you can fly."

"The name's Dallas. So when would be a better time? After we've crashed? After we let that poor guy on the PA fly us into the ground because no one was up there to read the instruments for him? Or do they have readouts in braille as well?"

"Brai . . . *what?* Certainly not," Britta replied. "But unless you're a pilot, you have no business on the flight deck at this critical moment, and we already have someone up there with pilot experience helping the copilot read the instruments." An image of the reporter sitting just behind the unlicensed pilot who occupied the captain's seat popped into her head. She tried to push the image away.

"I want to at least stick my head in," Dallas said, "and offer to help be his eyes and double-check whatever the other guy is doing. I know what I'm doing."

"How? *How* do you know what you're doing, if you're not a pilot?"

"Because I have hundreds of hours reading Boeing seven-forty-seven flight instruments during my years as an engineer, okay?"

Britta felt her mouth fall open. "A flight engineer? Well, good heavens, why didn't you tell me that before?"

No, Honey, Dallas thought, *as a bored broadcast engineer playing video games like Microsoft's flight simulator, but you don't need to know that!*

"Okay," Britta said. "Follow me, quickly!" She began to turn, then looked back at Dallas. "But if he asks you to leave for any reason, you must promise right now that you'll return to your seat instantly."

Dallas Nielson reached out gently and put her hand on Britta's shoulder, her voice warm and friendly and low.

"Honey, I'm about as subtle as a pig at a tea party, but I'm *not* the idiot who's going to distract a blind pilot trying to land a giant airplane that happens to be carrying my ass."

Britta motioned her to follow as she made her way through the cockpit door. She pointed Dallas to the lefthand jump seat behind the captain's position and quickly explained to the copilot why Dallas was there, then turned to leave.

"You can read the instruments?" Dan asked Dallas.

"You mean like the Attitude Deviation Indicator, the HSI, the altimeter, VVI, airspeed, and whiskey compass?"

"That's an A-plus answer, Ms. . . ."

"Dallas."

"Okay. Dallas. Mr. MacCabe, would you let her sit in that seat, please?"

Robert was already ushering Dallas to the jump seat behind the captain's seat.

"There's a second jump seat there in the middle, Mr. MacCabe. You have to fold it out from the wall."

"I see it."

"Okay, Dallas," Dan said. "Have a seat and back us up. The fellow in front of you is . . ." Dan took a long, deep breath before continuing. ". . . ah . . . Geoffrey Sampson. Listen to what I ask him, and speak up instantly if we don't get it right."

"You got it, Chief."

Britta had paused in the cockpit door behind Dallas, pleased that the woman had fallen silent and was studying the instrument panels with what appeared to be practiced familiarity. The realization sent a small jolt of hope through Britta's knotted stomach.

HONG KONG APPROACH CONTROL,
CHEK LAP KOK/HONG KONG INTERNATIONAL AIRPORT
NOVEMBER 13—DAY TWO
1:55 A.M. LOCAL/1755 ZULU

The chief of Hong Kong Approach Control and two of his controllers had been in urgent consultation over how to handle the emergency that Meridian Flight 5 had become. When ready, they would bring the flight in from the west, lined up carefully with Runway 7, the aircraft flying on autopilot and tracking in on the Instrument Landing System radio beams, which could guide it right through an imaginary target box fifty feet over the end of the runway. The expansive new Chek Lap Kok airport near Hong Kong had incorporated the latest electronic equipment, and the ILS system was new and reliable, sending steady radio beams back up the approach that gave pilots precise guidance. Any aircraft flying the ILS within normal tolerances would arrive fifty feet over the threshold precisely aligned with the runway.

The chief had authorized open phone lines to Meridian Airlines' operations center back in Los Angeles, and had spoken to several American officials, including the American Federal Aviation Administration, as well as officials in the Chinese Air Force. Even the local American Consulate had been fully briefed, since there were American citizens aboard and no one knew if the explosion could be a hostile act. Customs, immigration, the Hong Kong police, the appropriate fire departments, and everyone else on the emergency plan was ready.

No one knew anything about an explosion to the south, east, or west. The blinded copilot's initial mention of a distant nuclear detonation as the possible cause had touched a spark to a powder keg of official angst and reverberated all the way from Beijing to Washington, D.C. So, too, had the possibility that Meridian 5 had collided with the Global Express business jet that had disappeared from radar before the incident. The increasingly shrill question of what, exactly, *had* blinded the flight crew of Meridian 5 was a secondary issue to the facility chief, who, more than anything, wanted to see his men guide the 747 to a safe landing.

One of the controllers gestured west. "What do you think his chances are?"

The chief took a deep breath before replying. "Seven-forty-sevens land at our airport every day using their automatic landing systems."

"Yes, Sir. I understand. But you haven't answered my question."

UNITED STATES CONSULATE, HONG KONG, CHINA

After locking the door to the consulate's guest suite, Kat shed all her clothes and slipped between the elegant percale sheets of the king-size bed, enjoying the scent of flowers throughout the room. She had just closed her eyes when the phone rang. The consular officer who'd greeted her was on the other end with the news of Meridian 5's emergency.

Kat sat in stunned silence for a few seconds, holding the receiver. Robert was a target, and now his flight was in deep trouble and might have been attacked.

"I'll need immediate transportation to the airport," she said, rubbing her eyes.

There was a brief silence on the other end.

"Right now?"
"Right now."

ABOARD MERIDIAN 5, IN FLIGHT

The voice on the PA speakers was labored, but clear.

Ah, folks, this is your . . . pilot. I'm ready to start the approach to Hong Kong. Here's . . . what I wanted to tell you. I . . . have several people up here to help me operate the right, ah, controls, and read the instruments for me. As long as . . . all the automation works, it will be a gentle landing. I won't lie to you, though. If anything goes wrong with the automatic system, and I have to take over manually, it could be a rough ride. All I can say is I'll do my best. And whatever your religious beliefs, a few prayers right now would be appreciated. Please stay seated and strictly follow all instructions the flight attendants give you. They speak for me.

A stunned silence filled the passenger cabin as the PA clicked off, as if the announcement had reinstated a level of fear that most of the passengers had been able to reason away.

Britta Franz stood in front of the coach cabin feeling numb, aware of the sudden motion as over 200 people checked seat belts, adjusted pillows, held hands, and tried to reassure one another—some of them openly bowing their heads in prayer.

She issued a reassuring pat to Claire's shoulder and headed back up the stairs to report the cabin ready.

And who will reassure me? Britta thought, and was instantly dismayed with herself for even a moment of self-pity.

In the cockpit Dan Wade moved the landing gear handle to the Down position. The 747's four main gear assemblies and the nose gear shuddered into place, gently rocking the cockpit with reassuring vibrations.

"What . . . do you see now on those landing gear lights?" Dan asked.

"They're all green," Geoffrey Sampson replied. "Some were red, but now they've all turned green."

"Okay. Now . . . I need you to tell me what the number is in the mileage window," Dan said.

Sampson leaned forward again, his eyes searching the bewildering array of displayed numbers in front of him.

"You want the DME, Honey?" Dallas Nielson asked from the jump seat.

Dan turned his bandaged head to the left. "You understand DME?"

"Sure do. Distance Measuring Equipment. It's showing eleven miles, and I can see the lights of the airport out there at about the same distance. There's some lightning to the left, almost ahead, and some dark clouds over the airport. The altitude is still three thousand feet."

"That's correct!" Geoffrey Sampson echoed. "That's the very instrument you were pointing to earlier." He swiveled around to look at Dallas, who was sitting directly behind him. "Ms. Nielson, are you certain you shouldn't be sitting here?"

"No. I can't handle the controls, but I can help you guys with what I see."

There was another ragged sigh from the exhausted copilot. "Ah, don't hesitate to speak up, please."

Dallas Nielson chuckled. "One thing I've *never* been accused of is hesitating to speak up." She glanced over at Robert MacCabe and rolled her eyes with a huge smile that Robert couldn't resist returning.

Dan's right hand moved into position on the control yoke, even though the autopilot was flying. "In about two miles . . . we'll intercept the glide slope. The lights on that display I showed you . . . will change. Please tell me when it happens, and what it says. At that point, the throttles will come back some and we'll start down."

He leaned forward again, breathing hard, before raising his head. "And then I'll need to know how fast we're coming down. That's really critical."

"You mean the rate of descent?" Dallas asked.

Dan nodded. "Do you know where to look?"

"Sure do," Dallas answered.

"The display is changing, Dan," Geoffrey said.

"How?"

"It's—I think it's—like you said, captured the glide path. The button that has GS on it is now green, and the throttles are coming back."

"We are descending, Dan," Dallas added. "We're coming down about five or six hundred feet per minute." There was a small series of lightning strikes just to the north of the runway, but she was trying to ignore it. What could they do, go around?

The voice of the Hong Kong controller cut through the cockpit. "Meridian Five, cleared to land. Emergency equipment is standing by."

"Roger, Hong Kong," Dan replied. "Altitude?"

"Two thousand six hundred," Dallas replied.

"And airspeed?"

"One hundred sixty knots."

"I'm . . . moving the flap lever one more notch. One of you confirm it's at the twenty-five-degree position."

"It is," Sampson confirmed.

"And we're not rolling left or right? We seem steady?" Dan asked.

"Steady as a rock," Dallas confirmed. "We're two thousand feet now, and I can see the runway straight ahead. We're gonna nail this one, Baby!"

Dan fumbled behind the center pedestal for the interphone handset and pressed the buttons for the PA by memory. "Okay, folks, everyone into a brace position."

"One thousand five hundred feet," Dallas called out. "More lightning up there, Dan. Just to the left of the airport."

Dan nodded, his left hand fumbling for one of the knobs on the glareshield. "Do I have the airspeed knob?"

"No! That's altitude," Geoffrey said. "Next one to your left. Yes, that's it."

"We're at one thousand three hundred," Dallas said.

"What does the speed show?" Dan asked.

"One hundred sixty," Dallas replied.

"I want one hundred fifty. Am I going the right way?"

"Yes, keep coming. Two more clicks. One more. There! That's one-fifty."

"The throttles should come back a bit automatically," Dan added.

"Yes, they are," Geoffrey confirmed.

"One thousand one hundred feet," Dallas said, watching the approach lights crawling steadily toward them. The amazing glow of light from Hong Kong formed the backdrop to the east. "The runway's all lit up ahead."

Dan fumbled on the forward panel for the landing light switches, assuring himself that they were on.

"Nine hundred feet," Dallas said.

"Tell me instantly if anything goes off!" Dan said.

"Seven hundred feet. Runway's right ahead," Dallas added.

"Airspeed?" Dan asked.

"It's one hundred and fifty," Geoffrey replied.

"Six hundred feet," Dallas called out.

"Okay," Dan began, "at just under a hundred feet, the airplane will start to flare itself and the display will change like I told you."

"Four hundred."

"We should be about a mile out, and the runway directly ahead, right?"

"You got it, Baby!" Dallas said. "It looks beautiful! A row of jewels in the night, and we're at three hundred feet."

Robert MacCabe felt himself holding his breath as the huge jetliner floated toward what appeared to be a runway too short and narrow to accommodate such a huge machine.

"Two hundred . . ."

The intense flash of lightning ahead was followed by a sudden change on the forward panel as things snapped off and warning flags jumped into the display for the Instrument

Landing System—all of them warnings that would have told a sighted pilot that the ILS transmitter had just been knocked off the air.

"Something's happened, Dan!" Dallas said, her voice in control as she struggled to figure out what to say.

The Autopilot Disconnect Warning was going off, its import clearly understood by the copilot.

"Oh God!" Dan's voice was an agonized croak.

"We've got little red warning things on the instruments," Dallas said, "but hold her steady! Keep it coming down. The runway's just ahead."

"Talk me down, Dallas! Talk me down! Am I wings-level?"

"You're rolling to the right a bit . . . and the nose is coming up too much. Down . . . down more . . . and roll her back left . . . NO, DAN! You're still rolling too much right!"

"HOW HIGH?"

"Ah . . . one hundred, less than that, coming down now, but a bit too fast! Roll left! LEFT!"

Dan Wade snapped the yoke to the left, causing the 700,000 pound aircraft to roll sharply left with its wing hanging less than fifty feet off the ground. The huge airplane began to drift left toward the side of the runway.

Geoffrey Sampson's voice rang out from the left seat. "We're aimed too far left of the runway to land, Dan!"

"TOO MUCH LEFT! ROLL RIGHT, DAN, AND PULL!" Dallas bellowed.

The left wingtip struck the ground a glancing blow. The sudden left yaw was countered by the thundering impact of the sixteen tires of the main landing gear in the grass to the left of the runway. The nose began to come up in response to the blind copilot's frantic pull on the yoke.

"Going . . . around!" Dan Wade managed to say as his left hand jammed the throttles all the way forward. Instinct caused him to counter the left-hand lurch with right rudder and right roll, which guided the big jet somehow back into the air, nose high, robbed of airspeed, and hanging ten feet over the surface on the pressurized cushion of air created by its passage. "TALK TO ME!"

Another bright series of lightning strikes, accompanied instantly by a sudden crack of thunder momentarily boggled both Dallas and Geoffrey. Dallas found her voice first, but decided there was no point mentioning something the copilot couldn't see or do anything about anyway. "We're . . . we're holding . . . don't let it down any more! We're barely above the ground, but your wings are almost level. Runway's to the right! Pull her up some."

"AIRSPEED?"

"Jeez, Dan! One hundred . . . twenty!"

"Dan," Geoffrey Sampson's almost detached voice again, then, "DAN! THERE'S A TOWER AHEAD!"

Dan pulled sharply back on the yoke.

"OH LORD!" Dallas yelped, as the sight of a red-and-white checkered metal tower disappeared beneath the nose, followed by the sickening sound of a muffled metallic scraping noise. Another gigantic shudder rattled through the aircraft. The engines came to full power and the nose pitched up.

"GOD, Dan, We HIT it!"

"DALLAS! Can you tell me my pitch angle? How nose-up am I?"

"I'm looking! I think maybe ten degrees!"

"Help me hold it there! Am I wings-level?"

The sound of a muffled explosion on the left side was followed by a warning bell and a red light on the panel directly before them as the 747 yawed left.

"What the hell is that?" Dallas yelped.

"There's a red light in the handle up there!" Robert Mac-Cabe chimed in. "It has the number 'two' on it."

"That's a fire in number-two engine," Dan said, automatically pressing the right rudder pedal to oppose the unbalanced thrust from the right wing. "We lost number two. You gotta help me keep the wings level, everyone! Talk to me! TALK TO ME! Geoffrey, keep telling me the degrees of wing-left or wing-right!"

"Wings are level now, Dan," Sampson replied, his eyes huge.

"You're level and we're climbing quickly!" Dallas said, her breathing coming in short staccato gasps as she tried to keep up.

"How high?" Dan asked.

"Ah . . . three hundred feet. Still climbing."

Dan found the flap handle and snapped it to the fifteen-degree position. *Gear!* he thought. Should he dare? It might be damaged, but he needed less drag. It could wait a second, he decided.

His left hand released the throttles to find the engine fire levers.

"Altitude?"

"Five hundred and climbing. Airspeed one hundred forty now," Dallas said.

"Dallas, this is vital. The fire handle I'm touching, is that the one with the red light in it?"

"Yes!"

"Okay, and it says two?"

"YES! You need to roll a little to the right. JUST A LITTLE!"

"Left wing down three degrees," Geoffrey Sampson intoned. "Now down left two degrees."

Dan yanked the number-two engine fire handle and twisted it to set off the fire extinguisher. "ALTITUDE?"

"Eight hundred . . . still climbing!" Dallas said.

"I'm going to pull the gear up," Dan said, and his hand snapped the gear handle to the Up position. The sound of moving landing gear shuddered once more through the aircraft.

"Airspeed?"

"One hundred eighty . . . no, one-ninety," Dallas replied. "We're climbing through a thousand feet. Wings are still level, but we've lost lights in here, all but a few."

"Are we above the hills on the other side?"

"Yes," Dallas told him.

Dan moved the flap lever all the way up as he took a deep breath. "You're going to have to talk to me constantly! We need to go to the west and climb to five thousand. Don't let me get too nose-high or roll too far in either direction!"

"I can still see the instruments, but this side only," Geoffrey said.

"TALK TO ME, DAMMIT!"

"*Okay,* Dan!" Dallas responded. "Right wing's down a few degrees, your nose is about ten degrees up."

"I'm going to touch a switch called APU, Dallas. The Auxiliary Power Unit. Would you verify it says APU?"

"Yes. APU."

He snapped it on and pressed the Transmit button on the control yoke.

"Hong Kong Approach, Meridian Five. We may have taken out your ILS tower. I'll need vectors to a safe altitude while we try to figure out what to do."

There was no answer.

"Hong Kong Approach, Meridian Five, how do you hear?"

Dan Wade's left hand had found the glareshield panel again and was punching the Autopilot Connect buttons, but there was no response.

"Dallas? Geoffrey? Is the Autopilot Connect indicator here lit up?"

"No. It's dark," Geoffrey replied. "What does that mean?"

"Oh Lord. It means I don't have an autopilot. I'll have to fly manually. You've got a friggin' blind pilot flying manually!"

"Oh, no," Geoffrey moaned.

"Hong Kong Approach, Meridian Five. Please respond!"

The radio remained silent, as did Dan for an extended period, before Robert MacCabe broke the silence.

"Why aren't they responding, Dan?"

The copilot reached forward and put his finger on a small round compass dial containing two needles.

"Ah, are . . . there two red flags in here?"

Dallas Nielson leaned forward. "Yes. Two of them."

Dan pointed back to the center pedestal to one of the navigation radio dials. "Make sure it's on one-oh-nine-point-five, and then tell me if the flags are still there."

The sound of clicking filled his ears as Dallas made the adjustment. There was silence for a few seconds.

"The flags are still there, Dan."

She could see him slump. "Dan? You okay?" Dallas asked. "Roll right a bit, nose down a bit."

Dan began shaking his head. "We've lost it," he said quietly.

"Can't we try again, Dan?" Robert MacCabe asked, his voice strained.

Dan was shaking his head. "If I can't reconnect the autopilot, we can't do an automatic approach. And if we can't get the localizer . . ."

"I don't understand," Robert said.

"When we took out the ILS tower and our own ILS receiver back there," Dan said, "I think we destroyed the only equipment we had that could get us home."

chapter

12

"Where is he going?" The facility chief was leaning over the duty controller, watching the faint return from Meridian Flight 5 crawl away from Hong Kong.

"He's heading approximately zero-eight-zero," the controller said. "But his transponder is not working. All we have is the raw radar return."

The chief nodded. "I'm not surprised. He had to have lost equipment when he took out the Runway Seven-right ILS tower. I *am* surprised he's still in the air."

"Meridian Five, Hong Kong Approach. How do you copy?" The controller looked up at the chief. "I've been calling him constantly. He either can't hear us, or he can't talk."

"Maybe both," the chief replied. "Keep trying him, though."

"Meridian Five, do you hear Hong Kong Approach?" Still no response. "I've asked an outbound Cathay Pacific flight to look for him out there, but there's a thunderstorm cell to the east that may make it more difficult. Is there anything else we can do to help him?"

The chief thought for a long time before shaking his head again. "If he is truly blind, and if there are no other pilots on board to help him fly that airplane, his only chance is an automatic landing. The other ILS system is working for Seven-left, but he'll have to find the beam on his own. Make sure that ILS is up and monitored!"

"Yes, Sir."

The chief straightened up. "Keep calling him. Ask him to make turns even if he isn't responding, just on the chance that he might be able to hear us. If not—if you lose his radar return—note carefully his last position and call me upstairs."

The possibility that faulty airport equipment had almost caused a crash was politically intolerable—as intolerable as the idea that a brand-new, state-of-the-art ILS system could fail. The ILS had been hit by lightning. That was not their fault.

The thought of the hapless blinded pilot and his crew and passengers losing what might have been their only chance for a safe landing sickened the chief.

Maybe, he thought, *maybe there's another pilot on board after all.*

ABOARD MERIDIAN 5, IN FLIGHT

"What's our altitude now?" Dan asked.

"Climbing through five thousand steadily," Geoffrey answered.

"Your left wing is dropping again, Dan," Dallas said.

He rolled right in response as the interphone call chime rang. "How's that?"

"Good. Wings are almost level again. Now they're level."

Dan reached for a switch on the overhead panel, feeling it latch into place.

"Hey! That helped. The cockpit lights are back," Dallas said.

"Robert?" Dan said. "Grab that handset from the back of the center pedestal and see who's calling."

"You bet." Robert MacCabe pulled the handset from its

cradle to hear the shaking voice of a flight attendant from somewhere below. "Captain? I think we hit something. There's a terrible roaring under our feet."

Robert shielded the mouthpiece with his hand. "Hang on. He knows."

Dan reached to the center pedestal behind the throttles and changed his radio settings before calling Hong Kong again, but there was still only silence.

"Dan, the left wing is down five degrees," Geoffrey told him.

"Roll right a little, Dan," Dallas echoed, "and bring your nose down a bit. You're what I'd call about ten degrees up."

"Airspeed?" Dan's voice was little more than a hoarse croak.

"Two hundred sixty, no, two-seventy," Dallas shot back.

Dan Wade throttled back, listening to the distant whine of the engines. "Altitude?"

"Ah," Dallas began, "coming up to seven thousand feet."

"Help me level off, Dallas. I'm going to start pushing over now. Give me degrees of nose up."

"Okay, you're about ten nose up, now eight . . . five . . . three."

Dan pulsed the yoke back about an inch. "How about now?"

"Nose up about three degrees. You're dropping a little."

He pulled back slightly and triggered the elevator trim, which repositioned the horizontal tail up or down to reduce the need for back pressure or forward pressure on the controls.

Once more he called Hong Kong Approach.

And once more there was utter silence from the radios.

"That's . . . what I was afraid of," he said quietly.

"Get your nose up a little, Dan, and roll right a bit," Dallas added. "What were you afraid of? What does that tell you?"

Another long, ragged sigh from the right seat. "It . . . tells me we have no radios, no navigation radios, no autopilot. It tells me we crammed something into the electronics bay and my popping ears tell me we're depressurized."

"So what do we do?" Geoffrey Sampson asked.

"I can tell you this, folks," Dan said, his voice breaking. "I . . . cannot fly this way for very long."

Robert leaned forward and grabbed his right shoulder. "Dan, hang on. And this isn't a Leslie Nielsen speech. We're going to do this together. We're going to find a way to talk you through it, okay?"

Dan was shaking his head with increasing violence. "No! NO, NO, NO!" There was a sharp intake of breath and a sob from the right seat. "Don't you understand? I *can't* do this! We have no autopilot and now we have no contact. We're all alone up here. We can't talk to anyone, we can't navigate, and we've got no way to land! I couldn't even keep it flying straight through the last hundred feet."

"There's *got* to be a solution," Dallas said, her voice low and tense. "And Robert's right. You've got to hang on."

"GOD! Don't you think I *know* that?" Dan turned his bandaged head to the left. "Geoffrey, thank you for the help. Please get out of that seat and let Ms. Nielsen in it. Dallas? You're going to have to fly."

"Not on your life, Honey!"

"Britta said you were a flight engineer on seven-forty-sevens!"

"No. I'm a broadcast engineer who's logged hundreds of hours flying Microsoft simulators using a keyboard. 'Course, I might have forgotten to mention the broadcast part, but your flight attendant wasn't going to let me up here otherwise."

"Microsoft?" Dan asked incredulously. *"Microsoft?"*

"That's right," Dallas said. "It's an airplane computer simulation program you run on your home computer. They even have a seven-forty-seven cockpit, but since it was an office computer, all I had for a control yoke was the keyboard."

"Which is why you can read the basic instruments, right?" Dan asked.

"That's it," she replied. "And right now I read your left wing down. Roll right a little, nose back up a degree or two."

"Lord, if you hadn't been such a help, I'd throw you out

of here. But if you can read the instruments, Dallas, you can fly the plane," Dan said.

"Not only no, but *hell* no! I don't want to die that fast. I'd probably have us upside down before you could scream."

Geoffrey Sampson had quietly placed his hands on the control yoke. "Let me give this a go, Dan."

"You mean, try to fly it?" Dan asked.

"Indeed. Ms. Nielson? Would you assist me with the readings?"

"You bet your British backside I'll help you," she said, as Dan took his hands off the yoke and retrieved the interphone handset, punching up the PA.

Folks, this is me again, your pilot, Dan Wade. Obviously . . . the landing attempt was a disaster, and I'm terribly sorry. There was a lightning strike just as we approached the runway, and it knocked out the instrument landing system . . . and, ah, the automatic pilot can't land that way. We drifted off the runway and clipped the top of a radio tower and lost number-two engine on the left wing and now all of our radios are gone, and somehow . . . I've got to find a place to land and figure out how to do it without eyesight and without contact with the ground. I'll . . . talk to you again when we've got a plan worked out.

When something had crunched through the forward fuselage, Britta had jumped to her feet and raced downstairs from nose to tail, but other than terrified passengers, there was no visible damage. She'd turned at the rear galley to head back toward the front when a hand reached out and grabbed her arm.

"What?" she said none too gently as she turned. *Oh. The smart-mouthed kid with the radio.* Britta adopted a stern expression and looked him in the eye. "What can I do for you?"

"That guy's losin' it!" the boy said as he pointed to the

approximate position of the PA speaker. His accent was clearly American.

Britta frowned at him. "He's doing the best he can."

"Look, Ma'am, we're in deep shit if he's blind without an autopilot."

"Watch your language, young man! I don't have time for this."

"Do you need another pilot up there or don't you?"

Britta hesitated. Someone so young couldn't be of any help. Or could he? "Are you saying that you *are* a pilot?"

He nodded hesitantly. "This is a seven-forty-seven four hundred, isn't it?"

"Yes."

"Then I can make it fly."

Make it fly? Britta thought. *That's not the way a pilot would talk.* She leaned over and dropped to her knee, speaking directly to him. "Listen, I don't mean to put you down, but I have a hard time believing that someone your age has been trained in something this big. Explain how that could be."

"Look, we almost crashed back there and the pilot says he can't see. I know enough to do a better job than a blind pilot!"

"How did you learn to fly? *How?* I need specifics."

"My dad manages a pilot training simulator company. I can fly all of them. I don't have a license, but I can fly the seven-forty-seven four hundred simulator."

"Can you land?"

"Ah . . . sometimes."

"'Sometimes' isn't good enough."

"Yeah, well, I don't see any other pilots running to the cockpit."

"What's your name again?" Britta asked, suppressing her dislike of him.

"Steve Delaney," he shot back with an acidic tone. "What's yours?"

She ignored the retort. "I'll tell the pilot of your offer, Mr. Delaney."

"Yeah, sure."

Britta stood up and leaned over him. "Young man, when I say I'm going to do something, you may stake your life on it. I will brief the pilot and see if he thinks your expertise can help. If so, I'll be back to get you quickly."

She turned and moved rapidly up the aisle, working to stay upright as the aircraft began shuddering through turbulence.

"We've got a lot of lightning ahead, Dan," Dallas reported, her eyes flicking back and forth between the instruments and the clouds they were entering.

"Oh, God," Dan said, "I forgot the thunderstorms. Is the radar working?"

Dallas looked at the display screen and shook her head. "No, it's not."

"Then we could be in for a rough ride." He reached up to the overhead panel and fumbled for the switch that controlled the seat belt sign, flipping it off and on twice before reaching for the PA handset and ordering everyone to stay strapped in.

"Are we going back to Hong Kong, Dan?" Robert asked quietly from the jump seat behind the copilot.

"I, ah, don't know what we're going to do. There's . . . been no time to think about a plan." Dan turned toward the left seat. "Geoffrey, I need you to keep us level and slowly turn us back to the west. And I need all of you strapped in."

Geoffrey Sampson was fighting the airplane, overcontrolling on the upside, then on the downside, but slowly getting the hang of it, with Dallas's help.

"I'm trying, Dan. This is very hard. I seem to be out of phase."

"I can feel what you're doing. Hold that input, Geoff! Don't push down yet. Let it stabilize . . . there. Now push down. You're chasing it and getting too tense." Dan could feel the yoke being pumped first backward, then forward, then backward again, as the 747's pitch-up, pitch-down response became more pronounced with each circuit.

"I can't bloody well imagine why I'm tense. Can you?" Geoffrey snapped.

"I've got it, Geoff. Please let go for a few seconds," Dan said.

"Very well."

Dan took the yoke, instinctively dampening the porpoising effect. "Dallas, am I zero rate of climb and in a right turn?"

"Close," Dallas replied, noticing the lead flight attendant in the doorway of the cockpit. "Bring the nose down just a hair, and roll a bit left."

Britta had moved into the cockpit. "Dan, this is Britta."

He slumped a bit in the seat. "We . . . were almost there, Britta. Is everyone okay downstairs?"

"I heard your PA. Everyone's very scared, but no one was hurt. No internal cabin damage."

He nodded without comment. She could see his right hand holding the control yoke as Robert gave her a quick synopsis. Her eyes grew wider. "How can you fly by hand? I mean, can't . . . Mr. Sampson fly for you?"

"He's trying, but he has no experience."

"But how about the lady here? She has some experience."

Dallas Nielson held up her hand. "No! I told you I can read the instruments, but I can't fly this mother."

"Geoff, take it back now," Dan ordered. "Take it and just stay calm with your corrections."

Geoffrey Sampson's hands closed around the yoke as he swallowed hard. "Very well."

"So—" Britta's eyes were wide with fear as she looked around the cockpit and at the featureless black of night beyond the windscreen, punctuated every few seconds by lightning. The big ship shuddered through a small patch of turbulence, then steadied. "What, ah, what are we going to do?"

Dan sighed. "Britta, we're in desperate trouble. All our radios are out. We're deaf, dumb, and blind. We can't talk to anyone down there, and without the autoflight system, I couldn't set us up for another approach even if I could find an airport. There's another ILS at Hong Kong, but we can't use it even if I could find it. We may . . . have to ditch. If I can't do anything else, I . . . guess we could descend slowly into the water off a coastline somewhere. But we'd have to wait until daylight."

"But . . . can you . . . can we . . . oh, God!"

Dallas reached out and took Britta's hand.

The sudden impact of the 747 with a wall of hailstones was preceded by only a few seconds of rough turbulence as the jumbo flew blindly into the side of a thunderstorm cell. Britta and Robert were thrown into each other, and then partially into the air as the entire structure of the big Boeing flexed and lurched through the angry updrafts and downdrafts. Sheets of lightning played out in front of them, accompanied by real thunder audible through the skin of the ship. Dallas grabbed her armrests, then reached out to grab on to Britta. Beads of perspiration showed on Geoffrey Sampson's forehead as he fought to control the 747, his body straining hard against the seat belt with each lurch.

"Hang on to it, Geoff!" Dan called from the right seat. "Aim for three degrees nose up and wings level, and don't even worry about altitude or rate of climb."

"I'm trying!" Geoffrey managed, his voice strained and thin.

"Britta, Dallas, Robert? Are y'all okay?"

"We're hanging on," Robert MacCabe answered. Another thunderous impact of hail blotted out all other noises. The bouncing was too severe to read the instruments.

"What . . . is . . . the heading?" Dan asked, his voice nearly drowned.

"WHAT?" someone bellowed.

"THE HEADING. WHAT'S . . . OUR HEADING?"

"TWO HUNDRED FORTY DEGREES!" Dallas yelled back.

The hail ended as suddenly as it began, leaving a wall of rain in its place. Dallas could see Dan flailing around the overhead panel, feeling for a certain switch.

"WHAT DO YOU NEED, DAN?" She could hear his rapid breathing.

"ANTI-ICE. THERE!" He clicked on the wing and engine anti-ice systems, his hand repeatedly bouncing off

the overhead surface as they lurched through air currents
that seemed sure to tear the jumbo apart.

"Geoff! Roll back to the right," Dallas barked in his ear.

There was no reply, just a nod, but the 747 responded, the
roll to the right throwing all of them slightly to the left.

Again a wall of hail and rain and lightning and turbulence
engulfed them, and the altitude decreased as Geoff struggled
to keep the attitude and bank angle under control. The
impacts of flying into shifting air currents at over 200 knots
of airspeed bounced them too much to permit reading the
instruments at times, and moment by moment the passenger
flying in the left seat had to cope with recovering from a
severe roll to the left or right, or a severe nose up or down
attitude.

"GEOFF! WE'RE DESCENDING. WE'RE GOING
DOWN THROUGH THREE THOUSAND!" Dallas
shouted. "GEOFF! PULL IT UP!"

"I'M TRYING!" Geoff cried.

"THIS FEELS LIKE A DOWNDRAFT!" Dan yelled.
"ALTITUDE?"

"TWO THOUSAND FIVE HUNDRED. DESCENDING
FAST."

"PULL IT UP, GEOFF! NOW!" Dan ordered.

"WE'RE BELOW TWO THOUSAND!" Dallas yelled in
Geoff's ear, watching him haul back on the yoke timidly.
The nose came up to ten degrees as the altitude continued to
wind down.

"WHAT'S HAPPENING? TALK TO ME, DALLAS!"
Dan demanded, his hands holding on to the yoke and trying
to follow what was going on. "WHAT'S OUR PITCH ATTI-
TUDE?"

"TWELVE DEGREES UP!" Dallas yelled back. "AIR-
SPEED DECREASING, NOW TWO HUNDRED
TWENTY."

Dan grabbed the control yoke and yanked hard without
warning. "TELL ME WHEN WE'RE THIRTY DEGREES
NOSE UP OR LESS THAN ONE HUNDRED FIFTY
KNOTS!" he commanded.

"WE'RE DROPPING THROUGH ONE THOUSAND FEET, DAN!" Dallas yelled. "OH, LORD! WE'RE GONNA HIT!" Anguish was creeping into her voice as the 747 continued to descend, the remaining three engines at maximum power, the nose pitched up to a frightening deck angle. To her right, Robert MacCabe and Britta Franz hung on to the seat backs and watched the altimeter unwinding in detached silence.

"WE'RE THIRTY DEGREES NOSE UP. SPEED'S ONE HUNDRED SEVENTY."

"ALTITUDE?"

"COMING THROUGH FIVE HUNDRED FEET . . . FOUR HUNDRED . . . DAN, IT'S SLOWING, BUT WE'RE STILL DESCENDING!"

chapter
13

The facility chief sat down hard next to one of his controllers and shook his head, his eyes on the computer-generated control screen. "You saw him descending, and then lost the transponder?"

The wide-eyed controller nodded in a staccato motion. "Yes, Sir."

"Where did you lose him? What altitude?"

"Two thousand feet, descending at over two thousand feet per minute. He had made a broad turn back west."

"How long ago?"

"Seven minutes ago. I called you immediately."

The chief took a deep breath and shook his head, feeling the weight of the loss. There had been over 200 people on that aircraft, but if they had hit the water at a hefty descent rate in the middle of the night, the survival chances were minimal.

"Very well. Start the notifications. You know what to do."

The controller turned to the task of notifying rescue forces and the world that Meridian Flight 5 had crashed at sea.

THE WHITE HOUSE, WASHINGTON, D.C.

The President of the United States swept through the east door of the most familiar office in the world and nodded to the Air Force chief of staff—a four-star general—and the press secretary, who had assembled for an emergency telephone conference on the unfolding aerial crisis in Hong Kong. He shook the general's hand and settled into a chair near the lighted fireplace, looking to Jason Pullman, the press secretary, whose finger was poised over a speakerphone. "Who's on the line, Jason?" he asked.

"Richard Herd, the director of Central Intelligence; FBI Deputy Director Jake Rhoades; and Dr. Stella Mendenhall at the National Transportation Safety Board."

The President nodded and Jason punched through the conference call. There was a brief round of hellos.

"All right," the President began, "on this end we've got General Tim Bauer, Air Force Chief of Staff, and Jason Pullman, my press secretary. Now, who called the meeting?"

"I did, Mr. President," Herd, the DCI, responded. "The rumors are going to start flying on this one, and I felt you needed to be briefed immediately."

"What rumors, Richard?"

"Unfounded rumors that this Hong Kong situation is somehow connected to the SeaAir crash near Cuba, and that Hong Kong is, in fact, an act of terrorism."

"Is it?" the President asked.

"We don't think so on either count, Mr. President, but we don't know yet."

The President sighed. "Okay, Richard, give me the briefing."

The DCI filled in the facts to the moment, detailing the possibility of midair collision versus airborne attack before the President interrupted him.

"Wait a minute," the President said. "You say the remaining pilot also mentioned the possibility of a nuclear *detonation*?"

"Oh, it definitely wasn't that, Sir," the DCI replied.

"National Reconnaissance Office confirms their sensors have picked up nothing nuclear."

"What, then?" the President continued. "You said a midair collision or some sort of attack, but to have a midair, someone's got to be missing an airplane."

"Well, there is an aircraft missing," the DCI said, relating the puzzle of the U.S. business jet and the fact that FAA was still verifying who owned it.

The President leaned forward, twirling a fountain pen in his fingers, his eyes on the floor. "And the third possibility is some sort of attack? What sort of attack? Military? Terrorist? And using what, a missile?"

General Bauer raised a finger. "Sir, we have no reason whatsoever to suspect hostile military action. This was a scheduled airline flight, ten miles from Hong Kong's airport, on a normal departure track. No way would the Chinese Air Force be involved. Now, if we're talking about what kind of an attack could blind two pilots . . ."

"That boggles my mind," the President interjected, shaking his head. "The captain dead, the copilot blinded. How?"

The DCI spoke up before the general could answer. "Any large flash, such as a direct lightning strike or fuel exploding during a collision, could temporarily flash-blind the pilots. We know of nothing that could kill with a burst of light alone, but whatever happened probably triggered a secondary reaction, a heart attack or a stroke."

"General, you weren't finished?" the President said.

"I was going to say, Sir," General Bauer continued, "that the intensity of the so-called explosion this surviving pilot reported is not inconsistent with the burst of a phosphorous-based warhead at very close range. A lightning strike wouldn't do it."

"A *what*?" the President exclaimed, sitting up and cocking his head.

"Phosphorous, Sir. The flash against a nighttime background is devastatingly bright. If someone lobbed a small missile at them with such a warhead designed to explode just in front of the aircraft, I'm told it could seriously interfere with a pilot's vision for several hours."

"Flash blindness and a missile?" the President asked, watching the general nod in response. "Terrorist, in other words?"

The DCI spoke up again from Langley. "We don't think it likely, Mr. President. We think the most credible possibility is a midair collision and explosion. If this was a terrorist act, it would require a missile, a place to launch it from, and the uncertain assumption that flash-blinding the pilots would bring down the aircraft."

"Okay."

"Then, too, Sir," the DCI went on, "there's the matter of the type of missile required. It couldn't be a heat seeker because an infrared tracker would go for the engines. You'd have to have a pretty sophisticated missile to fly close to a cockpit and explode without physically damaging the aircraft, and we think that unlikely."

The President's eyes snapped to the Air Force chief of staff, who was shaking his head. "General? You disagree?"

"Absolutely. A sophisticated missile *is* likely. In fact, this is the signature of a laser-guided missile. That so-called missing aircraft could easily have been the target designator, holding what is essentially an invisible infrared laser dot on the seven-forty-seven while a confederate below fires the missile. All they'd have to do is program the missile to detonate by internal radar a hundred yards out."

"That's your guess?" the President asked.

"No, Sir. That's our assessment. It fits."

"A missile with a phosphorous warhead?" the President asked.

"Precisely."

"For the record, Mr. President," the DCI cut in, "CIA believes the more credible possibility is a midair collision. I mean, after all, that other aircraft is *missing*. If he was just the target designator aircraft, where is he?"

"Ah, Mr. President, Jake Rhoades here."

"Go ahead, Jake," the President prompted.

"We're told the missing business jet cut in front of the Meridian flight just before the explosion. We have that information directly from Hong Kong Approach. Whether they collided or helped fire a missile, that jet *is* likely to be involved."

The President was nodding slowly. "There is a similarity here to SeaAir. Both aircraft were over water. If a missile was fired from a boat in both cases, that fits."

"Sir," the DCI replied, "remember that we don't have any idea what brought down the SeaAir MD-eleven."

"True." The President nodded, glancing at the general. "Wait a minute. General, could a target designator damage a pilot's eyes?"

The general shook his head. "Not like this. Maybe over time, but it's an invisible infrared beam, Sir. It just puts an invisible hot spot of coded light on the side of whatever we want to hit, and the missile recognizes the dot and flies to it. The designator is not designed to do any damage itself."

"Okay."

"But a small phosphorous warhead or, to be fair, the flash of exploding fuel in a collision, as Director Herd postulates, could easily flash-blind."

Stella Mendenhall spoke up from NTSB headquarters. "Mr. President, two points of difference on SeaAir. First, the SeaAir accident occurred during bright daylight, and even a phosphorous explosion at close range would probably not be enough to temporarily blind a pilot. Could it hurt his eyes and make it difficult to see around the huge spot in the middle of his vision? Certainly. But in bright daylight the pupils will be contracted, and I doubt anything but a nuclear fireball could do the job. Therefore, I see no possible connection between these two incidents."

"Okay, but—" the President began.

"And," she continued, "one other point, please. I can't imagine how a seven-forty-seven could physically collide with a large business jet the size of a Global Express, create an explosion of fuel bright enough to blind both pilots, and not destroy the nose section and probably the cockpit of the airliner in the process. From what we're hearing, the copilot never reported any physical damage to the jet until they struck an ILS tower by the runway trying to land."

"But, Stella," the President said, "in theory, could Director Herd's assessment be right?"

"Could a midair, you mean, cause a big enough explosion to blind?"

"Yes," the President responded, knowing the NTSB official would choose her words carefully and try to refrain from crossing swords with the DCI.

"Sir, I can't say it isn't possible. I just don't know how."

The President sighed. "Fair enough. Okay. We may have a sophisticated attack, or we may have a midair collision, but what we don't have is a clear indication of which one and who, if anyone, attacked. That sum it up?"

"Yes, Sir, I believe it does," the DCI said.

"Jake," the President said suddenly, "what's the status of the Bureau's thinking on sabotage or terrorism in the SeaAir crash?"

Jake cleared his throat before answering. "Mr. President, all we have right now are deep suspicions. There are several minutes missing from the SeaAir cockpit voice recorder that probably could have given us substantial clues, but without that, or at least *some* physical evidence of sabotage, neither we at the Bureau, nor Stella and her folks at NTSB, can say what caused the SeaAir pilots to lose control, let alone answer the question of whether a criminal act is involved. We know the MD-eleven didn't explode. We have no evidence or reason to suspect a missile. It's as if the pilots just suddenly clicked off their autopilot and keeled over for no apparent reason. Naturally, all of us at the Bureau are haunted by the incorrect initial terrorist conclusion we jumped to in the TWA 800 disaster a few years back, and I know we're being super careful on this one, but the bottom line is, we just don't have any evidence as yet in either direction."

The President nodded. "As I said an hour ago, if anyone can prove to me that Cuba is responsible for downing that SeaAir MD-eleven, we'll hit Fidel immediately. But let's say that SeaAir is *not* Cuba's fault. Let's say you fellows and gals at the Bureau determine later that it is a terrorist act.

And let's say, further, that the Hong Kong thing is a terrorist act, and let me go even further into fantasy and speculate that we decide the same organization is probably responsible. Then we're facing a real specter: Who the hell is attacking airliners, how are they doing it, and what do they want? This is the second one inside six weeks. It seems to me those questions would become a matter of great national urgency, because we have no group taking credit, we have no demands, and that means we have a terrorist organization that will undoubtedly keep on doing whatever they're doing until they're ready to reveal themselves and tell us what they want."

"Mr. President," the DCI replied, "with all respect, is there a question in there somewhere that we can answer?"

The President shook his head. "I guess not, Richard. I'm just worried."

"Sir, as you know, other than the possibility of Cuban involvement, we simply do not see any substantive reason to believe that the SeaAir accident was terrorist, let alone a new terrorist group. Perhaps the best reason is the one you cited yourself, the utter lack of anyone taking credit. Any organization that *wants* to kill a jumbo jet and all aboard wouldn't hesitate to crow about it early on. And why be subtle about it? If you're going to mount an operation to bring down a civilian airliner and commit mass murder to make a point, why run the risk it will be labeled an accident?"

"Okay, Richard, the Company's caution is noted and appreciated. Stella? Is there any aspect of SeaAir that resembles what we know so far of Hong Kong?"

There was a long, uncomfortable silence from the other end before the NTSB board member responded. "Mr. President, only one thing. The flight path of the SeaAir MD-eleven resembles an aircraft devoid of pilot control. If the Hong Kong flight was, in fact, purposefully attacked, the objective was most likely the removal of both pilots' ability to control the aircraft, so it would crash. Somehow, one pilot managed to stay in control, but if they were attacked, the objective would be to take both of them out. If SeaAir was attacked with the same objective, then the answer is yes, I see a similarity. But in Sea Air, we haven't a clue yet as to what could have incapacitated the pilots, and a light burst, as I said earlier, just doesn't explain it."

"Thanks, Stella."

The President's secretary had quietly entered the Oval Office and slipped a note to the President. Those in the group who were watching him saw his face fall and his eyes grow dark as he read the message. The President looked up then and sighed, a sad and grim expression on his face.

"Folks, we've been keeping an open line to Hong Kong in the Sit Room. I'm . . . devastated to tell you that the Chinese air traffic people have just lost Meridian Five from radar, and believe he's crashed. The location"—the President referred to the note again—"is at sea, approximately thirty miles south of Hong Kong." He passed the communiqué to Jason Pullman, who shook his head.

"Okay," the President said with a loud sigh. "We have mysteries and no solutions. If this flight was attacked, we're at war with someone, and I need that target defined, whether it's Fidel, Saddam, Milosevic, or some other upstart group. I want a deep assessment of the possibility that we're looking at a new pattern using phosphorous-based warheads designed to flash-blind pilots. That, to me, is the most promising, and chilling, possibility. And, Jake, from the Bureau I want the earliest possible confirmation of terrorist activity in either of these two accidents."

"Yes, Sir," Jake replied. "We have two hundred and ten agents assigned to the SeaAir accident and I happen to have one of my best agents in Hong Kong right now."

The President got to his feet. "Good. We need to turn these questions into answers very rapidly. If the idea gets out that American airliners are being systematically targeted by some mysterious new group using some noxious new warhead on a laser-guided missile, we're going to see the airline industry paralyzed, and all of us held hostage by the panic. And with our luck, the damn missiles will probably have been made in the U.S."

•   •   •

In the FBI headquarters building, a short distance from the White House, Jake Rhoades clicked off the connection and got up from his desk. Two of his senior agents were waiting in his outer office and stood when he entered.

"How'd it go, Jake?" one of them asked.

Jake snorted and shook his head. "The Air Force used missile-speak to mesmerize the big guy. He likes a missile with a phosphorous warhead that magically knows just where to explode in front of a cockpit."

"And we don't?"

Jake shrugged and sighed. "I don't know what to think, except that the NTSB lady had it right. At this point, we're clueless."

HONG KONG APPROACH CONTROL,
CHEK LAP KOK/HONG KONG INTERNATIONAL AIR-
PORT

Kat Bronsky thanked the shift supervisor and pushed through the door of the radar facility, where the consulate car was waiting. She felt stunned, empty, and ill, and the supervisor's words rang in her ears in bits and pieces: "Terrible explosion . . . nuclear mentioned, but not possible . . . copilot blinded, captain killed . . . another aircraft missing in the same area . . . possible midair . . ."

The last radar return, the supervisor told her, had come during a rapid descent through 2,000 feet in the middle of a thunderstorm cell.

Kat closed her eyes and shook her head, trying to get the image out of her mind. Without question, the big Boeing was in pieces in the South China Sea. She thought of Robert MacCabe and the seat next to him, which she would have occupied if fate had not intervened.

"Where would you like to go, please?" the Chinese driver asked.

"What? Oh," Kat replied, fatigue weighing her down. "Give me a minute." She sighed and pulled the satellite phone out of her purse, intending to check in with Jake

Rhoades back in Washington, but the words of the Hong Kong Approach Control supervisor crystallized at the same moment: possible midair with another aircraft now missing. Which aircraft? She had been too shocked to ask.

She yanked open the car door and headed back into the radar facility.

chapter

14

NATIONAL RECONNAISSANCE OFFICE, MARYLAND
NOVEMBER 12—DAY ONE
1:48 P.M. LOCAL/1848 ZULU

The urgent call from Central Intelligence for satellite support in the Meridian 5 matter had triggered a flurry of activity in the NRO's surveillance center near Washington. As the newly targeted orbiting sensors peered intently at the Hong Kong area from space, three men and one woman gathered around a large, sophisticated video screen in a small room within the high-tech warrens of the cutting-edge installation. One of the men had been holding open a phone line to a CIA team in Langley, but he put them on hold to peer at the display screen, following the small pointer being used by the chief NRO analyst.

"This is Hong Kong over to the far right," Janice Washburn said. "The satellite we're using is approaching at almost ninety degrees overhead. There's a solid cloud cover both above and below the jet's altitude, so we're using a primary infrared depiction with an optics backup."

"We have this real-time, correct?"

"Yes, Sir," the woman answered. "But remember, this is a processed shot. Real-time information for a composite depiction. We've got the other stuff on tape."

"Bottom line, Janice, have you found anything?"

She nodded. "I've filtered out all other known air traffic being worked by Hong Kong, Vietnam, or any of the other air traffic authorities in the vicinity."

"And?"

"Take a look," she said, pointing to a tiny white dot southwest of Hong Kong. She repeatedly toggled a switch on the display to zoom the picture. "This is twenty-mile range from one side of the screen to the other. Ten miles. Five. Two. One." The target became progressively larger, streaming white plumes behind it as it moved to the southwest. "Okay, I'm zooming in to a matter of yards."

Suddenly the screen was filled with a white, ghostly shape that could only be a 747. The inboard power plant on the left wing was obviously not producing heat, since there were plumes from only three engines. There was another, smaller plume from the tail-mounted auxiliary power unit.

"Are we sure that's Meridian?" George Barkley whispered.

She nodded. "We've dovetailed the track of the aircraft from before the landing attempt back to when we could pick up the radar transponder. That's him, okay, and as you can see, he's still very much airborne and alive—though his course has been erratic. By the way, George, I'm told the Chinese have launched a search-and-rescue force. Are we going to be able to tell them the aircraft hasn't crashed?"

George Barkley shrugged his shoulders. "That's not our decision, but you know the concerns. Too much information about what we've seen and how we did it compromises our capabilities."

"In other words, probably not."

He nodded as he pulled the phone receiver to his ear and smiled. "At least I can tell our side, and it's going to feel good to relay positive news for a change."

ABOARD MERIDIAN 5, IN FLIGHT

Dan Wade had fully expected to die.

Unable to actually see the altimeter unwinding toward the surface of the South China Sea, and caught in the maw of a massive thunderstorm downdraft, he couldn't sense the sudden exit of the 747 from the downburst until Dallas Nielson's voice rang through his consciousness.

"There! Oh sweet Jesus, THERE! We're level. Three hundred fifty . . . no, we're climbing now! Thank you, Lord!"

The heavy turbulence continued bouncing them around. Lightning flashed ceaselessly outside the windows. Suddenly, a soul-shattering crack tore through the cockpit, lighting up everything and receding just as fast. The electronic flight instrument displays went dark, leaving only a few small instrument lights beneath the forward dash panel.

"WE'VE LOST POWER!" Dallas yelled.

Dan's left hand snaked up to the overhead and cycled two electrical switches, restoring the power. "Did that cure it?" he asked.

"Yes. What in hell was that?" Dallas asked.

"Lightning strike. Knocked off the APU, I think."

There were three more horrendous flashes of lightning not accompanied by noise as they flew through the lower western wall of the cell, and within a minute, a clear night sky opened up before them, framed by towering storms.

"Altitude?" Dan asked in a more normal volume.

"One thousand five hundred and climbing fast. Two thousand."

"Geoff," Dan said, "take over as I push the nose forward. Keep a positive climb . . . back to eight thousand, okay?"

"I'll do my best," Geoff Sampson replied, his voice thin and fatigued.

To the right, the top part of a cumulonimbus towering above 60,000 feet boomed away with lightning, and to the left, another wall of storms could be seen. But ahead there were stars and moonlight glinting off the ocean's surface.

"Good heavens! What on earth happened?" Geoffrey asked.

"We . . . blundered into a massive thunderstorm cell, I'm afraid, and a huge downdraft," Dan said, shaking his bandaged head carefully. "Is everyone okay?"

"That was one hell of a ride," Robert said softly.

"We're okay, Dan," Britta added as she pulled the interphone handset from the pedestal and punched in an All Call. She polled the flight attendants below before disconnecting. "No one's hurt below. They're all terrified, but no injuries. The galleys are a mess, of course."

"Geoff? You okay?" Dan asked.

"In all honesty, Dan, I think Ms. Nielson should consider taking over. I'm doing a frightful job. I nearly lost it."

Dan started to answer when the cockpit door opened. Britta turned around, shocked to see young Steve Delaney standing just inside with a hesitant expression and looking around with wide eyes.

Britta moved toward him instantly. "*Mr. Delaney!* I did *not* say you could come up here!" Britta's voice was sharp and irritated, and Steve Delaney backed up.

"What did we hit?" Delaney asked, his voice betraying fright.

"Who are *you*, Darlin'?" Dallas asked, looking at the teen.

"A brash young irritant who says he knows how to fly simulators," Britta said, turning to push Steve back out the door.

"Whoa, Brits," Dallas said, sliding out of the jump seat toward the door. "We aren't exactly running a surplus of pilots up here. What's your name, Honey?"

"I'm, uh, Steve Delaney."

"Can you fly this airplane, Steve?"

He nodded, repeating the information about his father's simulators.

"He taught you? Your dad, I mean?"

"No. He didn't want me near them, but I'd fly them anyway, at night."

"My *man*! Self-starter, then," Dallas said, offering him a

high-five palm slap, which he met somewhat timidly.

Dan Wade had been listening to the exchange without comment as Dallas turned to check the instruments. "Dan, pull the nose up a bit for Geoffrey and roll right about ten degrees."

"Thank you, Dallas," Dan replied.

"Just a moment here," Geoffrey Sampson said, his hands maintaining a death grip on the control yoke. "Look, it's time we faced the fact that I'm not helping you at all. I'm doing a horrible job. We don't have many options, it seems, so may I be so bold as to suggest that if this young chap thinks he can fly, why not give him a go?"

Dallas was nodding. "Geoffrey, why don't you climb out and let Mr. Delaney here get in."

"WHAT?" Dan barked the question.

"Hey," Dallas said, "maybe he can help. In any event, it's like chicken soup. May not help but it can't hurt!"

Dan Wade's head came around to the left. "Dammit, who's in charge here?"

The response from Dallas Nielson was instantaneous and sharp. "We thought *you* were, Danny boy, but you seem to be giving up, with this babble about ditching."

"The hell I am!" Dan interrupted. "Who the hell are you to—"

Robert MacCabe clamped his hand on Dan's right shoulder and shook it slightly. "Keep your cool, Dan. We won't make it without teamwork. The lady's got a good suggestion, and you should listen to it. It's not mutiny, it's teamwork."

"Listen, Daniel!" Dallas continued. "You've worked miracles to keep us alive, but you gotta open your mind to different ideas."

"I really . . . don't need . . . California hot-tub psychobabble right now, thank you!"

"I'm not from California, Dan," Dallas shot back, "my name's Dallas, and I don't own a hot tub, and you don't have a lot of options. Fact is, I was gonna suggest maybe we audition every passenger and find out who can learn to fly the quickest."

A sarcastic young voice spoke from behind, tinged with fear. "There's not much to flying this airplane, anyway. It's just a big video game with wings."

Dan turned his head to the left, in the direction of the voice. "You know what an attitude indicator is, son?"

"Yeah. And I'm not your son."

"Read my attitude indicator. Right now."

Steve Delaney moved forward past Britta and peered at the instrument panel in front of Geoffrey Sampson. "You're one degree nose-down, and you're rolling left about five degrees."

"I've got the airplane, Geoffrey," Dan said, making the corrections to raise the nose and roll back right. He began nodding slowly. "Okay, kid. Not bad. Just tell me the number of degrees of roll-left or -right, and degrees nose-up or nose-down."

"I'm not a kid, Mister. My name's Steve."

"Okay, Steve. Can you do that? Can you call out those corrections?"

"I just did."

Dan nodded again, this time more forcefully. "Okay, Dallas, I agree. Britta, help Mr. Sampson out of the left seat and put . . . Mr. Delaney in it. Quickly."

"All right, Dan," Britta said in a resigned tone, "but after that I'm going to check on things downstairs." She helped Geoffrey maneuver out of his seat and motioned for Steve to move in.

"In the captain's seat?" Steve Delaney asked, as Britta hurried from the cockpit, followed by Geoffrey.

"Yes. You're going to be my eyes and my hands. There's no autopilot. There's only me, and I'm blind. If someone else . . . can keep the airplane straight and level"—Dan stopped and took a long breath—"then maybe I can work on figuring out how to get us down somewhere alive. I need you to keep reading the attitude indicator . . . and using the yoke to keep the wings level and keep the little dot at about four degrees nose-up. Think you can do that?"

"Sure," Steve said. "Want me to program the flight computer, too?"

"You know how to do that?"

"Sure. I studied the manual."

"First," Dan said, "let's see if you can fly."

HONG KONG APPROACH CONTROL, CHEK LAP KOK/HONG KONG INTERNATIONAL AIRPORT

Kat thanked the Approach Control supervisor again and headed for the consulate car, the image of the radar tapes still playing in her mind. She was amazed they had been so open about something that would inevitably end up the subject of a major accident investigation, but the supervisor had hesitated only a few seconds before agreeing to show her the recordings.

The Bombardier Global Express business jet's transponder had blinked off without warning eight miles ahead of Meridian 5, but there had been shadowy skin paint returns. Kat knew transponders radioed back an electronic answer to radar scopes every few seconds, whenever they picked up an air traffic control radar beam interrogating them. But without an operating transponder, the only thing a controller could see on his scope was the echo of a raw radar signal bouncing off the metal exterior of an aircraft. The skin paint target had appeared just three miles to the side of the 747.

Kat had carefully plotted the speed and altitude of Global Express N22Z when it disappeared, and the speed of the skin paint return, and found they matched perfectly. The Global Express's crew had turned off their transponder and turned back to cross in front of Meridian 5. Not once, but *twice.* And the second time, at the very moment the Meridian pilot's eyes were hit, there were a few more skin paint radar hits, which the Hong Kong Approach facility chief interpreted as debris from a midair collision. The supervisor supplied the tail number of the business jet, explaining that it was operating as an air ambulance and had come out of the business jet terminal.

Kat slid into the backseat of the consulate car and gave directions to the driver to go to the business jet facility, then unfolded the satellite phone to call Jake.

chapter

15

Dallas Nielson had been unusually quiet for several minutes, her eyes following every move of young Steve Delaney's hands as he manipulated the flight controls and slowly calmed the 747's up-and-down motions.

Finally she leaned forward to speak in his right ear. "You're awesome, Steverino! You're staying within a hundred feet of your altitude now and staying just about on heading. I'm impressed. Are you watching the attitude indicator as your primary reference?"

"Yeah."

"I read a book about instrument flying, and that's what it said to do," Dallas added. "You're a natural."

Steve glanced around to his right and took his first deep breath in more than five minutes. "Yeah, thanks," he said.

Dallas turned to the copilot. "Dan, he's doing great. A virtual carbon-based autopilot."

There was no response. Dan Wade was hunched over the control yoke, his bandaged head in his hands.

"Dan? Dan, you hear me?"

She reached out and gently touched his shoulder, causing him to jump.

"Wha . . . ?"

"Dan, you've got to stay with us. Is that painkiller working?"

He sat motionless for a few seconds, then nodded. "It's making me sluggish."

"But are you hurting as much? Do you need another shot from the doctor?"

"No," Dan said, as if surprised at the realization. He began to straighten up, taking mental inventory. "No . . . it still hurts, but it's a helluva lot better."

"Thank God for that!"

Dan nodded again, then sat up suddenly as if shocked, his hands going instantly to the control yoke, his voice almost panicked. "Jeez . . . where are we?"

"It's cool, Dan!" Dallas told him. "Steve's been flying us, and he's got it under control. He's doing a great job."

"We're . . . stable?"

"Believe it or not!" Dallas replied.

"What's our altitude?"

"Eight thousand feet," Steve Delaney answered.

"Airspeed?"

"Two hundred ten knots."

"And heading?"

"Steering two-two-zero degrees," Steve said, "but I don't know where you want me to head."

"Dan," Dallas said, "we still have to decide where to go and what to do. Shouldn't we go back to Hong Kong? I was hoping you'd have some suggestions."

"Yeah. Too much happening too fast. All I was thinking about was staying in the air. I . . . thought we were dead back there."

"So did we," Dallas answered quietly. "But the Big Guy had other plans."

"The Big . . . ?" Dan began.

"God," Dallas said.

Dan swallowed. "Ah, first . . . I don't think we can chance another encounter with those storms, and that means

we don't dare . . . ah . . . go back, you know, to Hong Kong.
I remember the weather chart. It was pretty clear on the west
side of that line. We'll be okay in this direction, but not if we
turn around."

"But what's out in this direction, Dan?" Robert asked.

Dan took a deep, ragged breath. "Ah, Vietnam . . . Thailand. Look, there's also the problem of finding Hong Kong
and staying clear of the hills, even if we could get in. We
can't use any ILS now without a receiver, and it'd be too
dangerous to try to have you talk me down at night. I figure
we've got enough fuel for almost seven more hours of this
nightmare . . . but that's not enough to get us . . ." He paused
and took another deep, shuddering breath before continuing,
". . . not going to get us to Australia, or far enough south,
except maybe Sumatra, and frankly, I'd like more modern
facilities around if . . . if we need medical help. Technically,
we could make the Philippines, but thanks to the damage to
the airframe we can't pressurize, which means we can't get
above ten thousand feet, and there's a huge line of thunderstorms between Hong Kong and Manila. If we go north, we
get into mainland China. They wouldn't shoot us down, but
I don't know any of the airports there."

"So that leaves us nowhere to go but west?" Dallas
prompted.

Dan nodded. "Yeah. West to Vietnam, and Thailand on
the other side. I know Thailand. Bangkok has a long runway,
and so does the big air base south of there called U-Tapao.
It's long and flat, and the weather was supposed to be clear."

"But how do we find it?" Dallas asked.

"Oh, yeah. I guess I forgot to program the navigation
computer," Dan said. He looked left. "Steve, you said you
can handle the flight computer?"

"Yeah. It's pretty simple."

"That's arrogant as hell, kid. It takes most pilots weeks of
intensive training to master the thing."

"Doesn't say much for pilots, does it?" Steve Delaney
shot back.

Dallas saw the spark find tinder. Dan inhaled sharply
and sat up, his shoulders squaring for a fight. "And just

whom do you think you're talking to, young man?"

"Enough," Dallas said. "Steve, show a little respect for your elders, okay? You can trade insults after we land. Now is not a good time to start a war."

She could see the boy struggling with himself. "Sorry," he said at last.

"Okay, Steve," Dan said, "look at the Flight Management Computer screen on your side and tell me what it's showing."

"Nothing," Steve replied.

"You might want to turn up the intensity control."

"I already did, and the screen's still dark," Steve replied. "It's not working."

"Check the screen on my side."

"That one's out, too."

There was stunned silence from the right seat before Dan pointed at the overhead panel. "There's, ah, a control head up there for the inertial navigation systems. Do you see any lighted digits on the display face?"

Dallas placed a hand on Steve Delaney's shoulder. "I'll look, Steve. You fly." She strained to look up and shook her head before remembering Dan couldn't see the gesture. "That screen's dark, too, Dan."

"Oh, Lord! Okay, Dallas, I'm going to need you to check the circuit breaker panels." He relayed the name and position of the circuit breakers that controlled the various navigation and computer equipment, and Dallas checked each one.

"The breakers are all in. I pushed each of them to be sure."

Dan slumped in his seat again. "I can't believe this!"

"What?" Steve asked, apprehension audible in his voice.

Dan was shaking his head. "I can't frigging believe this!"

"Believe what, Dan?" Dallas added.

"What we hadn't already lost, that lightning strike finished off. We probably lost the transponder as well, so I'll bet they think we crashed. We really are deaf, dumb, and blind! I don't have an autopilot, I don't have navigation radios, I don't have anything to navigate with, I can't talk to anyone, the radar's out. . . . The only thing we have going for us is the fact the engines are still running and the flight controls still work!"

"So what do we do?" Dallas asked. "How do we find Thailand?"

There was silence from the right seat for several long seconds. "I guess," Dan began, "with enough fuel—if I can estimate about when we'll be over Vietnam, we could circle until daylight, then follow the coast around until we find Thailand."

"You mean, fly visually?" Dallas asked. "Just by looking outside?"

Dan nodded. "With your eyes and my memory and the map . . . if we could dig out the right map . . . we could do it."

"That's provided we can see the coastline," Robert said.

"I was thinking, too . . ." Dan said, ". . . that if anyone onboard has a radio or a cell phone and we could make contact with . . . with any air traffic facility . . ." His voice trailed off.

"Dan," Dallas said, "even if we find the right airport, how on earth are we going to land? Steve can keep it straight and level, but can the two of you land?"

Steve Delaney shot a silent, anxious look at Dan as the copilot turned his bandaged head to the left. "I'm not sure we've got a choice," he said at last. "First we've got to *find* an adequate airport. All I'd need is one global positioning satellite readout to let us know where we are and where we need to go. Even light airplane drivers have GPS these days, but here we sit, goddammit, in a hundred-and-seventy-five-million-dollar state-of-the-art airliner, and I might as well be navigating with Charles Lindbergh's equipment."

Robert MacCabe had been looking at the floor in deep thought. He looked up suddenly and snapped his fingers. "Wait a minute. I'll bet anything someone on this airplane has a portable GPS, one of those little portable units. They were even selling them in the duty-free stores in Hong Kong. I'll go ask the passengers." Robert unsnapped his seat belt and slid out of the jump seat as Dan turned toward him, speaking in the same slightly drugged meter.

"Robert, ah . . . ask if anyone has a cell phone, okay? Maybe we'll get a break."

MacCabe was back within ten minutes. "Dan, this is Robert again. I'm right behind you."

The copilot turned his head to the left to listen. "Go ahead."

"We're out of luck, I'm afraid. We did find a passenger with a handheld GPS, but it's in the baggage compartment in a checked bag."

Dan sighed. "Naturally. There's no way, of course, we can get into the baggage compartments in flight."

"But," Robert added, "Britta tells me she knows where we could go through the floor. It's somewhere behind first class."

"What?" Dan began shaking his head. "She's thinking about the floor hatch in first class. That only goes down to the electronics compartment . . . same compartment we ripped apart back in Hong Kong. That won't get you to the luggage, and it . . . ah . . . definitely won't get you close to the rear compartment. There's a huge fuel tank. And there's the wing structure in the way."

"I didn't know that," Robert said. "Hollywood had me convinced there were kitchens in the belly with doors to the baggage compartment."

"Yeah, well . . . those are called lower lobe galleys. Some types of jumbos had them, but not this one. I'm afraid we're out of business on that idea."

"Wait a minute," Dallas said. "You guys listen to yourselves! I don't *believe* this! Dan, you need that GPS to get us to a good airport in Thailand, right?"

Dan Wade thought for a few seconds before answering. "It would sure help. It's . . . going to be difficult to find our way without some form of navigation, and all we've got now are compasses. We can hold any heading, we just don't know which one to use without something like a GPS. But Dallas, if the only one aboard is in a baggage bin, forget it. I mean, even if we could get in there, we don't know which bin the bag's in, forward or aft."

"Actually," Robert said, "we do know. The man who owns it saw his bag being loaded in the rear bin coming up a long conveyor belt on the right side."

"Well," Dan began, shaking his head slowly, "we know it's in there, but there's no way to get to it. It was a good try, anyway."

Dallas Nielson snapped off her seat belt and stood up, her hands on her hips. "Wait just a *damn* minute here!" she said. "By the way, Dan, I'm standing right now and looking daggers at you! What the hell do you guys mean, *'good try'*?" She included Robert MacCabe in her sweeping, disapproving glance. "I haven't seen a *try* yet, let alone a good try, just a lot of defeatist talking!"

Dan sighed loudly. "Dallas, look. There are no cabin doors to the rear baggage compartment in flight. If that isn't clear enough for you—"

"Whoa, mister can-do attitude! Are we hauling around a rear baggage bin or did we leave that mother back in Hong Kong?"

The copilot turned farther around in his seat to face Dallas's voice. "Dallas, I'd like to get that GPS as much as you would, but—"

"I don't think so! Otherwise, you'd be trying to find a way to solve the problem instead of sitting here trying to justify why it can't be done."

"But it *can't* be done!"

"Bullshit, Baby! Where there's a will, there's a way."

Dan shook his head with an exasperated sigh "Lady, who in the hell *are* you, anyway?"

She laughed, short and loud. "I'm no lady, ace, I'm a woman who's learned a few things about surviving over the years, and lesson one is, you never, ever give up."

"I really resent that!" Dan snapped. "That's . . . that's the second time you've accused me of giving up. I'm *not* giving up, but I'm not going to sit here in blinding pain and argue about things we can't change."

Robert MacCabe leaned forward, his palm up. "Okay, boys and girls, look. This will get us nowhere—"

Dallas ignored him, the volume of her voice rising. "What are you *telling* me, Dan? You telling me there's no *damned* physical way to get to that baggage bin, or just no procedure?"

"I'M TELLING YOU THERE'S NO WAY TO GET IN WITHOUT CHOPPING THROUGH THE FRIGGING FLOOR!"

Dallas let silence fill the cockpit as Dan realized what he'd said.

"Sounds like a plan, Dan. Didn't I see a crash ax around here?"

Dan Wade stuck his palm out and shook his head. "Oh, no you don't! NO! You can't attempt that. You could end up cutting through a control cable."

"Are there any manuals around this bird that show where those cables are?"

"They run through the ceiling—" Dan began, then stopped himself suddenly. "Ah, as a matter of fact, they *are* in the ceiling. I'd forgotten that. They wouldn't be a factor. But there still may be electrical lines in the floor. That's a lot of metal to cut."

"The floor isn't that strong, Dan," Dallas said. "I've felt it bounce up and down just walking up the aisle. Does the crew downstairs know where the baggage bin is in relation to the floor?"

He thought for a second. "Maybe. But you're talking about major effort, peeling back sheet metal and chopping through fiberglass around the compartment."

"Dan, any *real* reason why we couldn't do it?"

He thought for less than a minute before shaking his head. "No. I guess not. Just make sure no one gets too energetic using that ax. Peel back the sheet metal after you cut it, and don't try to cut through any beams, however small. If you make a big enough hole, remember that cut metal is going to be very, very sharp."

"Let's get moving. Robert? If you'll grab that ax, we'll go bobbing for bags." Dallas turned to her left and patted Steve Delaney's shoulder. "You're doing great, Honey! Just keep her straight and level. You holding out okay?"

Steve nodded. "Yeah."

"How about cell phones?" Dan asked. "I hadn't asked you whether anyone came forward with a cell phone."

Robert cleared his throat. "Britta asked on the PA, and dozens of passengers offered theirs, but she couldn't get a signal on any of them."

"Okay. Tell Britta to ask if anyone has one of those new worldwide satellite phones, since the onboard satellite phones are out."

Robert nodded. "She tried. No one came forward."

"Wonderful," Dan said with a labored sigh. "Tell Britta to go ahead. Tell her I authorized this. She's very Germanic. She'll need specific assurance."

Dallas had already left the cockpit when Dan turned around once more, hoping to catch Robert on his way out. "Robert, wait a second!"

Robert stopped and turned at the cockpit door. "Yeah, Dan?"

"I forgot to tell you about the blowout panels back there . . . big panels under the rug. You'll see them when you pull back the carpet. They're there to prevent the floor from collapsing in case one of the cargo doors boomed open in flight."

"I'm not following you."

"If the underside of the floor were suddenly depressurized and the top side still had seven pounds per square inch pressure, the main floor would instantly collapse without blowout panels. Point is, if you find and cut through one of those panels, it should provide a quick path to the baggage bin."

One hundred and sixty feet to the rear, Dallas Nielson found Britta Franz in the rear galley and explained the plan.

"And he said this is okay?"

Dallas nodded as Robert, ax in hand, came down the aisle to join them. "Ask the *Washington Post* if you don't believe me."

"Oh, I believe you, Ms. Nielson," Britta said, glancing at MacCabe.

"You have any idea where to cut, Brits?" Dallas asked.

Britta grimaced and looked at the floor, then looked back at Dallas. "Yes. I've never thought about it, but I know exactly where all the bumping and knocking about comes from when the baggage people are in that rear bin."

"Shouldn't we tell the passengers what we're doing?" Dallas asked. "You should've seen the looks on their faces when Robert walked through cabin with that ax."

Britta turned and picked up a handset, punched in a two-digit code, and held it to her mouth.

Ladies and gentlemen, this is your lead flight attendant. We are going to be cutting a hole in the floor of the aircraft to try to gain access to the baggage compartment. One of our passengers has a bag down there with a navigation unit the pilot needs badly. Please help by staying out of the way and staying calm.

She moved quickly up the aisle and knelt to find a seam in the carpet. "Here!" She pulled at the edge of the seam and began to peel it back from the yellow adhesive holding it to the floor, exposing the edge of a panel that yielded to the touch. "Here it is. A blowout panel."

"Cut it here?" Dallas asked, down on all fours herself.

Britta said nothing and turned to MacCabe with her hand out for the ax.

"I can do it," Robert replied, moving forward.

Britta looked up at MacCabe, then over at Dallas with a determined expression. "If anyone is going to start chopping up my cabin, it will be me."

"Whatever you say, Honey," Dallas said, and looked up at Robert. "Give her the ax, Babe."

Britta lifted the crash ax and took aim, bringing the sharp edge down with a powerful stroke that immediately breached the surface of the floor. She raised it again, and began a rapid, rhythmic series of blows.

"One . . ."
Whap
". . . thing I want to . . ."
Whap
". . . get straight with you . . ."
Whap
". . . is the fact that my name . . ."
Whap
". . . is Britta!"
Whap
"Not 'Brits.'"
Whap
"Not 'Honey.'"
Whap
"But BRITTA!" She stopped and glared at Dallas. "Understand?"

Dallas raised her eyebrows. "You think I'm gonna argue with an angry woman carrying an ax?"

Britta was motionless for a moment, then nodded and took another swing.

"Okay, then."
Whap
"We should get along just fine."

Steve Delaney had said nothing since Dallas and Robert left the cockpit. His concentration on the task of keeping the 747 on the same altitude and heading was becoming progressively easier, leaving more of his conscious mind to face the question of what lay ahead.

"Are we going to make it?" he asked suddenly.

Dan Wade swiveled toward him and searched for an answer. "I, ah, Steve, there's no reason we can't make it, but . . ."

"But I'm gonna have to land it, right?" Steve said suddenly, his voice clearly conveying the tension he felt.

"No, we'll do it together."

"How? You're blind! How're you going to help?" Steve sounded increasingly panicky, raising caution flags in Dan Wade's head. There were only so many realities the kid

should have to face, Dan decided. His corrections were
becoming more pronounced and erratic.

"Look, kid—Steve—we're going to make it. Here's how
we'll do it. You'll tell me what you see and I'll tell you what
you need to do. It's going to be simple. I'll get the landing
gear and the flaps extended. The object will be to fly the airplane onto the runway and use the rudder pedals to steer, just
like you do in your dad's simulator."

"That's just pretend. This . . ." Steve was breathing hard.
"This is the real thing! If I crash a simulator, all I have to do
is hit the Reset button."

"Steve, listen to me. Calm down!"

"What if I screw it up and crash?"

"Not going to happen. You're doing great. Your dad
would be proud of you."

"Yeah, right!" Steve snapped.

"He would," Dan said. "You've been flying this airplane
like a veteran pilot."

"I don't want to be a damn pilot. Just shut up about my
father!"

"Hey, look, I may not be good with kids, but . . ."

Steve whirled on the copilot, his small hands shaking on
the control yoke. "You're just like *him*! Just like all damn
pilots. Anyone my age is just worthless till you need something, and even then no one can ever please you."

"Steve—"

Steve's voice rose to a mocking tone. "Why are you too
stupid to hold that flashlight steady, Steven? Steven, I knew
you'd screw this up when I asked you to do it. Steven, you
couldn't pour piss out of a boot if the directions were printed
on the heel." He paused for a second before continuing. "I
showed him how stupid I was. It took a lot of hours in the
simulators in the middle of a lot of nights, but I taught
myself how to fly his precious airplanes!"

Steve shot a quick glance at the copilot, then brought his
eyes back to the instruments. "I'm not just a kid, and I'm not
stupid! I'm flying your goddamn airplane, aren't I?"

"Yes," Dan said carefully, "you are flying this aircraft and doing a magnificent job of it, and I apologize for using the word 'kid.'"

"Yeah, you can say you're sorry now because you need me. If we were on the ground, it'd be different. Then it'd be, 'Go away, kid, you bother me,' one of my father's favorite expressions."

"I'm sorry to hear that, Steve."

"Yeah, sure."

"Look, you want me to treat you like an adult, and that's reasonable. But that means I've got to be able to speak frankly to you. Is that okay?"

Steve was still breathing hard and obviously frightened, but he nodded slowly.

"Yeah. That's okay."

"All right. We've got a job to do up here, you and I. You're the only one aboard with working vision who knows anything about flying a plane. I'm the only qualified pilot. If . . . we can successfully put our capabilities together, we can get through this. I need you to concentrate on the job and try to put both fear and upsets aside, *and,* before you say anything back, let me remind you that I have to do the same thing. I'm scared to death right now. I really mean that. I'm scared I'm going to screw up and kill everyone, myself included. I'm frightened I . . . may . . . never regain my eyesight, and therefore I'll never be able to do the only thing I know how to do, be a pilot. I'm kicking the hell out of myself for losing control and hitting that tower back there. And I'm in terrible pain . . . *and* . . . I need to go to the bathroom, which means I'm going to have to entrust the lives of the over two hundred people aboard to you."

There was a long silence from the left seat. "Now that *is* scary," Steve Delaney said at last, the shadow of a smile creeping over his face.

"Okay. So if we're both terrified, it's easy to strike out at each other, but we can't afford to do that. Deal?"

"You mean about working together?"

"That's exactly what I mean. Without comparing me to your father."

"Promise you won't call me 'kid' again?"

"I promise. But what if I get mad at you? What can I call you then?"

"Use 'Steven Julius Delaney.' That scares me more than anything when my mom uses it."

"Okay. Now, do we have a deal, Steve? And . . . please don't let go of the controls to shake my hand."

"Deal."

Steve heard a seat belt being unfastened. He felt his stomach flutter as Dan Wade lifted himself from the copilot's seat and carefully swung his leg around behind the center console, feeling his way along. He stood up and reached out to hang on to the back of one of the jump seats.

"I'll be in the bathroom just outside the cockpit, Steve. Two minutes max."

"What if something happens while you're gone?"

"Then you handle it. I know you can."

chapter

16

In the rear of the coach cabin, Britta Franz leaned against the back of an unoccupied seat and looked at the gaping, jagged hole in the floor. The struggle to enlarge it had taken more effort than she'd expected, even with Dallas and Robert MacCabe taking turns with the crash ax.

She could see Dallas's head moving among the bags below, using a flashlight to search for the one that held the handheld global positioning satellite unit. The PA announcement that they were going to cut through the floor had galvanized almost everyone aboard to wide-eyed silence while they hacked through the metal. As soon as the hole was large enough to climb through, Robert had gone back to the cockpit.

Britta glanced around the coach cabin, taking inventory of her passengers. Nine people had been moved forward to other seats to clear the aisle, most of them from the tour group, and at least a dozen were still standing at a respectful distance under the watchful eye of their tour director, Julia Mason.

Britta smiled encouragingly at Julia.

"You okay?" Julia asked in return.

Britta nodded. "Just tired," she fibbed, trying to keep the gnawing fear she was feeling from showing up on her face. *This has to be a nightmare. I'll wake up any time now!* she told herself, well aware it was real.

She thought of the passengers in first class, and the trade delegation. She'd paid little attention to them since the crisis began, but Claire, who was working the lower first-class cabin, had reported that everyone was calm. A third of the passengers in coach were Asian, men and women from Hong Kong and mainland China as well as other Asian nations. Most had remained in their seats with expressions ranging from neutral to barely masked panic, almost all of them searching Britta's eyes for some new glimmer of hope every time she came down the aisle. The professional responsibility for maintaining a believable smile had never seemed so onerous.

The sound of bags crashing to the floor in the baggage bin below snapped Britta's attention back to the baggage search.

"Dallas? You okay down there?" Britta called.

The answer came back with a disgusted tone. "Everything's fine, Britta. Once I shovel two thousand pounds of suitcases off my feet, adjust my attitude, and get past the next twenty years of trying to forget this night, I'll be just fine."

"Okay."

Dallas's head popped up through the hole, carefully clear of the jagged edges. "It was light brown, right, Britta?" Dallas asked.

"That's right."

"And the name was Walters?"

"Yes," she said, brightening. "Did you find it?"

Dallas shook her head. "No. But I think I know where to look now."

Once again she disappeared, and the sound of serious bag-throwing could be heard all the way to the main deck.

In the cockpit, Dan Wade held the controls while young Steve Delaney took his turn using the bathroom. Robert

MacCabe kept up a constant description of what the instruments were showing.

"You know, this is working pretty well," Dan said, as fourteen-year-old Steve came back in the cockpit. "I'm able to visualize the attitude indicator as you describe it, and fly what I visualize."

"Seems very steady to me," Robert said.

"Not enough to land with, of course."

"You certain?" Robert asked.

Dan turned slightly toward the left seat. "You ready to take over, Steve?"

Steve Delaney nodded before remembering that Dan couldn't see the gesture. "Yeah, I'm ready."

"You've got it," Dan told him. "Keep steering a heading of two-two-zero degrees on the lower instrument there."

"Okay."

Dan sighed and turned partially toward Robert. "I figure we'll cross the Vietnamese coast in twenty minutes, and daylight should overtake us in about an hour-thirty. Whatever we decide, we better have it figured out and rehearsed by then."

He heard Robert MacCabe get to his feet. "If you two are okay, I'm going to go back for a moment." Robert left the cockpit door ajar and moved back into the cabin with no particular goal in mind other than to escape the tension for a few minutes.

Susan Tash reached out and caught his sleeve as he passed. "What's going on up there?" she asked. Dr. Graham Tash was looking up expectantly as well, and Robert knelt down to talk to them both.

"Dan's holding out remarkably well, and the boy, Steve, is doing an outstanding job of flying, but . . ."

"Do we have a way to land?" Susan asked point-blank.

Robert sighed and smiled fleetingly. "I guess there's always a way, but it looks to me like young Steven is going to have to actually fly the plane down while Dan talks him through it. In any event, we're going to have to wait until daylight to find a long enough runway."

Susan pursed her lips and glanced at her husband's grim

expression before looking back at Robert. "They think they can do it?" she asked.

The veteran reporter searched her eyes, thinking how beautiful she was, before diverting his gaze to her husband and nodding. "I think they do. I think we all do."

"One hell of a story, eh?" Graham asked.

"Look, I'd . . ."

Graham raised his hand. "I don't mean you're up there for crass purposes, I just mean that if we get through this, it'll be a rare event to have a professional wordsmith who can appropriately describe it."

Robert thought for a second and smiled at the doctor, nodding slowly. "That's gracious of you, Doctor. I actually hadn't thought of it that way, but you're right. Gives me an even better incentive."

Susan squeezed his hand as he stood up. "Thanks," she said.

When Robert had gone, Graham stood and motioned Susan back toward the galley at the rear of the upper-deck cabin. The flight attendants were all downstairs, and Graham drew her in close against him and pulled the curtain closed, cupping the back of her head with his hand.

"Graham? Are you okay?"

"I don't know, Suze." He pulled back and looked her in the eye. "How are you holding out?"

"You tell me first. You look shell-shocked."

He nodded. "I can't recall ever being this scared, Honey. I'd . . . like to tell you I have faith it's going to be all right."

She started to giggle, leaving him slightly nonplussed.

"What are you laughing about?"

"Look at the situation. We're in a giant airliner, without radios, being flown by a blind pilot and a fourteen-year-old boy!"

Graham cocked his head and smiled thinly. "Yeah, I guess . . ."

"This is beyond ridiculous!" She kept on giggling nervously.

"Are you missing the seriousness of this?" he asked.

She stopped immediately. "No. I'm aware of the seriousness. It's just so ridiculous to think that there's any way out of this!"

"What do you mean, Suze?"

"We're screwed, Baby, that's what I mean."

"Wait . . . wait a minute! We've got a fighting chance. You heard what that fellow was saying."

She cupped his face in her hands. "Baby, I'm not saying we shouldn't try everything, and I'm not saying there isn't a chance it'll work out, but I think you and I better face the reality that we're probably not going to live through this."

He was silent for a few seconds as he studied her face, aware that tears were forming now at the corners of her blue eyes.

"Honey . . ."

"What we ought to do is go find that rest room and make love until we hit. If we've gotta go, that's how I'd like it."

It was Graham's turn to laugh.

"What? Good idea?" she said.

"I was thinking a while ago that you'd suggest just that if you were convinced we were going to die." He looked at her, watching the smile fade into a veil of tears. Susan pulled her husband to her and wrapped her arms tightly around his neck.

"Graham, I love you. Hold me for a few more moments. Don't talk."

In the aft area of the coach cabin, a sudden shriek of excitement wafted up from the jagged hole to the baggage bin. Britta jumped up to peer over the edge, and a bag came sailing up at her. She reached out by instinct and caught it.

Dallas's face popped into view with a toothy, ear-to-ear grin. "That would be the very bag, Ms. Franz!"

"*Wonderful!*" Britta replied.

"Is Mr. Walters around to fish out his GPS, or do I go through his underwear?"

Britta showed the bag to a worried-looking man standing fifteen feet away.

"You found it!" he said as he came toward her. He took the bag, unzipped it, and pulled the GPS unit from its depths.

Britta pointed the way toward the front of the 747 and the

stairway. "Let's get moving. The captain . . ." She paused, feeling off balance, the image of the captain's body curtained off in the small crew rest bed behind the cockpit filling her mind. A cold shudder ran down her back.

The GPS's owner had noticed. "You okay?"

She nodded. "The pilot," she corrected herself, "needs this immediately."

He pulled the unit from its case, punched the On button, and watched the small liquid-crystal screen show a procession of images as it began its search for satellite signals.

Britta motioned him to follow as she led the way to the cockpit. "Dan, this is Britta. We found the GPS unit!"

The copilot swiveled around. "Wonderful! But I'll need someone to help . . ."

"I've brought him," Britta interjected. "Mr. Walters? This is Dan Wade, our acting captain." She gently pushed Walters into the area just behind the central console, where he saw the copilot's outstretched hand and shook it.

"You've heard . . . my PA announcements, Mr. Walters? You know what we're facing?"

Walters was shocked at the effort it took for the copilot to talk. "Yes, and the name is John, please."

"Okay, John. You're not a pilot?"

"No, Sir. I have a sailboat. I bought this GPS for sailing."

"You know I can't see. The young man in the left seat here is Steve Delaney. Steve . . . has extensive flight simulator experience and is flying us right now. But we need to know . . . where we are and where we're going. Can you help?"

"You bet, Captain Wade."

"Just Dan, please. Is the antenna internal, or do you stick it on a window?"

"It has little suction cups. It goes in the window."

"Use the side window by the jump seat behind me. The other windows have little heating wires embedded in the glass that block satellite signals."

Dan could hear John Walters fumbling around in the jump seat Robert MacCabe had vacated. Finally he pushed the antenna onto the window's surface.

"John, will the unit tell you when it's tracking enough navigation satellites?"

"Yeah, it sure will. It beeps," John Walters replied.

"Then can you . . . put in the . . . coordinates of the airport we want?"

"Sure. It'll give us the speed, exact compass heading, miles to destination, and how many minutes."

"Does it tell you the course to fly?"

"Yes. This one is really designed for airplanes, but I use it on my boat."

There was a small electronic beep from the vicinity of the jump seat.

"There!" John Walters announced. "It's tracking."

"Here's an aviation map of this area. Can you find the coordinates on the map, then tell me . . . how far we are from the coast of Vietnam?"

Walters took the map gingerly and unfolded it. For nearly a minute he looked anxious, a demeanor that changed in an instant as he sat up. "I've got us. We're less than a hundred miles from the coast. We'll be passing about forty miles south of Da Nang and China Beach."

Dan cocked his head in puzzlement. "Are you ex-military, John?"

"Yeah. Ex–Air Force master sergeant. I was stationed at Da Nang during the war. How about you?"

"I'm ex–Air Force as well," Dan said. "I was a forward air controller for two very long years out here." He took a deep breath and rubbed his forehead again. "Here's what I need, John. I need you to look on the other side of the map and extract the coordinates for U-Tapao. You're familiar with U-Tapao, south of Bangkok?"

"Ridiculously familiar. I spent a year there one afternoon."

Dan paused, thinking that over. "Sounds like a story I'd like to hear later."

"Yeah." John chuckled. "I even remember her name."

Dan smiled slightly. "If you . . . can plug in U-Tapao and . . . give me a heading and the time en route at this speed, it will help immensely."

Walters worked for several minutes with the map and the GPS unit, then scribbled a number on a scrap of paper from his shirt pocket and held it out to the copilot, forgetting that Dan couldn't see it. He looked embarrassed as he pulled his hand back and read the heading out loud.

"You need to fly a heading of two-three-zero degrees magnetic."

Dan nodded. "So we guessed right. We've been on two-two-zero."

"So, two-three-zero now?" Steve asked.

"Yes. Just make a gentle correction to the right." Dan turned his bandaged head back to the left. "How far and how long, John?"

"To U-Tapao, four hundred eighty nautical miles and, at this speed, a bit under two hours." Walters paused, looking at Steve Delaney, then back at Dan. "Are you going to want me to stay up here and help?"

Dan hesitated less than a second in answering. "Yes. Not only to help with the GPS, but I've got another mission for you. We're going to need several people crammed up here reading the instruments out loud on landing. Steve will fly, I'll listen to the instrument readings, and I need you to be one of the voices."

"Sure, but . . . my God, will that work?"

Dan turned his head to the left again.

"It'll have to, John. We're out of choices."

CHEK LAP KOK/HONG KONG INTERNATIONAL AIRPORT

The fact that Meridian 5 was still airborne was classified, but Jake Rhoades made the command decision that Kat Bronsky had a need to know. The telephoned revelation came as a wave of relief to Kat, though it was painfully obvious to both of them that the crisis was far from over, and the cause still a mystery.

"Thank God! You don't know how . . . relieved I am," Kat said, surprised to be fighting back tears. She willed the emotion away before continuing. "In fact, Jake, I'm relieved, but very concerned that we get back one passenger in particular, because of what he may know about the SeaAir crash."

"Oh?" Jake replied, the caution audible in his voice.

"I'll have to brief you later."

"I guess I don't understand," Jake replied.

"You will. My main focus right now is what caused *this* disaster. What I'm sure of is that the Meridian copilot reported some sort of incredibly intense light from an explosion in front of them. I heard the air traffic control tape."

"And you're looking into that?" Jake asked.

"Actually, I'm trying to find out why that American business jet crossed in front of a commercial seven-forty-seven while operating as a medical evacuation flight, and then disappeared. They suspect a midair here, but there was no report of an impact. Jake, I need you to have someone get hold of FAA's Oklahoma City aircraft registration section and find out all you can about Bombardier Global Express November-Two-Two-Zulu: who owns it, who flies it, where's it headed, and whether it's been specially modified somehow."

"You think it's involved?" Jake asked.

"I don't know," Kat said, "but how often have you seen a business jet playing tag with a seven-four-seven? I have no idea what might have happened, but their transponder went off, and they flew dangerously close in front of the Boeing."

"The theories," Jake added, "range from a midair collision to a sea-launched missile with a phosphorous warhead guided by a laser designator aboard the business jet. And Kat, we're way ahead of you on looking up that registration info. I should have it in a few minutes."

Kat whistled beneath her breath. "Good show, Jake. I'll be waiting."

The local manager of the American-owned corporate jet facility had rushed eight miles from his home when he heard an FBI agent was asking questions of his workers at 3 A.M. Once he arrived, his assistance had proven invaluable. With permission to speak, the employees who fueled and serviced

N22Z gave Kat a detailed picture of the aircraft, its two pilots, and its two passengers—all male, all closemouthed and secretive, and all Americans, as far as they could tell.

When Kat was through, the manager escorted her back through the beautiful new private terminal and handed her a plastic bag containing the fuel charge slip.

"Hopefully, it will have some fingerprints for you," the manager said. "I also had our employee who touched the slip include a plastic sleeve with his fingerprints."

"Thank you. I appreciate your assistance," Kat said, smiling warmly.

"Can you tell me what this is all about, Agent Bronsky?" the manager asked.

She shook her head. "I'm sorry, but not yet. Perhaps next time I'm in town. But this is very important, and the FBI thanks you very much again for your help."

He smiled thinly and bowed as he held the door open.

Kat was approaching the consulate's car when the satellite phone in her purse rang. Jake Rhoades was on the other end.

"FAA's Oklahoma City people have reported in, Kat. The registration number 'November-Two-Two-Zulu' is not assigned to a Bombardier Global Express. It's not even assigned to a jet. The registration number on the plane you saw is definitely bogus."

"Bingo." Kat sighed and shook her head. "I expected that. It rather confirms that they're involved."

"Really?"

"Jake, there was no midair."

There was silence in Washington for a few seconds before Jake's strained reply. "Well, Langley's convinced there was. What do you know, Kat?"

"I know the radar signature of a small jet with its transponder, and I saw the radar tapes. He didn't crash. Trust me. He turned away from the antenna and dove to the surface to disappear. We need to know who owns that specific jet."

"We'll need the manufacturer's serial number for that," Jake said.

"The guys who fueled it here in Hong Kong didn't make

note of a serial number, but then they normally wouldn't. The registration number was painted on just like it should be, and their credit card was accepted for the fuel. I'll fax the charge slip after I dust it for prints."

Kat stopped for a second, realizing she was practically dictating to her superior. "Look, Jake, I know I'm not officially on this case yet, but I think I can make some significant progress before the NTSB gets in position. And correct me if I'm wrong, but the Bureau's going to be the lead agency on this anyway, correct?"

"If it's a criminal act, a sabotage or shoot-down, there's no question, Kat. At least the Air Force agrees with you. They think it was a missile."

"Are you okay with my pressing ahead?"

"Would it make a difference if I weren't?" he asked.

"Of course! Am I not your obedient servant, Mr. Deputy Assistant Director?"

Jake chuckled. "No way am I going to bite on that one, Kat."

"Smart man. But really, may I press ahead?"

"Absolutely. Screw Langley. What, exactly, do you suggest?"

"I . . . think I'd better hang right here with this consulate car and driver until the aircraft lands safely somewhere. I'm thinking out loud."

"Understood. Go ahead."

"Well, I think if they land in Vietnam or Thailand, for instance, I should probably cancel that meeting at the consulate and catch the first flight to Bangkok to interview the pilot and anyone else who can shed some light on what hit them."

"I concur. I don't know how we'll get the diplomatic clearances, but let's wait until we know where they've come down."

"Are we getting minute-by-minute intelligence updates from CIA?"

"Actually, Kat, Langley's relaying the updates from the National Reconnaissance Office. I'll call you back as soon as we have a resolution."

"But what's the latest?" Kat asked. "What's the aircraft's status?"

"It's still flying. Currently they're approaching the Vietnamese coastline. Langley thinks they have more than enough fuel to make Bangkok, and they seem to be headed almost directly there."

"Jake, the bogus 'N' number tells me this may be a sophisticated operation of some sort. It might be a really good idea if NRO could scan the airspace around that Meridian aircraft just in case Two-Two-Zulu is still in the neighborhood."

"You mean, could the Global Express still be out there shadowing Meridian?"

"Precisely. If they are, special security arrangements would need to be made the second that seven-four-seven lands, because the Global Express will undoubtedly touch down right behind him. If they're hostile, the occupants won't be happy Meridian hasn't crashed."

"I'll relay that immediately."

"You do understand my concern?" she asked.

She could hear Jake sigh on the other end. "Unfortunately, yes, I do. Whoever's flying and controlling that business jet is going to be determined to finish the job they started."

ABOARD MERIDIAN 5, IN FLIGHT,
OVER THE SOUTH CHINA SEA
NOVEMBER 13—DAY TWO
4:42 A.M. LOCAL/2042 ZULU

With the pain in his eyes significantly numbed and young Steve
Delaney flying the airplane with surprising smoothness, Dan
Wade had dared to hope again. He had sat back and breathed
deeply, forcing himself to think clearly, when the jarring
sound of a warning bell coursed through his consciousness.

*What the . . . ? Oh, Lord! That's an Engine Fire Warning
bell!*

Dan turned in sightless frustration to the forward panel,
wondering which of the four engine fire switches had a
bright red light showing in the handle, a light that would be
indicating a fire or overheat in one of the remaining engines.

"Wha . . . what's THAT?" Steve Delaney was already
asking from the left seat.

Dan could feel the control yoke bobble slightly as Steve
reacted to the adrenaline coursing through his system, propelled by the shrill cacophony of the bell.

"Engine fire warning," Dan replied. "Steve, follow
where I'm pointing. Quickly! One of those four handles
will have a red light in it. Which one? There's a big number
on the end."

"Ah . . . number one!"

Oh Lord, we've already lost the left inboard! Now I've got to shut down the left outboard.

Dan put his left hand on the engine fire switch for the out-board left engine.

"Am I touching the only handle that's lighted?"

"Yes," Steve replied, his voice betraying deep fright.

"Don't stop flying, Steve. She's going to want to turn left. Don't let her."

Keep your emotions in check! Dan told himself. *If you sound panicked, he'll panic. SLOW DOWN!*

"Okay, Steve. We have specific procedures for things like this, and I'm going to ask you some questions first, then we're . . . going to handle it."

"Okay."

"First, look down at the center instrument panel where I'm pointing. Are some of the engine instruments now show-ing in red?"

"Yes."

"Which ones?"

"Number one."

Dan took a deep breath, trying to muster strength. "Look down that row of instruments and find the one labeled 'EGT.' Read me the temperature."

"Uh . . . it looks like, seven hundred something."

"Is that reading going up?"

"Yes. Slowly."

"Okay, Steve. I'm . . . going to shut down number-one engine. I'm putting my hand on the lighted handle again. It is vital that I get the correct one. Is my hand on the lighted handle for number one?"

"Yes."

"You are certain."

"YES! You're holding number one."

"Okay, I'm pulling it and discharging the fire bottle. Did a light come on?"

"Yes."

Please let that be enough! Dan thought. *I've only got the one fire bottle left on that side.*

There was a sudden, seismic BOOM from the vicinity of the left wing, and the entire airplane shuddered.

Oh, God! It exploded!

"What was *that*?" Steve Delaney asked in a strained voice.

"Steve," Dan asked, "did the engine readings on the forward panel for number one all go to zero just then?"

"Yes."

"Is the red light out in the handle?" Dan asked, holding his breath.

"No."

It may take thirty seconds. Don't panic! But if the engine's gone . . . "Watch the red light, Steve! Tell me when it goes out, but keep flying the airplane."

"Okay. DAN, IT'S ROLLING TO THE LEFT!"

"Stay calm, Steve! Roll it back to the right. It will do what you physically tell it to. Look back at the attitude indicator. Make it go back to straight and level. I'm putting in rudder trim to the right, and that will help, too. You've got to remember that this airplane will fly fine with just two engines on one side."

Dan could feel the increasingly staccato gyrations on the control yoke as the boy in the left seat fought the airplane. Dan toggled the rudder trim several degrees to the right to counteract the loss of engine thrust on the left wing, ignoring the fact that the cabin call chime was ringing.

"Is she still wanting to roll to the left?" Dan asked.

"Yes! Not as much now, but I'm . . . I'm having a hard time holding it."

"I'm putting in more trim. Does that help?"

"I think . . . yes, it does. Much better."

"See the turn and slip indicator? It's below the ADI—the attitude indicator."

"I . . . think so."

"Is the little ball centered, or off to the left or right?"

"It's . . . a bit to the right."

Dan toggled in more right rudder trim. "And now?"

"Almost centered," Steve replied, his voice nearly an octave above normal.

"Okay. She should fly straight now. Don't let that right wing come up on you. All our thrust now is on the right wing, and it's going to want to roll left. Is the red fire light out?"

"No. It's still on."

The call chime rang again, and this time Dan swept his left hand back to scoop up the handset.

"Yes?"

"Dan? This is Britta! Our left wing is on fire!"

"What . . . you mean, left engine? The outboard engine on the left wing?"

"No, Dan. It's in that vicinity, but the wing is on fire!"

"Oh, wonderful! Ah . . . Britta, make sure everyone's strapped in. Report back to me every three minutes or so on . . . how bad the left wing is. Okay?"

"Right."

"Okay . . . ah, Steve, what's our altitude?"

"Eight thousand."

"And airspeed?"

"I CAN'T DO EVERYTHING AT ONCE!"

"Hang in there, Steve. You're doing fine. You're not going to lose it. She can fly on one engine if necessary."

"I know that."

"Now I *do* need you to glance at the airspeed."

"Ah . . . two hundred and . . . ah . . . five."

"Okay. Don't let it get under a hundred and sixty until I tell you."

"What do I do?"

"You tell me if I get too slow and I'll push up the power." Dan turned partially to his left. "Mr. Walters? Are you still there?"

John Walters's voice reached him immediately. "Yes!"

"Okay. Can you punch in the coordinates for Da Nang, Vietnam, and give me a heading and distance?"

"I . . . I think so. Hold on . . ."

Dan heard the sound of a map being hastily unfolded. "Take it easy, John," he said, breathing hard. "Just do it methodically."

The cabin call chime rang again and Dan pulled the handset to his ear.

"Dan. Britta. It's still burning! A long plume of flame off the left wing, maybe twenty or thirty feet inboard from the wingtip. The passengers are freaking out! It's getting very red out there, the metal I mean! Can we do something?"

"I'm . . . trying, Britta. Keep calling."

He punched in the number for the PA system. *"Robert MacCabe . . . Dallas Nielson . . . to the flight deck immediately, please. Folks, we're going to attempt an emergency landing. Strap in."*

Dan could hear heavy breathing from the young boy in the left front seat. "How're you doing, Steve?"

"I'm holding it, but it doesn't want to fly straight."

"Three hundred forty degrees, and about forty miles!" John Walters said.

Dan nodded. "Steve, you'll need to make a gentle right turn. That's to the right. Come right to a heading of three hundred and forty degrees. Okay?"

"Yeah."

"Once you have it turned, we'll work on getting the altitude down carefully."

Dan could hear people bursting in the cockpit door. "Who's there?"

"What's left of Dallas, Honey!" Dallas Nielson said.

"And this is Robert, Dan. What's happening?"

"Okay . . . here it is. We must have damaged the left outboard engine back in Hong Kong. I think the engine exploded a few minutes ago and probably . . . peppered the wing with shrapnel. I'm guessing it breached a fuel tank, which is now feeding a fire. We have no choice but to land or ditch. We're forty miles from Da Nang, Vietnam, where there's a big runway. I don't have time to plan this. Dallas? Please sit behind Steve and help him . . . strap in and make sure he stays under control. Start a gentle descent now, to five thousand feet on a heading of three-forty, and don't let the airspeed get below one hundred sixty. Robert? In the middle jump seat, please. John? I'll need you standing for now, and strapped in back in the cabin before we land."

Dan could hear Dallas talking low and soothingly to

Steve Delaney. "Steve, Honey, take a deep breath and stay calm. You're doing fine."

"What's your plan, Dan?" Robert asked, his voice low and urgent.

Dan reached for a leather-bound book of instrument approach procedures and handed it behind him to Robert. "I need you to find the pages for Da Nang. They're organized alphabetically . . . look under Vietnam. They're instrument procedures. I need a runway heading and . . . John, please make sure the GPS has the precise airfield coordinates." Dan stopped, lowered his head, and took several ragged breaths.

"Hang in there, Dan!" Robert said, frantically flipping pages.

Dan nodded. "I am. I am." His head came up again. "Here's the deal. Steve will physically fly. I'll follow him on the controls. Dallas?"

"Yes, Baby?" she responded, her eyes glued to the forward instrument panel.

"I'll need you reading out the heading and . . . the airspeed. Okay?"

The cabin call chime rang through the cockpit again, and Dan yanked the handset to his ear once more.

"Yes?"

"It's still the same, Dan," Britta reported. "Some of the metal is getting cherry red out there! Can't you do something?"

"I'm trying, Britta. Keep reporting." He dropped the phone in his lap once more. "Okay, people . . . if we can't make the runway, we're going to ditch. We don't have long with that fire. Steve? Dallas? Can you see anything outside?"

"It's black out there, Danny. Still nighttime. I can see lightning up to the left, but . . . what am I looking for?"

"You're looking for a large group of lights on the coast, about thirty-five miles ahead. We should still be over water. Da Nang's runway is north-south, I think. That's our only chance, but we have to see it to use it."

"So, I'm looking for city lights?"

"And an airport."

"Okay. I'm looking."

"Let's descend carefully to two thousand feet. No more than one thousand feet per minute descent rate. Dallas, make absolutely sure Steve doesn't descend through one thousand for now. Go, Steve."

"All right."

"Robert? I'll need your voice calling out descent rate and altitude. Do it like this: down one hundred, at two thousand three hundred feet. Can you handle that?"

"I think so," MacCabe replied.

"It's this display," Dan said, pointing in the direction of his own set of flight instruments in front of the copilot's control yoke.

"Down eight hundred, at four thousand eight hundred feet now," Robert said. "That's the way to do it?"

"Yes. Yes, that's good. Okay, and John?"

"Yes?" John Walters replied.

"Can you read the attitude indicator? Do you know what that is?"

"No."

"Dallas? Could you quickly show John Walters how to do that?"

"I'll try," she said. Dan could hear her pull the man toward her and begin talking earnestly in his ear.

"Down one thousand five hundred, at three thousand eight hundred feet, Dan."

"Thanks, Robert. Steve? Slow your rate of descent. What's your airspeed?"

"Two hundred fifty."

Dan reached up and pulled back the throttles for engines three and four on the right wing slightly. "I'm reducing power to keep the airspeed in check. Does it want to roll back to the right now?"

"No," Steve replied.

"Is it flying straight?"

"Yes."

"Good. Is it slowing?"

"A little. Two-forty-five now."

"And can you see any lights ahead?"

"Some. But I can't look at those and at the instruments at the same time."

The cabin call chime rang again. "Dan? Britta. The fire's diminishing a bit. I don't know what you did, but it's getting better."

"Maybe airspeed is helping. Thanks, Britta."

Dan could hear Dallas finish with John Walters.

"John?" Dan asked. "How many miles now?"

"Twenty-eight. We're on the right heading . . . dead on," he replied.

"Okay. Dallas, we're going to have one shot at this. When we slow down further, that fire is probably going to flare back up. Can you see an alternating green-and-white beacon ahead?"

There was silence for a few seconds from the left before Dallas replied.

"You know, I expect a refund for this flight if I'm going to be a damn crew member!" she grumbled. "YES!" Her voice was tinged with excitement. "I've got it, Dan! Dead ahead."

"All right," Dan began, taking a deep breath. "We will probably not see the runway lights until the last minute or so. We need to aim for that beacon, but remember, it will not be on the end of the runway. Robert? Have you found that approach sheet in the book?"

"Yes. Just now."

"See if you can find anything that indicates . . . I don't know how to say this, but there may be a way to manually control the runway lights there by clicking the radio."

"Do we have a radio we can use?" Robert asked.

Dan hung his head. "Damn! No, we don't. Forget that."

"Down one thousand, at two thousand three hundred," Robert said.

"Steve, start pulling her back to level flight, which will be about three to four degrees nose-up on the attitude indicator. Okay?"

"Yeah," Steve replied.

"Dallas, are we still aiming directly at that beacon?"

"Yes, we are."

"Can you see anything that looks like an airport?"

"I—not yet, but we're aiming the right way."

"Okay. Airspeed?"

"Two hundred sixty," Steve said.

"I'm going to slow us down now, Steve. She'll take larger corrections with the yoke, and will seem a bit more sluggish." He pulled the two throttles for the engines on the right wing back and changed the rudder trim and the pitch trim, keeping a hand on the yoke to feel what Steve Delaney was doing. Thirty seconds crawled by like an eternity.

"Airspeed?" Dan asked again.

"One hundred ninety," Steve said.

"Altitude, Robert?"

"Level two thousand feet."

"Exactly?"

"Dead on."

"Great job, Steve! Keep her there a bit longer. John? How far out?"

"Seventeen miles."

"Okay. The field is at sea level. At seven miles out we need to start down at no more than seven hundred feet per minute. Robert? You understand that?"

"Yes."

"If you see a descent rate greater than seven hundred to eight hundred feet per minute, tell Steve to pull it back a hair. You'll be talking directly to Steve, and I'll be helping. Steve? Even if you feel me moving the controls, you hang on and keep on flying. I might make corrections, but do not let go! Okay?"

"Okay."

"Airspeed?"

"One hundred seventy," Steve replied.

"I'm going to try to get flaps out. Robert? See the flap position gauge up here?" Dan waved his finger at the appropriate gauge. "See the two needles?"

"Yes."

"If they start to split apart, yell 'STOP FLAPS!'"

"Okay."

"Okay—Flaps One." Dan moved the flap handle to the first detent. "Steve? The airplane is going to want to jump up a bit and climb, so I'm toggling in some nose-down trim."

"Okay."

"Flaps Five." Again he moved the handle, and the sound and feel of the giant 747 flaps moving into position rumbled through the cockpit.

"Robert, are the needles pointing to five?"

"Yes, Dan. Together."

"Okay. Flaps Fifteen. John? How far from the airport?"

"Fourteen miles."

"Altitude?" Dan asked.

"Still steady at two thousand," Robert answered.

"And airspeed?"

"One hundred fifty," Steve said.

"Dan!" Dallas broke in. "I can see what looks like runway lights up there."

"Good! Is there a series of flashing white lights leading to the runway lights, or any patch of white approach lights?"

"Yeah, something like that," Dallas responded.

"So, we're still headed right for the end of that runway?"

"Looks like it," Dallas said.

"Keep helping Steve to aim right at it. Now for the landing gear."

Dan held his breath as he moved the gear handle to the Down position, but the sound of the gear moving out of the underbelly and into position was unmistakable.

"How many green and red lights do I have up here?" Dan asked, his hand on the appropriate gear light panel.

"All green, Dan. No red," Robert said.

"Hallelujah!" Dan replied. "How far, John?"

"Eleven miles."

"How does it feel, Steve? Are you pushing or pulling to keep level?"

"I'm pulling."

The sound of the trim wheel operating filled the cockpit for a moment as Dan toggled it nose-up. "How about now?"

"That's better."

"If you let go, does the nose go down or up?"

"It pretty much stays the same."

"And airspeed?"

"One hundred thirty."

"Oops!" Dan pushed the throttles up and changed the rudder trim. "Now, tell me when we reach one-forty. We want no less than one hundred forty knots."

The cabin chime rang again with Britta on the other end.

"It's flaring up, Dan. It's really burning out there."

"Strap in, Britta. We'll be on the ground in . . . three minutes."

"Okay. I'm just behind the cockpit on the upper deck, Dan."

"Okay." Dan replaced the handset in his lap. "Miles to the field?"

"Eight miles," John Walters said.

"Okay, folks. We're gonna do this!" Dan said, pumping as much energy into his voice as he could in an effort to convince himself.

"Dan, there's lightning ahead. Looks like a storm's on the other side of the airport, and when it flashed, I was able to see the airport and the runway."

"Okay, Dallas. Now, Steve . . . the object will be to keep a steady descent and not try to flare. Just keep her aimed at the runway, and when we're down to a hundred feet or so, just make very, very gentle left-and-right movements to keep her between the lights on the runway. She'll touch down hard, but it'll be okay. This is a tough bird. She can take it."

"All right," Steve replied.

"The wings must be level on touchdown, understand?"

"Yeah."

"Distance?"

"Seven miles," John Walters said.

"Okay, Steve, start her down. No more than seven hundred feet per minute. I'm going to nudge the power back and change the trim slightly."

"Okay."

"John? Give the GPS to Robert, show him how to read mileage, and strap in."

"I'll stay here."

"NO! There's no other seat for you."

"Six miles. I'm staying, Dan."

Dan hesitated, then nodded. "Your choice, John. Thank you. Altitude?"

"Down eight hundred feet per minute, at one thousand eight hundred feet."

"Got it. Dallas? Start your call-outs now."

"Heading is three-five-zero degrees, speed one-fifty."

"And John? Attitude?" Dan asked.

"Ah . . . plus one degree. Is that how you want it?"

"Yes!" Dan replied. "Distance now?"

"Five miles," John Walters said.

"Dallas? Are we lined up with the runway, or are we angling to it?"

Steve answered before she could reply. "It's angling off to the left—maybe twenty degrees left. WHAT DO I DO?"

"Okay, Steve. *Carefully, gently* bank the airplane to the right ten degrees, then turn back gently just before the runway comes into alignment. Understand?"

"I . . . think so."

"Turn NOW! Keep it gentle! Robert?"

"Yeah, uh, down eight hundred, and . . . altitude fifteen hundred."

"Heading three-six-zero," Dallas added. "Steve, turn it back left now."

"Okay," Steve replied.

"Airspeed, somebody?"

"One-forty-five," Dallas said.

"There!" Steve Delaney said. "I'm lining up! It's good!"

"Robert?" Dan prompted.

"Down six hundred, altitude twelve hundred," Robert replied.

"Attitude, John?"

"Plus one degree."

"Steve, keep it steady . . . keep it lined up. Make small corrections, *very* small corrections, in roll and pitch. Okay?"

"Yeah!"

"Robert?" Dan prompted again.

"Down eight hundred now, altitude just under a thousand."

"We should be three miles, John. Right?" Dan asked.

"Yes. Three."

"Dallas, can you see the runway clearly? Does it look empty?"

"Yes. The runway looks clear, but there's lightning on the north side."

"Concentrate on the runway. Does it have lights on each side?" Dan asked.

"Yes."

"Down nine hundred, six hundred feet."

"Steve," Dan said, "I'm pulling back gently. We want the descent rate a little less. Now, is the end of the runway coming up in the windscreen, or moving under us?"

"Ah, it's . . . ah . . . moving under us."

"Speed?"

"One-forty."

"Steve, let the nose down just a hair," Dan added. "Is the end staying in the same place now?"

"Yeah, I think so," Steve replied.

"Down nine hundred, two hundred feet," Robert said.

Dan reached up and verified by feel that the landing lights were on. "Okay . . . are we headed straight down the runway?"

"Yes!" Steve replied. "But something's wrong! There's . . . a . . . OH NO! THERES A BUILDING IN THE MIDDLE OF THE RUNWAY!"

"Dallas? What does he mean?"

"Jeez, Dan, this isn't a runway! There's . . ."

"DAN! This is a taxiway! It ends in a building!"

Dan Wade's left hand crammed the throttles forward and pulled back on the yoke, pressing the right rudder pedal hard to keep the airplane aligned.

"We're going around!" Dan croaked. "Max power. Steve, keep wings level!"

"I am!"

"Are we climbing?"

"Yes, a little!" Steve said.

"I'm . . . guide us straight out, Steve. Are we clear of hills?"

"I don't know . . . *there's* the runway, under us! Oh, man, I lined us up on the wrong thing!"

"Steve, keep us climbing gently straight ahead. Let's go up to a thousand feet and turn east. It'll want to turn left. Don't let it."

"There's a hill over there . . . in front," Steve yelled. "And a lot of lightning just ahead."

"Steer us away," Dan replied, feeling the yoke go to the left.

"We're climbing eight hundred, at five hundred feet," Robert said.

"Airspeed?"

"DAN! WHICH WAY DO I GO?"

"Steve, stay calm! Hold on to the airplane and aim to the left of that storm and keep us clear of any hills. Most are to the west. Keep climbing."

"Gotta come left more," Steve said, his voice high and strained. "Lightning!"

"Yes, to the left!" Dallas echoed. "I can't tell how far. Can't see for these clouds. We're in the clouds now, Dan."

"Steady, Steve. Keep her climbing, and keep her going straight. We'll go back around to the east, around the storm, and try it again."

Unseen by the copilot, a tremendous flash of light illuminated the cockpit.

"Dan, we've flown into a storm," Robert said, as calmly as he could.

"DON'T TURN, STEVE! Just keep climbing on this heading. We'll have to take the bumps."

Another lightning flash flooded the cockpit with a ghastly light, followed almost instantly by a gigantic booming sound.

"SWEET JESUS, HELP!" Dallas exclaimed.

"DAN," Steve yelped, "we're right in the middle of it!" The aircraft had begun to heave and buck in the violent air currents of a thunderstorm cell.

"Keep climbing. Robert?"

"Ah . . . up . . . ah, one thousand, and altitude now at one thousand two hundred."

"Airspeed, someone?" Dan asked.

"I can hardly see after that flash!" Steve said.

"One-sixty," Dallas said. "And heading two hundred eighty degrees."

"I CAN'T SEE ANYTHING, DAN!" Steve yelled.

Dan raised his left hand. "Wait, did you say *two-eight-zero degrees*?"

"Yes," Dallas said.

"NO!" Dan said. "Aim more north! Use your instruments now. Turn right. Keep climbing. I'm going to raise the gear." Dan reached out and snapped the landing gear lever to the Up position, feeling the undercarriage respond. "Altitude?"

"One thousand seven hundred, but we're not climbing," Robert said.

"Attitude, John?"

"Ah, up five degrees."

Robert's voice cut in. "Dan, we're descending three hundred feet per minute."

"Watch your pitch, Steve!" Dan shoved the throttles as far forward as they would go as he added back pressure to the yoke to pull the nose up. "Attitude?"

"Up seven, no, eight degrees."

"We've stopped descending, Dan, but we're at one thousand three hundred."

The sound of a call chime rang through the cockpit, unheard by Dan. Dallas answered it, then replaced the handset. "Dan, the rain's put the fire out!"

"Thank God," Dan said. "We turn north now, we'll be over the coastline. Need more altitude."

A tremendous burst of wind slammed into the 747 at the same moment another round of staccato lightning strikes all but blinded everyone but Dan. The gut-wrenching sound of repeated thunderclaps coursed through their souls as the turbulence became severe; the instruments bounced too wildly to be read.

"HANG . . . ON . . . EVERYONE!" Dan shouted. "STEVE . . . IT'S UP TO YOU TO KEEP THE NOSE UP! KEEP IT AT FIFTEEN DEGREES UP! AIRSPEED, ANYONE?"

"CAN'T READ IT!" Dallas cried.

"HEADING? *HEADING PLEASE!* "

"TWO HUNDRED SOMETHING . . ." Dallas yelled.

"NO! NO, NO, NO!" Dan yelled. "THERE ARE MOUNTAINS TO THE WEST. TURN RIGHT!"

"DAN, WE'RE DESCENDING AGAIN!" Robert yelled. "WE'RE HOLDING AT A THOUSAND . . ."

A sudden massive impact threw them all forward against the shoulder straps with incredible force as the belly of the 747 found a ridgeline. John Walters felt himself propelled forward, his body frozen for a split second by another lightning strike. The mountain ridge ripped off all of the engines and most of the flaps, leaving the remaining structure of wings and fuselage skittering in disintegrating confusion at more than a hundred knots past the ridge and settling progressively into the mountain jungle canopy. The airframe rapidly decelerated as flaps and wing panels, engines and lower fuselage parts were ripped away. The lower deck and coach cabins, galleys, seats, and passengers were progressively yanked into the thickening buzz saw of passing trees as the 747 spread its parts through the jumble of vegetation below.

For those in the cockpit, the sensory overload became total. The unbelievable sequence unfolded too rapidly to grasp or see or understand. The airplane disintegrated like a block of cheese skimming a kitchen grater, shedding more and more parts and ribs and components until only a portion of the liberated upper deck of the 747 remained intact. And finally, all that remained habitable of what had been an enormous airplane slid to a halt in the middle of a verdant jungle clearing.

In the minutes that followed, the thunderstorm moved east, leaving behind the normal sounds of a misty predawn jungle, broken in places only by the sound of liquids hissing on hot metallic objects.

chapter

18

Janice Washburn gently touched the sleeve of the technician next to her and gestured for him to zoom in closer. Normally the scenes they monitored from orbit carried no emotional reaction, but this was different.

The computer-generated picture assembled itself at last from the transmissions of two different satellites, causing her to gasp. "Am I seeing . . ."

"I'm afraid so, Janice. This is the hot spot I found a few minutes ago, right on the track they were flying, and there are no longer any airborne seven-forty-sevens within their flight range from the previous contact. They're down."

The picture coalesced to a field of intense white images defining the wreckage path of Meridian Flight 5.

"How about survivors?" she asked, in little more than a whisper.

"Could be, but it just happened. So far, I'm not seeing any."

She whirled around to search his eyes. "That aircraft carried over . . ."

"Two hundred. I know, Janice. We just have to wait."

"That's the *best you can do*?"

He nodded. "This whole debris field is too hot, too many fires. The heat is masking any survivors who might be there. Remember, we're looking at infrared."

She lifted the receiver she'd been holding to relay the news to her senior, George Barkley, then back to the technician. "George wants to know if you could bring back the shot of that small jet?"

He nodded, entering a flurry of keystrokes into the keyboard. A still infrared image of a small two-engine jet appeared on the screen.

"Where is he?"

"When this was taken, he was ten miles east of Da Nang, off the coast. But we've lost him beneath a thunderstorm that moved over Da Nang a little while ago. He was right over the crash site earlier, but flew back offshore. He's just orbiting."

"What's our confidence level he's been tailing the seven-forty-seven?"

The technician said, "High. Very high."

Janice raised the phone to her ear, still curious, reminding herself to feed the latest reports to Langley immediately.

IN THE JUNGLE,
12 MILES NORTHWEST OF DA NANG, VIETNAM

The realization that he was alive came slowly to Robert MacCabe.

Aside from the flickering orange light of countless fires somewhere in the distance, it was dark—and cold. The feel of damp air on his face and the lack of familiar background noise of commercial flight jolted him back to the reality that he wasn't awakening from a nightmare, he was still living it.

We were trying to fly . . . no, to land . . . and something happened . . .

Robert tried moving his right arm, and found it still attached and usable. He checked his left, and progressively his entire body, finding everything intact.

Where am I? Total confusion reigned for a few seconds

until his short-term memory flooded back, causing him to sit bolt upright in what was left of the right cockpit jump seat.

Oh my God! We've crashed!

He tried to stand, but couldn't. *I must be hurt!* But there was no pain.

Robert reached down with rising apprehension to feel his waist, the concept of paralysis hovering in the back of his mind.

He struggled again, hearing twisted metal parts rocking against one another. Still he couldn't stand. Something was preventing him from moving his lower waist. Something was binding him to the ruined seat.

The seat belt!

With great relief, Robert reached down and snapped off the belt, standing up gingerly, his mind confused by the flickering images and ghastly shadows everywhere. He was in the remains of the cockpit, and the shell of the window frame was still intact.

There was a form slumped forward just below the broken windows. Robert moved to it, stumbling over debris that held his feet in the darkness. He pulled the body back, recognizing the bandage over the eyes. The copilot.

"Dan! Dan, can you hear me?" Robert doubted he was hearing his own voice at first. It was oddly pitched and strained. "Dan! Answer me!"

The figure stirred and tried to sit up. "Wha . . . ?"

"Dan, this is Robert MacCabe. Can you hear me?"

Dan shook his head. "I . . . I can't see you . . ."

"We've crashed, Dan. Somewhere in Vietnam. Do you remember?"

There was a sound to the left, a low moan, and Robert glanced over at the remains of the captain's seat, now dislodged, the bottom end showing in his direction.

Dan was nodding, his hand on his head. "Oh my God."

"Stay put, Dan. I've got to check on the others." He picked his way through the jumbled debris on the floor of the cockpit and pulled the captain's seat back upright, bringing Steve Delaney with it. He, too, was coming around, and basically uninjured except for a few minor cuts to his head.

Dallas was trying to dig herself out. She was dazed and shaking like a leaf.

John Walters had not been strapped in at the moment of impact. He was lying lengthwise on the broken front of the instrument panel. Robert reached for his wrist, aware of the awkward position of the man's head and neck. There was no pulse.

"Where the hell are we?" Dallas mumbled, holding Robert's shoulder.

"Dallas, are you okay?"

She nodded, her hand to her head, her dark face barely visible in the orange light. She sat on a remarkably intact jump seat. "Depends . . . how you define okay," she mumbled. "How 'bout you?"

Robert sank back on the remains of his jump seat and tried to clear his head. "I don't know. I don't know why we're alive."

Thirty-five feet away in the shattered forward half of the upper deck first-class cabin, Dr. Graham Tash worked to extricate himself from the tangle of wires and tubes that engulfed him, the remnants of the overhead panels. He vaguely remembered feeling the jet pull up from a landing, but what had happened then?

Susan! he thought suddenly. *Oh my God!*

Graham turned to his left and began pawing through the debris that covered the aisle seat, exposing his wife's blond hair.

"Susan!"

She stirred, giving him hope as he worked rapidly to free her from the tangle.

"Graham?"

"Honey! Oh my God, are you okay?"

There was a long hesitation as she took inventory, then nodded and opened her eyes, blinking at the reflection of fire on his skin and wondering why there was a campfire nearby. His voice seemed to fade away into a void.

Susan Tash sat up abruptly and looked around in shock. The remains of the 747's upper deck still resembled a passenger cabin, but it was little more than the shell of sidewalls and windows attached to the floor that remained. Some of the seats were still visible as well, but most of the ceiling had collapsed, and she realized that there was nothing but debris behind her.

She took a ragged breath. "Graham . . . what . . . what . . ."

"We crashed, Suze! We crashed, but we made it!"

The airline CEO who had been sitting in the first row had not fastened his seat belt. The impact had catapulted him into the forward bulkhead where he now lay, moaning quietly.

Susan got to her feet, grabbing for support against rubbery legs, and tried to move toward him. "Graham," she said, as her husband held her and guided her toward the front, "he's hurt. We'll need a flashlight."

A beam of light snapped on by her shoulder, pointed at the shattered floor.

Susan looked over at the silhouette of a disheveled woman she finally recognized as Britta.

"We always carry these," Britta said in a matter-of-fact manner.

"Are you okay?" Graham asked Britta.

Britta nodded, a shaky right hand brushing back what had become a wild mane of hair, while she tried to straighten a hopelessly torn white blouse.

There was a commotion ahead of them, and Britta raised the beam of light directly into Robert MacCabe's face as he stumbled through what used to be the cockpit door.

"Ow!"

"Sorry," Britta said, lowering the flashlight beam to the torn and littered floor.

"Who's there?" Robert asked, his voice unreal and raspy.

"Britta Franz and two passengers. Doctor . . ."

"Graham and Susan Tash," Graham said.

Robert nodded drunkenly. "Dan and Dallas," he began, stopping to clear his throat, ". . . and . . . and . . . Steve made it," he said. "They're up front. Be careful. The floor is jagged in places."

Britta nodded.

"How is everyone downstairs?" Robert asked.

Britta looked at him blankly, her right hand rising, then falling limply to her side, an apparent attempt to gesture somewhere behind.

"I . . . can't find it. There's no . . . stairway either."

Graham had been focusing on Rick Barnes's prone body, preparing to kneel beside the man and examine him. He turned and looked behind them at the field of orange flames burning and flickering in a thousand places, all radiating toward what was becoming a light purple glow on the horizon.

A lightning strike somewhere in the distance shot a bolt of terror up Graham's spine as if it had struck him directly. He realized he was looking at the remains of the storm that had almost killed them.

"I think . . . the others must be somewhere back there," Britta said, looking blankly in the same direction, obviously in shock. "We . . . we've got to find them."

Graham followed her gaze, recognizing the clearing of broken trees as the final flight path of the 747. He could see shapes in the distance, bits and pieces of fuselage, a shell with windows on one side, and other terrible shapes in the dark, but nothing as large as a survivable part of an airliner cabin.

There were over two hundred people on this airplane! he thought. *My God! There could be hundreds injured back there!*

"Doctor. Please. Mr. Barnes is injured," Britta was saying.

Graham turned to look at the airline CEO and knelt down as Britta played the flashlight over his face. "Can you hear me, Mr. Barnes?" Graham asked.

Rick Barnes moaned, but didn't speak.

Britta found the aircraft first-aid kit, and Graham went to work on the obvious facial injuries, stabilizing Barnes and concluding there were probably internal injuries in addition to a serious concussion.

"If you're done for now, Doctor," Britta said, "I need the flashlight to check the others." Graham nodded, and she swung the flashlight forward at the tangle of debris in her pathway, stepping in toward Dan, Dallas, and Steve.

To the east, a pronounced glow was filling the horizon as dawn overtook them. They could hear a host of nonthreatening jungle sounds of birds and wind and the occasional buzz of an insect.

Graham Tash stood up and held Susan for support as he looked behind them at the wreckage path. "Susan, there will be others in terrible shape, wherever they are. We should go help."

She nodded without a word and lifted the first-aid kit. Graham took the flashlight from Britta and stepped out of the wreckage onto muddy ground before turning to help Susan down the eighteen-inch drop. The air reeked of jet fuel. The two of them stepped carefully past jagged remains, wincing at the unique smell of the burning rubble to the east as they walked fifty yards away, then turned to look back.

The entire upper deck with the cockpit attached had sheared away from the rest of the fuselage. Somehow, the forward half had slid mostly intact into what was apparently a natural clearing, the lower fuselage having absorbed most of the speed and impact.

Behind them—toward the highway of flames and wreckage—the outlines of broken trees marked the final flight path of the disintegrated Boeing. Using the flashlight, they made their way in that direction. Susan stumbled in her low heels and twisted her ankle as they stepped gingerly through the macabre landscape of debris, both natural and man-made. They moved steadily, without speaking, until the first encounter with crushed seats and fragmented human bodies announced the western extent of the remains of Flight 5's main cabin.

After ten minutes of searching, it seemed obvious they were wasting their time.

Susan and Graham made their way back toward the

remains of the upper deck, stopping at the edge of the clearing to hold each other for what seemed like an eternity. The enormity of being unable to find a single survivor from the main cabin was too much to bear.

"When I was an emergency room nurse," Susan said, "I . . . had to deal with survivors who couldn't understand why they were spared, and others in an accident died. The 'why me?' syndrome, you know? Why did I survive?" Susan breathed heavily and Graham held her as tightly as he dared. She flailed a hand in the direction of the main wreckage, tears streaming down her face. "I've . . . never experienced it myself. But now—here *we* are alive, and . . . and all of them . . . are *gone*! Why?"

She buried her face in his chest and cried soundlessly, her shoulders heaving. Graham held her close, tears streaming down his own face as he tried to erase the images of the broken and torn human remains he had just seen.

"Let's keep moving," Graham said, as gently as he could. "We do have some of the living to care for."

She nodded in staccato fashion, hanging on to him as they again picked their way toward the dark outline of what used to be the upper deck, the unique whalelike upper hump of a Boeing 747's fuselage.

Dallas had lost consciousness again, for how long she didn't know. The memory of Robert talking to her was there, but she had felt tired all of a sudden and had sunk back into the jump seat, intending to rest for a few seconds. Slowly she forced herself to swim up through the fuzzy layers of fatigue and shock to consciousness, vaguely aware that someone who sounded a lot like Britta was helping Dan Wade out of the broken cockpit.

Dallas got to her feet once more and turned to follow. She was almost at the rear of the wrecked flight deck when she remembered Steve Delaney. She turned back just in time to catch him in her arms as Steve tripped over something unseen in the still-dark cockpit.

"We didn't make it, did we?" Steve asked her, his voice shaking and reedy.

"This ain't a ghost you're talking to, Darlin'. Yes, we *did* make it, but we sure banged up Dan's airplane."

Steve was breathing hard, almost in a panic. "I . . . tried my best . . ."

"What?"

He was shaking his head, his entire body quaking, his right hand gesturing to the front of the broken cockpit. "I tried . . . I pulled up . . . and . . . I didn't mean to line up on the wrong lights . . . I . . ."

Dallas turned and seized the fourteen-year-old by the shoulders. "Look at me. LOOK AT ME!"

Steve looked up, his eyes huge with shock.

"You did everything right. You hear me? You did everything right, Steve! This just—happened."

He began hyperventilating and she hugged him tightly, rocking him gently as they stood in the darkness of the wreckage.

"It's okay, Steve! This is NOT your fault. It's not your fault."

There was no response.

"Do you hear me?" she shouted, satisfied only when he nodded his head. "Okay, Baby, let's get the others and get to safety." Dallas moved through the jumbled mess of the cockpit's rear entrance and onto the buckled floor as Britta came forward again.

"We need to get out of here," Britta said, finding another flashlight and snapping it on.

"You're right about that!" Dallas agreed. "Who's back there?"

Britta turned slowly, supporting herself on the broken wall of the cabin, as Robert reappeared.

"The doctor and his wife have gone to help the others," he said. "Everyone else, the galley up here, all the other seats—they're gone. And I can't . . . find the downstairs."

Dallas heard the words, but the statement made no sense. How could one fail to find a downstairs? They had climbed to the upper deck originally, therefore . . .

She looked out to the side of the wreckage while Britta played her flashlight into the darkness. Where there should have been airspace some thirty feet above the ground, there was the ground itself, and branches, and shrubs, and trees at the same level. They had been in a heavily loaded 747.

This makes no sense! Dallas thought.

"We have the doctor and his wife, plus Mr. MacCabe, plus Mr. Barnes, plus you, Dallas. We have Dan, and . . ." Britta gestured to Steve.

"Steve?"

"Yes," Britta said.

"How about the rest of them?"

Britta shook her head.

"Where the hell is the *rest* of this airplane?" Dallas asked in amazement.

Britta gestured toward the avenue of burning debris behind them, and Dallas's eyes followed her, the reality pressing in slowly. Britta saw Dallas Nielson's shoulders slump a bit as her mouth came open.

"Oh my dear Jesus! All of them?"

Britta shrugged, her voice barely above a whisper. "I don't know. But so far, there's only us."

chapter
19

A last line of thunderstorms had pelted the airport with hail the size of golf balls and moved on, leaving a resplendent starry sky in the hour before sunrise.

Kat had spent the previous hour sitting and thinking in the backseat of the Consulate's car while the driver slept in the front. She startled him awake by getting out to stretch and look at the stars at the same moment Jake rang her satellite phone.

"Kat? Langley's relayed the word that Meridian has gone down in Vietnam."

Kat felt her legs get rubbery and she leaned against the car. "Oh my God!"

"All I have is a potential crash site, nine miles west of the coastal city of Da Nang, Vietnam, in some low mountains. No information on survivors."

"Did it come down intact?" she asked, knowing instinctively that a jumbo jet couldn't withstand a high-speed encounter with a forest.

"Ah . . . they mentioned a debris field almost a mile long, Kat, with active fires in the area. That doesn't sound hopeful."

The image of the cabin in which she had sat for a brief moment was etched in her mind, but she forced her eyes open and made herself concentrate.

"Okay, Jake, here's what I propose to do." She stood away from the car, commanding her legs to support her. "I should get the first flight into Vietnam and get to the site as fast as possible. Can you formally approve that and assign me to the case, and get me out of that obligation at the Consulate? I think we'll also have to coordinate with NTSB."

"I'll need twenty minutes."

"Call me back. I'm going to go pick out a flight. Oh . . . Jake, did they ever see that Global Express in the air?"

"Langley said no."

"Can we check with NRO directly?"

Again Jake fell silent on the other end, long enough to register extreme discomfort. "You realize, Kat, that NRO is probably monitoring this call."

"On tape, yes. But I have a reason for not trusting Langley on this. Methinks they doth protest too much on the subject of accident versus terrorists. If NRO saw the Global Express, Langley will want to discount the identification because it disproves their midair theory and leaves us with a terrorist attack. Therefore, they're getting in the way of a criminal investigation."

"You said the magic words, Kat. You don't think much of them, do you?"

"I'm just a neophyte regarding CIA, but—let's just say I think they're developing a pointed habit of not wanting the Cuban crash and this one to be terrorist-related, and I don't trust their motives. Heck, Jake, they're trained to shade things. But we need their help. That Global Express crew is still a big threat in this situation."

"How do you mean?"

"They're going to be very concerned now that they've got a loose end. If anyone survived the Meridian crash, and there's a chance that evidence of what the Global Express did has been left behind, they'll have to go in and clean it up. That crash site needs to be found and protected quickly, and any survivors recovered."

IN THE JUNGLE,
12 MILES NORTHWEST OF DA NANG, VIETNAM

The first glow of dawn had begun to illuminate the jungle, revealing the details of individual branches where only dark outlines had been minutes before. The small group had helped each other out of the wreckage, and found a large metal panel to sit on by the time Graham and Susan Tash returned with ashen faces.

"What did you find?" Robert asked.

Graham Tash merely shook his head. There was silence for a few telling seconds before Dan raised his head in response. "Why is no one saying anything?"

Graham Tash knelt beside the copilot. "Dan, Susan and I went back to the main wreckage. It's strewn behind us for a thousand yards, at least." Graham stopped and cleared his throat. "We found no one alive back there."

Dan Wade sat in stunned silence for a moment. "You . . . you mean everyone . . . down below and . . . in coach . . ."

"I'm afraid so. The entire lower portion of the airplane was . . . I don't know any other word for it . . . shredded. Somehow the forward part of the top section, with us in it, came through, but nothing below. There are no other survivors."

"Two hundred . . ." Dan said, almost in a whisper. "My God! And Mr. Sampson, who tried so hard to help—did he . . ."

"He had gone back to sit with his wife in coach, Dan," Britta said, touching his shoulder. "He isn't here."

Robert MacCabe was pacing. "So what's our plan?" he asked. "We need to formulate a plan."

"I guess we sit here and wait to be rescued," Dallas said.

Britta's hands were in the air in a gesture of frustration. "But why aren't they here already?"

Robert started to answer, then pursed his lips. "We can all walk, right?"

"Except for Mr. Barnes," Britta replied.

"Okay," Robert said. "We flew right over Da Nang just before the crash. I figure we're no more than ten miles from there because we weren't in the air very long. The jungle in here is pretty sparse and scrubby. Dan? You know the area from your Air Force years, right?"

Dan nodded slowly.

"Any reason we shouldn't just walk out of here?"

Dan sat for several long minutes with his head in his hands before raising his head and speaking. "In daylight, without snipers trying to kill you, it won't be that hard a walk."

"Dan," Dallas began. "Wouldn't they be sending rescue choppers, or ground parties, or *something*?"

He shook his head vigorously. "They probably don't even know we've crashed. We flew past a bunch of primitive facilities on a deteriorated airfield in the middle of a night-time storm and disappeared into the darkness, and we haven't been in radio contact since Hong Kong. Who in hell is going to know we're here?"

"Well, wouldn't there be villages around here?" Britta asked.

Again Dan shook his head forcefully. "No. Not in these mountains. There's a road not too far from here called the Ho Chi Minh Trail, but no one would have seen or heard us crash if we're where I think we are. Charlie—" He stopped himself.

"Who's Charlie?" Britta asked.

"The Vietcong," Dallas answered for him. "Right, Dan?"

Dan nodded. "It's hard to shake the old cautions, but I do know we're almost certainly alone up here. We must have hit a mountain plateau."

"Well, *eventually* someone will show up, right?" Dallas prodded.

"Sure," Dan agreed. "Eventually. But God knows when."

"So what do we do?" Britta asked.

"We walk out of here," Robert MacCabe said, noticing how fast Dan nodded in response. "And if it's only six or eight miles back there to the ocean, at most it'll take us five or six hours." The image of his computer flitted across his mind, and the fact that he'd just seen it on the floor. Robert returned to the remains of the cabin and climbed inside to retrieve it, finding it still intact.

"What happens if we take off walking and *then* rescue arrives?" Britta asked.

"Then Mr. Barnes gets help even quicker, and we end up in a thinly disguised physical fitness run," Robert replied, as he joined them again.

"Barnes is semiconscious," Graham Tash said. "We need to leave a note or something, so if someone does come, they'll know we're walking out."

"We'll do better than that. If they come, I'll tell them," Susan Tash said. Graham looked at her in alarm.

"I'm going to stay here, Graham," she explained. "I'm a nurse, remember?"

"No, Suze! I'll stay."

She shook her head. "My ankle is hurting and I'm wearing heels. Walking any distance is just not an option for me in bare feet or heels."

"Well, then, I'll stay, too," Graham said.

"No, Graham. You're a good hiker, and if anything occurs with the rest of the group . . . if there are injuries we don't know about, you need to be there. I'll be fine. Heck, I'll probably get rescued first."

"How about tigers and snakes and such?" Dallas asked.

Graham's worried eyes were firmly on his wife, his mind registering the fact that her bright yellow dress was becoming more visible by the second in the growing light of dawn. After several long seconds he shook his head. "Tigers don't exist around here, and you'd almost have to look for a snake to bite you. Only monkeys. Thousands of them."

Dallas looked at each of them in turn. "Okay. Dan, are you staying here?"

"I'm going," the copilot said. "Anything's better than just sitting here in agony. I'll . . . just hang on to someone's shirttail."

"We should get moving, then," Robert prompted.

Britta looked around uncomfortably, weighing her sense of duty with her sense of revulsion at remaining one minute longer than necessary in the midst of such carnage. "I'll go, too, unless Susan wants to borrow my shoes."

Susan shook her head no.

Dr. Graham Tash gently tugged at Susan's sleeve as he looked at the others. "Ah, give me just a minute, will you? And Britta, we'll want to take a few basics with us from the first-aid kit, just in case."

Britta nodded and turned back to the wrecked upper cabin. Graham and Susan walked a few paces from the group to talk. He turned at last and put his hands on Susan's shoulders. "Honey, I'm terrified of your staying here alone."

"Nonsense. We're both still in shock, but other than my twisted ankle, we're physically okay. That man needs help and the rest of the group may need you. We're professional medical people, Graham. This can't be personal."

"The hell it can't! You're my *life*, Honey. I love you!"

She put the palm of her hand on his cheek. "And I love *you*. But I don't believe God kept us alive just to tear us apart. Now keep these folks safe and go get help. No one's shooting at anyone in Vietnam these days. I'll be fine."

Graham pulled Susan to him and hugged her tightly, stroking her hair until she pulled away. She smiled and kissed him lightly, then turned and headed back to the wreckage.

ABOARD GLOBAL EXPRESS N22Z, IN FLIGHT, NORTHWEST OF DA NANG, VIETNAM

Arlin Schoen sat on the edge of a plush leather armchair and took the receiver to the satellite telephone, pulling it to his ear and nodding to the broad-shouldered, heavyset man who'd taken the call.

The thoroughly controlled voice of the man on the other end spoke with unhurried ease, as though nothing had gone wrong. "What's your status, Arlin?"

"I was going to call you. They went down about twelve miles west of Da Nang, in the mountains. We're orbiting off-shore, undetected so far."

"Did you fly over the site?"

"We did. Couldn't see a thing except the fires. That was before dawn."

There was a sigh on the other end. "We can't rule out survivors. But I can't get you any more assets out there now. You're on your own to solve this."

Schoen shifted the receiver to the other hand, weighing his words carefully. "I know. Some could have made it. So far no rescue forces have launched. I don't think these local morons realize anyone crashed."

"We must stay on schedule. No loose ends, or loose lips, to tell tales and undo everything we've put in motion. You know that."

Schoen took a deep breath. To go in was a huge risk, but to imperil the operation after all that had happened was unacceptable. "We're going in, of course."

"I agree," the voice on the phone replied. "Get in and get out fast. In twenty-four hours the entire world will be crawling all over this one. Don't forget the timetable."

"I won't."

"This was your show, Arlin. I had your assurances it was the best solution and that you could make it work."

"It is, and I will. Relax."

Within five minutes, the Global Express touched down on Da Nang's runway under an emergency declaration, leaving the tower operators in a state of confusion over where the sleek business jet had come from. A quick exchange of American currency at the door of the jet produced the local military garrison commander, a bored Vietnamese army officer who emerged ten minutes later with a smile and a briefcase containing $200,000 U.S. small bills.

Within fifteen minutes, the leader and crew of the American business jet lifted off in an ancient, American-built Bell UH-1 helicopter.

chapter
20

Robert MacCabe squinted at the eastern horizon, trying to calculate the distance they'd come in almost a half hour of walking.

Maybe a quarter mile. Maybe more.

After a lifetime of backpacking and hiking, taking the lead was a natural role, even if the northern coastal jungle of Vietnam was unknown to him.

Vietnam was someone else's experience—the name of a war his father had fought as a Navy staff officer in the Pentagon; something that had caused the previous generation to break out in a serious case of hysteria and protesting hippies. The rest was merely a tumultuous chapter in American history to be studied in school. He had been a child when the helicopters plucked the last Americans off the Embassy roof in Saigon.

Robert looked around at Britta as she helped the copilot back to his feet. For the third time in less than ten minutes, Dan had stumbled on jungle undergrowth, his hand slipping away from Britta's as he plunged forward into the fragrant but insect-laden vegetation. She helped him up, and Graham looked him over.

"Dan, are you okay?" Robert called.

"Yeah, I'm okay." The copilot nodded, brushing twigs and leaves out of his hair and water droplets off the uniform coat Britta had retrieved from the cockpit.

Robert shivered suddenly, wishing for his sport coat, which he'd put on Rick Barnes, the injured airline CEO.

Robert nodded, checked his watch, and motioned for them to follow.

Dan and Britta moved out, followed by Graham Tash, Steve Delaney, and Dallas Nielson, all of them once again trudging toward the sunlight now streaming over the eastern horizon.

The smell of the sparse jungle in the early morning hours was foreign to all but Dan, who had experienced it before in a far more dangerous time. The cool air, heavy with humidity, melded with the numbing effect of walking as a welcome salve on everyone's psychological wounds.

A chorus of birds chirped and sang in the growing light, the songs echoing from all angles. The low banana trees mixed with taller trees that rose to fifty feet—not the impenetrable canopy of the tropical rain forests to the south, but a jungle nonetheless, replete with mosquitoes and huge flies.

"Wait!" Robert's voice rang out as a command, and he held his hand up.

"What?" Dallas asked.

"Sh-h-h!" he replied, cocking his head, listening intently. "I hear something."

The lights of Da Nang were almost in view down the mountainside in the distance, and the noise was coming from that direction. The faint sound of . . . *something* . . . began to assert itself, the volume growing louder, transitioning to a low-frequency hum of intermittent thumps that Dan recognized immediately.

"Choppers!" he said, excitement driving his voice. "At least one helicopter!"

"Maybe they *are* aware we're here," Dallas said.

The sound of the onrushing helicopter was growing by the second.

"He's coming from the Da Nang area. Has to be a rescue effort!" Dan added.

"We're not that far from the crash," Robert said. "I'd say let's turn around and get the hell back there."

"Damn right!" Dallas replied. "But no need to rush, Robert. Once they find the crash, they're not going to go away."

The helicopter flashed overhead suddenly as the survivors turned to follow, increasing their pace behind the journalist as he retraced their steps through the jungle.

It took fifteen minutes of forced marching before the distinctive sounds of a hovering helicopter became audible. The helicopter was moving, apparently circling over the crash site looking for survivors.

"He's . . . obviously found the main wreckage . . ." Robert said, puffing slightly as he hurried them along.

The intermittent image of the American-made Huey could be seen in the early light through the trees as they approached the area where the 747 had first struck the tops of the vegetation. Initially, Robert had led them along a primitive path that kept them in the jungle, but parallel to the path of wreckage. They moved back along the same route now as fast as they could.

"Look, I'm going to sprint ahead," Dallas said over her shoulder as she pulled abreast of Robert. "Y'all follow at a rational pace. I'll make sure they know where everyone is." She broke into a run, leaping over branches and snags as she closed the distance to the clearing that held the remains of the cockpit and upper deck.

When less than a hundred yards remained between Dallas and the edge of the clearing, she slowed to a walk and glanced behind her. The others were too far back to be seen. She looked forward again, relieved to see the helicopter touching down. There were still bushes and trees between her and the clearing, but Dallas could make out several figures as they jumped from the sliding door of the Huey and moved toward the wreckage of the upper deck. She blinked in the growing light, trying to focus the image, wondering why Vietnamese rescuers would arrive at a crash site wearing business suits. No matter. She would ask them, if they spoke English.

Where are the stretchers? Dallas thought in puzzlement. Maybe this was just an advance crew, and the main rescue would follow in a few minutes. She was within fifty yards now, and heard the sound of a female voice in the distance— obviously Susan Tash, indecipherable but distinctive under the sound of the helicopter's idling engine and swishing blades.

Dallas rounded the last berm between the wreckage and a row of banana trees at the edge of the clearing. She could see the men standing amid the wreckage, yelling something to each other. *Good!* Dallas thought. *They'll get the injured guy out of there quickly, before waiting for more choppers to arrive.*

But something ahead wasn't right, and Dallas stopped without fully knowing why, keeping herself behind the row of trees.

Two of the men were hauling something out of the wreckage, handling it roughly and carelessly, which made no sense. *What is that?* Dallas wondered. It was hard to see. The men were on the other side and the wreckage blocked her view. She could hear Susan's voice, yelling, it seemed, as if she were angry about something.

At last the men reappeared around the wreckage, still pulling the object, which finally coalesced into a recognizable shape. *My God! That's the injured airline guy! What in the world are they doing?*

The two men reached the Huey and shoved a limp Rick Barnes inside.

Dallas glanced behind her, but there was still no sign of the others. She looked back at the clearing, noting two other men in the wreckage. There was a flash of yellow to the left, and Dallas realized with a chill of terror that now Susan Tash was being hauled bodily from the cabin, protesting loudly and trying to fight the crewmen who were holding her. The other two men returned from the helicopter to subdue her, grabbing Susan by the feet and shoulders and carrying her to the open door of the machine, where they tossed her in like a sack of flour.

Dallas sank to her knees in the undergrowth, completely confused and desperate to remain out of sight. She saw one of the men stand back and draw a pistol, pointing it at Susan, and she could see Susan cower in the corner as she looked around at the motionless form of the injured airline chief who had been her patient. There were sounds in the jungle vegetation behind her, signaling the approach of the others; the trees effectively screened their presence from the men in the clearing. She moved in tighter behind a large group of ferns, watching the men jump back aboard the helicopter, one of them sliding into the pilot's seat. The engine power increased, and the noise washed out all possibility of being heard. Dallas turned and motioned frantically to the others. Robert saw her first and acknowledged her signal with a worried expression, as he brought the others toward her.

The helicopter was lifting off and moving away, gaining altitude slowly.

"What's happening?" Robert asked, as he came up beside Dallas.

"Get down!" she said.

Dr. Graham Tash was beside her now, wearing a puzzled expression. She grabbed his arm, pulling him down as she motioned the others to get down as well.

"Susan's in the chopper. They pulled her in along with Barnes."

"Okay . . . but why are we hiding?"

Dallas looked at him, unsure what to say. She could hear the Huey circling overhead. They would be safe beneath the trees, but if they moved into the clearing . . .

Graham took her by the shoulders and turned her toward him. "Dallas, what's wrong?" There was a frightened, feral expression on his face.

"They handled both Susan and Barnes very roughly," Dallas said, jumping up and out of Graham's grasp. She moved forward and motioned for him to follow. Together they carefully moved closer to the edge of the clearing.

The helicopter was hovering directly over the wreckage of the upper deck and cockpit, sitting motionless perhaps two hundred feet in the air.

"I don't understand," Graham said. "What are they doing?"

The door to the helicopter had been closed, but as they watched, it slid open.

Arlin Schoen stood in the doorway of the Huey and glanced out at the rising sun. They would have only minutes to get what they needed and figure out the rest on the run. Incredible luck, he thought, that the very passenger they were looking for was right there, still alive, his business cards in the pocket of his coat even if his messed-up face was unrecognizable.

The woman in yellow, however, was a regrettable problem.

"This a good enough altitude?" his pilot bellowed back into the cabin.

Schoen nodded, his eyes darting to the men holding guns on the survivors. He looked at the male survivor and stabbed his thumb toward the ceiling. "Get up!" he commanded.

The man was obviously badly injured, his face puffy beyond recognition. No matter, Schoen concluded. It was MacCabe. There was enough in the coat to positively ID him even if the team had only had a quick glimpse in Hong Kong.

"Bring him over here!" Schoen commanded. One of his men yanked the injured man to his feet and threw him toward the open door. Schoen watched as the man's arms flew out to brace against falling, his frightened eyes looking at Schoen.

"Okay, MacCabe, where's your computer?"

"What?" The question was barely audible, and Schoen moved toward Rick Barnes like a striking cobra, grabbing his collar and thrusting him partly out the door.

"You either tell me where you put your damned computer down there, or out you go. Your choice, but you've only got ten seconds, and you might think about the fact that what you transferred onto your hard drive is not worth your life."

"I . . . don't know what you're . . . talking about!"

What little he could read of the man's expression bespoke puzzlement. His mouth was moving, but Schoen had to haul him close to hear the words.

"I'm . . . not . . . MacCabe. I'm Rick . . ."

Schoen shoved the man halfway out the door again, watching him flail air until he pulled him close again.

"Where is it, MacCabe? Was it in the overhead? Last chance before your flight lesson begins."

The man was shaking his head furiously. "I'm . . . not MacCabe! He . . . he was in the cabin . . . I met him . . . but . . ."

With an angry heave, Schoen propelled Rick Barnes toward the back of the helicopter, watching as he lost his balance and landed heavily on the floor just in front of the bench seat that spanned the rear of the Huey's cabin. Schoen glanced at the terrified blond in the yellow dress, felt an uncharacteristic twinge of regret, then motioned to one of his men.

"Bring her!"

Susan reached out to fight off the burly arms that grabbed her, but she was no match for the man as he hauled her over to Arlin Schoen.

"Tie her hands!" Schoen ordered. A plastic tie was produced and cinched around her wrists with her hands in front.

Schoen grabbed Susan by the wrists and nodded toward the metal steps built into the frame of the Huey. "Stand on the bottom one!" he commanded.

"No! Why are you doing . . ."

A burst of automatic rifle fire from one of the men in the cabin whistled past Susan's head. Slowly she complied, stepping gingerly onto the top, then the bottom step as she tried unsuccessfully to wrap her fingers around Schoen's hands.

"Okay, MacCabe!" Schoen shouted at the man in the back of the helicopter. "Answer the question or I'll drop this pretty woman two hundred feet."

Once more the man spoke up, yelling with all the volume

he could muster. "My name is . . . Rick Barnes! I'm . . ."

Schoen shook his head, stopping the protest, and pushed Susan's wrists farther out until she was too far off balance to recover if he let go.

"Look, PLEASE!" the injured man yelled from the corner. "I CAN PROVE IT TO YOU!"

Arlin Schoen realized with a start that the man was reaching around to the back pocket of his pants. Had they checked there for a weapon? Schoen reacted instinctively. He grabbed with his free hand for the 9mm pistol in his belt, pulled it free, and raised the barrel, letting panic guide his aim as he squeezed off four quick rounds, two tearing through Barnes's chest, the other two through his already bloodied face.

Schoen watched the body slide to the floor with a thud, a pool of blood forming beneath. His right hand flopped down and released the object that had triggered Schoen's response: a leather wallet, which now slid toward the edge of the door. The Huey pilot had reacted to the sudden shots by bobbling the cyclic control stick and tilting the helicopter's deck suddenly to the right, throwing Schoen off balance.

Arlin Schoen fought to regain his footing while hanging on to the woman's wrists as he watched the object slither toward the abyss. It was a wallet, not a gun, that the man had tried to grab. Schoen thought of lunging for it, but the weight of the woman was dragging him out the door as well. It was an easy decision to let go of her and grab the door jamb as he watched the wallet fly out into space.

The terrified blond began to fall, but Schoen heard a heavy impact on the right side of the Huey and peered over to see that the woman had caught the right side landing skid and was hanging on, even though her wrists were still bound together. Her fingers were white as they held a death grip on the tubular metal.

Too bad, he thought. *She's a fighter, and beautiful, but . . .*

He raised the barrel of the 9mm and aimed between her eyes, using thirty years of professional detachment to ignore her pleading expression. It was more humane, anyway, he thought. Save her the horror of feeling herself fall to her death. They would have to land and bag the body, of course. A dead passenger with a bullet in the brain would be evidence he couldn't leave behind.

He willed himself to get it over with, but still his finger hesitated.

"WE'RE NOT THE ONLY SURVIVORS!" she yelled, staying his trigger finger.

"WHAT?" Schoen yelled back at her.

"THERE ARE OTHER SURVIVORS! THEY KNOW I'M ALIVE!"

Schoen snorted and lowered the gun, thinking fast. Probably a ploy, but if she was telling the truth, they had some sanitizing to do. He stuck the gun in his waistband and motioned for one of his men to take over and pull her back up and in. The end result would be the same. She would have to die, but he'd let her buy some time until he'd analyzed the situation.

From the point of view of the crash survivors huddling behind bushes at the edge of the clearing, the inexplicable sight of the Huey hovering 200 feet above the wreckage with an open door and Graham's wife aboard had been as puzzling as it was terrifying.

Maybe they're just looking for other survivors, Graham had thought, trying to understand how Susan could have been so roughly handled.

Maybe Dallas got it wrong.

They could see one, then two, men in the doorway, but as the helicopter rotated slowly around in a circle, they lost sight of the men altogether.

Suddenly the door faced them again, and Susan's yellow dress and blond hair were clearly visible. She was being forced to stand on the landing skid outside the chopper while one of the men held on to her hands. The sight was a horror beyond Graham's worst nightmare. There was no possible reason or explanation, and therefore it couldn't be happening. What rescuers would threaten survivors of a plane crash?

"MY GOD, NO! DALLAS, WHY?" Graham cried, as he watched, powerless, from below. The sound of gunfire came as distant pops as the Huey bobbled and Susan began to fall.

His heart had all but stopped before he saw her catch the landing skid.

Once again the helicopter rotated around, obscuring the door but not Susan as she struggled to hang on. When the door was visible again, another man could be seen balancing on the skid and reaching down to pull her back to safety.

A bizarre feeling of gratefulness swept through Graham, as if he owed the men who had almost pushed her to her death great thanks for saving her life.

Dallas had been holding Graham down, knowing instinctively that if he ran into the clearing it would mean death for them all. But with an anguished cry, Graham slipped from her grasp and scrambled to his feet, his mind intent on getting beneath the helicopter in a doomed effort to catch Susan if she fell.

Dallas lunged out and tackled him, pulling him to the ground again as Susan flailed the air 200 feet overhead. Susan's entire weight was supported now by nothing more than the hand of her kidnapper, and he was having trouble pulling her up. Dallas could feel her own legs moving for Susan, as if she could propel her up and get her leg over the skid.

Slowly Susan succeeded, wrapping her leg around the skid and rotating on top of it, letting the man pull her up so she could stand on the skid beside him. She tried to swing her left leg into the door, but her right foot slipped at the same moment and she fell backward in what appeared to be slow motion. Dallas could see Susan yank at the man's arm and pull him down as well. She saw him lose his balance, unable to shake loose from her desperate grip. Two hundred feet up the man grabbed helplessly for something to hold on to, but Susan's body was already accelerating away from the helicopter, her iron grip taking her assailant with her as they fell headfirst. Their bodies accelerated toward the wreckage below, legs and hands kicking uselessly.

From Graham Tash's point of view, the fall lasted forever. He lay transfixed in agony, watching his wife as her dress streamed indecently over her head like a blindfold until she thudded into the mass of jagged metal below.

The sound of the two bodies striking the razor-sharp wreckage at nearly 200 miles per hour permanently imprinted itself on the minds of the observers. It was followed by an unearthly howl that emanated from the depths of Graham Tash's soul. Both fists were against his mouth, his body shaking, as Dallas held onto him.

"Get down! *Get down, Doc!*" Dallas snapped. "Or they'll be back to get all of us! She's gone!" She enfolded Tash, pulling him down and falling on him.

The helicopter descended. Dallas could feel the rest of her group hunkering down in terrified silence, and she could feel Tash's grief turning to homicidal rage.

Robert MacCabe had watched the unfolding drama in utter disbelief, too caught up in the absolute horror of what he saw to analyze why. The obscene sound of bodies colliding with the wreckage had all but frozen him in place, his eyes recording what his mind could not accept as real.

The Huey reached the surface of the clearing and touched down. The door facing the hidden group opened, and two men in business suits leapt out, both of them moving toward the spot where the two bodies lay. Halfway across the twenty-yard distance, the first man stopped and looked up, scanning the sky in Robert's direction, his gaze brushing past their hiding area. His face, for one moment, was clearly visible. Robert could feel his stomach contract into an icy knot. He recognized the face. It was one of his Hong Kong assailants.

Suddenly it all made twisted sense: It was all about him! The attack on the 747, the crash, the loss of over 200 lives, the arrival of the helicopter, and the murder of Susan Tash, all designed to prevent him from divulging information he didn't possess.

He wasn't prepared for the tidal wave of guilt that suddenly rolled over him, muting even his fear of the murderous bunch, who were apparently trying to decide what to do with the two bodies in the wreckage.

Robert watched in a fog as Susan Tash's body was wrapped in some sort of plastic sheeting and carried to the helicopter. He could hear Dallas struggling to keep Graham Tash quiet and on the ground as he tried to break free, presumably for a suicidal run to retrieve his wife's remains.

The three men came back for their comrade, hoisting his wrapped body to the Huey in the same manner and tossing it in on the blood-slicked metal floor before climbing in themselves. The helicopter lifted off and flew in a slow circle as it climbed, then turned southwest, moving out rapidly over the jungle along the ridgeline, away from Da Nang.

For several minutes there was no sound at the edge of the crash site except the agonized, muffled sobs of Graham Tash. Dallas released him at last and he got to his feet in a stupor, stumbling forward to the spot where his wife's ruined body had lain.

Dallas got up as well, but could not force herself to move. She heard several of the others coming up behind her, but her eyes remained on Graham and the surreal things she had just witnessed. Her whole body was shaking, her mind reeling. They were survivors of a plane crash, and the men in the helicopter were their rescuers . . . weren't they?

Dallas heard someone move beside her. She forced herself to glance over and recognized a badly shaken Robert MacCabe. She looked back toward the wreckage, her voice coming as little more than a strained croak.

"Why in God's name . . . ?"

Robert said nothing at first, but Dallas could hear him breathing hard.

Dan Wade was on his feet, leaning on Steve Delaney as they came up behind Dallas. Britta had described to Dan part of what was happening before the words caught in her throat. She finished as the helicopter disappeared

"Who," Dallas said behind a cascade of tears, "who *were* those animals?"

Robert MacCabe answered quietly, his eyes still on the

remains of the 747's cockpit. "The ones who killed the captain and blinded Dan."

"What?" Dan gasped. "What do you mean?"

Robert didn't answer, but Dan grabbed for the approximate location of his voice, finding his shoulders and turning him around. "I said, WHAT DO YOU MEAN? WHO ARE THEY?"

"I don't know," Robert replied, his eyes staring blankly at Dan with a gaze the copilot couldn't see.

"Come on, man, ANSWER ME! What were they after?"

His face bloodless, his eyes pools of agony, Robert Mac-Cabe sighed and looked down, barely mouthing a reply.

"Me."

chapter

21

"Where are you, Kat?" Jake Rhoades asked over the satellite phone.

"Standing near the Air Vietnam counter at the airport. I've already bought my ticket to Ho Chi Minh City—Saigon, by any other name," Kat reported. "I'm leaving in about an hour, if it's on time. I've still got to book a flight on to Da Nang."

"Okay," Jake replied. "You're formally assigned to this case as on-scene commander. That title won't last more than a day, but it will get us started. But you said you're leaving in an hour?"

"Yes. Maybe. They won't confirm they're on time."

"Kat, I'm not sure an hour gives us enough time for the diplomatic clearances. We've requested help from the State Department on getting you into 'Nam, but so far the Southeast Asia desk hasn't come through."

Kat hesitated for a second, letting the name of the State Department merge with the image of Jordan James, her father's lifelong friend and the newly appointed acting Secretary of State.

"I think I know who to call. Don't ask me who. I'll call you right back."

IN FLIGHT,
22 MILES SOUTHWEST OF DA NANG, VIETNAM

"Arlin, YOU'D BETTER LOOK AT THIS!"

Arlin Schoen turned his eyes from the passing beauty of the Vietnamese coastal mountains below and looked at one of his men in the back of the Huey. He was leaning over the bloody remains of Rick Barnes and holding something up.

"WHAT?" Schoen yelled, trying to be heard over the noise of the helicopter.

"I FOUND A KEY CASE ON THIS GUY, WITH A NAME INSIDE," the man yelled back.

Schoen moved to him quickly and took the key case, looking carefully at an identification card with the name of the owner: Rick Barnes, CEO, Meridian Airlines.

"What the hell is this?" Schoen mumbled to himself. "WHO IS RICK BARNES?"

The subordinate pointed to the body. "HIM."

Schoen shook his head. "NO! WE CHECKED . . ." Schoen leaned toward his subordinate so they could stop shouting. "We checked his coat pockets. He had business cards and receipts and all of them said MacCabe!"

Schoen knelt and inspected the pockets of the man's blood-soaked sport coat. There were two more receipts, one an American Express charge slip with MacCabe's name on it, which he handed to the other man.

"See?" Schoen proclaimed. "I told you. This guy was Robert MacCabe, and . . ." His eye caught a difference between the sport coat and the pants, and he peered more closely, realizing with a start that they didn't match.

"Oh, Jesus H. Christ!"

Schoen examined the right pants pocket, turning it inside and finding two more charge receipts. Each bore the name of Rick Barnes.

Arlin Schoen got to his feet in disgust. "Godammit! We've blown it!" Schoen held on to the door frame and took a deep breath, shaking his head and trying to think. He had killed the wrong man and let an innocent woman fall to her death for nothing, not to mention losing one more of his team. Somehow the man named Barnes had been wearing MacCabe's coat.

Schoen's assistant was at his side, looking worried. "What are we going to do, Arlin?"

"Just a second. I'm thinking," Arlin snapped, and turned to the pilot. "Land this damn thing in the nearest clearing. Make sure no one's anywhere close."

The pilot nodded and banked the Huey to the right to find a spot. Schoen turned to the other man. "We'll dump the bodies, clean out this interior, and get back to the crash site to search for the bastard."

"Who?"

"Who do you think? MacCabe. The only reason we penetrated this stinking place was to make sure MacCabe was silenced."

"So he's probably dead in the wreckage back there, and this guy just used his coat. We need to get out of here before that pipsqueak commander in Da Nang decides to double-cross us and impound the jet. We don't have much time."

Schoen was shaking his head, his mouth a thin line. "That guy was wearing MacCabe's coat because MacCabe survived. We know he was assigned a seat in the upper-deck section and our search proved his computer was not there. If he has his computer with him and gets back to civilization with that disk drive intact, we're toast. We've got to find him. They're out there trying to walk to the coast."

Schoen could see the sudden panicked look on his assistant's face.

"What?" Schoen demanded.

"I . . . was just thinking. We got there pretty quick after the crash. If that was me trying to walk out, and I heard a helicopter arriving on the scene, I'd turn around and go back, figuring it was a rescue force. They could have seen us dump the woman."

Arlin Schoen looked back out the door, an old fear gripping his spine: the fear that a loose end could suddenly whip around and snare him in his own trap. His man was right. There could be witnesses to two cold-blooded murders.

Schoen turned back to his subordinate. "We've got to kill anyone who might have seen us back there. We don't have a choice."

"What if we're talking about twenty or thirty people, Arlin? We can't just shoot all the survivors."

The Huey was thirty feet off the ground and settling toward a small clearing.

"Yes, we can. For Chrissake, man, we just blew away a seven-forty-seven full of people. We don't have the luxury of quibbling over a few more. And may I remind you what's at stake? A couple of billion dollars and our lives."

CHEK LAP KOK/HONG KONG INTERNATIONAL AIRPORT

The warm rumble of the familiar voice on the other end of the satellite phone brought back a lifetime of happy memories.

"Katherine, how are you?"

"Just fine, Uncle Jordan, but a bit pressed for time and in need of a favor."

"*Where* are you? Not that your dad and I ever knew where you were."

"Hong Kong, and in immediate need of diplomatic clearance into Vietnam." She briefed him quickly on the mission and the problem. "This one has me spooked. I was pulled off that very flight to do an FBI favor for the Consulate here."

"Good heavens, really?" Jordan replied, shock evident in his tone. "My God, Kat, that's too close. I had no idea State was involved with anything you were doing."

"Well, you promised Dad you'd look after me, and you did this time, too."

"Indirectly, perhaps, but thank God. You said you're leaving in a half hour, so I'd better get busy. What number do I use to call you back?"

She gave him the satellite phone number.

"Uncle Jordan, are you going to get the permanent

appointment as Secretary of State?" For decades he'd been known as the quintessential Presidential Adviser.

"I don't want it, Kat. I didn't want this acting position, but when your President calls, you come. Give me ten minutes."

"Thanks, Uncle Jordan."

IN THE JUNGLE,
12 MILES NORTHWEST OF DA NANG, VIETNAM

Robert MacCabe stood at the edge of the clearing, still clutching his computer case, his eyes wild as he begged the other five survivors to run before the helicopter came back. He explained his suspicions about Walter Carnegie and the possible connection to the SeaAir crash and the attempted Hong Kong kidnapping, and finally convinced them that he could be right.

With Graham Tash all but catatonic, the rest of them looted the remains of the upper deck of first-aid kits, blankets, food, water, and various bags to carry them in, while Steve Delaney managed to find the backpack he'd left outside the cockpit. The helicopter had been gone less than ten minutes when they assembled back at the edge of the clearing, ready to go.

"Question is, which way?" Britta asked.

"Back to the coast as fast as possible, kids," Dallas said.

"No!" Robert replied, breathing hard. "No. They'll be expecting just that. They'll look along that pathway, and there isn't enough jungle vegetation to hide under on that eastern slope. You saw it."

"Where do you want to go, then?" Dallas asked, her hands on her hips.

"West. As fast as we can. More vegetation, more hiding places, and they wouldn't start the search there."

"So what's to the west, Robert?" Dallas replied.

Dan's voice reached them before Robert could speak. "West from here goes through a number of miles of this type of jungle, but empties to a flat valley five or six miles away. On the ridge going down to the valley, if we need them, are a lot of very deep caves that the Vietcong used to use. There's a highway around here, too, which runs from Da Nang to the valley, and there're probably some airfields in the valley."

"So we want to stay away from highways, right?" Dallas asked.

Robert pointed west. "We need to stop debating and move. Let's go!"

Dallas looked at the reporter with undisguised irritation, wondering when he'd been elected to take over. The fact that he was still clutching his computer case was irritating as well. But what he said made some sense, and there was no doubt in anyone's mind that the men in the Huey were killers uninterested in leaving witnesses.

"I saw all I needed to convince me," Dallas said, looking at Britta, Dan, Steve, and Graham in turn. She looked down at the silk pantsuit, knee-length brocade vest, and soft pumps she was wearing, then glanced at the others. "We may not have the right clothes or shoes for this little hike, but I hear my momma's voice saying, 'Girl, get your tail out of there now!' and I always listen to my momma. Let's move!"

The makeshift backpacks were shouldered quickly as Britta leaned down to help Graham to his feet.

"I'm not going," Graham said. His eyes were swollen and red and his face bore the ravages of a man thirty years older.

"You have to go," Britta said.

He shook his head slowly. "My life died with Susan. Go. I'll tell them I'm MacCabe."

"You don't look anything like Robert MacCabe, and I'll not lose another passenger. Now, come on, Doctor."

Robert retraced his steps to their side and heard the exchange.

"Doctor, either you get up, or I'll pick you up myself."

Graham sat completely still, his eyes focused on the wreckage. There was a faint sound to the east, and Robert looked eastward with growing fright.

"Doctor, for God's sake, you're going to get us all killed if you . . ."

"I said, go on without me!" Graham snapped, not looking up.

Britta knelt beside him, speaking urgently in his ear. "Doctor, we can't leave you, which means our lives are in your hands. And we've got a badly hurt pilot who is going to need your help through this ordeal. But there's more. If Susan could materialize right now, from what I saw and heard of her, I'm absolutely sure she'd tell you to get up and get out of here. She'd want you to live, not follow her in a suicidal refusal to keep trying."

Graham looked up at Britta. "I appreciate what you're trying to do, but . . ."

"That's it!" Robert said suddenly, putting his computer case on the ground and leaning down to thread his hands beneath Graham's arms and yank him up. He turned the doctor around to face him, a maneuver Tash did not resist.

"Look!" Robert said, his words coming in terse, urgent packets. "I can't . . . begin to . . . *know* how you feel . . . but . . . I swear I'll slug you into a coma and drag you if you don't come voluntarily. Please! *PLEASE!*"

Graham sighed and looked down. With tears pouring down his face again, he turned to Britta, catching her eye.

"You're right about Susan, you know."

They moved rapidly into the brush and trees bordering the western end of the crash site just as the thumping noises in the distance rose significantly in volume and definition until the rotors of a rapidly advancing helicopter could be clearly heard.

"Come on, y'all! Hurry! Hurry!" Dallas shouted, breaking everyone into a jog. She held the doctor's hand and pulled him along.

A brushy landscape of low-growing banana trees mixed with palms and sporadic taller trees lay before them, little of it conducive to evading a helicopter—and the one they were hearing was approaching rapidly, now little more than a mile away.

Robert turned, walking backward for a moment as he yelled, "Over here!" He motioned to them to hurry, pointing to a thicket of trees surrounded by dense ferns which formed a low-hanging canopy over the ground. "Down! Just get in there and sit." Robert pulled Dallas and Steve in as Britta guided both Graham and Dan under the canopy.

The distinctive whap-whap-whap of a Bell UH-1 Huey grew to thunderous proportions behind them, then suddenly diminished.

"He's landing," Dan explained.

"What do we do now, Robert?" Dallas asked in a loud whisper. "We don't have any guns. Shouldn't we keep moving?"

"I expected them to come our way," Robert explained, still breathing hard from his exertion. "We don't want to be spotted from the air."

"But if they come looking for us on foot?" Dallas added.

"They're still on the ground back there," Dan said. "I think . . . we're in more danger from a ground party, especially since they can follow our footprints."

There was a sudden rustling to one side and Robert looked over, startled to see Dallas scrambling to her feet and clawing her way out from under the brush. "Dallas!"

"Dallas yourself!" she shot back. "Let's get the hell out of here."

Britta hesitated, watching Robert MacCabe's face in the partial shadows and wondering what to do. Suddenly he was in motion as well, pulling them out of the hiding place. He checked a small compass as they resumed walking as fast as possible to the west and into deeper jungle, with the vivid memory of Susan Tash's long fall from the helicopter filling everyone's mind.

Behind them, at the crash site, a Vietnamese search-and-rescue helicopter was touching down.

CHEK LAP KOK/HONG KONG INTERNATIONAL AIRPORT

Kat folded the antenna on the satellite phone and turned toward the departure gate for the flight to Ho Chi Minh City. Jordan James had sliced through all the red tape to arrange her entry into Vietnam and promised to relay the word to Jake.

Kat hesitated at the podium and turned, spotting a tall, sandy-haired Caucasian male in a business suit a hundred feet away pretending not to be watching her. But he had been, and Kat suppressed the feeling of apprehension, the feeling that she was missing something very significant, and very dangerous.

She looked again, but the man had gone.

MERIDIAN 5 CRASH SITE,
12 MILES NORTHWEST OF DA NANG, VIETNAM
NOVEMBER 13—DAY TWO
7:23 A.M. LOCAL/0023 ZULU

The presence of another helicopter at the crash site was an unwelcome surprise to Arlin Schoen as they approached from the south and circled at a discreet distance. He shook his head in disgust and sighed, his eyes scanning the eastern horizon as he wondered how many more helicopters would be coming now that the crash was officially discovered and broad daylight filled the landscape.

"What do you want to do?" the pilot asked, gesturing at the occupied clearing.

"Stay at least a mile distant and bring us to the western side. We can't go look around the wreckage for footprints, but if they're on the run, they'll be running west."

"And if we find them? What then—shoot them one by one from the air?"

Schoen nodded. "If we can find them."

"And if not?"

"Then we get the hell back to Da Nang and try to get out of here." He leaned forward. "How much fuel does this thing have?"

"About three more hours, depending on how much you make me hover."

"Arlin," one of the men in the back said, grabbing his shoulder. "If we don't get back there and get our plane, they'll nail it down, either with red tape or something worse. And if they do that, we won't get out. Please! Let's abort this and go. I think we've lost them anyway."

Schoen shook his head no. "It's not over. It's not compromised unless that reporter surfaces."

"Dammit, who are you, Captain Ahab? We've lost this round. They wouldn't crash where they were supposed to, and now we're flying around a friggin' jungle acting like Vietcong looking for downed GIs. Let's just get the hell out of here!"

"I said no."

"Why, man?"

"Because what that damned reporter has is worth the risk."

IN THE JUNGLE, WEST OF DA NANG, VIETNAM

Dark clouds looming ahead, heralded by the boom of distant thunder, increased the anxiety of the six survivors as they stumbled and pushed their way through the increasingly dense jungle vegetation. The sound of monkeys chattering away and racing around blended with the eternal buzz of flies and other flying insects. The humidity made even the diminishing cool of the morning seem oppressive.

Robert MacCabe looked back over his shoulder for the hundredth time, making sure everyone kept up with the frantic pace he'd set. His head was still spinning with the horror of seeing one of his Hong Kong attackers at the crash site. And he felt the crushing guilt that flowed from his panicked determination to get out of Hong Kong without thinking about the risks to others. That selfishness, he'd decided, was the primary reason over 200 innocent people were now dead. And then there was Susan Tash.

There had been no time to question the copilot on what might have exploded just outside the cockpit of the Meridian jumbo, but the face of Walter Carnegie kept haunting his thoughts, along with the increasingly logical conclusion that somehow they were victims of the same terrorists who'd destroyed the SeaAir MD-11.

Robert thought about Kat Bronsky and how incredibly lucky she'd been to get pulled off.

Unless . . .

He rejected the thought as fast as it had formed. The possibility that Bronsky was somehow involved was just too bizarre. He had searched her out. She'd already had a reservation. Yet her removal was strange. But then, she was FBI, so maybe it wasn't so strange.

He wondered whether Kat knew of their crash yet, what she was thinking, and what she would do when she found out. *How would it feel,* Robert thought, *to know that the flight you got off of by chance had gone down?*

He heard someone stumble behind him and looked back to see Britta helping Dan to right himself. Robert stopped for a second to search the green tangle ahead for the best path and decided to go slightly left. The sound of water somewhere ahead had wafted in and out of his ears for the past few minutes. Where there were rivers, there were often settlements, and the Vietnamese people would be no threat. If he could just get them to a village and alert the authorities, they would be safe. But if their pursuers spotted them first, he had no doubt they'd all be killed.

The horrific reality of the carnage behind them was never more than a thought away. Robert tried to block the images. He took a deep breath of the jungle air, laden with moisture and the fragrance of flowers, then pushed off again, ignoring the insect bites that were itching and stinging their way into his consciousness. It was his responsibility to keep these people safe. That would be only a small act of atonement for the events his presence had set in motion.

Robert pushed through several large fronds, ignoring the possibility of snakes and dangerous insects as the sound of water grew louder. Dallas Nielson appeared beside him, matching his pace. His attention snapped back to his present surroundings.

"Robert MacCabe, let me ask you a question."

"Go ahead," he replied, trying unsuccessfully to read her expression as he stepped over a log and pointed it out to her. "But we need to keep our voices low."

Dallas hopped over the log and continued. "You told us back there those goons tried to kidnap you, probably kill you, because they thought you knew something that would connect that crash near Cuba to a terrorist group, right?"

"Essentially," Robert replied, holding a huge frond aside for her to pass.

"Thanks. And you *had* to figure that they might be the same terrorist group, right? I mean, since you weren't working on any other secret spy stuff, the connection's pretty obvious, right?"

Dallas pushed through a dense overhead of branches.

"Something like that," Robert said, following her.

"Right. So when you headed for the airport, would you tell me why a big, world-class, Pulitzer reporter like you didn't say to himself, 'Gee, if people who zapped a big airliner out of the sky are trying to kill me and still have the capability to do so, d'you think maybe they would shoot down another airliner to shut me up?'"

Robert grimaced as Dallas pushed several ferns aside to let him through, then moved ahead to watch his expression.

"I mean, *Robert*! Come on! Shouldn't you have said, maybe I'm endangering everyone by getting on this airplane? I mean, *Robert,* DUH!"

He nodded. "I know."

"Well, I'm pretty ticked that you nearly got me killed, and oh, by the way, we're missing about two hundred and fifty others."

Robert let out an agonized breath and closed his eyes, his chin down, his lips tightly together. He looked up at last, eye to eye with her. "Dallas . . . I'm sorry. I would never have stepped on that flight if I'd thought for a moment that an entire airplane could be targeted just to get me."

She began moving again, looking back over her shoulder. "You just don't happen to be my favorite human being right now. Maybe that's uncharitable of me, but if you get tired of kicking your ass, I'll be happy to take over."

Robert started to respond, then stopped suddenly, listening carefully. "I keep hearing a running river somewhere ahead."

"Is that good?" Dallas asked.

"I don't know," he said, his eyes ahead as he tried to part a series of large ferns for the two of them, "but we've got to keep moving." Robert stumbled and almost lost his balance, but righted himself and started pushing through another set of ferns.

"STOP!" Dallas barked suddenly.

Robert braked to a halt, realizing his foot was resting on the edge of a hundred-foot drop-off. A river full of shallow rapids ran below, both embankments steep, vine-entangled products of erosion.

"Good Lord!" he said, putting a healthy distance between himself and the ledge.

Dallas whirled around and yelled a warning to the others, who approached the edge carefully. The sound of a vehicle in the distance reached their ears.

"I hear a truck," Steve Delaney said, pointing over the river.

"Me, too," Britta chimed in. "Should we hide from it or try to flag it down?"

Dan stood behind Britta, holding her hand tightly and cocking his bandaged head as the sound increased in volume and then receded. "Probably the highway they made out of the old Ho Chi Minh Trail," he said.

"And conveniently placed on the other side of a river," Robert added.

"How . . . ah . . . far have we come, do you think?" Dan asked, his voice betraying crushing fatigue. His breathing was labored.

"Maybe two miles. Maybe a bit more," Robert replied.

"So . . . what's the plan?" Dan directed the question toward Robert's voice.

"How about to get away and live happily ever after?" Dallas laughed ruefully, then grew serious again, noting Graham's numbed look as he stared at the ground, with his hands in his pockets.

Robert cleared his throat. "Look, here's what I think. We have to keep on moving as fast as we can along this bank of the river until we find civilization, or get out of these mountains."

The sound of a shortwave radio made them all jump and look around. Steve Delaney was fiddling with something he'd fished out of his backpack.

"What the heck is that, Steve?" Dallas asked.

"Aviation band. It can also send out a distress signal to the rescue satellites. Should I turn it on?"

"Wait!" Robert replied, his hand up. "We'd better think this through. Who could track that?"

Dallas's eyebrows climbed almost to her hairline. "How about an American-built helicopter full of English-speaking cutthroats looking to nail our"—she hesitated, looking at Steve—"posteriors."

Dan was shaking his head. "It's true, Dallas, that . . . the basic signal could be tracked by any . . . aviation radio equipped with a direction finder, but . . . the special search-and-rescue satellite system wouldn't help whoever was in that helicopter. It's . . . designed to look for . . . for distress signals from downed airplanes . . . and relay the information to legitimate search forces."

"So, the bad guys don't have direction finders?" Dallas asked.

"Unlikely," Dan replied.

They all exchanged glances, trying to decide. Robert broke the silence. "Let's wait. Let's get farther away," he said. "It's still midmorning, and it won't be long before the crash site will be swarming with rescue forces and Vietnamese military. Then it would probably be safe to turn it on. I just wish we could transmit a voice message on that thing."

"We can," Steve said, holding up the handheld radio. "It's a new type. If the satellite can hear the beacon, it can hear what you transmit, and it's got a GPS in it, so it transmits our exact location digitally."

"What does all that mean?" Britta asked.

"It means," Dan began, sighing deeply, "that when we turn it on, we can tell the world where we are. We'd just better be ready for the consequences."

"Wait!" Dallas held up her hand, her eyes up as she cocked her head to listen.

"What?" Robert said in a low voice.

"I hear a helicopter over there, somewhere," she said, pointing west.

"And the crash site's behind us, right?" Britta asked.

Robert nodded. "Probably not the same one," he said. "He'd be searching along this direct pathway if it was."

"How much longer?" Britta asked.

"What do you mean?" Robert replied.

"I mean, how much longer do you think it's going to take to get out of here and get to safety?" Britta's chin was trembling slightly, her emotions cracking through the calm facade she'd been keeping intact. She tried to smooth her hair with her right hand, embarrassed to be shaking. "I, ah, I'm exhausted, thirsty, hungry, scared to death, dirty as a bum, flea-bitten and scratched to shreds, and I just . . . I just wanted to know if I should be planning on sleeping in this horrible place, too."

"Not if we're lucky," Dan said softly. The sound of his voice triggered tears Britta instantly regretted.

"Oh, Dan! I didn't mean to cry." She swatted at the tears, her mouth opening and closing as she tried for control. "I mean, I know you can't see them, but what *you're* going through—what the doctor's going through—and here, I'm bitching like a little baby. I'm sorry."

Dan put his arm around her shoulders and gave her a small squeeze, his voice soft in her ear. "Come on, Britta. You're not made of steel. It's okay."

"We *are* going to make it, aren't we?" she said. She looked around at the others. "Dammit, we can't bring them back, but we can get out of here and make sure the world knows what those bastards did."

IN FLIGHT,
18 MILES WEST OF DA NANG, VIETNAM

"Where, Arlin?" the pilot asked in a disgusted tone. He'd picked nearly a dozen clearings to land in, and Schoen had rejected every one.

"There!" Arlin Schoen said as he pointed into the distance.

"All I see is jungle," the pilot replied.

"Follow my finger. It's a wide clearing by that river, with a highway bridge on the other side. If they come this way, they'll be funneled right into that location."

The pilot nodded and began planning his approach. They would land, Arlin had decided, camouflage the helicopter with whatever brush they could find, and wait for MacCabe and whoever was with him to come walking out of the jungle.

"And if you're wrong?" one of the men had asked.

"Then we crank up and fly this bucket back to Da Nang, collect our aircraft, and get the hell out of here."

The man shook his head. "Always have an answer, don't you, Arlin?"

chapter

23

Kat Bronsky walked briskly through the door of the aging Air
Vietnam jetliner into a wall of fragrant humidity. She followed her fellow passengers through the tropical decay of
the airport terminal to the long line that led to customs. Kat
stood waiting, holding her passport and FBI credentials, as
she recalled Jordan's words on the satellite phone just before
boarding in Hong Kong.

"I'm glad you're letting me help, Katherine. You don't
want to experience what everyone else does entering Vietnam."

"That bad?"

"Well, from French colonial officials, the Vietnamese
learned bureaucratic arrogance and how to dither endlessly
over meaningless details. They polished that knowledge
with the dizzying duplicity *we* taught them during the war.
And then they folded in a heavy dose of Marxist intransi-
gence before topping that off with the innate suspicion
inherent to an abused culture whose every contact with the
West in the past century has been an utter disaster."

"Meaning?" Kat had asked, worried he might have failed to get her clearance.

"Meaning that for the normal passenger, especially an American, getting through Vietnamese immigration and customs inside a week is a small miracle. For instance, if they run out of ink for their mind-numbing collection of itty-bitty rubber stamps, the country comes to a complete, screeching halt."

"Jordan, I really have to board now, if I'm going. Am I going?"

"I'm sorry, Kat. Here I am telling colorful stories. Yes. You're all set."

"You don't like the Vietnamese much, do you?"

"Love the people, hate the bureaucracy. You'll see."

"That bad?"

"Let me put it this way. If Bethlehem had been in Vietnam, we wouldn't be wearing crosses. Jesus would have died of old age waiting to clear customs."

A police officer was waving frantically at the line Kat had joined. She could hear him issuing the same Vietnamese command with increasing urgency as he tried to wave them through a doorway. An Asian couple in the lead had been fumbling for something in a small jump bag. They straightened up suddenly and moved obediently through the door, and Kat and the others followed.

An array of uniformed men stood waiting on the other side, each in a tiny booth arrayed with the predicted rubber stamps. One by one they sucked in the passports and papers proffered by each passenger through a small slit below the window of the booth, examined each in minute detail with intense fervor, followed by a flurry of energetic pounding of rubber stamps before the passport—and the passenger—were allowed passage to the next gauntlet.

Kat was next in line, wondering why no one had singled her out, when a hand clamped down none too gently on her right shoulder and she turned to find several uniformed men regarding her unsmilingly.

"Passport!" one of the men demanded. Kat handed the

small blue booklet to him, and he quickly examined it before saying something in Vietnamese to the others. He looked back at Kat and nodded toward a distant door.

"Follow!"

The self-important choreography of the customs and immigration dance had been amusing, but she was relieved when the man led her away from the normal processing arena, through a second, then a third, door, and into a dingy office of decaying off-white tiles and stained laminate floor. He motioned her to a rickety chair next to a metal desk that was undoubtedly left over from American surplus in 1974.

"Sit now."

"Okay. How long?"

"Sit! Sit sit sit!" he demanded in a flurry of staccato gestures. The officer carefully took off his hat and placed it just so on the desk before seating himself on a swivel chair and grabbing the phone. As Kat prepared to speak again, he angrily gestured for her to be quiet. Two other officers, probably police, had appeared at Kat's side, their faces deadly serious.

There was an elaborate ritual of dialing the ancient phone, followed by what appeared to be a curse in Vietnamese. The officer slammed the phone back in its cradle and reached in his pocket. Kat looked at her watch and frowned. The officer pulled out a tiny GSM cellular phone and extended the antenna before punching the keypad and placing it to his ear.

The exchange was brief, but among the Vietnamese words, she clearly heard her name, followed by much nodding and the hint of a smile. The officer stood suddenly and looked at her. "You wait now!" he commanded, turning and rushing out the door.

Kat looked around at the other two unsmiling officers, neither of whom wanted to meet her eyes. "Either of you fellows speak English?"

There was no response.

"Not even a little bit? *Parlez-vous français?*"

A calm, cultured male voice rang out from behind her in

answer, the words spoken in lightly accented English. "Not if they want to keep their jobs, they don't."

She turned to face a short, overweight man in a business suit with a security card clipped to his pocket.

"Hello?" Kat said, raising her eyebrows.

He stepped forward and extended his hand. Kat got to her feet to take it.

"I am Nguyen Thong, immigration director in Ho Chi Minh City. We've been expecting you."

"I appreciate that," Kat replied.

"We are happy to respond to the request from your ambassador in Hanoi. He called as you were leaving Hong Kong," Nguyen continued, "and explained that you are from the American FBI and that you would be the advance representative for the American accident investigation team. They asked us to help get you on your way to Da Nang, and so we shall. We've arranged a helicopter to take you directly to the crash site, and we've had your bags cleared and put aboard."

"A helicopter? That's wonderful."

"Vietnamese Air Force. You will board the helicopter right here. Vietnam is determined to do what we can to help. The location is around six hundred kilometers from here, roughly four hundred miles. It will take about three hours."

"That's very kind of your government, Mr. Nguyen. Speed is vital here."

"I understand. I'm truly sorry about the circumstance, but welcome to the new Vietnam, nonetheless."

"Your help is greatly appreciated, Sir."

He smiled at her as the other officer entered quietly with Kat's passport in his hand. He held it out to her and bowed slightly.

"Thank you," Kat said to him, observing the frightened look on the man's face as he glanced at the immigration director and backed quickly out of the room. She turned back to Nguyen, noting his eyes happily exploring her body in an appreciative manner. She lowered her head slightly, looking at him through upturned eyes as if reproaching a misbehaving adolescent. He smiled and shrugged, dropping his gaze to the curve of her breasts once again before looking her in the eye. His left arm swept toward the door in an exaggerated gesture.

"You are a beautiful woman, Miss Bronsky."

Kat regarded him with raised eyebrows, her relief at the sudden offer of help eclipsing her natural tendency to bristle at sexist remarks.

"*Really?*" she said, letting a guarded smile take over her face. "Thank you. Actually, this is just a disguise. Underneath, I'm really just an FBI agent."

IN THE JUNGLE, NORTHWEST OF DA NANG, VIETNAM

Britta Franz had stepped away from the others to look for a place to relieve herself. When she had readjusted her torn clothes, she glanced up, surprised to see what looked like a path ahead.

Britta could see Steve Delaney moving parallel to her position, following Robert, whose arm was around Dan. Dallas had moved back to encourage Graham to try to keep up. Steve was an unhappy kid, Britta realized, but a smart one. Britta's initial judgment of him as a repulsive, spoiled brat had softened to an almost maternal feeling of protectiveness. He had tried his best in the cockpit, and felt responsible for the crash.

The image of the disaster loomed up again, bringing the sickening thought of the more than 200 passengers and crew who hadn't lived through it. The faces of her flight attendants paraded before her, triggering tears. Nancy, Jaime, Claire, Alice—all dead. And Bill! Her friend for decades. Solid as a rock. How could he be gone? She thought of his three boys, the triplets, all in college, and of his wife, all of them about to go through incredible grief when the rescuers returned with the word that there were no survivors.

Oh my God! Britta shook her head to expunge the shock. They'd think she, too, had died! They would notify Carly if she couldn't get word back. The thought of her daughter getting the news that her mother had been killed in a distant jungle was unacceptable. Phil, she knew, would protect Carly as long as possible from the conclusion that there was no hope, but with so many shredded bodies, who would know? Despite their divorce and his custody of Carly, he had always been wonderful about nurturing Carly's love and respect for her absentee mom.

Britta forced herself to shake off the panic. Carly would find out in due time that her mom was alive. For that matter, Britta chided herself, the grief for her comrades and her passengers would have to wait as well. The first order of business was survival of those who had made it through.

Britta looked ahead at the trail she had spotted. It seemed to lead in the same direction they were going, to the west. *A little overgrown, but definitely a trail.* She yelled in the direction of the group, "Hey! I've found a path!"

She had just pushed past a small tree that overhung the trail when a half-dozen objects slammed into her. She stopped, puzzled, realizing she had walked into a small man-made web of cord laced with heavy Coke cans. She was completely entangled, but something told her to hesitate before just pulling herself away.

What in the world? "Everyone wait a second. I'm tangled up in something."

Nearly eighty feet ahead, Dan grabbed Steve's arm, his voice tense. "What did Britta say back there?"

"She found a trail, and now she says she's tangled up in something."

"Oh my God!" Dan cupped his hands and yelled in her general direction. "BRITTA! FREEZE! DON'T MOVE A MUSCLE! DO YOU HEAR ME?"

There was no response.

Dallas and Robert whirled around to see what the commotion was about. "What's the matter?" Dallas asked, completely puzzled, as Dan told Steve to lead him toward Britta.

"Robert? Follow us, please," Dan yelled over his shoulder. Steve pushed through the undergrowth with Dan holding his arm and keeping pace. Robert broke into a run to follow them.

"BRITTA! FREEZE! DON'T MOVE!" Dan yelled as he ran, repeatedly tripping and righting himself despite Steve's best efforts.

There was an answer from Britta's direction. Steve shoved aside one last fern and stumbled into the middle of the same pathway Britta had discovered.

"We're on the trail now," Steve said.

Dan yanked him to a halt. "Don't move! Can you see Britta?"

"No," Steve answered, looking up as Robert and Dallas came up behind them.

"Who's behind me?" Dan demanded.

"Dallas and Robert. Graham stayed behind."

"Freeze!" Dan commanded. "Don't move past me, no matter what."

"What on earth is this all about?" Dallas asked.

"Britta?" Dan called ahead, ignoring their questions for the moment.

"Here, Dan." Her voice came from the left.

"Robert," Dan asked, "can you see her?"

Robert looked down the trail, seeing only vegetation at first. "Britta, where are you?"

"Down this way. I'm tangled up in a bunch of tin cans or something."

"Oh, God! DON'T MOVE!" Dan yelled. "BRITTA? DO YOU UNDERSTAND ME? DO NOT MOVE A MUSCLE. DO NOT TRY TO GET YOURSELF UNTANGLED, UNDERSTAND?"

Dan leaned close to Robert and Steve. "Listen to me very, very carefully. I should have warned us all not to get on anything that looks like a trail. This country, and this area in particular, was lousy with Vietcong booby traps during the war. Some of them are still here."

"Jeez!" Steve said.

"You've . . . got to guide me closer to her," Dan said, "and then describe in minute detail what we've got. Let's get everyone away from this path. Go around it, and carefully penetrate the wall of the trail adjacent to where she is."

"DAN?" Britta was calling.

"HOLD ON, BRITTA. STAY PERFECTLY STILL."

"YOU'RE SCARING ME, DAN," she replied.

"Steve, you stay here," Robert said, watching the flash of anger on Steve's face as he released the copilot to Robert's care.

Robert guided Dan carefully away from the trail Britta had found. "Dan, I can see her through the ferns now," Robert said.

"Carefully part the ferns, but if you see any wires or anything man-made, don't touch them." Dan could hear Robert reach out and rustle the plants slightly.

"I've got a good view now," Robert said. "She's only about eight feet away, standing in the clutch of a banana tree, her shoulders and arms dripping with a tangle of what appears to be just some old Coke cans."

"Worst case!" Dan muttered under his breath. "Okay, Robert. Look closely. Are there bottoms on those cans, or are they cut off?"

Robert looked carefully before answering. "The bottoms look open."

Britta was watching them from across the trail. "What have I gotten tangled up in, fellows? Please! You're really scaring me now," she said softly, watching the expression on Dan's face.

"Stay still, Britta. I'll explain in a second. Just, for God's sake, do—not—move."

"Dan," Robert reported, "the cans are all connected by some sort of cord."

Dan shook his head. "And each can has the bottom and top cut out, and each is connected to the others, right?"

"That's right. What are they?"

"Any one of those could blow her apart," Dan said, too low for Britta to hear.

"Come on, what are you men saying over there?" Britta snapped.

"Britta, stay still!" Dan commanded. "Don't talk unless I ask you something. Whatever you do, do NOT move a muscle. Move your lips and face as little as possible, okay?"

Britta's eyes grew huge, darting all around her as she

tried to speak without moving her mouth. "What . . . what's wrong? What are these things?"

Dan was breathing rapidly, trying to figure out how to handle it without being able to see. He turned to Robert. "Everyone must stay back at least twenty yards."

Robert relayed the command.

"Okay," Dan said, "first, without moving your head, Britta . . . can you glance through the open top of any of the cans? DO NOT NOD. I can't see the gesture anyway. Just do it, and tell me what you see."

"Well . . . there's something in there that looks metallic and bronze, and it has something clipped to the top of it. Some mechanism."

"Do those seem heavy?"

"Yes. Very."

He nodded, taking a deep breath, his mind racing. "Britta, you've blundered into what's left of an old Vietcong booby trap, probably from 1969. The brown things in each can are hand grenades."

"Oh, God!" she said, flinching slightly. "How do I get them off of me?"

Dan held up his hands. "Stay frozen! That's the first rule. That's called a daisy chain. The grenades are"—he tried to slow his breathing—"delicately suspended in there with the pins pulled. As long as they don't fall out of the cans, we're safe, but . . . there's a big trip wire around here somewhere and a bent-over tree that's connected to it."

"I don't understand!"

"They were . . . designed to kill our troops, Britta. Some poor lieutenant would come down the trail leading his patrol, thinking *he* was taking the greatest risk by being in the lead. He'd hit the trip wire, yanking out the little strings holding the grenades in the cans. They'd all fall down along the trail at the feet of his soldiers, and before anyone could react, the poor guy had lost up to a dozen of his men."

"Are they still . . . deadly?"

"Britta, we're going to get you out of there, but yes. Any one could kill you."

"Oh, God!" Britta swallowed hard.

"This trap is old, Britta. That means it's even more dangerous. It will have deteriorated, but the grenades will still be lethal."

"Can't I just take these off?"

"NOT YET! We're going to need to study it for a second. We've . . . got to make sure we don't hit the trip wire getting to you. Especially now that we've disturbed it. It's sat here for decades without going off, but now that the apparatus has been disturbed, it could be a hair trigger."

"What do we do?" Robert asked.

Dan was still breathing hard. He gripped Robert Mac-Cabe's shoulder. "I . . . don't know how I can ask you to risk your life, but I can do nothing without seeing."

"Forget that!" Robert commanded. "I'm responsible for getting all of you into this, and I'll do whatever I can to get you out."

The words stopped Dan for a second, but he recovered and continued.

"All right. Let me describe this in great detail . . . then *you* tell her what you're going to do. Basically, it's two things. First, you have to make sure you don't hit the master trip wire getting to her. That means slow, deliberate movements across the trail. No sudden footfalls. Second, you have to . . . cup your hand under each can so the grenade can't come out. Then cut the can loose, being . . . absolutely certain that the action won't cause another to drop. Then you place each can gently on the ground. If the grenade doesn't come out, it simply can't explode. Okay so far?"

Robert nodded, his mouth as dry as cotton. He was familiar with grenades and mines and much of the killing paraphernalia that armies used, but since he had never been trained as a military man, manipulating such things was something entirely different. He felt the perspiration beading up on his forehead as Dan walked him through all the things he could think of that might help avoid a fatal mistake.

"Okay, Britta," Dan said, "now, I'm going to turn you over to Robert. I've told him everything he needs to know."

"Can you, ah, hear me, Britta?" Robert MacCabe asked.

"Yes."

"Okay. First, I'm going to move very slowly toward you."

"Please be careful."

"I'm going to." Robert stopped to look at her and saw huge tears running down her cheeks. "I'm going to get you out of this, Britta. It's going to be okay."

"I . . . I don't want to die, Robert."

He shook his head vigorously. "You're not going to die. Stay calm and still." He gingerly moved his foot up and forward in an exaggerated, slow arc, carefully testing the foothold before shifting his body weight.

"Robert?" she called. "Dan? Something's stinging me on the back."

"Bear with it, Britta. Don't flinch!" Dan called out. "But speak only to Robert. I'm here, too. We mustn't jostle those cans."

Robert could see Britta's face contorting in pain. "Is it bad?" he asked.

"Yes. Maybe a scorpion or something, but I can stand it."

There was a rustling in the leaves behind her. "Britta, are you moving?"

"No. Robert, how are you going to do this?"

He repeated the instructions Dan had given and glanced back to see Dan giving him a thumbs-up sign.

"And if a grenade falls out?" she asked.

"We'll have ten seconds to grab it and throw it away. *You* don't do that. I'll dive in to do it."

A small monkey skittered by and stopped to look at Robert, sending a shiver up his back until he saw what it was. The monkey jumped onto a nearby tree and watched him. Robert kept his concentration on Britta, ignoring the chattering of the small primate, which was quickly joined by a second and third.

"I think," Britta said, "that there must be three or four of these grenade cans hanging on my back. They all whacked me when I stumbled in here."

Eight feet separated Robert from Britta, most of it fairly clear of deep underbrush. He looked carefully at one of the cans hanging in front. There was something—perhaps a shadow—at the bottom. As he looked, the picture coalesced.

Oh, God, the bottom is protruding! The retention line at the bottom of the can must be gone. That one could drop at any second.

He ran his eyes over the other cans he could see. On all the others, a small-gauge piece of fishing line was still in place, giving each grenade something to rest on, but each line was now taut and running off into the underbrush, waiting to be yanked away. If he so much as touched one the wrong way . . .

"All right, Britta, I need for you to actually hold one of those things in its can. Now, very carefully and very slowly, move your right hand up an inch at a time until you're touching the bottom of the can that's hanging on your stomach. Cup your hand around the bottom and make sure the grenade stays in."

"Okay," Britta said, trying to stay in control. Slowly, gingerly, she did as directed until her shaking hand had secured the errant grenade.

"Well done, Britta! That's one down. When I get to you, I'll get the others."

There was more chattering from the left as a small race broke out among the three monkeys. They dashed along the pathway left to right in front of Britta and clambered up an adjacent tree.

"Damn things!" Dan said. "They taste terrible, too."

"I don't really want to know," Britta said. "I've sort of lost my appetite."

The distant sound of a helicopter reached their ears, the chillingly familiar whump-whump sound rising slowly in volume.

"Ignore that chopper, Britta," Robert ordered. He stopped, his foot in midair, feeling an obstruction. He looked closely, seeing only a vine, and pushed his foot past it to the ground. "Just a little bit more, Britta," he said as confidently as he could manage. "And then I can start pulling them away."

As Robert continued to move in slow motion toward her,

Britta's eyes fixed on Dan. Dallas had come up quietly behind him.

"Dallas?" Britta said. "Are you there?"

"I sure am, Britta," she replied, causing Dan to jump slightly.

"I thought I told you to stay back?" Dan hissed at her.

"Sh-h-h!" Dallas told him.

"Dallas, would you do something for me?" Britta asked.

"Sure will, Honey."

"If . . . something happens, could you take a message to my daughter, Carly?"

"Of course I will, Britta, but you're gonna be able to do it yourself."

Britta's face was glistening with tears. She bit her lip. "I hope so! But . . . I've got these things all over me. Down my back, between my breasts, on my shoulder . . . there's even one between my legs. Oh, God!" Her body was shaking visibly.

"Britta!" Robert said. "Calm down! You're going to be fine. No defeatist thinking, okay? But you've got to be still."

"I don't want to die this way," Britta said in a small, strained voice. "But I think you'd better get back, Robert. I'm too tangled up."

"Bull! I'm getting you out of there. We've just got to do it methodically."

Robert worked on planning his next step forward as Britta shut her eyes, holding still for a few moments until a sudden gasp racked her body.

"Dallas . . . if I'm . . . gone, tell Carly . . . her mother loved her endlessly."

"Britta—" Dallas began, but Britta stopped her. "No!" she said, her voice tremulous but insistent. "Tell—tell her I love her, and . . . I'm proud of the strong young woman she's become . . . and . . ." There was a choked sob and a shudder through her body that alarmed Robert.

"Britta! Please stay still! Please!"

"And tell her I'm so . . . *very* sorry"—she was trying to keep from moving but the sobs were racking her body—"we had so little time. That was always my fault."

Dallas had to fight back a growing lump in her throat to answer. "Britta, it's gonna work, Honey. Hang in there. Robert's gonna get you out."

Britta was shaking her head slightly. "No. No, he's not. Robert, get out of here. I feel one slipping down my back. Please! Go."

"Britta, stop that!" Robert ordered.

"This isn't going to work, Robert, and I don't want to take any of you with me. I can feel it slipping."

"If one slips out, I can throw it far enough away. Calm down."

A sudden round of chattering and screeching broke out from the three monkeys on the right, sending chills down Robert's back. He struggled to ignore the primates as they jumped back to the floor of the trail without warning and scampered off into the brush at high speed, one of them running headlong into a thirty-year old cord now stretched taut across the trail from Britta's collision with the daisy chain.

Robert glanced to the right, sensing the sudden motion. He was helpless to stop the movement as the monkey's impact yanked the aging release lines from the bottom of each can, leaving the six heavy objects inside free to thud onto the trail at Britta's feet.

There was an endless second of stunned silence before Britta's voice cut through the moment, surprisingly strong. "Run, Robert! Don't argue. Run!"

"Hell NO!" he replied. Time seemed to dilate as his mind raced through the possibilities. He could dive for the grenades and scoop up a few, but how many? Four? Five? Could he find them all in time? Could he heave six away in time? No! Get her out! If he could yank her away from the cords . . .

"BRITTA!" Dallas yelled. "PULL YOURSELF LOOSE AND RUN THIS WAY!"

Robert crouched to spring toward Britta, but Dallas had already leaped across the path and grabbed his collar with surprising force, yanking him backward. Britta shook off her stupor and started fighting to disentangle herself, thrashing and pulling against the cords. She lunged almost two feet away, but one of the lines around her waist was anchored to a tree. She turned to wrench it loose without success, acutely aware that the seconds were passing.

"NO!" Robert yelled helplessly as he fell backward in Dallas's grip, furiously trying to break away from her as she dragged him over the top of a large log and fought his efforts to break away. Robert could still see Britta across the path. She was giving up! Turning and shaking her head and mouthing the word "go" at him.

One more time she tried to pull loose, tears streaming down her face. He saw her shake her head finally and stand, her shoulders slumping. She turned toward them and calmly closed her eyes, taking a deep breath before lowering her head.

"KEEP TRYING, BRITTA! TRY!" Dallas's voice was a shriek in his ear, but it was too late.

"LET GO OF ME!" Robert yelled.

"DOWN, DAMN YOU!" Dallas snarled, jerking him behind the log into the moist dirt and falling on top of him at the very moment the first trigger completed its deadly work.

The thunderous impact of six simultaneous explosions fifteen feet away rocked the jungle as it sprayed shrapnel and vegetation and Britta just inches over their heads, the blast dissipating before reaching the others.

Robert angrily shoved Dallas off him and scrambled to his feet, tears in his eyes, his mind disoriented as he stumbled toward the scorched spot where Britta had stood. He couldn't believe she was really dead, but everywhere he looked, his eyes confirmed it in gruesome detail.

"GOD DAMN YOU, DALLAS!" His voice, a guttural cry through gritted teeth, partially covered the sounds of someone running through the brush.

Steve skidded to a halt by Dallas, his eyes looking at the torn and ravaged portion of the trail where Britta had been. "Oh God! Where is she?" he asked, his voice shaking.

"Steve," Dallas said, trying to put her arm around him. Steve pushed her away and stepped forward, his eyes scanning frantically to the right and left, trying to find an explanation for the explosion that would still leave her alive. Instead, his eyes fell to the spot where she had stood and slowly focused on the shredded pieces of flesh and bone, and one identifiable portion of a foot.

Steve leaned past Dallas and began throwing up violently. Dallas held him, tears coursing down her cheeks as she tried to comfort both of them.

"It's okay, Honey. It's okay. It's okay."

chapter
24

It was too much to absorb in a single pass.

Kat Bronsky rubbed her eyes and asked the helicopter pilot to circle the perimeter of the wreckage a second time. What had appeared at first as a dark gash in the midst of a verdant jungle had grown rapidly as they approached, becoming an ugly expanse of blackened vegetation, coalescing into a gut-wrenching killing field of twisted aluminum, shredded seats, and human bodies.

The Vietnamese Air Force major nodded and banked the craft to one side.

"My God!" Kat said to herself, the contrast of clear blue skies overhead and total destruction below an upheaval in her mind. She felt a tap on her shoulder and turned to find the government interpreter she'd been assigned leaning in her direction.

"I'm sorry, Agent Bronsky. I did not hear you."

What was his name? Kat asked herself, remembering at the same moment. *Phu Minh. That's right. And his western name is Pete.*

She shook her head. "I was just talking to myself, Pete."

She looked back at the wreckage and gestured toward it. "I just can't believe this." Her stomach was hovering on the edge of nausea.

The helicopter flew slowly over the narrow point of first impact and the broad swath of destruction plowed by the disintegrating jumbo jet to the final resting place of the upper deck and cockpit area. It was twisted and shattered but recognizable, as it sat in a natural clearing over a mile distant from the point where the jungle first snagged the wings of the huge Boeing.

She snapped several pictures, knowing they could never transmit the full effect of the horror laid out before her in three dimensions. Once again she tried to put out of her mind the prospect of seeing Robert MacCabe's body.

"Again?" the pilot asked in English.

Kat shook her head no and motioned toward the area around the forward section of the jumbo where a small group of men was waiting. She watched the pilot set the Huey on the ground with effortless precision, remembering the two hours of dual instruction she'd had in a much smaller helicopter back home. The memory was a momentary escape from the carnage spread out before her.

The on-scene commander was a Vietnamese colonel with an ashen face who met her at the door of the Huey.

Kat greeted him and stepped out, gesturing to the wreckage. "Did . . . did anyone survive?"

She felt herself go cold when he shook his head no.

"No one alive here," he said. "I am waiting for our aviation ministry from Hanoi. I understand you are from the American accident agency?"

She nodded. "Technically, Colonel, I'm a special agent with the FBI, but I'm here to take a first look while all the other investigators are on the way."

"You will not . . . disturb anything?"

"Of course not."

"Please tell me if we can help."

"Just let me walk around and get a feel for this accident," Kat said.

The colonel nodded and turned away.

Kat walked quickly toward the main wreckage of the 747's upper deck, the only large part still discernible. She climbed carefully over the sharp, ragged sides and stepped into the main aisle of the first-class upper-deck cabin. She felt suddenly light-headed as she spotted her seat.

She moved carefully toward it, then stopped in shock. The window seat where MacCabe had been sitting was completely intact and devoid of blood stains. The aisle seat where she would have been sitting was a different story. The seat itself was intact, but a jagged piece of aluminum had been propelled through the seat back. It would have passed through her chest.

My God! Kat said to herself. *There's no question. I would be dead now.*

She shook herself back to the present and looked around. MacCabe's body was nowhere to be seen.

So where is he?

The break in the cabin was behind the fourth row of seats, and Kat searched carefully both inside and behind the wreckage. *Anyone back there would be gone, but anyone strapped in up here might have survived. The impact forces were obviously low.*

There was a torn sheet of black plastic draped over one side of the wreckage where the left side windows had been. Kat moved carefully toward it. All her work as a police intern during college years had left her hardened to the ravaged bodies accidents could produce. She braced for the worst, her memory replaying some of the more gruesome things she had seen: indelible images of small aircraft victims, auto accident victims, suicides involving twelve-gauge shotguns, and one woman who chose to dive through a ten-story window, reducing herself to a mound of drained, gelatinous flesh on the concrete below.

Kat pulled the plastic back, somehow expecting to find Robert MacCabe, but there was no body beneath it. Instead, copious amounts of blood and some human tissue were embedded in the razor-sharp metal. *They must have already started removing the bodies. That's the only reasonable explanation.*

Professionally, the thought was worrisome. The NTSB couldn't control an investigation of a crash in a foreign nation, but they could provide expert professional advice, including the universal recommendation that bodies and wreckage be left wholly untouched until a preliminary examination had been completed. Nations unsophisticated in accident investigation often let bodies and wreckage be moved far too early, obscuring major clues, and sometimes hiding the true causes of the crash.

She replaced the plastic sheet and began moving carefully around the tortured floor of the upper deck, looking for clues. There was a general lack of blood on all but one of the passenger seats. Even in the cockpit, the only sign of severe body impact was around the forward windscreen, and that victim—a man in civilian clothes—was still draped over the center throttle console, his neck obviously snapped. The copilot's body, however, was nowhere to be found.

Wait a minute. A blinded copilot would have had others in this cockpit, not just the one guy on the glareshield. So where are the rest of them? There was no blood on either of the pilot seats or the two observer seats, even though all of them had been partially dislodged from the buckled cockpit floor.

Kat snapped a series of pictures before finding the small sleeping compartment behind the cockpit. The captain's body was crammed against the forward bulkhead of the compartment, but without major wounds. She reached past the buckled wall and turned him over. He appeared uninjured, though as she looked more closely at his face, there was something about his eyes—his pupils—that looked very odd. It was as if he had cataracts in each eye. *Probably related to the explosion,* Kat thought. *It must have been terribly intense. We desperately need an ophthalmologist on the autopsy.* She took note of the torn uniform shirt and several marks on his chest. *CPR, I'll bet.*

Kat emerged from the cockpit and moved back through the truncated upper deck before climbing down. She glanced at the ground she had stepped on, noticing the unusual number of footprints emanating from the wreckage of the upper deck where stepping to the ground was the easiest. The ground was muddy, and many of the footprints were deep. A few led back toward the main debris field, but several people had moved around to the west and the north, heading into the jungle.

Kat knelt to read the prints more closely. Two were clearly women's pumps, the small heel unmistakable confirmation that a woman had stepped from the wreckage. And a third, even smaller woman's heel led off in a different direction.

Kat walked to the Vietnamese commander as her interpreter rushed over. "Colonel, have there been any other women up here on the rescue force?"

The colonel frowned and shook his head. "Only men."

"One more question, please," Kat replied. "Have *any* bodies been removed from the forward section?"

"No. None. May I ask why?"

Kat pursed her lips and nodded. "I'm wondering where the rest of the flight crew and the passengers in the upper deck are."

The colonel frowned again. "I do not know. This is how we found it several hours ago."

Kat returned rapidly to the same spot, making mental note of the number of different shoes impressed into the muddy soil along with several sets of men's footprints moving toward the west, one of them walking backward, the prints deep enough to indicate something heavy was being carried.

She spotted something else in a small puddle alongside the prints and knelt down with a stick, poking at the substance.

Blood! Lots of it. Someone was carrying a body, and it was bleeding out.

Kat reentered the wreckage of the upper deck and sat in one of the intact passenger seats.

Okay, what went on here? There should have been survivors up here. Were there? Did Robert make it?

She remembered her question to Jake about the Global

Express. The Company had said nothing about NROs seeing evidence that the Global Express was shadowing the 747, but had they been? Could they have reached the crash site first?

The footprints told a tale. At least three females must have survived, and several males. But where were they?

Kat got to her feet and looked back to the east, toward Da Nang. *If I found myself alive and knew there was a city back there, would I walk out?*

Kat moved to the black plastic sheet and looked underneath. *Someone impacted this spot at substantial speed.* She could read the bent metal now: The crushed beams held a completely different damage pattern than the rest of the wreckage. *Is there a way a body could have catapulted here in the crash?*

Something shiny was visible at the corner of one piece of bent aluminum. Kat had to crawl up to get to it, reaching carefully into the tangle and moving aside a piece of human tissue to retrieve it. She stood up again and looked at what was unmistakably a woman's pierced earring.

Oh my God!

Kat jumped out of the wreckage and carefully followed the footprints to the south, to the edge of the clearing, and then to the east, toward Da Nang. She was about to turn back when a disturbed area of soil and brush caught her eye, an area filled with footprints heading in the opposite direction, to the west, into the heart of the jungle and mountains. She knelt to examine the footprints carefully.

At least four males, but only two females. One's missing. The one with the smallest heel.

Once more she returned to the plastic sheet. Beneath the twisted metal she had recalled seeing a flash of yellow. It took several minutes of digging, but the search finally yielded a woman's yellow pump, ripped and blood-soaked—a shoe that matched perfectly one set of footprints by the wreckage, footprints missing from the group that had headed west from the edge of the clearing.

Kat left the shoe in the wreckage as she fought a primal

urge to run to her helicopter and get out of there. The woman with the yellow shoes had been alive and walking just after the crash. Later, she had fallen from a great height into the wreckage. Had a helicopter rescue attempt gone bad?

Or was she dropped intentionally?

The survivors running into the jungle undoubtedly knew, and they wouldn't be running, she concluded, unless they had seen something that panicked them. *The bad guys got here first! Whoever was in that Global Express was here.*

Kat motioned to the interpreter and headed for the helicopter. "I need you to fly slow and low directly to the east," she told the pilot, "following the same path anyone would follow if they tried to walk out of here."

She saw the question in his eyes. "Don't ask. Just please, let's go."

"I will need to refuel in Da Nang," the pilot said, "but okay for a while."

Pete Phu jumped aboard as the rotor blades began to turn. Kat settled in the cloth seat nearest the open door, snugly buckling her seat belt, well aware that she was breathing hard.

It was MacCabe. Wherever he is, this whole disaster was to get him.

It was an illogical conclusion on one level, but on another, it was something she should have seen in Hong Kong, and the thought made her sick.

IN THE JUNGLE,
NORTHWEST OF DA NANG, VIETNAM

The five remaining survivors of Meridian Flight 5 sat huddled together in shock on a mossy log in a pouring rainstorm, slightly more than a hundred yards from the spot where Britta had died.

The cloudburst had begun several minutes before, but they sat wordlessly until Dallas Nielson finally looked skyward, blinking back the water flowing into her eyes. "Thank God for small favors. At least the flies are gone."

Robert MacCabe shook his head and sighed as he straightened up and took inventory. Dallas was coping, as was he, but he could tell that Dan was convulsed with agony and blaming himself for not warning about the dangers of booby traps.

Young Steve Delaney sat staring at the ground, his shoulders shaking slightly as he tried to come to grips with the nightmare he'd seen.

And then there was Graham Tash, whose expressionless face and wordless demeanor reflected the unfathomable shock of watching his wife murdered. MacCabe wasn't sure if Britta's death had truly penetrated Graham's consciousness.

I've got to get us moving! Robert concluded as he got to his feet. "I think it's time," he said, inclining his head toward the west.

One by one they rose from the log and followed.

The jungle vegetation was unbelievably slippery beneath their street shoes, and all of them fought a constant struggle to stay upright as they tried to ignore the misery of being soaked to the skin.

The expensive beige silk and brocade outfit Dallas had worn from her Hong Kong hotel now lay plastered to her body. Her hair was soaked, giving her the appearance of a moving apparition emerging from a swamp. She kept losing her wet shoes in the underbrush and thought longingly of the comfort of her dry, soft satin slippers at home.

"Robert?" Dallas called. "What's the plan?"

He stopped and turned. "Get to that road, I guess, and then trigger Steve's radio to call for help."

For what seemed like hours they moved steadily downslope as the storm passed and the sun came out, filtering through an overhead jungle canopy that was sometimes sparse, sometimes heavy. Steam rose from their bodies as their clothes slowly dried, and as the patina of moisture evaporated from the ferns and plants of the jungle floor, their footing improved. Noises flowing through the underbrush from unseen creatures were a constant companion, as was the sound of hands slapping at the returning clouds of flies and mosquitoes—a steady, annoying counterpoint to the footfalls of five terrified people pushing through the underbrush.

DA NANG AIRPORT, VIETNAM
NOVEMBER 13—DAY TWO
4:45 P.M. LOCAL/0945 ZULU

The helicopter carrying Kat Bronsky flew over the western border of the former American air base at Da Nang and slowed for a landing. With both of the sliding side doors open, Kat and her interpreter had spent the twenty-minute flight in a fruitless search for the survivors, but the failure merely reinforced her suspicion that they were probably headed west, and running for their lives. The pilot touched down in front of a shabby servicing facility on a decaying concrete ramp that held several small aircraft, a scattering of military helicopters, and one luxury business jet, the latter looking decidedly out of place.

Curious, Kat thought, looking at the jet and not recognizing its form at first. *I wouldn't have expected to find a corporate jet. . . .* She leaned slightly out the door for a better view, blinking against the windblast, and read the jet's registration number: N22Z.

Oh my God!

It was the Bombardier Global Express from Hong Kong.

I was right. They were here. No, she corrected herself, *they* are *here! Now what?* she asked herself as the rotor slowed. The pilot was looking back at her, but Kat was suddenly too off balance to give a normal response. She struggled not to show her confusion and smiled at him, flashing a sophomoric thumbs-up sign.

"What you want to do?" the Vietnamese major asked.

"Ah . . . after you refuel, could you just wait here for me?" Kat asked. "We'll need to go back up and keep searching until dark."

The major nodded, but Kat's attention had already shifted back to the $40 million world-girdling Global Express, which sat by itself on the ramp with its doors closed. There was a figure walking around the nose of the jet, a lone Vietnamese soldier standing guard duty with an AK-47.

Kat stepped carefully from the Huey and walked around the rear of the helicopter, taking care to keep out of sight while she pulled out her satellite phone. It would be almost midnight in Washington. She'd memorized Jake Rhoades's home number and punched it in, listening to it ring after only a few seconds, expecting Jake or his wife to sound cross at getting such a late call.

Jake himself answered, and she could hear him yawn on the other end as they exchanged quick hellos.

"What do you have, Kat?"

"A very scary discovery here in Da Nang!" she said, keeping her voice low. "I'm looking at that Bombardier Global Express, November-Two-Two-Zulu."

She could hear Jake sit up in bed and whistle. "Whoa!"

"Jake, the crash scene about nine miles from here is predictably horrible. Over two hundred people were obliterated—shredded—in the breakup as the seven-forty-seven slammed into the ridge."

"No survivors, then?"

She cautioned herself to breathe and slow down. Her voice was sounding shaky and unprofessional. "Ah, that's the point. I'm told no one has been found alive, but I've found very convincing evidence at the scene, around the remains of the cockpit and upper first-class cabin, that at least five or six people survived, possibly including the copilot and the person I alluded to earlier . . . a reporter who approached me in Hong Kong with information about SeaAir."

"Then where are they, Kat?"

"I think they're on the run in the jungle, trying to stay away from something murderous they witnessed at the crash site." Kat gave him the details, including the clues that led her to the conclusion that a female survivor had been murdered.

"You see any other rational explanation, Jake, from what I just told you? The blood, the shoe, the footprints, the earring?"

There was a long hesitation and then a sigh. "No," Jake said, "I'm guided to the same conclusion."

"Now that I find this jet here, it makes twisted sense."

"Kat, is anyone hanging around that jet?"

"There's a soldier guarding it. I haven't approached it."

"We need that serial number. I'm told it will be on a metal plate under the tail. If you could safely get that, and maybe get a look inside . . ."

"Understood. I'll try to see if they're any special weapons installed, too, like that target designator you said the Air Force was talking about."

"I don't want to push you into doing anything dangerous, Kat, but the Bureau is getting kind of desperate for some answers back here. I have to tell you, the media is all but labeling the Meridian crash a terrorist act because of the copilot's transmission about something exploding in front of him, and Langley's attempts to call this a midair had pretty much evaporated before your call. Obviously there was no collision. The possibility that this is number two in a series of terror attacks, beginning with SeaAir, is already being openly discussed from *Larry King Live* to NPR."

Kat chewed on her lip a second. "I hate to say it, but that pretty accurately sums up *my* fears!"

He snorted. "I know it. Mine, too. But Langley's trying to blow it off."

Kat had been moving steadily around the back of the helicopter's tail boom as they talked, watching the lone soldier pace slowly around the Global Express, but something Robert MacCabe had said in Hong Kong snapped back into her mind and she dropped her eyes to concentrate.

"Jake, on the subject of Langley, is there a chance they might be soft-pedaling this because they really *are* afraid it's a group they don't have a handle on—maybe one sophisticated enough to steal one of our missile-based weapon systems?"

"I don't know, Kat. I try to leave the politics to others."

"Did Langley flat-out say that NRO never saw this business jet from space?"

There was a hesitation before Jake replied. "No, they didn't."

"Okay, because I'll bet NRO could see this bird from orbit, and Langley decided not to share the information. Can you find out?"

Jake's voice changed slightly, his tone shifting. "Kat, you're pushing into a delicate area here. Why?"

"Something that reporter said to me. The one I'd dearly love to find alive."

"Something about Langley's fears and reaction?"

"Yes."

"Well, you've virtually nailed my own suspicions. I'll call NRO. I'll bet you're right, although I don't know what it proves. And for us, it changes nothing."

Kat looked back at the soldier, who was now sitting on the ramp and obviously bored to tears. "I'd better go," she said.

"Be careful! But call immediately if you get anything, whatever the hour."

She punched the phone off and returned to the interior of the helicopter to find the interpreter, who had been relaxing on the back bench.

"Pete? See that jet over there? I need you to help convince that soldier that I have official authorization to look at that aircraft."

Pete Phu's eyes grew large. She held up a hand and smiled. "Just tell him I love that type of plane, Pete, and I just need an excuse to look at it."

After a moment he nodded his head. "I think . . . I can do that."

• • •

The soldier was appropriately suspicious for only a few seconds as Pete explained in Vietnamese the official role of the American woman he was escorting.

"Big, important official from the United States. Hanoi has provided this helicopter, and me, and is asking everyone to cooperate."

The soldier nodded as he stepped aside.

The main entry door was locked, as she expected, and with no ground power hooked up for air-conditioning, it was undoubtedly too hot inside for anyone to be hiding in the cabin. The crew and occupants didn't seem to be anywhere around.

Kat walked casually beneath the tail, cataloging the fact that there were no external rails from which a missile could be fired. *Must have been fired from a boat below, or another airplane,* she thought. She found the production plate and memorized the serial number as she smiled and pretended to be enjoying the experience of seeing such an aircraft up close.

The aircraft appeared to be standard in every way—except for the registration numbers on the sides of the fuselage. Up close, it was obvious that a portion of the original number had been painted over, and new numbers added. The job was sloppy, and she could almost make out the original N-number beneath.

The baggage compartment was locked as well, and she drew a startled look from the soldier when she tried the latch. She smiled back and waved at him as she nodded to Pete and headed back to the Huey, which now had a fuel truck in front of it. It would take a few minutes to fill the tanks, and she had a decision to make.

Kat glanced back at the Global Express, torn between returning to look for MacCabe and any other survivors, or staying to find a way into the Global Express. She paused to lean against the tail boom in thought, weighing the options. Whoever had flown the jet into Da Nang had undoubtedly followed Meridian and knew exactly where the 747 had crashed. There was probably a pile of evidence aboard, and maybe even the target designator. The key to a dangerous mystery might be no more than a hundred feet away.

But there were also survivors moving through a hostile jungle, possibly being stalked by whoever had occupied the business jet.

Kat thought about the alternatives that would have faced the Global Express crew around dawn. If they were truly the assassins of Meridian 5, they would be desperate to finish the job by going directly to the site, which they couldn't do by road.

Kat stood upright suddenly, watching the Vietnamese fueler. She moved to the cabin and caught Pete's attention again, motioning him close.

"Pete, I need you to do something else for me."

He nodded hesitantly.

"Would you go ask the guy fueling us when the people from the jet we just looked at will be returning in their helicopter? If he acts like he knows what you're talking about, ask him if it was a Huey like this."

Pete Phu climbed out and engaged the fueler in conversation, the colorful tones of the Vietnamese language wafting in the door, accompanied by spurts of laughter. In a few minutes he was back, leaning toward Kat.

"He says he doesn't know, because they took the helicopter just about sunrise. And he said yes, it's just like this one."

Kat thanked him and pulled out the satellite phone again to pass the information to Jake.

IN THE JUNGLE,
NORTHWEST OF DA NANG, VIETNAM

Arlin Schoen stood momentarily exposed in the broad expanse of the jungle clearing and tried to spot the helicopter they had just finished camouflaging.

Good job! he told himself. By turning the machine nose-on to the heart of the clearing, they only needed a little greenery to make it blend with the background.

He checked his watch and looked up, calculating how fast the quarry would have been walking. The river had them neatly boxed on one side, and with the highway on the other side of the river making itself known with every truck and car that rumbled past, the survivors would probably move along the south bank to look for a place to cross.

And the bridge a thousand yards downstream from where he would be waiting could be seen a half mile up the small gorge, which meant, he concluded, that as soon as they spotted the bridge, excitement would outweigh caution, leading them right into his trap.

Perfect.

He turned back to the hidden helicopter, covering the distance in a quick jog, in a hurry to prepare the weapons.

Less than a mile to the east, Robert MacCabe motioned for the others to stop as he stepped toward the riverbank to peer down the river.

Dallas Nielson had been guiding Dan Wade with her arm around his shoulder, while Steve Delaney helped Graham Tash. They came to a halt and waited, emotionally and physically exhausted.

"Ah . . . Dan, Graham here."

They all turned at the sound of his voice. "Do you . . . ah . . . need another shot?"

Dallas looked at the doctor in surprise. *Good,* she thought. *He's beginning to reach outside himself.*

Dan shook his head slowly. "I may just be too numb, Doctor, but I'm not hurting much right now. Not my eyes, at least."

"Okay, ah . . ." Graham sighed. "Let me get Susan and . . ." Graham's eyes fluttered open at the recognition of what he'd just said, and the loss of his wife crashed in on him again. He staggered back slightly and sank in uncoordinated confusion to the ground, his head down and shaking back and forth. "I'm . . . sorry. I'm . . ."

Dallas knelt beside him quickly and put an arm around his shoulder. "It won't be easy, Doc. But you've got to hang with us."

Robert reappeared, his hair standing on end from brushing under a branch. "I think I see a bridge way down there," he said. "That'll be our ticket out of here. There's been enough traffic on that road."

Dallas started chuckling, and the spontaneity of it startled Steve into the beginning of a smile.

"What?" Robert asked, looking suspicious.

"You look like you just plugged your finger into a light socket," she said, grinning broadly as he reached up and smoothed his hair.

"Good grief, Dallas," he replied.

"Well, you did look funny."

"For crying out loud," he said. "I hardly see what's funny—"

"I guess," she said, her smile receding, "I guess I'd rather laugh than cry, and that's the first thing even remotely funny I've seen today."

Robert paused, then nodded, his eyes on Dan and Graham. "I understand."

"But seriously, we've got to get out of here, and I've got a question for you," Dallas said. "If we walk out on that road and flag someone down, how do we know we're not flagging down our killers?"

"They had a helicopter," Steve interjected.

"Which they could have traded for a truck by now," Dan added.

Robert took a deep breath. "What are you thinking, Dallas?"

"Well," she began, "Stevie here said that radio of his can transmit our precise coordinates and a voice message. Maybe we should stop short of that road, stay hidden, and turn that thing on. Any real rescuers can come right to us, provided the bad guys can't get that information."

"It's digital," Steve said. "It goes to a special satellite."

"So," Robert said, "it's probable whoever's chasing us won't have access to that information. Okay. Maybe a half mile more."

With Robert in the lead, the small group resumed walking, moving faster than before as the vegetation thinned somewhat next to the south bank of the river. The temperature was still mild and the sun at a steeper angle on the western horizon. In less than twenty minutes they stopped at the edge of a broad clearing, staying out of view as Steve pulled out the emergency radio, turned on the GPS function, and turned on the beacon. That done, he handed the radio to Dan to transmit a voice message.

"Mayday, Mayday, Mayday. We are five of the eight survivors from Meridian Flight Five. Two others were murdered by the occupants of an American-built helicopter, a Huey, that arrived at the crash site just after dawn. A third has been killed by . . . an explosion in the jungle. We need immediate aid and protection at these coordinates. Mayday, Mayday, Mayday."

DA NANG AIRPORT, VIETNAM

Kat watched the state-of-the-art Global Express business jet drop away as her Huey gained altitude, and wondered if she'd made the right decision. If it was gone when she returned, it would be all but impossible to track. With over a 6,000 mile range and the transponder turned off, they could escape to practically anywhere on the planet, moving out of radar coverage almost immediately.

The flight back to the crash site seemed very brief. When the pilot pointed to the ugly gash marking the site, Kat slipped carefully over the barrier separating the passenger seats from the front and into the left copilot's seat.

"Okay, bring us down to treetop level and start from the northwest corner of that clearing, heading west."

The pilot nodded and moved the controls to comply as Kat wondered why she was hearing a new sound above the native roar of the helicopter. It was intermittent and high-pitched, like an electronic warble, and it was very distant. She tried to concentrate on scanning the landscape ahead of her, but the sound kept interceding until its origin finally dawned on her.

Kat turned and motioned to Pete Phu, pointing to her purse. He handed it to her and she yanked open the flap to pull out the satellite phone and unfold the antenna.

"Hello?"

The voice on the other end was too soft, and she struggled to raise the volume.

"Hold on! I'm in flight and it's hard to hear." She toggled it up to maximum and held it to her ear again.

"Kat, can you hear me?"

"Who is this?"

"Jake!" he replied.

"Okay, Jake. Talk loud."

"We've received an emergency message by satellite, Kat. You were right. There were eight survivors. Three are dead. Five need immediate rescue." Jake repeated the message that had been recorded, and gave her the coordinates.

"Thank God! We can do it, Jake. I'll call you as soon as we have them," Kat promised. She disconnected and leaned toward the pilot. "Do you have a GPS?"

He shook his head no.

"How about a map?"

The major nodded and handed over his area navigation chart. Kat buried herself in it with the coordinates and a pen, finally bringing the lines together and circling the resulting point on the surface. She looked closely, following what appeared to be a river to a point just east of a highway bridge, and handed the folded map back to the pilot.

"Here. We need to pick up five people right here."

The major looked skeptical as he brought the Huey into a left-hand orbit and began matching the features below with the map. After a couple of minutes, he looked up, smiled at Kat, and pushed the cyclic control forward as he inclined his head to the west.

"About six miles," he said. "No problem."

chapter

26

Dallas placed her hand gently on Dan Wade's shoulder, causing him to jump slightly.

"It's Dallas, Danny. How're you doing?"

He reached up and patted her hand. "Better, I think. I mean, maybe it's false hope, but I'm daring to think that maybe the damage to my eyes isn't permanent. The pain has diminished. Whatever it was that got us, I only got a glancing blow."

"Are you seeing any light through that bandage?" she asked.

"I think so, but Graham said to keep it on for now."

She squeezed his hand. "Here's hoping and praying."

"What do you see out there?" he asked.

"Well, we're about ten yards back from the edge of a clearing. I guess you'd call it a clearing, or sort of a natural open space in the jungle. It's pretty wide, probably about a quarter mile across to where the trees get thick again. I gotta tell you, Dan, this isn't like the scary, snake-infested, tiger-prowling jungles I expected, although the bugs aren't far from the stereotype."

"Those jungles are to the south, Dallas. They're beautiful, but can be deadly, too."

The distant sound of rotor blades slapping the air at considerable forward speed vibrated into their consciousnesses.

Dallas turned to Steve. "I think that radio of yours attracted some attention."

"Hope so," Steve said, his eyes scanning the sky behind them, where the sound seemed to be coming from. The volume increased steadily. Robert got to his feet and joined Steve Delaney's attempt to spot the source of the sound in the eastern sky.

The helicopter popped over a ridge, the rhythmic noise slapping at them until it flew directly overhead and pulled its nose up, slowing rapidly before turning and descending into the clearing. The pilot brought the craft to a hover less than fifty feet from the eastern edge of the clearing, moving along slowly as a figure in the open left door stood and waved.

"That's a woman," Dallas exclaimed, looking startled.

"My God in heaven," Robert MacCabe said under his breath, his eyes fixed on the face of the female in the doorway. "I don't believe it. That's Kat Bronsky!"

Kat leaned toward the pilot, trying to make herself heard. "Keep coming forward slowly. They're out there somewhere." She resumed waving as broadly as she could, her eyes scanning the perimeter of the clearing, but seeing no one at first.

Without warning, five figures suddenly burst into view, running toward the Huey and waving back.

"There!" She turned to the pilot. "Land! Now!"

He turned and tapped his ear, then understood her gesture and unloaded the blades, lessening the lift they produced and letting the Huey drop rather smartly onto the surface.

Kat jumped from the open door, waving at what appeared to be a black woman, a man with a bandaged face, a young boy, another man . . . and Robert MacCabe! She felt a small shiver of excitement as he waved back.

Pete Phu had jumped to the ground as well, and the two of them helped the five refugees into the Huey, with Kat bringing up the rear. Robert reached out to help her in, pulling her up and into his arms for a surprising bear hug and kiss, a broad grin on his face as he aped a very bad Bogart accent. "Of all the sleazy meadows in all the sleazy jungles in all the backwaters of the world, you fly into mine!"

"You have no idea how glad I am to see you alive," Kat said, pulling away from him to close the door and order the pilot to take off. "Okay, let's get back in the air and . . ."

There was a popping noise from somewhere to the right and glass shattered in the cockpit. The possibility of a mechanical problem crossed Kat's mind as she wondered why the pilot was leaning so far to the left. There was a broken window on his right as he continued to fall over the center console.

"Somebody's shooting at us!" Dallas yelled from the back, and another voice ordered them to hit the floor. Kat moved forward to the pilot and lifted his head, then lowered it, realizing her fingers were red with blood. There was a simple entry wound in his right temple.

More bullets whizzed through the cockpit, one barely missing her nose. She clawed away at the dead pilot's seat belt and hauled his body out of the seat and into the back in one desperate motion.

Kat slid into the right seat, ignoring the blood, her left hand grabbing the collective control—a lever to the left of the seat with a motorcycle-style throttle in the handgrip. There was no time to debate whether she could fly the chopper without crashing; the alternative was to sit and die in a hail of bullets from unknown assailants. She twisted the throttle, boosting the rotor RPM, which was just below take-off speed. She searched the instrument panel for the right gauge and found the rotor RPM needle coming out of the red as she pulled up on the collective. She felt the Huey stand up on its skids and lighten as the rotor bit into the air, the blades creating enough lift to counter the weight of the helicopter. Another quarter of an inch up and they were airborne, drifting backward as another slug ripped through, this time leaving a jagged hole the size of a large fist in the windscreen in front of her.

"Please, Jesus, get us the hell out of here!" Dallas's voice moaned in the back.

Kat's feet found the rudder pedals, and she pushed the left one hard now to swing the tail toward the shooters, masking the cabin. The trees on the eastern edge of the clearing were perhaps fifty feet tall, and she knew she would have to gain enough altitude to get over them before gaining forward speed.

The Huey wobbled violently as Kat worked the cyclic control stick between her legs back and forth, fighting for some semblance of control. She shoved the stick forward much too fast and the Huey responded by dropping its nose and changing its rearward motion to forward motion, trading some of the lift for forward speed as the ground rushed up toward the machine.

"Yikes!" she heard herself shout as she jerked the collective up again, barely missing ground impact with the forward skids.

The Huey rose again, but not fast enough, and the trees ahead rushed toward the nose as several more bullets pinged through the cabin.

Once again she pulled on the collective, taking the throttle as high as she dared. She felt the machine shudder as it clawed the air in obedience, and she realized they were not going to clear the trees.

The UH-1 hit the tree line with twenty knots of forward airspeed, the Huey's huge rotor blades chopping through the top ten feet of the foliage as easily as a hedge trimmer through a bush. The blades mowed down the top five feet of an adjacent tree before the helicopter popped up over the remaining ones. It continued to climb and accelerate, apparently no worse for the experience.

"This . . . is supposed . . . to handle just like an airplane above forty knots!" she told herself out loud, remembering what her instructor had said several years back. She looked for the airspeed indicator and spotted it sitting on thirty knots and accelerating, as she worked the two controls to get the helicopter under control.

They were considerably above the trees now and stabilizing, the engine sounding steady with no warning lights visible on the forward panel—though the windblast was becoming a bother as she accelerated through fifty knots. She checked to make sure she was flying an easterly course back to Da Nang, and kept climbing.

Someone appeared at Kat's left elbow and she glanced over to see Robert MacCabe, his eyes huge as he looked at her. "Thank God you're a helicopter pilot, Kat."

She shook her head. "I'm not. I have almost no idea what I'm doing."

He looked at her with disbelief, and she smiled. "Welcome to my first helicopter solo. I only have a fixed-wing license. I do have an instrument rating, though."

"Will that help?"

"No."

"Oh, wonderful. Can you land?" he asked.

"Don't know. Never tried. Should be interesting." She smiled again, amused by his discomfort. "Is anyone hurt back there?"

"Well, Steve has a new part in his hair, but other than that, no."

"What?" Kat asked, only half paying attention.

"One slug almost nailed Steve, but all it did was take a line of hair off the top of his head. It's superficial."

"Thank heavens."

"That doesn't include the poor pilot, of course. He didn't make it. Do you have any idea who was shooting at us?"

She shook her head, the motion causing her to move the stick too abruptly, almost knocking Robert off his feet.

"Sorry. No, I don't know. I never saw them. It came from the right. The people you've been evading may have come in by road."

He was nodding. "Probably. What can I do to help you?" he asked.

She turned and grinned. "Pray a little? Or maybe open the operations manual to the chapter on how to land, and read it to me very slowly."

Robert MacCabe shook his head. "Okay, now I *am* terrified!"

• • •

The frantic efforts of the three men at the western end of the clearing to yank the camouflaging vegetation off the HU-1 took less than two minutes. The pilot jumped in the right seat and hit the Start switch as the last branches came off, bringing the rotors up to takeoff speed as fast as he could. Arlin Schoen pulled himself in and slid the door closed just as the pilot lifted off, accelerating in the direction of the departed Huey to the east, while the men in the back reloaded their guns.

"Maximum speed! Whoever's flying that crate isn't an experienced pilot. You should be able to catch him."

The pilot nodded, barely clearing the trees at the east end as he used the engine's best effort to gain speed first, then altitude, bringing the Huey above a hundred knots, the blades slapping the landscape ahead with a horrendous noise.

Within five minutes the outline of the other helicopter appeared on the horizon, moving at half normal speed.

"How do you want to do this, Arlin?" the pilot asked.

"Come to their five o'clock position, stay one ship high, and I'll guide you."

"You gonna try for the engine?"

Schoen shook his head no. "He might be able to autorotate and put it down. No, I need to get the rotor hub and put them completely out of control."

"That rotor head's a pretty tough assembly, Arlin. I'm not sure we've got enough firepower."

"Okay, what do you suggest?" Schoen asked.

The pilot motioned ahead. They were less than a mile now and closing.

"If I stick our skid into their blades near the center, I may be able to knock them down."

"Jeez! How about us?"

"It's a risk."

"No. We go back to Plan A. I'm gonna shoot. Bring me in."

Schoen moved back and slid open the left door, securing himself to a safety strap. His partner did the same. Schoen cocked the Uzi slung around his neck and checked the .45 automatic in his belt. When they were less than a hundred yards away, he could see the pilot intermittently through the window. Schoen realized with a start that it must be a woman. Her chestnut-colored hair was whipping around and streaming partly out of the broken side window.

Schoen motioned to his pilot to come forward a bit more, then hold position as he took careful aim at the rotor hub assembly and squeezed the trigger.

Kat felt a sudden series of staccato impacts in the Huey's controls, and an echo of something outside the right window. Dallas could feel it as well, and moved to the right to press her face against the glass of the sliding door.

"There's another helicopter back there," Dallas yelled. "He's firing at us!"

"Hold on!" Kat commanded as she jammed the right rudder pedal down, shifting the pitch of the tail rotor, which swung the Huey around to the right in a gut-wrenching maneuver that threw them all to the left.

The other Huey suddenly filled the right-side windows as the startled pilot of the trailing helicopter pulled up sharply to avoid a collision.

Kat thought over the possibilities as fast as she could. Too wild an evasive maneuver, and she could lose control of a machine she didn't really know how to fly.

Another round of bullets rattled the cyclic, forcing a decision. Kat pulled back and kicked the Huey into a tight left turn, reversing course and climbing as she slowed, pirouetting around before the pursuer was able to react. It was a gamble whether she could do it without stalling, but she had to get out of their sights.

Kat could see the other helicopter now through her left window. The shooters in the doorway hung on for their lives as the pilot tried to turn left to get behind her again. She pulled a bit tighter, feeling the Huey respond and steady out, the feedback vibrations on the cyclic stick reassuring her that she wasn't pushing too far.

No way in hell are you getting on my tail again! Kat thought to herself, her teeth gritted, as she continued the turn, spiraling closer above the other helicopter. The two of them were essentially circling each other. She could see the two men in the open door trying to regain their balance, one of them obviously yelling instructions forward as the pilot tried to give the shooters a stable firing platform.

Kat looked at the airspeed. She was down to thirty knots and the Huey was beginning to wallow, the stick becoming mushy and more finicky as her control inputs grew frenzied. She tried to stabilize her heading while she waited for the other chopper to reach her altitude; they were climbing fast. As soon as they reached her level, she shoved the collective lever to the floorboard, causing the helicopter to drop almost in free fall, her stomach immediately protesting the maneuver.

"What the hell are you doing up there, girl?" Dallas yelled at her as the other Huey shot up in her perspective, the pilot caught off guard by their sudden maneuver.

Kat watched her altimeter unwind, and at a thousand feet, she began pushing the nose down to pick up forward momentum as she brought in the collective and leveled out, kicking the Huey around to the right in another tight turn.

As expected, the other pilot had followed her down, dropping rapidly, and was now flattening out his descent as he dropped below Kat.

Now you're vulnerable! she thought, aiming straight toward him and shoving the stick forward to race at and just over the top of the other UH-1.

I've almost got this thing under control! Kat told herself, with a flash of relief, as she shot fifty feet over the top of the confused adversary and kicked her machine around to the left, staying behind and above him as he turned to find her.

The airspeed was dropping again, changing the requirements from basic stick-and-rudder flying to the skills of a helicopter pilot as she fought to stabilize her control inputs. But suddenly it wasn't working. Her hand jerked the stick around, her rhythms and ability to commune with the machine suddenly compromised. The Huey was beginning to wobble off on its own, the airspeed now down to less than twenty as she tried to hover, gyrating left and right and even up and down as she fought to dampen her inputs and regain control. Sweat was breaking out on Kat's forehead as the other pilot seized the moment to maneuver back into firing position.

Dammit! Fly! she snarled to herself, bringing the rudder pedals into the destabilized ballet as well, which worsened the gyrations.

The other Huey was turning on Kat's right, bringing its open left-hand door into view. As she struggled with the bouncing, turning machine, she could see the two shooters raising their guns for another try as they came along her right flank. The advantage she had gained had been lost just as fast. She'd reverted to being a sitting duck, too low to use the sudden-drop maneuver, and too underpowered and out of control in a hover to suddenly pop up. The other helicopter was close now, the pilot controlling his speed of passage to give the gunmen plenty of time.

Robert MacCabe had been holding on just behind the center console. He spoke up suddenly. "Kat, they're going to strafe us!"

"I know."

"We'd better turn—or something."

She nodded, her right hand finally reacquiring something close to a usable rhythm on the stick. The Huey settled down and moved forward, correcting to the right to aim directly at the oncoming machine.

"Kat! Ah . . . I don't think ramming him is the solution," Robert said as she accelerated directly at the windscreen of the onrushing Huey. She could see the pilot's head moving as he altered his course to her right, unprepared for her maneuver.

Kat pulled up suddenly, trading the small amount of forward speed for altitude as the attacker slid below her.

More slugs tore through the Huey, most of them along the left side.

"Now!" Kat barked out loud as she kicked the rudder and banked excessively to the left, feeling the HU-1 almost stall as she tried to slip behind him.

Oh, no! Too much! They were heeling left at a violent angle, the side window suddenly filled with the top of the other machine.

"Kat! LOOK OUT!" Robert yelled. The tail boom of the other helicopter rose toward them at a frightening speed as they slipped to the left at too great an angle to recover.

"NO!"

The shuddering impact of the left skid with the whirling tail rotor of the other helicopter produced a momentary buzz-saw sound of colliding metal and threw them all to the right in a violent roll. Their destabilized chopper staggered sideways in the air before recovering, its basic airworthiness remarkably undamaged—but its left landing skid was a twisted mess, after an amazing shower of sparks.

"Good Lord, Kat!" Robert exclaimed.

"Wasn't planned." She banked to the right and skidded around the turn, expecting the other pilot to be lining up for another shot.

Instead, the sky to the right was clear.

Kat kept turning, scanning ahead, thoroughly startled when Robert grabbed her shoulder and pointed below.

"There!"

"Hang on!" the pilot had shouted to Arlin Schoen and the other man in the door as he pressed hard on the vibrating rudder pedals and tried to stop the world from whirling. He'd dropped the collective and tried to descend as soon as he realized that the other pilot, however inexperienced, had succeeded in damaging his tail. There was no doubt the tail rotor was in deep trouble, because the ship was vibrating at a furious rate. But the blades must still be there, so maybe he still had some control.

With a sudden lurch, the vibrating stopped as the damaged tail rotor flew off its hub, leaving him with no turning control. Instantly the spinning of the helicopter around the main axis of its rotor became worse. The pilot used all the tricks in the book: forward airspeed, unloading, sudden throttle pullback, but nothing worked. He was losing it, and the jungle floor was rising fast in a spinning, spiraling blur.

The crippled Huey slammed into the first of the trees, the tail boom swinging into a tree trunk and flipping the body of the helicopter over with a horrendous sound as the fuselage dove the remaining fifty feet to the ground.

The plume of flames and dust following the impact below heralded a crash too severe to be survivable, Kat figured. She kept her Huey moving at greater than forty knots as she circled at a distance and watched the funeral pyre of smoke rising from the wreckage.

"Incredible flying, Kat!" Dallas Nielson said, clutching the back of Kat's seat.

"That . . . was actually a lucky mistake," Kat replied. "I thought we were dead."

"You got them, Kat," Robert added quietly, his eyes on the smoke below.

"The question is," Kat replied, "who *were* they?"

She tore her eyes away from the smoke and concentrated on climbing back to a higher altitude. Da Nang couldn't be more than ten miles away to the east, and a plan, however improbable, was beginning to form in her mind—provided she could figure out how to land the old Huey without killing them all.

In the middle of a thicket of ferns, bushes, and brush some forty feet from the burning remains of the borrowed UH-1, something moved. A massive tangle of branches had cushioned the fall of a body thrown from the door of the crashing helicopter as the tail boom struck the tree trunk.

The figure stirred again, and tried to rise.

Arlin Schoen rubbed his eyes and looked around, the receding sounds of the helicopter he had intended to destroy in his ears as he spit out part of a branch, took inventory of his limbs, and calculated his remaining options.

chapter
27

The Da Nang Airport ramp was less than five miles ahead.

Kat squinted to see through the steady hurricane of wind blowing through the hole in the windscreen. She slowed the Huey as much as she could and motioned Robert and Dallas close to the back of her seat.

"Robert, do you have any idea . . . who those assassins were?"

He nodded. "On the ground at the crash site, I recognized one of them from Hong Kong. One of the goons who tried to snatch me."

"So, as I figured, they were trying to keep you from talking," Kat said, working hard to keep her control movements conservative and the Huey flying smoothly.

"But as I told you, I really don't know anything yet to talk *about*," Robert said. "That's the ridiculous part. They've validated the fact that Walter Carnegie really had stumbled onto something, but I still don't know what."

"Robert, we don't have much time, and I've got to try to land this thing, but"—she looked back over her shoulder at him—"they left their business jet up ahead."

Dan had been standing beside Dallas and behind Kat. He

reached out and grabbed Kat's shoulder. "This is the copilot, Dan Wade. Who *are* you?" he asked.

"Special Agent Kat Bronsky of the FBI, Captain Wade. I'm sorry, there was no time to—"

"Don't apologize! You rescued us. There's no better introduction. But you mentioned a business jet?"

"Yes."

"What kind? Not a Bombardier Global Express, by any chance?"

Kat turned partially in the seat to try to see Dan Wade's face, but he was standing directly behind her and the momentary diversion caused her to bobble the controls. She turned her attention back to stabilizing the Huey and slowing.

"Dan, it *is* a Global Express. I think it may be the same one that shot, or sabotaged, your plane."

There was a long pause before Dan spoke. "It was a Global Express that took off ahead of us, all right. He had to be part of it. There may have been a fighter out there too, because someone fired a missile that exploded in front of us."

"The Air Force thinks it may have been a special phosphorous warhead, designed to flash-blind you," Kat said.

"Yeah. That would be about right. It was hideously bright. I thought at first it was a nuclear blast in the distance, but since we immediately hit a shock wave, it had to be an exploding missile."

Da Nang was on the nose now, two miles away. Kat felt her frustration rising that the small necessity of figuring out how to land was blocking some key questions. She looked hard at the ramp up ahead, relieved to see the Global Express was still parked in the same place. Kat turned slightly in Dan's direction. "We'll talk later. In the meantime, I plan to steal their Global Express, search it, and fly the evidence home."

"You can do that?" Dallas asked, her eyebrows up. "You can fly a jet, too?"

"Well, I'm not trained in a Global Express, but I can fly it safely . . . with help." She worked to find the right combination of power and pitch to slow the Huey a bit more and continue to lose altitude, aiming for the same spot they had occupied a few hours before, a hundred feet from the Global Express.

"Okay, everyone, this could get rough. Everyone please strap in!"

"You need me up here, Kat?" Robert asked, pointing to the copilot's seat.

She turned quickly and nodded. "Yes. Moral support, at least. Wait! First, look out that left side and tell me whether I've got enough of the landing skid remaining to support this machine's weight."

She pulled back slightly on the stick, forgetting to lessen the pitch angle of the rotor blades—and the lift they were generating—with the collective lever. With less of the lift going to forward motion and more directed upward, the Huey began to climb sharply.

Gotta remember, down on the collective when I'm slowing like this. She made the adjustment and started descending again. The airspeed was less than thirty knots, and this time she was forcing herself to feed in some rudder to keep the Huey from turning as she slowed.

Robert was back, climbing over the center panel to get in the left seat. "Kat, the forward strut is gone, but the back strut is still there, and I think it'll hold. The skid itself is partly there, attached to the rear strut."

"If it doesn't hold," Kat said, "she'll fall to the left on touchdown and the blades will hit the ground."

They were less than a hundred feet from the target spot on the ramp, still moving forward at ten knots. Kat milked the stick back slowly and lessened the collective to compensate for the changing flight dynamics. She felt herself working the rudder pedals too much, and the nose swung back and forth, left and right, as she coaxed the Huey into what could pass for a hover and let it continue to descend. Her inputs on the stick were much calmer now, but still causing the helicopter to dance around.

She could see the Global Express just ahead, and she could see something else, which chilled her: The forward door was open and the stairs had been extended.

The momentary loss of concentration was too much. Suddenly she was behind the machine again, nudging the stick left when it should have gone right, and shoving it right when it needed only a nudge left, until they were rocking violently back and forth in all three axes as she struggled for control.

"DAMPEN YOUR INPUTS!" Dan Wade yelled forward, feeling the gyrations. "Easy does it! THINK the controls. Don't move them!"

Kat felt herself tensing. Her hands shook, defying her attempts to relax. Any correction on the collective lever, and they were either dropping dangerously or rising precipitously. For every axis she brought under control, another would slip away into a left pirouette, a forward or backward motion, or just another severe case of the wobbles.

She was breathing hard, holding on, calculating the distance to the ground at twenty feet as she held the stick fairly still and forced herself to merely *think* the collective down a hair.

Obediently, the Huey began moving down ever so slightly, but going sideways to the right. *Think it left!* she commanded herself, amazed when the sideward movement ceased. *Ten feet! Okay, just hold this, hold this. . . .*

They settled to within three feet of the ramp, all forward motion now stopped. The Huey slowly turned to the left as she successfully tried the new technique again and felt the skids touch with surprising gentleness, the one on the left giving a little, then rocking them forward.

She felt her heart jump into her throat as the body of the helicopter suddenly shifted forward and to the left. The arc of the blades descended toward the tarmac as she instinctively hauled back on the cyclic stick, raising the blades even as the motion continued, then suddenly stopped. The blades were still whirling without obstruction, with the lowest point of the arc mere inches above the concrete.

Kat slowly let the rest of the collective down, reducing the lift to zero. She reached out, then, and cut off the fuel, shutting down the turbine engine rotor as the blades slowed and stopped.

"You okay?" Robert asked, watching her breathe hard, her hands still welded to the controls, and her head caged straight ahead. He saw her eyes flick over to him, then a smile began to play around her mouth. There was a nod, followed by a tremendous sigh of relief.

When the rotor blades had stopped, Dallas, Graham, Dan, Steve, and Pete Phu began helping one another up to move across the tilted floor toward the left door. A loud crack reverberated through the helicopter, throwing them farther to the left as part of the mangled skid gave way, leaving the Huey with the left forward part of the fuselage resting on the ground.

A military jeep was approaching fast. Kat found the release on the pilot's door and climbed out, jumping to the ground in time to summon Pete Phu, the translator.

"Pete, this is very important. Whoever these guys are, explain to them what happened, that we were attacked, and the major . . . the pilot . . . was killed. Explain that the attackers got into a midair collision with us and damaged this helicopter. Do NOT, please, tell them that the attackers are from that Global Express over there, okay?"

He nodded. "No problem."

"If he wants us to go in somewhere and—I don't know, fill out reports or something bureaucratic, tell him we'll do so in an hour. Not now."

"You want to stand here on the ramp for an hour?"

"No. Tell them that's our airplane, the Global Express over there. We need to check out something onboard first."

A strange expression clouded Pete's face, but he nodded anyway and turned toward the occupant of the jeep, a Vietnamese Army captain. A certain amount of arm-waving and examination of the damaged Huey ensued, the captain looking at every bullet hole and the shattered window before speaking into his walkie-talkie.

"What's he saying?" Kat prompted.

"A lot of reports are needed," Pete said. "Government property has been damaged and the pilot is dead. But he wants to know who these people are." He motioned to the survivors.

"Tell him . . ." Kat hesitated, thinking fast. "They are survivors of the airline crash, and all are American citizens under my protection. Ask him if he needs to talk with the ambassador in Hanoi about this."

Pete grinned. "I don't think he will." He turned to relay her words, watching the eyebrows of the officer suddenly rise when offered the option of checking.

"No, no, no! You will all wait here. My colonel says everyone must wait here," he told Pete in Vietnamese.

"May they go over to check on their jet?" Pete asked the officer. "Remember, these are guests of our government in Hanoi. I don't think your colonel is going to want to get in trouble with Hanoi."

The captain thought for a second as he looked at the Global Express, then nodded. "Okay. But wait at the airplane."

As the exchange continued, Kat moved to Robert's side and motioned Dallas over, speaking quietly. "I'm going to go over to the Global Express and try to secure it. I don't know why it's open, and I don't know if they left anyone behind. Stay here, and if you see the landing lights blinking on and off, bring everyone and come get aboard. I've held off the local officials for a few minutes, but if we don't get in motion rapidly, we're going to get stuck here."

"Why?" Dallas asked.

"Somebody let those cutthroats park their jet undisturbed this morning and let them take a very expensive helicopter, and I'll bet you anything it was all without customs or immigration or diplomatic clearance. That means a lot of money changed hands, and the recipient's going to be very nervous right about now over all that's happened with the crash, and now this damaged chopper. He's very likely to do unpredictable and dangerous things, using his official position."

"Understood," Robert said, and Dallas nodded in agreement.

"Please bring my bag when you come," Kat added. "I'm going to . . . get something out of it now and leave the bag with you."

She moved into the Huey and retrieved a 9mm pistol

from the dead pilot. She opened her shoulder bag and rummaged quickly for the plastic flex cuffs she always carried, verifying she could pull them out quickly.

The short walk to the business jet was a circuitous affair. It was a Global Express, the latest of the rarified breed of multimillion-dollar business jets that could span almost seven thousand miles without refueling. It sat delicately on its tricycle landing gear, its wingtips turned up in fuel-saving winglets, a vision wholly out of place with the impoverished backwater that postwar Vietnam had become.

With the sun hanging low on the horizon and shining in her eyes, Kat circled casually off to one side and came up behind the aircraft, invisible to anyone inside. She walked the length of the fuselage just to the right of the belly, and slipped around and up the entry stairs as quietly as she could.

She stopped near the top of the stairs, hearing someone snoring rhythmically inside. Quickly glancing around the cockpit bulkhead, she spotted a Caucasian male in a white pilot's shirt snoozing in the right seat.

Kat took a deep breath to steady herself, checked behind her, then looked to the right, into the cabin. The interior was beautiful, empty, and typical of an executive jet. She could smell the aroma of rich leather from within.

Kat backed through the cabin, keeping her eye on the cockpit as she checked the bathroom and rear cabin. Both were empty. She slipped off her shoes, kept her gun at the ready, and moved forward again through the cabin and past the entry, stepping gingerly into the alcove just behind the cockpit. With a sudden movement, she leaned forward and jammed the barrel of her gun against the pilot's head with one hand while flipping out her leather ID wallet with the other.

"FBI! Freeze! DO NOT MOVE!"

The shouted command brought the wide-eyed pilot bolt upright, and his head crashed into the overhead panel. "Ow!" he said, trying to turn to his left, but freezing at the sound of the 9mm being cocked. His eyes finally found her, and he raised his hands to the ceiling. "Okay, okay! What is this, a joke?"

"On the ceiling! NOW! Put your palms flat against it!"

"What's this all about? Where are the others?"

"As if you didn't know, scum. You're under arrest for the murder of over two hundred civilians, among other things."

"Mur . . . *murders*? I'm just a corporate pilot!"

"Sure you are. Understand this clearly. This is a hair trigger and I have every incentive to blow your miserable brains out, so *please,* go ahead and give me an immediate reason. Go ahead. Flinch, try to move, say something smart-ass." He didn't move or speak. "All right," Kat continued, "you're going to keep both those hands touching the ceiling as you ooze slowly out of that seat and walk back here, kneel, and put your hands behind you."

"Yes, Ma'am!" he said forcefully, his head bobbing up and down. "*Please,* don't get trigger happy! What is this, a problem with rival factions in the Bureau?" The pilot was in his forties and extremely nervous. Sweat covered his brow, and his eyes were wide as he complied precisely with her orders.

Kat flex-cuffed the pilot and carefully frisked him, taking his wallet and leaving him facedown in the aisle as she moved forward and flashed the landing lights twice. She looked through the wallet quickly, memorizing the name on the various licenses.

"Is this jet fueled?" she asked.

"Yes, Ma'am."

"Range?"

"Ah . . . over six thousand miles."

"Where are you planning to take the others when they get back?"

He was trying to shake his head, rubbing his chin on the floor in the process. "I . . . don't know. The captain ordered me to put on a full load of fuel, coffee, and ice, and then stand by."

"You leave from Hong Kong last night?"

There was a long hesitation and Kat kicked him hard. "Answer the question."

"Ah . . . yes. I don't know if I'm supposed to tell you anything."

"You're going to tell me anything I ask. For instance, did you take off in front of a Meridian seven-forty-seven?"

"I don't recall."

Kat kicked him harder.

"Hey!"

"Remember, Pollis, if that's your real name, I've got the option of killing you right here, right now. The ACLU is six thousand miles away. They can't help you. You have three seconds to answer."

"Look . . . *yes.* Probably."

"And why did you turn off your transponder and fly in front of that jumbo?"

"Because I had a guy as mean as you ordering me to shut up while he did the flying. I couldn't figure out why he wanted to play chicken with a jumbo jet."

The answer stopped Kat. *Clever,* she thought. *Fiction writing under pressure.* "What are the names of the men you were with?"

"I . . . only know two of them. Arlin Schoen. He was the boss. The captain's name was Ben Laren."

"And the others?"

"Honest. I don't know the other names. Ma'am, why are you doing this? I'm on your side."

There were sounds outside and Kat turned to see Dallas and Robert helping the others up the stairs. She pointed to the prisoner and explained the situation. "Just step over him, and when we crank up, I'll need one of us to cover him."

"Excuse me," the pilot said.

"What?" Kat snapped.

"Are you qualified on this type of jet, Ma'am? Or do you have a pilot?"

"No. I'm it, and all I can fly are little Cessnas," Kat told him, watching the reaction. "This is going to be on-the-job training."

"Ah, look, if you're planning to . . . to . . . fly off with me on board, then let me help you do it right. I don't want to get shot, but I also don't want to die in a plane—"

A crushing blow from Dan Wade's right shoe slammed into the midsection of the man, causing him to gasp and cry out in pain. "WHAT? WHAT DID I DO?" he yelped, gasping.

Dan leaned down, following his voice, and yanked him halfway off the floor by his hair, speaking millimeters from the back of his head. "I'm the first officer of Meridian Flight Five, you fucking murderer! You and your henchmen killed my captain, you've probably blinded me for life, and you've murdered over two hundred passengers and crew members, some of them my dear friends. I want you to know that you're never going to reach a jail, because I'm going to dismember you alive."

The cuffed pilot was frantic, his eyes huge. "I DIDN'T KILL ANYONE! I was just hired to fly this trip, and then . . . they were doing something back there, I don't know what."

Dan let the pilot's head thud to the floor. "When we get airborne, I'm going to take a small knife and start removing your favorite body parts until we get the truth."

Dallas put a firm hand on Dan's arm and her mouth next to his ear. "Danny, I feel like killing him, too, but it's probably not the best of ideas to do it or even threaten it in front of the FBI, know what I mean? They make pretty devastatingly honest witnesses when you have to explain why someone ended up in a couple of plastic garbage bags."

Kat was studying the instrument panel as Robert leaned close to her. "You can only fly little Cessnas?"

She shook her head. "Actually, I'm typed . . . qualified . . . in Learjets and Cessna Citations, just not something this new and fancy."

He exhaled and smiled. "I was hoping you'd say something like that. I've seen quite enough on-the-job flight training for a lifetime."

chapter

28

There was a flurry of activity at the rear of the cabin. Dallas turned to look as Robert emerged from a curtained area with a large metal box.

"Look what I found!" he said. He set it on the floor and opened it, pulling out a heavy object that resembled a couple of diminutive scuba tanks with a telescopic sight on one side, along with a small liquid-crystal control panel. He turned it around, finding an aperture on one end, and a hand-grip on the other.

"What the heck *is* that?" Dallas asked.

"I don't know," Robert said as he moved to the prisoner to yank his head up, aiming the object's small aperture directly at his face. The man didn't flinch.

"What is this thing?" Robert asked.

"I honestly don't know," the pilot said.

"Then you don't mind if I fire it at you?"

"Hell, man," the pilot replied, "I'm apparently dead meat anyway. Frankly, I think you're all crazy as loons. First I get hired by the guys you apparently have a beef against, and now I've got the paranoid agents from hell. Do whatever you want. I've never even seen that thing before."

Kat had reappeared. "Do you normally fly captain or copilot, Pollis?"

"Uh, copilot. Right seat, but I'm a qualified captain on this bird."

Kat nodded as she pulled out a knife and cut the flex cuffs. "Well, now you're going to upgrade. And Mr. Mac-Cabe here is going to have a gun with orders to kill you if you so much as raise an eyebrow, understood?"

"Yes, Ma'am."

"Get up there in the left seat and get this machine started. Do NOT touch the radio, and do NOT put on a headset."

She repeated the instructions to Robert and passed him her 9mm pistol.

"Oh, and Pollis? Understand this. I can fly this thing if I have to without you, so don't think for a moment that you're indispensable."

"Ah, Agent?" Steve Delaney had been looking out the left windows.

"I'm Kat," she said.

He nodded. "Kat, some cars with armed soldiers are coming out there."

"What are they doing?" she asked.

"They're standing and pointing, and I think they're talking about us."

"Which means," Kat concluded, "at best we've only got a few minutes." She glanced at the others. "Buckle up. We're getting out of here."

Kat turned and moved to the entryway to say good-bye to Pete, who was waiting at the bottom of the stairs. She stowed the stairs and closed the door before moving into the cockpit. Pollis was already running the prestart checklist in the left seat as she slid into the right-hand copilot's seat and fastened her seat belt. He started the auxiliary power unit and clicked it on-line for electrical power, as he read the checklist items aloud and began starting the left engine.

Kat adjusted the headset she'd found on the copilot's side and checked the frequency for Da Nang Ground Control on the approach plate still clipped to the yoke. She dialed in the frequency and pushed the Transmit button on the control yoke. "Da Nang Ground, Global Express Two-Two-Zulu."

There was a short hesitation before a high, nasal voice came back, struggling with an approximation of English.

"Two-Two-Zulu," Kat began, speaking slowly, "must do an engine run for maintenance purposes. We will start engines and taxi to the end of the runway, then come back to this location. Roger?"

The controller's voice came back again, slightly more understandable. "Two-Two-Zulu . . . approve request . . . taxi runway. Running of engine okay."

"Roger," she said.

The left rear-mounted engine was at idle, the right one winding up.

"Pollis, soon as you can, head for the south end of the runway."

He nodded.

"Steve?" Kat yelled over her left shoulder. "Check the left side and see if those goons are still following us."

There was a small interlude of silence before Steve answered. "Yes. Three jeeps filled with men. Soldiers, I think."

The end of the runway was just ahead, and Kat checked to make sure the approach was clear of any landing aircraft before directing Pollis to taxi toward it, then quickly turn the Global Express 180 degrees to face the oncoming jeeps, all of which braked to a halt.

"Set your parking brake," Kat ordered. He complied quickly. "No," she countermanded, "push up the throttles and aim us directly at those vehicles until all three drivers have turned around."

The Global Express moved toward the jeeps and Kat watched with satisfaction as all three drivers turned quickly and raced off to a safer distance.

"All right, Pollis. Run your before-takeoff checks, then I want you to suddenly swing the bird around and taxi onto the runway in one fluid motion. Understand?"

He nodded as he worked his way through the list. "Are you ready?" he asked her.

"Go!" she ordered.

He pushed the throttles up and continued moving away from the runway for a few yards, waiting until the jeeps began moving away in the same direction.

"Is the runway clear over there to the right?" he asked.

"Yes," Kat answered, before Robert could look and reply. "Well, about halfway down, there's a fire truck sitting there on the taxiway, but he's not blocking."

Pollis swung the Global Express around.

"Here we go," Kat said as she punched the Transmit button. "Da Nang Ground, Two-Two-Zulu needs to go to the end of the runway again. Approved?"

"Roger," was the response.

With a rapid movement of her left hand, Kat gestured for Pollis to position the aircraft on the runway, watching carefully as he complied. "Okay. Takeoff power. Let's go," she said. "And remember, there's a gun to your head, Pollis."

The Global Express moved onto the runway and accelerated. Pollis reached over and engaged the automatic throttles, and Kat watched as both throttle levers moved smoothly to the maximum thrust position.

"The jeeps are moving, Kat. On your left. They're going to try to get in front of us," Robert said. "That fire truck way up there is moving in, too!"

"Let's go," Kat ordered. They began to accelerate down the runway.

"These bastards are liable to shoot," Pollis said, worry tingeing his voice.

Kat glanced at the airspeed depiction on the glass cockpit's electronic flight panel. They were above a hundred knots, accelerating toward the rotate speed of 135.

"The jeeps have chickened out, Kat," Robert reported.

"Is anyone shooting?" she asked.

"Not yet," Robert said, as he strained to see out the pilot's side window.

One hundred ten! she told herself, watching the large fire truck pick up speed as it raced toward the next taxiway intersecting the runway.

"He's going to beat us there!" Pollis said.

The Global Express was accelerating, but not fast

enough. The fire truck was clearly moving from left to right in their perspective, meaning he would reach the center of the runway before they arrived at the same spot.

One twenty.

"Ah, Kat . . ." Robert began.

"I'd better abort," Pollis said, stunned when Kat's hand firmly covered his right hand on the throttles to prevent his pulling them back.

"Don't even think about it," she ordered. "Steady on!" Kat's concentration shifted to the airspeed and how fast it was rising.

"I'm not kidding, Agent . . . we're not gonna make it!"

"KEEP GOING!" she yelled.

The fire truck was at the entrance to the runway, moving at perhaps thirty miles per hour, when the forward door flew open and the driver jumped to the tarmac, leaving enough momentum for the truck to roll to the center on its own.

"Kat . . . KAT . . . !" Robert's voice was rising in pitch and volume.

The truck was less than 2,000 feet ahead, moving slower now, but still in their path, no matter how hard she might try to steer to the right.

"WE'RE NOT GONNA MAKE IT!" Pollis called out in genuine alarm.

"Yes we will. STEADY! I'll call your rotate!" she barked *One thirty. That's enough.* "OKAY, ROTATE NOW!"

Pollis pulled back smartly on the yoke and the jet's nose rose rapidly through ten degrees up, but the main wheels remained on the runway.

The truck was directly in front of them, less than 500 feet away, with the Global Express moving toward it at 222 feet per second. Kat grabbed the yoke on the right side and pulled the nose up sharply until the heavily loaded jet leapt from the surface and began to climb. Simultaneously she reached for the gear lever and snapped it to the Up position.

The fire truck disappeared beneath the raised nose of the business jet as it sped upward. The main wheels retracted sideways into the belly and reached a forty-five-degree angle at the moment the Global Express flashed over the fire truck.

The partially retracted main tires cleared the top of the machine by less than a foot. The underside of the tail, however, clipped the top of the truck a glancing blow, creating an incredible metallic thud that reverberated through the fuselage and scared everyone into silence.

Pollis's voice rang out as they pitched up to more than twenty-five degrees. "Whoa! Too much pitch!" He pushed forward on the yoke, lowering the pitch angle. "We only want about eighteen degrees," he explained. With the pitch angle under control, Kat felt herself begin to breathe again. The jet settled into a rapid climb, the airspeed sitting at a safe 180 knots.

"We hit it, didn't we?" Robert asked in a strained voice.

Kat nodded. "We touched it, but everything looks normal and feels normal."

"Except my heart rate," Robert added.

"Flaps up," the copilot said.

"Flaps up," Kat repeated, her hand shaking slightly as she reached to the center pedestal and raised the flap lever to the fully retracted position.

"Okay, break to the right, Pollis. Right around that hill. Keep it fast and low."

He banked the jet tightly to the right, flying just north of the hill to the east and keeping the climb rate to a minimum as they picked up speed. At 300 knots he pulled back and began a shallow climb.

"Where's the transponder?" Kat asked.

"There," Pollis replied, pointing to the control head. "You want it on?"

"No, I want to make sure it's off." She reached out to make certain the switch was in the right position. "Okay, Pollis. You're going to talk me through this as you set up the navigation system to go direct to Guam, understood?"

"Whatever you say, Ma'am. But do you really want to do this without an air traffic control clearance? Some countries get really nasty about that sort of thing."

She gave him an acidic glance. "When I want your opinion on my strategy, I'll ask for it," Kat snapped. "Meantime, do precisely what I order you to do."

He looked over at her. "I know this probably cuts no mustard with you, Agent, but would you *please* consider that I might be telling the truth? I was just hired to fly copilot for this trip, and I honest-to-God had no idea what they were doing. I don't even know where they leased this airplane, since I doubt the Bureau owns it."

Kat shot him a puzzled glance. "What are you talking about, 'the Bureau'?"

"FBI."

"*What?*" Kat asked, cocking her head with a pained expression.

"You're an FBI agent, just like them, right?"

Kat shook her head as if to clear the confusion. She could see Robert leaning forward in the jump seat to look at Pollis's face. "All right, Pollis," she said. "Are you attempting to tell me that the people who hired you to fly this aircraft represented themselves to be FBI agents?"

"You mean they weren't?" he said, with an expression of pure shock.

This guy is a really good actor! Kat thought. His eyes were now huge, and his voice shook slightly.

"I . . . Ma'am, they told me they were FBI agents. They had IDs just like yours."

Robert MacCabe's left hand lashed out to grab Pollis's collar, getting a tight grip on it as Pollis fought to keep the aircraft steady. "Hey! You want me to lose control?"

"How long," Robert began, snarling his words, "have you been working on that stupid story?" He aped a whining, high-pitched voice: "If I'm caught, I'll just pretend I was hired by the FBI."

"It's the truth!" Pollis replied. "Every time I asked what they were doing, the head guy would warn me that I was interfering with a federal operation."

Robert tightened his grip and shook Pollis hard. "Now what's the *real* story, bastard? Who're you really working for?"

"I told you. *I* thought they were FBI. But they *weren't* federal agents?"

Kat's eyes were on the instruments and outside the aircraft, searching the sky ahead. She knew his ploy didn't justify a response, but she couldn't help herself. "Whatever you might think, Pollis, and whoever you really are, the fact is, FBI agents do not run around the world like CIA covert operatives destabilizing governments, and we don't shoot down jumbo jets."

chapter
29

Jake Rhoades had slept no more than two hours on his office couch when he was jolted awake from a deep REM sleep by a call from Kat Bronsky.

"I hate to ask where in the holy hell you've been," Jake said, trying to adjust his eyes to the ceiling light his assistant had flipped on, "but where in the holy hell have you been?"

"Where do you *think,* Jake? Taking a city tour of Hanoi?" she asked, sounding slightly hurt.

"I've just been worried," Jake replied. "It's been hours. What's your status?"

"A lot of missions accomplished, Boss. In a nutshell, we picked up the five survivors, including Mr. MacCabe and the copilot, and in the process we were fired on by the same people, I believe, who flew the Global Express into Da Nang."

"So where are you now?" Jake asked.

"Flying the same Global Express *out* of Da Nang. We've left Vietnam."

Jake transferred the receiver to his other ear. "You're *what*?"

"There's a lot to tell, Jake." She gave him the details of the rescue and the ambush. "Our Vietnamese helicopter pilot was killed before we lifted off, and then we ended up in a midair collision with the attackers' helicopter."

"How'd *that* happen?" Jake asked.

"I made a mistake and hit him."

"You . . . hit him? *You* were flying the helicopter? How?"

"We were fresh out of pilots at the time, and it was raining bullets."

"Kat, I didn't know you could fly helicopters."

"Neither did I. Funny what you can do when someone's hosing you down with assault rifles."

"I know you're a pilot, but . . ."

"Actually, I had a couple of hours of helicopter instruction last year. Anyway, the group that was trying to kill us gave chase and kept shooting at us until we collided and they crashed. We don't think there were any survivors."

"So naturally . . . you flew to Da Nang and took their aircraft."

"Correct. Global Express November-Two-Two-Zulu, or at least the bogus version. That's where I'm calling you from now. But there's more."

"I was afraid of that," Jake replied, rubbing his forehead.

"They left a pilot behind. I arrested him and have him in custody. Actually, he's flying this aircraft for us under guard, and I've left him in the cockpit with one of our survivors holding a gun on him." She passed on the names of the prisoner and the two men he'd identified.

"Your . . . prisoner is flying the airplane? No, wait. Don't explain."

"It's complicated," she said. "He's told us nothing useful yet besides those two names. You also need to know that I elected to leave Da Nang without authorization or takeoff clearance, which may cause diplomatic problems, and our current status is that we're in flight in the Global Express headed for Anderson Air Force Base on Guam, where I'm going to need all sorts of coordination."

Jake had started taking notes furiously. "You've been a busy lady," he said, plopping in his desk chair. "I'm ecstatic you found and rescued the survivors, but I can't believe you took that jet!"

"Hey, Boss, I'm a federal law enforcement officer recovering stolen property."

He thought for a second before answering. "Yeah, you're right."

She told him about the copilot's assertion that he believed himself to be working for the FBI.

"That's absurd!" Jake responded.

"I know it's absurd, but he claims they represented themselves as FBI, and frankly, I don't know whether to believe him or not." She relayed the numbers on Pollis's passport, pilot's license, and driver's license. "The pictures on those IDs match his face," Kat said, "for what that's worth, but I want to turn him over to our people in Guam, I want him charged with enough counts of murder to hold him through the next Ice Age, and I want to protect him from any cleanup assassins."

"We can handle all that, I think. Hold on a second." Two other agents had been sitting in Jake's office. He motioned them over to the desk and ripped off the sheet of yellow legal pad on which he'd been writing. "Run a full ID cross-check, and get FAA out of bed in Oklahoma City to do a complete check on this guy's record as a pilot. Then get me our Senior Resident Agent on Guam."

Jake put the receiver back to his ear. "By the way, Kat, we matched up the serial number on that jet you're flying."

"Oh? And from whom was it appropriated? Is this Warren Buffet's personal jet, or does it belong to Ross Perot?"

"Close. It's brand-new, and belongs to a corporation in Dallas. It was in San Antonio for some custom electronics work but disappeared eight days ago. The company in San Antonio thought the owner had taken it early. They're all a bit upset. The aircraft is worth over forty million."

"Good grief! Well, it *is* pretty." Kat's voice became low and serious. "Jake, we found something here on this jet that may be a key to the whole mystery"

"What is it?"

"I don't know exactly what it is, but let me describe it." She gave Jake a detailed rundown of the odd-looking device.

"Two small tanks, you say?" he replied. "Any idea what they contain?"

"Not a clue, but there is definitely an aperture in the front and a telescopic sight, so this fires something, and since there are no unusual openings on this bird, it has to be fired through the window. You said the Air Force was voting for a phosphorous warhead on a missile guided by some sort of laser target designator?"

"That's right."

"My best guess is we've found a target designator, the thing that puts a laser mark on a target so a missile can find it. I've never seen one, but it fits."

"How about identification plates?"

Kat sighed. "No names, but a lot of numbers and some cryptic instructions."

"What language?"

"You sure you want to know? How secure can we consider this satellite phone line?" Kat asked.

"It's digital," he replied, "but it's commercial and not encrypted. Nothing classified should be discussed."

"I was afraid you were going to say that. Okay. I'll just tell you this. There are markings on this contraption, but a *much* higher pay grade than you or I is going to have to decide what the implications are."

"Go ahead and tell me, Kat. Time is too critical."

"Okay. The markings are in English, Jake. Whatever this thing is, it looks American, and it looks military, and it looks like a sophisticated piece of equipment, not some one-of-a-kind backroom zip gun."

There was a long sigh from Washington. "I was afraid of that."

"We still don't know where the missile came from, but the copilot confirms the explosion could indeed have been phosphorous. And one last point before I let you go. I can tell you that this organization, whoever they are, are slick and well-financed and very determined. Can I prove all that in a court of law? No. Not yet. Some of this is intuition and extrapolation, but unless they've surfaced with demands, I'd say we're going to lose more airliners before this is over. Somehow we've got to find out the rest of the equation, like where they're getting the missiles and whether that's what happened to SeaAir."

"The NTSB doesn't think so, Kat. They feel SeaAir couldn't be the same kind of blinding scenario, and they know from the wreckage it wasn't actually downed by a direct hit from a missile."

"Well, maybe they're varying their tactics, but whatever this organization wants, they haven't achieved it yet, or they wouldn't be so incredibly desperate to turn off a potential leak like Robert MacCabe."

"Understood."

"Jake, maybe the Air Force could scramble an SR-seventy-one to Anderson Air Force Base to take this thing we found back for analysis. That's the reason for Guam."

"Got it."

"Oh, and one other thing. Could you have one of our people check with the NTSB's investigator in charge of the SeaAir accident and track down whether or not enough of the pilots' bodies were recovered to analyze the condition of their retinas."

"Their what?"

"I'm no doctor, but maybe it's possible to find out whether the pilots' retinas show any evidence of damage. In other words, can they find any evidence of flash trauma to their eyes. If so, that would conclusively tie these two accidents together."

Kat disconnected and folded the antenna of the satellite phone after passing on to Jake an estimated arrival time and arranging for an ophthalmologist to meet Dan Wade on arrival. She returned to the cockpit and slid past Robert into the right seat.

They were level at 42,000 feet, flying an odd and unauthorized altitude in order to stay clear of any other air traffic. "We're probably invisible to all but satellite surveillance right now, because our transponder is off," she'd explained to Robert out of Pollis's earshot. "Dan told me how to do it.

At worst, we're a phantom target that keeps appearing and disappearing on various radar scopes."

She scanned the instrument panel and the electronic flight information system screen, which showed their heading, planned route, and destination, and rechecked the fuel. They had more than enough fuel to make Guam and Anderson Air Force Base, and even enough to make Honolulu, but the West Coast of the U.S. was out of range.

Dallas had come forward twenty minutes before to fill Kat in on the details of what had happened in the cockpit of Meridian 5, as well as the murder of Susan Tash, and the gut-wrenching loss of Britta Franz, whom Kat remembered.

Suddenly, an electronic chirping began somewhere in the cabin, and Dallas came back up.

"'Scuse me, Kat, but there's a telephone ringing back here, and we're sort of wondering whether you want to answer it, considering the fact this isn't our airplane."

"How far back?"

"Midcabin. You want me to . . . sit down with Robert and watch things up here while you get it?" Dallas asked, feeling her stomach turn over at the thought of repeating the odyssey she'd been through in the cockpit of Meridian 5.

"Are you okay with that, after what . . . you know."

Dallas smiled and nodded. "I'm totally numb. But I'll be okay as long as you don't bail out."

Kat hesitated less than a second before unsnapping her seat belt, wondering whether the phone would keep ringing until she got there.

She recognized the airborne satellite phone as one of the best on the market. The number could be dialed from anywhere in the world, but at considerable expense. Kat reached for the receiver and hesitated, calculating how to handle whomever she encountered on the other end. It could be the real owners, or Jake, or even a wrong number, she thought as she picked it up.

"Yes?"

"Here today, Guam tomorrow, eh, Agent Bronsky?" The

voice in her ear was masculine, toxic, and chilling, and the words came at the laconic pace of a death sentence: slow, threatening, and final.

"Who is this?" she asked, trying to sound in command.

"Shall we say, someone who is not appreciative of your sophomoric interference? Or, perhaps, someone who is looking forward to evening the score?"

"Who is this? What do you want?" Kat asked as calmly as possible, his venomous presence and unruffled, emotionless tone sending chills up her spine.

Unhurried and deliberate, the man on the other end hung up the receiver very slowly, the sound of squeaking leather filling her ear as if he had leaned forward in a plush chair, being careful to slowly position the receiver in its cradle— the performance of someone in total control and sending a clear message.

Kat replaced the receiver and looked up to find Robert MacCabe standing beside her, his eyes questioning what had happened. She pulled her hand back to hide the fact that it was shaking, and smiled at him.

"I guess the mastermind doesn't appreciate our breaking up his plans."

"What'd he say, Kat? Was it a he?"

She nodded. "Oh, yeah! Smoothest, scariest voice I think I've ever heard."

"What did he say?" Robert asked again.

"He's rather ticked and letting me know we're dead meat if we land in Guam."

"He knows we're headed to *Guam*?"

Kat nodded. "Yeah. He used a pun: Here today, Guam tomorrow."

"How could he know we're headed there?" Robert asked, his eyebrows flaring.

Kat felt her head spinning slightly. *How indeed?* She hadn't made the decision where to go until after takeoff. She hadn't even thought about it. She snapped her eyes toward the cockpit. "Who's watching the prisoner?"

"Dallas. But I've got your gun."

"Pollis has been under observation every second, right?"

Robert nodded. "Absolutely. I was watching him, now Dallas is watching him. I know what you're thinking, but there's no way he could have communicated."

"Then it's pure logic."

"What?"

"The nearest purely American facility to Vietnam these days is Guam. He was guessing, and I don't know whether I inadvertently confirmed it or not."

"But we're headed to an Air Force base, right? How could they infiltrate a base that fast?"

Kat was shaking her head. "I don't know, but they simply can't be everywhere. If there's any chance there's really a threat in Guam, we can't go there."

"Where, then?"

"Oh, shit, Robert!" Kat's arms dropped as she sat back and rolled her eyes.

"What?"

"My satellite call to Jake was intercepted. That's got to be the explanation!"

"You mentioned Guam?"

"Anderson AFB, everything. Lord. That *has* to be how he knows."

"How could they know you have a satellite phone?"

She sat on the armrest of a plush swiveling chair, stroking her chin in thought, vaguely aware of young Steve Delaney in an adjacent seat as he punched up song after song on the sophisticated flight entertainment system.

"No," Kat said, almost under her breath. "That can't be right. My phone is digital, and even though we don't consider them secure, they're extremely hard to intercept, especially with the new satellite network I'm using."

"Then we're back to logic? He figured it out on his own?"

Kat looked up at Robert and thought of another chilling possibility she didn't want to discuss with him or anyone: the potential for a leak at FBI headquarters.

She got to her feet and headed back to the cockpit, waving Dallas back down when she started to get out of the right seat. "Not yet, Dallas."

"Kat, by the way," Dallas said, "they've got a galley with

food and water and Cokes and coffee on this baby. We all
needed to eat something. When you're ready to get back in
up here, can I bring you a snack?"

"A bit later, yeah," Kat said with a slight smile. She
looked over at Pollis. "Can you ask this flight computer
questions about the distance to another location without
causing a change in course?"

"Sure," he replied. "What do you want to see?"

She hesitated a second, wondering if he could find a way
to communicate any change in destination to his employers.
Not if we watch him like a hawk, she concluded. "Program in
direct to Los Angeles," she ordered.

"Ah, that's much too far." Pollis punched the appropriate
buttons and waited for the result. "There," he said. "We're six
thousand, two hundred fourteen miles, which would be about
thirteen hours, depending on winds. We can't make it."

"Try direct Seattle."

Once again he complied, getting a slightly better, but still
impossible result.

"Erase that and punch in direct Honolulu," she said.

The result was under 5,000 miles distance remaining. *Ten
hours. And we have twelve hours of fuel.* "Okay, Pollis. Exe-
cute that flight plan direct Honolulu."

Kat watched as the new destination entered the computer's official flight plan. The airplane made a subtle turn as
the autopilot altered course to accommodate the change.
They were now headed on a direct, great circle course to
Honolulu International Airport.

"Dallas, I'll be right back. Make absolutely certain he
doesn't touch a radio or type anything on any keyboard."

"You got it," Dallas replied.

Kat returned to the cabin and sat by one of the windows,
enjoying the feel and smell of the soft leather seat. A minute
later, she unfolded her satellite phone and began punching in
the after-hours number that would connect her directly to
Jordan James.

chapter

30

"Kat? Wake up. It's Robert," a voice said somewhere just beyond the fog surrounding her head.

"What?" Kat opened her eyes, blinking at the brightness of the sun glinting off the Pacific Ocean some 42,000 feet below. She tried to reconcile the ringing sound with Robert MacCabe's presence in the cockpit.

"Your phone's ringing, Kat," he said, inches from her right ear.

She had dozed off in the right seat, for how long she wasn't sure. She sat up with a start, her eyes going to the distance-remaining numbers on the face of the flight computer.

Calm down! she told herself. *We're still three hundred miles out.*

Pollis was still in position in the left seat, watching her passively.

Kat turned to Robert. "Have you been here all along? Has somebody . . ."

He nodded. "Someone's watched this guy every second, Kat."

She unfolded the antenna on the portable phone and punched the button. "Hello?"

"Agent Bronsky?" a male voice asked.

"Right here. Who's this?"

"This is your contact at CIA headquarters at Langley, calling on behalf of your superior, who wants to avoid direct contact for the reason you worried about earlier."

Kat felt a chill ripple through her that Jake felt a breach of security at the Bureau was a possibility. Jordan James had been skeptical about a leak, but had agreed nearly nine hours ago to find a safe back-channel to Jake Rhoades's ear. Obviously Uncle Jordan had done what he promised, as usual.

"Okay, I understand. Is he satisfied that *this* channel is not compromised?"

"He is, but he thinks a plumber is needed at his home location."

"I'm . . . very sorry to hear that," Kat said. "What do you have for me?"

"On arrival at Honolulu, taxi directly to the corporate fixed-base operation. The Bureau's team will meet you there."

"They have a replacement pilot for us?"

"No. You and the others are to be transferred under assumed names to a commercial flight to D.C. Arrangements have been made to get the item you found aboard that aircraft to the appropriate location on a special Air Force flight."

"Why can't we just go on the same flight? Why go commercial?" Kat asked, sitting up and rubbing her left eye.

"That, ah, type of aircraft can't carry passengers."

Kat nodded to herself, envisioning the very thing she'd suggested, an SR-71, capable of streaking from Honolulu to Washington in approximately two hours, or anywhere else in the continental U.S. with the same lightning speed.

The underwire in Kat's bra had been progressively digging in to one of her ribs for the past several minutes, and it was getting close to intolerable, but there was no way she could discreetly adjust it with Robert MacCabe standing so close beside her. "Look," she said, rolling her shoulders in a wheel-like motion to try to relieve the pressure, "I'm really concerned about the commercial idea. My entire group is a target, especially myself and one other. I do not want another commercial flight placed at risk of attack because of our presence."

"That's all been handled, Agent Bronsky," the CIA contact said. "Your presence on the appropriate flight will be known only to us."

"It still worries me. Please relay . . . to my superior . . . that I'd like him to think that over."

"I will, but do not, repeat, do not attempt to call him directly. Understood?"

"Yes, Sir. That's clear enough. Is the home leak caused by an electronic problem, or a human problem?"

"I can't say, Agent. I don't have that information."

"Give me a number for you in case I need it."

He passed a phone number routed through the main Langley switchboard, but cautioned her to use it in an emergency only. She recognized the exchange.

Kat shifted the phone, looking back and smiling briefly at MacCabe. "Also, confirm that an ophthalmologist will meet us on arrival?"

"That's correct."

"And has anyone arranged our entry into Hawaiian airspace?" she asked.

"I was coming to that. Your transponder code is four, six, six, five. Your call sign is Sage-sixteen. Call Honolulu Center two hundred miles out." He passed the correct frequency and ended the conversation, leaving Kat agitated. She folded the antenna and checked the mileage remaining. *Two hundred eighty miles.*

Kat looked over at Pollis. "Got a pencil?"

He nodded.

"Then write this down." She passed the same information to him on transponder code and frequency.

"Where's Dallas?" Kat asked.

Robert disappeared, returning a bit later with Dallas to trade places with Kat.

Kat and Robert moved into the cabin, out of earshot of Bill Pollis.

"So," Robert began, "not that I was listening, but I missed some of that."

Kat filled in the blanks in the conversation. "Apparently I was right, Robert. There was a leak in D.C. That's how they knew we were headed to Guam."

"But we're okay now?"

She nodded and sighed. "I think so. That was a CIA contact relaying for Jake, my boss. This operation should be secure."

"But they're putting us on another commercial flight. Why?"

"I don't know, and I don't like it," she said. "They're not thinking it through."

"Kat, we're targets. At least, I'm a target, and after that spooky phone call last night to the sky phone, I'd say putting any one of us on a commercial flight is a dangerous idea. I am *not* comfortable with that idea."

She could see his agitation increasing and raised her hand to stop him. "Neither am I, Robert. But we'll work on it when we get in. I just want to get that weapon on the way to wherever, and get Pollis placed in high-security custody." She inclined her head toward the cockpit. "Mr. Innocent up there is sticking to his act, which is helpful. As long as he tries to convince us he's a good guy, he'll behave. He's hoping we'll eventually think he's the victim."

Robert looked out an adjacent window. "How much longer?"

"About thirty minutes, I think, before we should start descending."

Robert stood with one hand on a bulkhead for balance, very close to Kat, and looked at her quizzically.

"What?" she said gently.

"I was just thinking how much both of us have been through in the past, what, twenty-four hours?"

"More than that," she said.

"Not much more. Seems like a year ago that we were standing and talking in Hong Kong about that Cuban crash and my deceased friend Walter Carnegie."

She shook her head. "Well, it's about over, Robert. One way or another, we'll get our survivors back there debriefed and returned home, then you and I will need to sit down somewhere and go over every nuance of what you have, what you think it means, and where you think the Bureau can find what we need to find out. I . . . assume I can depend on your cooperation, and that you'll hold off publishing for a few days?"

He looked at her with a hurt expression. "I came to *you* for help, remember?"

She smiled and patted his arm. "Just . . . call it protocol. I don't like to make glib assumptions."

"Don't you think that thing we found is going to answer a lot of questions?"

"I hope so, but it's still worrying the heck out of me. If that is a target illuminator, or—what's the word they used?—designator, there's got to be a boat or a plane or something from which to fire the missile it's supposed to guide."

"Why is that bothering you?" Robert asked. "Because of the coordination required to get a missile into position in Hong Kong?"

She nodded. "Robert, how long had you had that return Meridian reservation?"

He thought for a few seconds. "I'd changed my reservation. Originally, I was on a return flight the next day."

"I thought I remembered that. So, if we assume they were after you, they had to change everything to intercept the new flight."

"But what if they weren't after me?"

Kat nibbled her lip in thought before shaking her head. "No. Too coincidental. They've done too much to try to find you personally, as far as I can tell."

"Okay," Robert began, "but I guess I'm still not tracking what's concerning you about that target designator laser, if that's what it is."

"How heavy would you say that thing is?" she asked.

"Maybe thirty-five pounds. Pretty hefty."

"Five feet long? And thirty inches around, including the two tanklike things?"

"Yeah. It almost looks like one of those water rifles for kids, with two water tanks on top of the barrel, plus the electronics that are obviously part of it."

"That's a lot for a simple infrared laser, don't you think? I mean, laser pens used in lectures can fit in your pocket. What if it's something more, Robert? What if there's no missile, just that thing?"

"*That* thing?" He looked back in the cabin as she continued.

"Other than a phosphorous explosion, how could you flash-blind a human in a cockpit in flight? What kind of technology?"

Robert shook his head with his right hand out palm-up. "I don't know . . . maybe some sort of particle accelerator? You know, like they were trying to develop for the Reagan Star Wars missile defense system. Fires a powerful stream of subatomic particles at an incoming missile."

"I'm thinking of something even more simple," Kat said. "Why use an expensive missile in a difficult-to-achieve flight path? Why not just use a powerful shoulder-mounted laser gun and do the job directly?"

Robert inhaled sharply and glanced toward the back of the cabin. "Of course. Why didn't we think of that earlier?"

"Because we've been busy, and because Washington's talking missiles."

Robert MacCabe was nodding energetically. "This could easily be what brought SeaAir down, too."

"If so, there's a radar record of another airplane nearby. Could be this one."

"That would open up an entirely new method of terror attacks, Kat!"

"And what if it's made in America?" she continued. "What if someone's stolen one of our military projects and started using it on us? I mean, I have no clue what they want, whoever 'they' are. Is this a strike against the Great Satan, as the criminal government in Iran calls us? Is this some sort of privateer group with the grandiose scheme of a James Bond villain trying to blackmail the world?"

"In other words," Robert said, "are we going to get a note after the next six accidents demanding a billion dollars if we want the crashes to stop?"

"Something like that. But my God, Robert, if this is an American laser now being used to destroy human eyesight . . ."

"Did you get a chance to question Pollis?"

"Yes," she replied. "Several hours ago, while you were asleep."

"Did you get anything useful?"

Kat shrugged. "If he's lying and playacting, then anything he told me was for the purpose of throwing us off the right trail. If he's telling the truth, then he amounts to no more than an involved observer. He says the leader, Schoen, spoke with a heavy accent, and he suspected the man was CIA instead of FBI, as he claimed. He said they simply didn't tell him what they were up to. He claims he didn't know your flight had crashed, and that he had no idea they were shooting anything out the window."

"Remember the old conundrum, that if everything I say is a lie, then I'm lying when I say that I never tell the truth, which means that sometimes what I say is true?"

"I'm too weary to figure that one out, Robert."

"It fits him. We can't trust a word he says."

"I know it."

With Kat back in the right seat, Dallas returned to the rear section of the elegant cabin, where Steve and Dan were sitting with Graham. She plopped down on the leather sofa next to Graham and reached for his hand. He responded slowly, trying to smile as he fixed her with a haunted look of utter despair.

"I, ah . . . want to ask how you're doing, Doc, but . . . I know the answer," she said softly. "It just . . . takes time, you know?"

His eyes dropped again to the floor.

Steve Delaney had moved to sit beside her. "Dallas? How much longer?"

"Not long. Then we change planes in Honolulu."

"I want to call my mother. D'you think Kat will let me?"

Dallas shook her head. "Stevie, we're still number one

on somebody's people-we'd-most-like-to-kill list."

"Just a quick call from a pay phone. Collect, even."

"Not without Kat's approval, Steve. You gotta trust her."

She saw him nod, and knew full well he was going to try it anyway.

chapter

31

The sleek new Global Express settled effortlessly onto Honolulu International's Runway 8 Left and slowed as Pollis taxied clear of the runway to a ramp crowded with other corporate jets. Ramp attendants guided them close to where three official-looking black sedans and five dark-suited men were waiting.

Kat waited for Pollis to finish the shutdown check before pulling out another pair of flex cuffs and resecuring him. "If you're telling me the truth, Pollis, your cooperation will go a long way to vindicating you. If you've misled me, God have mercy on you. No one else will."

"It was the truth, Ma'am. I hope you catch them."

She got out of the seat to open the door to a balmy wave of Hawaiian breeze and the fragrance of bougainvillea. One of the men was waiting at the bottom of the steps with his credential case open, the light splayed on his face through the moving branches of a palm tree.

"Agent Bronsky? I'm Agent Rick Hawkins, Honolulu office. These are Agents Walz, Moncrief, and Williams."

She shook Hawkins's hand as she studied his face. In his

late thirties, she figured. A strikingly handsome black man with a smile that reminded her of a dear friend in college. Rick Hawkins was just under six feet with a muscular physique and a cultured voice and she smiled at him in spite of herself. He motioned in the direction of the cabin.

"I understand you have a prisoner for us?" he asked.

Kat sighed and brushed back her hair with her right hand, while her left hand stayed within her handbag to quietly slide the safety in place on the 9mm pistol.

"Yes. Identifies himself as one Bill Pollis. We need to hold him on suspicion of grand theft for being in possession of a stolen aircraft of U.S. registry transported across state and international boundaries, and over two hundred counts of first-degree aggravated murder, and if that's not enough, I'll come up with some more."

Hawkins smiled and grunted agreement. "I doubt he'll be going anywhere for a long, long time."

"You'll find the scum flex-cuffed in the cockpit," she said. "But first, let's get our Meridian pilot to the doctor."

"He's waiting inside," Agent Hawkins told her.

As soon as Dan Wade had come down the stairs to be escorted to the private jet terminal's comfortable lounge, two of the other agents scrambled up to retrieve Pollis. Rick Hawkins stepped closer to Kat and lowered his voice. "And I'm told there's a very important item that needs to go express back to the mainland, correct?"

Kat nodded. "In the back. In a metal case. Top security, top secret, top everything. Lose this, don't bother coming back. That level of security."

"Understood," he said.

The agents marched Pollis down the stairs. He tried to catch Kat's eye, but she ignored him and turned as Graham, Dallas, Robert, and Steve emerged.

"Wait for me in the terminal over there, okay?" Kat said.

Robert hesitated while the others nodded, but Kat flashed him a no-nonsense look accompanied by a toss of her head toward the door.

Hawkins adjusted his aviator glasses and smiled broadly, obviously in love with the image he cut. He turned and motioned another agent into the cabin to retrieve the weapon case, then inclined his head toward the main commercial airport building visible in the distance across the runway. "We've got an office in the terminal cleared out, a safe area where you can wait to board your flight. We have it worked out so you won't be seen when you board. The flight leaves in about four hours. We have your tickets, and full security."

"I want a favor, Agent Hawkins."

"Rick, please."

"Okay, Rick. I appreciate all the arrangements, but if there's an Air Force flight going back, I'd much rather we be on that. The people we're dealing with are ruthless killers, and I do not want to imperil another airliner."

"I understand. Ruthless killers, huh?" He shook his head, looking dismayed. "I do have my orders, but I'll see what I can do." He leaned closer and touched her arm. "Agent Bronsky, this is very important. You are not to try to call anyone while on the ground here. That order is a security item and comes directly from Assistant Deputy Director Rhoades. Complete blackout. That means your satellite phone, too."

"I understand."

"They hammered that one into me," he said, smiling, then let his expression return to seriousness. "I understand these people have been through hell."

She related the basics of the crash and the rescue under fire, but stopped short of discussing the details of her suspicions, or the device they'd found.

"We should go inside," he said, motioning toward the lounge.

"I agree. I want to see how Dan Wade is doing."

"Can I ask you an off-the-record question?" Hawkins asked.

"You can ask," Kat said with a chuckle.

"Did you find any evidence that the SeaAir Cuban crash and this thing in Vietnam had the same cause? I assume you're on that case, too."

Kat drew a deep breath, thinking over the evidence, and momentarily stepped away from her normal caution about discussing potentially sensitive details. "Well . . . that's a very good question, but I'm going to let the higher pay grades in our esteemed Bureau make that determination, if you don't mind."

"Okay. Sure," he said, shrugging. He reached out to open and hold the door for her, then looked startled, like he'd been caught doing something wrong. "I'm sorry, I wasn't trying to be sexist."

Kat cocked her head and smiled as she patted his shoulder. "Don't ever apologize for being a gentleman, Rick."

He smiled in return and followed her in.

The ophthalmologist had examined Dan in a darkened inner office. He emerged about the time Kat walked in, and sat with her to explain. "He's got a chance for at least some vision to return. The receptors—the cones and rods on the retina—have been damaged, but they have not been eradicated. He can see light, but he needs that bandage and he simply needs time. If you're heading back to D.C., I'd suggest Johns Hopkins, but most of this is the body repairing itself."

"Thanks, Doctor."

"I was sorry to hear about your captain."

"Doctor, how could a beam of light or energy kill a man through his eyes?"

The doctor shook his head and shrugged his shoulders. "I don't know, unless it was so powerful it burned through the back of the eyeballs and caused a massive hemorrhage. Or the trauma of the pain could have caused a heart attack."

"Could a laser do that? A very, very powerful one?"

He hesitated and studied her before shrugging again. "Maybe."

"How about a particle beam?"

The doctor smiled and rolled his eyes at the ceiling. "Look, I'm not technically oriented outside of medicine. You're way over my head with *Star Wars* stuff like particle beams. Lasers, though? We use them now for cosmetic purposes, to burn off skin one layer at a time, and to cauterize small blood vessels. Could a really powerful laser do extreme eye damage? Absolutely. Could it kill? I don't know."

chapter

32

The trip from the private jet facility to the main passenger terminal took only five minutes, but the convoluted entry into the building, up a loading dock and back stairway, took longer. With Hawkins in the lead, Kat and Robert escorted Dallas, Steve, Graham, and Dan to the airport office arranged for them, a modest room with several metal desks and a sweeping view of the boarding ramps and central concourse. Sandwiches were brought in, but for two hours they cooled their heels with periodic visits from Hawkins and strict instructions ringing in their ears to call no one. Repeated requests to get them to a shower facility had gone unfulfilled, and despite their best attempts at grooming and rinsing out clothes on the way from Vietnam, the entire group looked bedraggled.

"We're having a group bad-hair day," Dallas had quipped.

At fifteen minutes past four, Rick Hawkins appeared again. "Kat, we've got you on an Air Force flight. It leaves in an hour."

She smiled and thanked him, locking the door from within as he departed. Robert MacCabe, she noted, had a strange look on his face. "What?" Kat asked.

He hesitated. "Nothing."

She walked over and pulled out a chair for him. Dallas lounged on a couch while Steve searched the airport with a pair of binoculars found on the windowsill. Dan, meanwhile, talked quietly to Graham about the ophthalmologist's diagnosis.

Kat pulled up a chair for herself and sat facing Robert, her leg brushing his knee for a second, a tiny stimulus that surprised her by resonating through all the fatigue and adrenaline. She discreetly pulled her leg back, worried she'd sent him an unintended message. But Robert seemed oblivious to the encounter.

"Something's bothering you, Robert," Kat said. "What is it?"

"Something he said about thirty minutes ago when he brought our Starbucks order in here."

"Hawkins?"

"Yeah. I mean, you're the FBI agent, so if it rings true to you . . ."

She leaned forward with her hands clasped in front of her, her eyes on his. Her hair cascaded around her face. "I'm a psychologist by training, Robert. I've been an FBI agent a little under three very fast-moving years. I don't know everything about FBI-speak, and I'm not a member of the good-old-boy network."

"'I was never a Marine.'"

"What?"

"That's what he said when I asked him when he first trained at Quantico. He chuckled and said he was never a Marine."

"Well, Quantico is primarily a Marine base."

Robert nodded vigorously. "I know. But it's also the location of the only FBI Academy you've got, and correct me if I'm wrong, but you don't get to be an FBI agent without going through training at Quantico. Correct?"

Kat looked at him for several seconds without moving. "That is strange, but he's FBI, all right. His ID was standard issue. There's even a . . . well, I can't tell you, but there are methods we have of instantly authenticating one of them, and I did."

Robert raised his hand in a dismissal gesture. "Good. I was hoping that was paranoia talking."

There was the sound of a key in the door and Hawkins reappeared, sticking his head just inside. "Okay, Agent Bronsky. The Air Force is ginning up a crew to fly all of you in one of their Gulfstreams back to Andrews. We're making the arrangements now to move you over to Hickam to board the plane."

Kat stood up, smiling. "That's great." She began walking in his direction. "Say, I was trying to place your name a while ago, and I was wondering if you were at the Academy about the time I was."

Hawkins smiled and raised a finger. "I need to get back down the hall, here. We'll talk in a few minutes, okay?"

"Okay," she said, and stood with her arms folded as he closed the door.

Kat turned and looked at Robert as she chewed on her lip. She moved swiftly to one of the desks where a computer screen was displaying a screen saver full of *The Far Side* characters and tapped on the keyboard. The screen snapped to a standard Windows program and she entered a flurry of keystrokes to call up an E-mail form.

"What're you doing, Kat?" Robert said as he quietly moved up beside her.

She looked up at him and shook her head. "Just checking."

She turned her concentration to the keyboard and entered a quick message routed as a "Deliver Immediately—Emergency" communiqué to Jake Rhoades.

JAKE . . . PLEASE CONFIRM USAF TRANSPORT FOR ALL 6 OF US FROM HONOLULU TO ANDREWS AFB IS OKAY. ALSO, CONFIRM ACTIVE-ASSIGNMENT STATUS OF FBI HNL FIELD AGENTS HAWKINS, WILLIAMS, WALZ, MON-CRIEF, ALL OF WHOM ARE HERE WITH US. REPLY ONLY TO MY NATIONWIDE BEEPER W/ ALPHANUMERIC ANSWER. KB

She hit the key to launch the message and waited while the computer dialed itself into a network and flashed confirmation on the screen. She erased the message and dug her beeper out of her handbag to make sure it was on before sitting down with Dallas and Dan.

Within six minutes her beeper began chirping. Kat pulled it out of her handbag again and casually punched the button, causing the message to pop up.

WHERE ARE YOU? SECST.JJ INFORMED ME DEST. WAS HNL, THEN REC'D WORD YOU DIVERTED MIDWAY ISLAND. ARE YOU IN HNL? ALSO, NO SUCH FBI AGENTS ASSIGNED TO HNL OFFICE OR ANYWHERE ON WEST COAST. BE CAREFUL.

Kat suddenly felt the room undulating, as if they were rolling through an earthquake. She glanced at a hanging light fixture, but it was motionless.

"Kat?" Robert said, startled at her response.

She said nothing, but bolted from the chair and walked quickly to where Steve was standing at the window. "I need your binoculars. Quickly!" she said, her voice terse. Wide-eyed, Steve handed the binoculars to her. She raised them to her eyes, adjusting them as she searched back in the direction of the private terminal where the Global Express had been sitting since their arrival.

It was gone. She scanned the airport and found it at the end of Runway 4L.

"Oh shit!"

"What, Kat?" Robert prompted. *"WHAT?"*

She pulled the glasses away and pointed. "See that jet starting takeoff?"

He nodded.

"That's Two-Two-Zulu." She lowered the glasses, her shoulders slumping. "My God, Robert. I've lost the weapon, I've lost the jet, and I'm sure I've lost Pollis, too." She handed him the beeper and he read the message quickly.

Kat turned into the room, surveying the others. She

turned back to the windows and began searching for a way to open one of them.

Dallas noticed Kat's agitation and moved over toward them. "What's up, boys and girl?"

Robert held up a finger to silence her, then dashed to the far end of the window array and turned back. "Kat, there's a section here with a ledge that leads to a fire escape!"

"Get it open. Break through with a chair if you have to."

"Hey, what's going on here?" Dallas was asking.

Kat took Dallas by the shoulders, her gaze moving rapidly between Dallas and the others in the room. "I've screwed up big-time, Dallas! These guys are not FBI. They're the enemy. There's no time to explain, but we've got to be gone before they come back."

"I thought we were going over to the Air Force," Dallas said.

"Dallas, if we get in their van, our bodies will never be found."

Dallas swallowed hard. "Well, that's pretty definitive. Let's go!"

Robert and Steve had been struggling with a window lever. "Got it, Kat!"

"Okay. Graham, take Dan. Dallas, you and Steve go out together. Robert, lead us out of here. We need to get to the concourse unseen."

Kat stopped and looked at her roll-on bag, trying to decide whether to risk bringing it. Graham, Dallas, and Dan had rescued nothing. Robert had his computer, and Steve his backpack. Steve noticed her hesitation and dashed over to get her bag.

"No, Steve! I'll leave it," Kat said.

"Not a problem," Steve said, and shoved it through the window.

The balmy humidity of the Hawaiian air flooded into the room from the open window. They rapidly stepped out and onto the fire escape, following MacCabe as he moved quickly to a ladder. They descended two stories before running across a tar-and-gravel roof to a metal door that was already propped open.

"This way. Quick," Robert said to each of them as they ran through the door. Kat pulled him along and shut the door behind them.

"Okay, hold up," she said, moving past several closed office doors through a hall to a glass door that opened into one of the main concourses outside security.

Kat turned and motioned them together in a huddle. "We're outside the security perimeter. I can't get us all in by flipping my badge, and if we force open the wrong door, we'll set off alarms. The concourse security screeners will act like morons, so our best bet is to come out of this door, go through security like normal, then regroup on the other side. There are three lanes there, so we split up."

"Where on the other side do we meet?" Dallas asked.

Kat licked her lips and shook her head. "I don't know. There's a gate right over there. Let's assemble in the waiting area, then we'll go from there. Dallas? You and Dan and Steve first. We'll follow. Hawkins is likely to find us gone any minute."

Dallas nodded and opened the glass door, escorting Dan as Steve followed, carrying his own backpack along with Kat's roll-on bag. When all three were safely through, Kat motioned for Robert and Graham to move.

"You coming?" Robert asked.

"Yeah," Kat said. "I'm trying to decide what to do about my gun."

"Use your badge. You don't have a choice."

Kat nodded and followed, staying back as first Robert, then Graham, cleared the metal detector and reclaimed their pocket change on the other side.

She stepped up to the guard and motioned toward the police officer standing in the background, flipping open her ID wallet. "FBI agent. Will you please ask your officer to step over here?"

The security woman's eyes grew big. She disappeared and returned with the officer. Kat handed him the credential case, speaking in an urgent, low voice. "Whatever you do, do NOT call attention to me, okay? We're on an active stake-out, something has gone wrong, and you'll blow a federal investigation if you so much as raise an eyebrow. I am armed with a standard nine-millimeter weapon, but I am a federal peace officer and authorized to enter secure areas."

"Yes, Ma'am," he said, his eyes wide.

"When you're satisfied with my ID, slip it quietly back in my handbag and instruct the security guard here to let me through without comment. Understand?"

"You got it, Agent Bronsky," the officer said.

Kat could hear voices shouting and footsteps in a full run behind her as she cleared the security area and motioned to the others to follow her down the concourse. She chanced a look behind in time to see Hawkins skid to a halt at the same portal and pull out what was obviously a well-done fake ID.

There was a departure reader board next to them, and Kat scanned it quickly, choosing a Seattle-bound DC-10 several gates down that was boarding. "This way!" she commanded, breaking into a trot. The others followed. Hawkins and his two compatriots were streaking into the main concourse now, looking both directions. Kat slipped in front of Robert, and they moved as fast as possible without breaking into a full run.

"Don't look back!" she told Robert as she peeked around him.

Hawkins had stopped and was jerking his head in both directions. He dispatched two of his men to the east concourse while he headed west. Kat realized Hawkins had not seen them, but he was coming in the same direction they were.

"Okay! In here!" Kat ordered, guiding the six of them to the right and out of sight behind a concrete wall that formed the boundary of one of the gates.

The gate was still open, and the airline gate agent was fanning the computer boarding cards she'd collected before closing the door.

Kat ran ahead and identified herself. "You don't have time to think about this!" she told the agent. "On my authority, I'm commandeering us aboard this aircraft, and you must close the door behind us and say absolutely nothing to anyone else except your operations people."

The woman's eyes were huge, and her mouth was moving up and down. "I . . . I . . . don't—"

"Is this flight full?"

"No, but—"

Kat motioned the others past her. "Get on! And have the lead flight attendant standing by to get me to the captain."

She reached out and turned the agent's face to hers. "This is a matter of life and death for the six of us. There is a man about to appear around the corner. He has fake FBI credentials and he is armed and dangerous. If he sees me here talking to you, or you help him in any way, he will probably end up killing you as well as me. Understood?"

The gate agent nodded and swallowed hard.

"Good. I'm gone. Remember, my last name is Bronsky. Call the local FBI office. They will validate me through Washington. Now put your head down, sort your cards, and wait a full minute. Close the door naturally."

Kat turned and ran through the door, disappearing down the jetway at the very moment Hawkins walked into view, scanning the gate and the agent as she worked with her boarding cards. He hesitated briefly, then moved on, having noticed a glut of people around the next gate.

Kat sailed through the entry door of the DC-10 and into the face of an agitated flight attendant holding on to Robert. Kat flipped open her credential case and explained.

"You say somebody's chasing you, Agent?"

"Yes."

"You say they're pretending to be FBI, but they're not?"

"Correct."

"With guns?"

"Probably."

Dan Wade had hesitated just inside the door, pulling Dallas back toward the sound of Kat's voice. Kat could see him listening, then fumbling for his wallet and opening it as the lead flight attendant asked her questions.

The flight attendant shook her head. "Miss . . ."

"Bronsky. Special Agent Bronsky."

"Look, you come running down here to board six disheveled people without tickets on the strength of an ID—

how do I know *you're* not the one with false ID?"

Dan's hand was flailing the air near the flight attendant's shoulder. He connected at last, turning her around to face him.

"Look in this wallet. Find my ID card and pilot's license."

"What?" she asked.

"Just do it! Did you hear about the crash of the Meridian seven-forty-seven yesterday in Vietnam that killed over two hundred people?"

"Yes," she replied, as she tentatively flipped through the plastic sleeves and stopped at his airline ID.

"Okay, sister. I was the copilot. We were shot down, and I've been blinded. The woman you're questioning here plucked us out of a jungle in the middle of a hail of bullets. She is precisely who she says she is, and if you don't help, we're dead."

The woman looked hard at the Meridian ID, and flipped to his FAA pilot's license before closing the wallet and handing it back.

"Stand back," she said, and turned toward the door to wrestle it closed, waving the wide-eyed gate agent back. "Pull the jetway and stand by. You didn't see any of this, okay?"

The agent nodded.

As soon as the door was closed, the flight attendant motioned toward the front. "Let's go. The captain needs to hear all this."

With Dallas and Dan following, Kat and the flight attendant entered the large DC-10 cockpit, where Kat repeated the explanation. The captain sat with his right arm partially over the back of his seat, listening and looking hard at the group that had invaded his airplane, saying nothing as the nervous flight attendant added that she had seen the blinded copilot's ID and license as well.

Kat felt her apprehension rising as the captain waved the flight attendant away and sat motionless for a few seconds, leaving an uncomfortable silence unbroken by the copilot or the flight engineer. Finally, the captain held out his hand.

"I don't need an ID, Agent Bronsky. I'm proud to have you aboard. You bet I'll help."

"Thank you, Captain."

"I know what you did to end the AirBridge hijacking last year, and how humanely you treated that poor captain." He looked at the flight attendant. "Judy? Get them all into first class if we've got it, take good care of them, and give Agent Bronsky anything she needs. She's a fellow pilot, too. Commercial and instrument rating, if I recall correctly, am I right?"

"That's right," Kat said. "Thank you, Captain . . ."

"Holt. Bob Holt," he said.

"Captain Holt, when we get to Seattle, I'll arrange payment of the fares."

"Tell you what, Agent Bronsky," the captain said. "After we get up to cruise, have Judy bring you back up here and let me ask you a whole bunch of things, okay?"

"You got it."

Kat started to turn toward the door, but a sudden, chilling connection finally snapped together in her mind. She sat down hard on the jump seat behind the captain with her index finger in the air. Meridian 5 had been attacked by the weapon they had found aboard the Global Express, and now the weapon and the Global Express were airborne in the vicinity of Honolulu, from which they were preparing to depart. *What if they've discovered where I am . . . where Robert is? I can't let them fly into the path of another attack, unaware!*

"Ah, Captain Holt," she said, taking a breath and shaking her head, "there's one more thing I'd better explain to you in detail right now, because by stepping aboard, I may have just placed you fellows at risk."

HONOLULU INTERNATIONAL AIRPORT, HAWAII
NOVEMBER 13—DAY TWO
4:40 P.M. LOCAL/0240 ZULU

A young couple in a holiday mood moved toward a public telephone along the concourse, laughing and talking. The man reached for the receiver, but another arm was already in front of him, reaching for the same instrument. The young man kept one arm around his girlfriend and adopted a reproving glance at the interloper, who in turn fixed the pair with a cold, reptilian stare, his demeanor a whirlwind of fury and challenge.

The young man backed up immediately, pulling his girlfriend with him and raising his free hand. "Oops! Sorry about that." The adjacent phone booth was empty, but the couple ignored it and quickly headed down the concourse.

The man who'd identified himself as Agent Hawkins yanked the receiver to his ear and punched in a series of numbers. He was perspiring from the marathon search among the various departure gates, and trying to figure out where his charges had gone. The possibilities expanded with each passing second as flight after flight pushed back. The six had vanished without a trace, and the heavy-handed use of the FBI badge had netted him nothing but hostility from the various gate agents.

"Yes?" The voice on the other end was slow and deliberate and in control, quite the opposite from the way he felt.

"This is Taylor, in Honolulu."

"You're certainly not going to tell me you've lost them, are you?"

"Unfortunately, that's exactly what I have to report. I'm sorry—"

"You certainly are," the voice interjected, the slightest hint of anger tingeing the otherwise rock-steady control. "Schoen screwed up, and now you."

"Sir, look. We did get back the jet, the item in the box, and one of our pilots."

"Wonderful," was the sarcastic response. "But the jet can't run to the wrong people with information that can ruin this entire enterprise, now can it?"

"No, Sir. We did the best we could. They went out a window."

"We're almost out of time before the next phase commences, Taylor, and I've got too many of you in the field running around on unplanned cleanup missions. Schoen's the only one left from the Hong Kong debacle, and he's on the way back. And now this." There was a long sigh. "Do you believe them to be still in Honolulu?"

"No. We think they slipped on an outbound flight somehow. I'll have it figured out in a half hour. They're headed to Los Angeles, Denver, or Seattle."

"When you're sure, coordinate the intercept with San Francisco directly, since you have descriptions and names. Provided you follow through in the next half hour, they have time to get in position anywhere in the West. Tell them to expect the FBI to be there in force wherever they land. Those six will have to be taken cleanly before the feds get a chance to get close. And Taylor, my orders are simple: Take those six to the nearest warehouse, shoot them, make absolutely certain they're dead, secure MacCabe's computer and destroy it, then ditch the bodies where they won't be found. Ever. As soon as that's done, I want everyone to reassemble here."

"Yes, Sir."

Kat left the cockpit and gently closed the door behind her, feeling profound relief that they'd reached altitude safely. *If there's a medal for commercial airmen who go above and beyond the call of duty to help the FBI, these guys qualify,* she thought.

Captain Holt had listened carefully to her worries that the crash of Meridian 5 could have been the result of an attack against the eyesight of the pilots, and the fear that the same group could come after his aircraft. At the flight engineer's suggestion, they used maps and pillows and a blanket to block the windscreen on the copilot's side.

"That," the captain told her, "leaves at least one of us fully functional. I don't care what they use, unless they blow up the cockpit, they can't hurt an eyeball they can't see."

"Maybe," Kat suggested, "that's the best way to protect all airliners against a Meridian-type disaster."

"If," Captain Holt told her, "it's some kind of anti-eyeball device, and if every flight crew blocks their cockpit windows as soon as they're airborne, then yes, it will work. But how about takeoff and landing? How about the situation where there's a hillside or a building nearby that someone could use as a platform to fire that thing you described? As commercial pilots, we're still going to be vulnerable on every flight, because ultimately, we've got to see outside."

"So there's no way to defend against someone trying to flash-blind pilots?"

Holt shook his head. "Kat, if somebody's really going to make a habit of this, we're sitting ducks. Hell, even an ordinary laser could damage our eyes. It's happened twice in Las Vegas in the past four years from nothing but show-business lasers. What if that thing you found is an antipersonnel version?"

"Antipersonnel?" Kat echoed.

"I'm an Air Force reservist," he said, "now retired, but I . . . let's just say I knew my way around the intelligence sector during my years in the saddle. I can tell you that one of the things that terrorized us in the fighter community was the prospect that one day the Russians or the Chinese or someone in the Mideast who doesn't like us a lot would decide to develop a powerful handheld laser for the simple purpose of destroying a pilot's eyes with one burst."

"The Air Force studied that?"

He nodded. "For decades. For nuclear blasts, we gave B-fifty-two pilots solid gold-foil eye patches, so they'd have one good eye left if someone touched off a nuke a hundred miles ahead of the attacking bomber. But fighter pilots have to use both eyes, we don't fly all that much by instruments, like the transports. So what happens when *we* can't look without losing our eyes? Simple. We can't see, we can't fight."

"Was anything developed that you know of to—to—"

"Neutralize the threat and protect the eyes? They tried. Nothing worked well enough to be foolproof. A laser or particle beam travels at the speed of light. Any shutter device or goggle device takes too long to close up. If the blast is powerful enough, it's going to fry your retina. I mean, literally, instantly, and permanently."

"Good grief!"

"Can you imagine the value of that to a pipsqueak nation with a pitiful air force who's purchased a hundred or so eye-killing light weapons? They could use Cessnas to neutralize F-fifteens. Bit of an overstatement, but the point is valid."

"Captain, did we build any? You know, we may want to stamp out biological weapons, too, but if there's a suspicion the other side's going to have them, we've got to have an even bigger, better arsenal."

"Ridiculous cycle, isn't it?" the captain replied evenly.

"But you didn't answer my question."

"I don't need to, Kat. You just answered it yourself."

She hesitated, smiling thinly. "What was your rank, Captain Holt?"

"In the Air Force? Brigadier general."

"I rather thought so. Your level of knowledge sounded flag rank."

"And you'd like to ask me more, wouldn't you?"

She nodded. "Such as, whether there's a stockpile somewhere of American-built antipersonnel laser guns."

Holt smiled. "It's too bad I can neither confirm nor deny that possibility."

Kat felt a shiver ripple down her back, but hid it and smiled at Holt as she turned to go.

The captain caught her sleeve. "Kat? If that's what was used against Meridian and SeaAir . . . in other words, if those things are being sold . . . you've got to get the word out, no matter how that impacts the economics of airline flying, and no matter where they were built."

"Understood."

"No, I mean it. No one's going to want to hear it. The FAA will want to run for cover and study the threat for a year while the Air Transport Association will want to flatly deny it could happen again. Meanwhile, whatever intelligence agencies screwed up and didn't see this coming will want to bury the whole thing while their covert-ops people move frantically to crush the organization that decided to use it this time. The public, for their part, will want to stick their heads in the sand and call the threat too technical to understand, and Congress, as usual, will sit around and convince each other that no action is needed. But if these weapons are really out of the bag now and being sold—we've got to ban them worldwide, just like land mines."

Judy, the lead flight attendant, spotted Kat entering the cabin and showed her to the first-class seat next to Robert, who had been looking out the window at the last glow of sunset behind them. Kat saw the wave of recognition cross his face, leaving behind a broad smile.

"Kat! I missed you."

She returned the smile, feeling extraordinarily good about sitting next to him, as if they'd known each other as old friends for years instead of hours. She could see Dallas sitting with Steve, and Dan seated next to Graham Tash, who had been sleeping but woke up suddenly, turning to look around at Kat.

"How're you doing, Doctor?" she asked.

He rubbed his forehead and sighed. "Trying not to dream or think," he said, settling back in the seat.

"How're you holding out?" Robert asked her.

"You mean, fatigue?" Kat laughed. "I'm walking wounded, and didn't even have to survive a crash . . . or see all the horrors you all witnessed at the crash site."

She started to stand, to pull her satellite phone and a fresh battery out of her purse, but the thought of the captain's words caused her to sit down again and turn to Robert. "We've got to talk. Carnegie knew something very, very vital, and we've got to figure out what that was. We don't have much time."

"I figured you'd be convinced," he said.

"Robert, I'm convinced of something else. Regardless of what happened to that SeaAir MD-eleven, the more I've thought about it, the more I'm sure that thing we found on the Global Express was an eyekiller. A laser, a particle-beam weapon, an exotic new ray gun . . . *something* designed to destroy eyesight. Apparently our military has been studying these things for decades, and that means we've been building them as well. I think some very clever bunch of cutthroats has found a new tool to use for international terrorism-for-hire, and they probably stole it from us."

"Where are you going with this, Kat?"

"To the phone, in a second. I've got to report in to my boss, and we need to find out what kind of eye-killing weapons are secretly stockpiled somewhere, and have someone go check to see if there aren't a few of them missing."

"The ID plate on that thing did look military and American-made."

"My point exactly." She tried to stifle a huge yawn and inclined her head toward the aisle. "I'm going to go splash some water on my face and try to get my hair under control, but if you can stay awake, I think we're going to need to connect up your computer to one of the skyphones and go fishing. We've got to find out what your friend knew."

He nodded. "I don't know how we're going to do that, but sure, I'll be awake. I'm too exhausted to sleep, anyway. And

I've probably crossed the threshold into social unacceptance by now."

She chuckled, shaking her head. "You know, for someone who's not only slept in his clothes but survived a major plane crash, a race through the jungle, and a helicopter ride with a maniac for a pilot, you look 'mah-vellous.'"

"As long as I'm not too ripe. We all used that tiny shower on the Global Express, but I still feel grubby."

"Well, Sir, you sure don't look it. Call it jungle chic. I think it suits us."

Her left hand was resting on the divider between the seats, and Robert had covered it with his right hand so gently she hadn't noticed until she started to get up. She looked up at him with a little smile and he smiled back and squeezed.

"You know, I like the 'us' part of that, Ms. Bronsky, Ma'am."

"You *do*?" she asked, feigning surprise. "And why is that?"

"I don't know. It's just that girls with big . . ."

"What?" she shot back, interrupting him, her eyebrows arching up.

"*Guns!* Girls with big guns."

"Uh-huh. And what about them?"

"They turn me on," he said.

"It's only nine millimeters," she added.

"I'd hate to have you say that about me," he replied.

Kat pulled herself up from the seat, rolling her eyes and trying not to laugh as she pulled the battery and satellite phone from her purse and looked down at him.

"You worry me, MacCabe."

After coordinating with the flight attendants, Kat and Robert unfolded the antenna on the satellite phone, positioning it against the Plexiglas window and verifying the signal indication before she punched in the number of Jake Rhoades's cell phone.

He answered on the first ring.

"Jake? Kat."

"Good Lord, Kat, what the hell is going on?"

"There's been virtually no way I could call before now."

"Okay, okay. Where are you?"

"Where are *you*, Jake? Not at headquarters, I hope?"

"No. I came home for a few hours. How'd you know to use this line?"

"I needed to talk to you with minimal chance of being monitored. My previous call to you was intercepted somehow. I think we have a leak at the Bureau."

"What?"

She gave him a quick synopsis of the bogus FBI team and their near success.

"Jake, I'm . . . ashamed to tell you this, but we lost the jet, the weapon, and the prisoner." She filled in the details of watching the Global Express depart, presumably with the weapon aboard.

There was a long sigh from the other end. "Oh, boy. I though we had it just about cracked, Kat. That weapon, or whatever it was, was pivotal."

"You saved our lives with that fast message response a few hours back. We were in the middle of a lethal charade."

"I couldn't fathom what you were doing in Honolulu when we'd been told you were on approach to Midway Island. We had no one waiting in Honolulu. So those names you sent were the aliases."

"That's right," she said.

"They were that convincing?"

"Even the special ID marks and the hologram on the ID card, Jake. These guys, whoever they are, are consummate professionals with access to the best equipment, and on top of that, they're good actors. I didn't have a clue."

"Then there's nothing you could have done, except, I suppose, call on arrival."

"They told me Assistant Deputy Director Rhoades had issued a specific order that I was to call no one."

"Wait a minute, Kat, they used *my name*?"

"They did. He did. The one calling himself Hawkins. As I said, there was virtually nothing that didn't fit, until it was almost too late. Do you have any idea how all that information could have fallen into their hands?"

"Did you tell anyone else you were coming, and where? I mean, it may be your satellite phone that's being monitored."

"Highly unlikely, given the digital, scrambled nature of the signal. Remember our briefings? We were assured this was one short step down from encryption, and my name isn't listed anywhere in association with the number of this phone."

She thought of the conversation with Jordan James, but decided to ignore it. After all, she had never mentioned their destination in that call. "You want to know how I can say conclusively that the leak came from my call to you, Jake?"

"How?"

"An ophthalmologist was waiting. That request was passed only through you."

"Good Lord," he said quietly.

"And, Jake, there's something else. I got a call in flight on the way into Honolulu that was supposedly from someone at Langley. You need to know about this, because the call set me up to believe the show they'd put together."

"You're not alone, Kat. We were thrown off, too, probably by the same person falsely claiming to be one of our liaison people at CIA."

"So what do you make of this?" she asked. "Who on earth are we up against?"

"There's a theory running around here . . ." Jake's voice trailed off.

"Yes?"

"Well, the thing that stopped me is that everything you just described to me reinforces that theory."

"Which is?"

"That we're finally encountering what some analysts predicted all along, a terrorism-for-profit organization, and they're simply clearing their throat to get our undivided attention."

"You mean mercenaries?"

"Worse. They may be working for themselves—an

organization determined to establish their power before they demand a huge ransom not to kill."

"I hate to say it, but that thought had crossed my mind, too."

"Kat, this morning the National Transportation Safety Board held a news conference in response to all the media speculation and, in essence, confirmed that SeaAir very likely resulted from the simultaneous loss of both pilots in flight."

"In other words, the same scenario as Meridian."

"Except in Meridian, one of the pilots refused to die," Jake added. "NTSB isn't saying how the pilots were taken out, and even though the press asked about the possibility of things like explosions and toxic fumes, NTSB says they don't know."

Kat thought for a few seconds before replying. "If true, Jake . . . if the same organization is responsible for both and it's the start of an unprecedented extortion scheme . . . then the fact that they have *not* gone public with any demands means they definitely *will* strike again."

"Precisely. That's the assessment."

"Good Lord! But would such a group pull out so many stops to kill Robert MacCabe and the other survivors just on the outside chance they knew something?"

"Considering the magnitude of what they've already done and the worldwide scope of their operations, I'd say it makes perfect sense for them to bend heaven and earth to get rid of MacCabe and anyone he might have talked to."

"Including me, of course," she said.

"Including you. Now. Where do we go from here?"

"Aren't I supposed to ask *you* that?" Kat rubbed her eyes and sighed. "I'm exhausted, Jake. We all are." She gave him a rundown on the condition of the survivors. "I'm not even sure that Honolulu ophthalmologist was legitimate."

"What I meant, Kat, was where do we meet you when you arrive? This one has *got* to be done right, and since we're dealing with a commercial airline, we shouldn't have another diversion problem."

"Sea-Tac Airport in Seattle," she said, passing the expected arrival time.

"We'll be there in force, Kat, at the gate."

Kat hesitated, holding back her burning desire to raise the issue of eye-killing weaponry possibly built by the U.S. military, but the question oozed with political danger. Perhaps she should think it through a bit longer before discussing such suspicions with the deputy director of the FBI.

"I'll call you from Seattle, Jake," she said instead. They disconnected, and Kat glanced at Robert before sitting in silence a few moments. She wondered if conspiracy theories tended to multiply in direct proportion to fatigue. Why had she held back with Jake Rhoades?

The sudden ring of the phone caught her off guard, and she jumped, losing control of it, batting it in the air and barely catching it and regaining her grip. Robert was trying to suppress laughter, and she smiled somewhat sheepishly as she punched the button and unfolded the antenna.

"Katherine? Is that you?" Jordan James asked.

"Yes, Jordan! And you don't know how good it is to hear your voice . . . but where are *you* calling from?"

"I'm at home, using the secure line State installed last week."

"No one else there?"

"No. Why?"

Once again she ran through the particulars of what had happened, ending with the potentially offensive question she couldn't avoid. "Uncle Jordan, I hate to ask you this, but are you sure of whomever you talked to at Langley? Because someone intercepted everything I said to you."

She heard him clear his throat.

"That's why I've been frantic to reach you, Kat. There's a very serious leak."

"What are you saying?"

"I'm saying the problem isn't Langley or my phones, the problem is at the Bureau. You can't tell them anything until the leak is plugged."

"That . . . that's just . . . that doesn't make sense."

"Nevertheless, you've been targeted by someone, and all the information they needed originated with your call to Jake Rhoades."

"He's my boss, Jordan! Jake absolutely can't be—"

"Of course Jake's not involved. I would be flabbergasted if any *real* FBI agent is involved, but someone's got access to the Bureau. You have to trust me now, Kat. Didn't you just tell me the IDs of those guys in Honolulu were flawless?"

"Yes."

"Most likely because they were genuine."

"No! We don't have any agents by those names—"

"Not the point, Kat. The IDs may well have been fabricated by the same office that prepared *your* ID. These people have found their way inside. Didn't they know the language? Didn't you say they *sounded* like your fellow FBI agents?"

"Yes." She felt her head spinning, her resistance to this bizarre idea crumbling in the face of his authority and logic.

"Kat, the problem is deep. Whoever is running this show has access to everything they need to target you and your entourage. I can't tell you how I know this, because it comes from a startling source, but my one hope is that it's only a single mole at the Bureau, and most likely clerical."

She said nothing for a few seconds as she sat with her pulse pounding in her ears, wondering just what was real.

"So what do I do, Jordan?"

"First and foremost, you *cannot* trust any of your compatriots at the Bureau until we know where the leak is. You have to assume that virtually every conversation goes right offshore to whoever is behind this operation."

"Offshore? We're sure of that?"

"Nothing else fits. Remember when I headed the CIA fifteen years ago? You don't forget the earmarks."

"You've had so many important jobs, Uncle Jordan, I forgot about CIA."

"Well, trust me, Honey. Where are you headed right now?" he asked.

She thought quickly and decided one communication had been enough. "Jordan, I . . . don't think I should speak the words on this line."

"Of course. That's a good precaution. But, did you tell Jake Rhoades?"

"Yes."

"I was afraid of that. Okay, Kat, now listen to me. Whatever you do, do *not* get off that aircraft the normal way, or run any risk of being intercepted by, or going with, anyone purporting to be FBI agents. If you've told Jake, there will most certainly be a party waiting for you, but not the one you want."

"But Jake will make certain that doesn't happen again."

"He got outfoxed in Honolulu, didn't he? Whoever these people are, they'll find a way to divert, contain, distract, or otherwise neutralize whomever Jake sends. We do not know what's real here, and until I can get to the bottom of this—and by the way, I'm taking this to the White House in the morning—until we know where the leak is, you're going to have to stay out in the cold and tell your own people nothing, because when you do, the information goes right to the enemy."

"Jordan . . ."

"No questions, Katherine. Just do it. Your life depends on it. Understand?"

"Yes, but Jordan, I'm an FBI agent. How can I run from my own people?"

"If you don't, Katherine, I'll lose you, and we'll lose those survivors you brought out with you. Look, before your dad died, I promised him I'd try to look after you as much as I could, and this is one where I can guarantee he'd say the same thing: Find a hole, take the others with you, and go hide in it. When you're secure and certain that no one knows where you are, call me. But not at State. Only on this phone. We need time to ferret out who's behind all this. And we *will* find them. Your responsibility is to protect yourself and the five people with you. Just concentrate on that."

"Okay, Uncle Jordan. Thank you."

"It's going to be okay, Katherine."

She disconnected and sat rubbing her forehead, more confused than ever, and aware that Robert was about to burst with questions.

"An uncle?" he asked, as tentatively as he dared.

She nodded, explaining who had been on the other end of the line.

"*The* Jordan James?" Robert asked, his eyes flaring as he sat forward. "You know *him*?"

She nodded. "Longtime friend of my dad's and a Dutch uncle all my life."

"I'm impressed, Kat! James is in the same league with John Foster Dulles, Clark Clifford, and Henry Kissinger. The perpetual presidential adviser."

"That's my Uncle Jordan." Kat turned to look Robert in the eye. "Robert, wouldn't Walter Carnegie have found a way to safeguard what he'd discovered and get it to you somehow?"

Robert nodded slowly. "If there was any way he could. I mean, I don't know what scared him away or kept him away from our meeting. But he was the typical scientist, and he would have been obsessed with safeguarding whatever he'd found."

"Then somewhere out there is a predeath message to you from Carnegie with the information we need, or at least clues on how to find it. You agree?"

"Yeah, but where? In a letter? In my E-mail? Stuffed under my doormat? I mean, the possibilities are endless."

"Not to a panicked man, Robert. We have to think like he was thinking, and see only the options he would see, and we don't have much time. I've got the sick feeling our murderous little terrorist group is getting ready to strike again somewhere, and whatever Carnegie was trying to pass you is the antidote."

Robert MacCabe sighed. "Then let's connect the laptop to this incredibly expensive seat back phone system and get busy."

chapter

34

For nearly two hours, Robert MacCabe had tried various ideas through the connection of his computer to the seat back phone system. Personal E-mail, his electronic mailbox at the *Washington Post,* a manual search by his secretary ordered by E-mail, and an hour's worth of attempts to hack into Walter Carnegie's E-mail account had turned up nothing. With the DC-10 beginning its descent for landing in Seattle, frustration was growing.

"Do you have any other Internet accounts or E-mail accounts?" Kat asked.

"No," he replied, sitting in thought for a few seconds. "Wait a minute." He entered a series of commands and the computer began dialing another number.

"What?" Kat asked.

"A brainstorm, and probably useless," he replied. The logo of an Internet service appeared on the screen, and Robert waited with his fingers poised over the keyboard.

"YES!" he said in a loud voice, startling Kat.

"Yes what?"

"Just . . . a second," he said, typing in a response to a

password request. The first two attempts were rejected, but the third worked, and he turned to Kat with a triumphant look. "Walter created a new account under my name at his Internet service, and used his own name as the password."

"How'd you figure that out?" she asked.

"Pure guesswork."

"Pretty impressive, Watson," Kat replied. "It says there's a message waiting."

"I'm pulling it up now," he said, as it assembled itself on the laptop screen.

Robert,

Since you've found this, many weeks have probably elapsed and something has happened to me. I figured that when you saw the bill on your American Express for this new E-mail account, you'd go probing. I also figured anything I sent to your regular account would be monitored.

I apologize profusely for missing our appointment. I was being followed and had to go elsewhere, and didn't want to endanger you by any other contact. I don't know who these people are, but I can assure you I'm not seeing things, nor am I becoming delusional. Someone, or some group, is highly incensed that I wouldn't just go back to my office at FAA and shut up. So, wherever I am, it's time you saw what I've seen. Maybe you can piece the rest of this together and get it exposed.

The following message is generic, with appropriate references I hope you'll follow quickly. First, there's a man you need to find ASAP. Remember our discussion about your piece on Desert Storm vs. technology, and what you said about Uncle's other tricks? Okay. This guy knows the new tricks, and why they've stayed invisible. You will have already received his name and locale by the time you find this, though you may not have recognized the message. Look again. It ends with the number 43. The main file you need to see is LOC'd up at my favorite hangout using the name WCCHRN.

One more thing. Remember Pogo's admonition about the identity of the foe, and be very careful, because they <u>are</u> out to get us!/Walter.

Kat pulled out a steno pad and copied the message carefully. "Okay," she said at last, looking at Robert. "What the heck does he mean?"

"The Desert Storm discussion and the reference to Uncle is probably about new military hardware, but . . . I don't really remember. It's been a long time."

"How about his favorite hangout?"

"I suppose he means a restaurant, and probably the one at the Willard Hotel, but why would he store a disk or something there?"

"You're assuming it's a disk, right?"

"Yeah, knowing Walter. He thought best on a computer."

"But why the spelling 'LOC'?"

Robert sat scratching his chin for a few seconds, then shook his head. "I don't know. I'm going to have to think about that. I wonder if he means his house?"

"Where is it?"

"Arlington, Virginia. A small house. He divorced a few years back. She wanted to enjoy life, he wanted to enjoy work. The house suits—*suited* him, poor guy. It's furnished in Early Federal Disaster Area."

"He'll probably come back and haunt you for that slam. One more question, Robert. He referred to a message you should already have received, but you've checked every message service you have, right?"

"Aha!" Robert disconnected his computer from the phone and raised the handset to dial in an 800-number. He punched in some additional numbers and looked at Kat while waiting for it to answer. "I lost my beeper somewhere in the jungle back there in Vietnam, but the host system stores messages for weeks." He hunkered down to listen as the distant computer replayed the messages of the previous week, then reached over to write them on the steno pad in her lap. He sat up suddenly, smiling as he wrote down another name and the words "Las Vegas," then disconnected.

"That was it, Kat! Walter sent it through my beeper. The name of his deep-throat source is Dr. Brett Thomas of Las Vegas. The message ended in forty-three."

"We'd better find him quickly. We won't be the only ones looking."

SEA-TAC INTERNATIONAL AIRPORT, WASHINGTON

Kat had returned to the cockpit jump seat as the big DC-10 rounded the south end of Puget Sound. She watched as the copilot reached up and pulled the pillow and map off his glareshield as the aircraft made a wide right turn over Elliot Bay and settled on to the ILS approach for Runway 16 Left at Sea-Tac Airport.

"Landing gear down, before landing checklist," Holt called as they intercepted the glide slope and began the steady final descent to the runway.

"Jerry?" he said to the copilot. "I want you to bottom your seat out and make sure you're not looking outside, just in case."

"All the way to touchdown?" the copilot asked.

Holt nodded, turning to the flight engineer. "You, too, Joe. Stay sideways. I know it's against procedure to land that way, but I want you shielded, too."

"You're worried someone might fire at us from the buildings off the approach end of the runway, right?" Kat asked.

The captain nodded. "Any air crew is vulnerable on final approach. With what you told us, and having you on board . . ."

She nodded. "Understood. I appreciate the caution."

"Five hundred feet, no flags," the copilot called, reading the instruments as the three-engine jumbo jet descended through an altitude of 500 feet above the housing areas below.

Without incident, the DC-10 transitioned smoothly over the highway bordering the north of the airport and settled gently onto the runway. Holt deployed the speed brakes and lifted the thrust reverser levers as he kept the nosewheel on the center line.

Kat's attention shifted to the North Satellite terminal on their left. She could see the large sign designating the gate they were supposed to taxi into, and she could see a significant number of black sedans and police cars arrayed around the jetway.

A cold chill of reality reverberated up and down her spine. She had briefed Robert and the others to stay seated and arranged for the crew to close the main door after all other passengers had left, but was that enough? Judy said she would leave it closed until Kat could call and verify the names of the agents meeting them.

Even so, Jordan James's warnings were ricocheting around her mind, mocking her decision to trust Jake's assurances. *They're there, as Jake promised. But what if Jordan is right?*

They were rolling past the North Satellite now, adjacent to the main terminal and decelerating smoothly. The tower controller directed the captain to turn off the runway at the very end, adding a postscript Kat almost missed.

". . . and your company operations need you to contact them immediately."

The copilot toggled in the company frequency and called in.

"Roger, Seven-thirty-two," operations replied. "Change in plans. Due to . . . a request from U.S. Customs and the FBI, we need to park you briefly at the South Satellite, Gate S-ten. Keep everyone on board. When the powers that be are finished doing whatever it is they're there to do, we'll have a tug tow you to N-eight."

Kat could feel her heart rate accelerating as the captain turned around in his seat to look at her. "Kat, it looks like your people are taking extraordinary precautions for you. We never park at the South Satellite on domestic flights."

He guided the DC-10 through a left turn off the runway as Kat sat in stunned silence behind him, thinking as fast as she could. *There were police and unmarked cars at the north gate. Suddenly they change us to the south terminal. Why?*

Jordan's words came back to her: "Whoever these people are, they'll find a way to divert, contain, distract, or otherwise neutralize whomever Jake sends. We do not know who is trustworthy."

The DC-10 was on the taxiway moving northbound, with less than a quarter mile separating them from the South Satellite terminal.

Kat leaned over Holt's right shoulder. "Captain, please listen to me. I believe my people and I are being set up. I saw the police cars at the north gate. This diversion has to mean the people we don't want to meet are waiting at the south."

He turned. "No problem. We'll just taxi to the north gate and ignore them."

"No!" Kat said. "That . . . that could put everyone aboard in jeopardy. No. Stop just ahead here, then go toward the south gate."

"What are you planning?" he asked.

"We're . . . going out your right rear door on the escape slide."

The captain thought for a minute and nodded. "Okay. I'll stop where that maneuver can't be seen from the terminal, then have Judy pull the pins after you're off. We'll just let the slide blow off, but I'm going to need your corroboration within a week, because my company's going to want to fire me for throwing a slide out."

"I will. I promise."

"What do we tell them at the gate?" Holt asked.

"That you have no idea what they're talking about. You saw nothing. Buy me some time. One of those groups will *not* be legitimate FBI agents. If you say you're going to check their names with FBI headquarters and they leave, you'll know."

"You got it. Go. Call me on the interphone before you open the door."

Kat patted his shoulder and thanked him as she turned and left the cockpit. She tried not to look panicked as she collected the others. Steve grabbed her suitcase from the overhead compartment without being asked and hurried after her toward the back of the DC-10.

The aircraft was moving too slowly, and the ground controller had noticed. "Seven-thirty-two, Seattle Ground. You have a problem, Sir?"

"Negative, Ground. Just a passenger out of his seat too soon. We need to hold here until we coax him back in."

Kat had briefed Judy on the way to the rear of the aircraft as they tried to avoid the startled looks of the other passengers. Judy pulled a curtain separating the last row from the entryway and placed her hand on the door lever as Kat phoned the cockpit.

"Captain? We're ready," Kat reported.

"Okay," Holt told her on the interphone. "We're depressurized and stopped. Do it. Be careful going down that slide, and Godspeed."

Kat breathed a thank-you as she hung up, and Judy opened the door, letting the large emergency escape slide fall from its housing and start inflating.

"Stand by!" Judy said. "When I give the word, jump and sit, and run when you hit the bottom."

"Jump, *then* sit?" Dallas asked. "Are you sure that's the right sequence?"

Judy nodded. "We do it all the time."

Dallas looked genuinely startled. "Passengers leave like this all the time?"

Judy smiled and shook her head. "Only in training. Now GO!"

Steve went first, followed by Graham and Dan, who was helped to the edge and guided by Judy. Robert followed, but Dallas stood to one side of the open door virtually immobile, her eyes following the others.

"*DAMN*, that's a long way down!" Dallas said.

"We don't have time to debate it, Dallas," Kat told her.

"Honey, you guys go on, and I'll just hide in the rest room till spring."

"No."

"I don't want to go down that slide, Kat! Gravity and I don't get along."

"It's simple," Judy offered.

"Then you go in my place. A little dark makeup, you

could pass for me. I could stay here and serve the drinks and pamper the pilots."

"DALLAS!" Kat snapped, taking her by the shoulders. "NOW!" She half kicked Dallas out the door, listening to a war whoop as Dallas's rear landed on the slide about a quarter of the way down. She slid off the bottom to the waiting arms of Steve and Robert as Kat turned to Judy. "He said to release it after we're gone."

"I will. Go. The bags come next. Good luck."

Kat's trip down the slide was fast. She stumbled at the bottom and righted herself, then turned around in time to see Steve's backpack, Robert's computer case, and her roll-on bag coming down behind her, followed by the large emergency slide fluttering away as Judy jettisoned it, waved, and closed the door.

"Okay, Kemosabe," Dallas yelled in Kat's ear, trying to be heard over the noise and jet blast of the engines as she brushed herself off. "What do we do now?"

Kat had seen the makeshift private aircraft facility at the south end of the field before. They had bailed out next to it, unobserved in the darkness.

"This way!" she said, running toward the trailer that doubled as an office, past two Learjets, a Cessna Citation, a King Air, and a Gulfstream, all of them parked on the small corporate ramp bordering the large Alaska Airlines maintenance complex.

With Robert running in step beside her, she glanced back, satisfied that all of them were keeping up. She slowed her own pace to keep everyone close.

"Hurry! Come on!"

Kat slowed to a walk as she climbed the steps to avoid bursting through the door of the office, where two men were working on a computer behind the counter.

Both of them jumped from their chairs. "Hi! We . . . didn't miss an arrival out there, did we?" one of them asked.

Kat smiled and shook her head. "No, we're from the Gulfstream. You fellows have a way to get us to the terminal?"

"Sure," the older man said. "Right out back. Come on."

Robert was giving her a quizzical look as they all followed the man through the doors to a van with the facility's name printed in bold letters on its side.

"What are you doing, Kat?" he half whispered. "I thought we were trying to avoid the terminal." She put a finger to her lips and motioned him inside the van, bringing up the rear and closing the door.

The driver dropped them off inside the airport's parking structure adjacent to the terminal, and Kat handed him a twenty-dollar bill as they got out.

"Hey, not necessary!" he told her.

She leaned over and lowered her voice. "No, but it's both a thank-you and silence money. You didn't see us, and neither did your coworker."

He smiled and put the van in gear. "You got it, Ma'am, and Jerry's going off duty as soon as I get back."

With Steve and Dallas bringing up the rear, Kat quickly guided the little group to the northern-most parking elevator. They rode it down to the first floor, and she briefed them urgently before the door slid open.

"Okay. Walk to the right, all the way to the end of that driveway where it rejoins the main drive. Wait there and be ready to jump in when I get there."

"What are you doing? Renting a car?" Robert asked.

"Sort of," she said, smiling. "We broke up a ring of car thieves doing exactly what I'm about to do. So don't ask, and don't hesitate when I reach you."

Kat found the appropriate part of the rental car return drive, positioning herself well away from where the other rental car company employees were standing. There would only be minutes left before the men waiting for them at the South Satellite realized they'd been outfoxed. With Jake's team converging as well, they had one chance to escape before even the airport exits might be closed.

A subcompact car entered the car-return area, and she let it pass, along with a midsize car behind it. A minivan turned in with a couple and three kids, and Kat stepped forward, checking a clipboard she'd taken from an unattended counter.

"Hi! And you folks would be the . . ."

"Rogers," the man volunteered.

She looked at the clipboard and smiled. "Yeah. The Rogers clan. You guys are the last customers I've got today before I can go home. Okay! We've got a new program for families, to get you into the terminal with less stress by getting you on this north elevator. You have your contract?"

The man nodded as he put the minivan in park and unstrapped his seat belt.

Robert squinted to see who was inside the dark-green minivan that slowed to a halt beside them. The door swung open, revealing Kat frantically motioning them inside. In five minutes they were speeding onto the northbound lanes of Interstate 5.

Dallas Nielson leaned forward from the middle of the bench seat in the second row and shook her head. "Honey," she said to Kat, "I've been on some scary adventures in my time, but that slide ride takes the cake. In fact, I could've sworn someone shoved me out the door back there."

"No!" Kat said, feigning shock. "Really?"

"Yeah, really. I was thinking of complaining to the FBI, but what the heck."

Kat grimaced. "Probably just some pushy teenager."

"Hey!" Steve said from directly behind her.

Dallas patted Steve on the right knee as she craned her neck to look at Kat. "All seriousness aside, Kat," Dallas said.

Kat glanced at Dallas. *"What?"*

"Sorry. Old radio term we'd throw out when we got bored."

"You were a DJ?"

"Broadcast engineer, actually. In New York. But I DJ'd, too. But then I won six million in the lottery and retired."

"The lottery. Really?" Kat asked.

"Yep. Really. But now I have a question for *you,* Jane Bond."

"And that would be?" Kat asked, shaking her head.

"Having survived a major plane crash," Dallas began, ticking off the points on the fingers of her left hand, "watched Graham's wife fall to her death and my friend Britta being blown to bits, been rescued under fire in a helicopter flown by someone who didn't know how to fly one, escaped from a commie country in a stolen business jet with a criminal for a pilot, fled from a team of FBI agents who weren't, and sneaked onto a flight that threw us off in the middle of the night somewhere short of the gate in Seattle, could I please ask when the hell this ride is going to be over? I mean, enough is enough, okay?"

"Did I forget to mention," Kat said, chuckling and holding the palm of her right hand out parallel to the floor, "that you have to be this tall to go on this ride?"

"So *that's* the problem!" Dallas snorted.

"I think what Dallas is trying to say," Robert began, but Dallas turned and glared at him in mock indignation.

"Hey, my man! Dallas can say what Dallas was going to say, okay?"

"Yup. Sorry," Robert replied.

"I should think so!" Dallas sat for a few seconds, then turned back to Robert. "What was I going to say?"

The comic relief broke them all up, all except Graham, who sat silently, staring out the window.

"Oh, yeah. I remember," Dallas went on. "You appear to be heading someplace, Kat. Would you please tell us where?"

"A cash machine first, then an all-night grocery store," Kat said.

Dallas looked at Robert and nodded with an exaggerated thumbs-up sign as if affirming a great new idea. "Right. Then what do we do? Buy a quart of milk?"

"In part, yes. We're going to buy enough groceries for a week. Food, milk, coffee, paper products, personal items. Everything. Then we go to the upper end of a fifty-mile-long inaccessible lake on the other side of the Cascade Mountains where there are virtually no telephones, no traffic, and no assassins, and we hole up there while I try to figure out exactly whom we can trust, and who, on the other hand, is trying to kill us . . . not to mention shoot down airliners."

Kat turned to the others. "I . . . can't force you to go, but

Graham, Steve, Dallas—you're all in grave danger if you try to go home or call anyone."

Steve shrugged his shoulders. "My mom will already have freaked."

Dallas nodded, but Graham Tash spoke for the first time in hours. "I'm . . . in no hurry, Kat."

"And Dan?" Kat continued.

"Whatever you think best," he said firmly. "I'm single."

Dallas raised her hand. "'Scuse me. One amenities question, please. Are we talking tents, sleeping bags, a Motel Six, or is there, perhaps, a four-star resort nearby?"

"My mother's brother owns a cabin there," Kat replied. "He's never there this time of year, and I have access."

"Kat," Robert said. "Are you saying no phones, no sheriff, and no escape?"

Kat nodded. "Except for park rangers. It's a National Recreation Area."

"Are you sure we want to be that isolated?"

She negotiated a turn onto the freeway and looked over at him with a sigh. "Robert, I'm making this up as I go along, but the only person in D.C. I can trust my life to told me to find a hole and pull it in after us for a few days while he tries to sort out what's going on. The best hiding place I know of is Stehekin, Washington."

"Somehow," Dallas said, "I get the impression you know this area."

Kat nodded. "I love the Pacific Northwest, and the Seattle–Tacoma area. I've come here many times over the years."

There was a small, insistent beeping from Kat's purse, and she fumbled with her right hand to extract the pager while keeping her eyes on the road. She handed it to Robert, motioning for him to read the message out loud.

"It says, 'Where are you? What happened in Seattle? By the way—NTSB pathology confirms destroyed/burned retina one SeaAir pilot.'"

"Good grief!" Kat muttered.

"What does that mean?" Dallas asked from the back.

Kat turned her head slightly. "It means that the same type of attack that hit you, Dan, and killed your captain, hit at least one of the pilots in the SeaAir crash near Cuba. And that confirms we're dealing with serial terrorism."

"Kat," Robert continued, "he's also ordering you to call ASAP."

She shook her head. "That I cannot do."

SEA-TAC INTERNATIONAL AIRPORT, WASHINGTON
NOVEMBER 14—DAY THREE
1:30 A.M. LOCAL/0930 ZULU

The two FBI agents searching the main terminal below had moved on. On the second-story mezzanine, a slim, dark-haired, pock-faced man in his late thirties carefully peered around a column to make certain they hadn't returned. Satis-fied, he lifted his arm and spoke softly into a hidden micro-phone wired through his clothes to a transceiver clipped to his belt.

"Rolf, are you in the clear?"

The response came back in his tiny earpiece. "Yes. We're both here. Where are you?"

"Stuck at the moment. Two feds are a floor below me, asking about us. I'll come off this perch as soon as they're gone. Have you called in yet?"

"You sure you want to hear that now?"

"I'm sure."

"Well, our leader is not happy. In fact, I'd say our leader's just shy of homicidally mad, although he's always so con-trolled it's hard to tell."

The man leaned slightly over toward the balcony, check-ing the progress of the two genuine FBI agents who had fanned out in the airport after discovering the charade at the

South Satellite. It had taken less than ten minutes for the FBI team waiting at the North Satellite to catch on, not enough time to thoroughly search the DC-10 a second time. Somehow the six had escaped, but it seemed impossible.

The man looked down each hallway, satisfying himself it was safe to venture out. He triggered the microphone again. "I knew he'd be furious, but did you tell him clearly what happened?"

"He called it a bad excuse. When are you coming out of there? We need to disappear fast."

"Why? What are you seeing?"

"Nothing we can hide behind for long."

"I'm coming out now and I'll—" The man emerged and turned directly into the barrel of a cocked handgun.

"Freeze!" the gunman snapped. "FBI! You're under arrest for—"

The bogus agent slammed a left fist into the belly of the genuine agent and rolled away from his extended gun as he grabbed it and diverted it upward. There was an "oof" and the sound of a body impacting the floor. The FBI agent scrambled to right himself, but the sound of four muffled pops put an end to the effort. The agent slumped to the floor in a growing pool of blood, his vision receding into a distant point as he lost consciousness, completely unaware of the presence of a cold metal barrel to his temple that would conduct the coup de grâce.

The shooter moved immediately down the hallway, slipped into the nearest stairwell, and walked calmly past two uniformed airport police officers to the door of the terminal and directly into a waiting van, which pulled away from the curb as soon as he was in.

"Trouble?" one of his companions asked.

"Scratch one fed," he said, patting the gun beneath his coat for emphasis. "What're the instructions?"

The driver sighed. "Word for word, you don't want to hear. Lots of accusations of terminal stupidity, yadda, yadda, yadda. We're ordered to spare no expense, and use no compassion in tracking down those six people and doing them."

LAKE CHELAN, STEHEKIN, WASHINGTON

The single-engine float plane was too familiar a sight to attract much attention as it banked over the verdant alpine valley just north of Lake Chelan. The DeHavilland Beaver she had rented at the south end of the lake was a blunt-nosed thing of beauty to pilots who knew her in the North country, as well as those she supplied. A veteran design from a Canadian company conceived in the 1940s and kept forever young by high demand, what the Beaver lacked in streamlined beauty it made up for in brute reliability. Uncounted times in her history, her large, radial engine and three-bladed propeller had rescued some miscalculating bush pilot from an otherwise fatal mistake. Beavers were slow but forgiving, rugged and accomplished mariners, and Kat had always felt a thrill in watching them touch down on water, the floats kissing the surface with a finger-light touch as they slowed suddenly in a cascade of spray and settled down to float instead of fly.

The half-hour flight just above the glassy blue surface of the fifty-mile-long lake had been spectacular; the small aircraft surrounded the beauty of the sharp snow-covered peaks rising to 7,000 feet on either side of the fjordlike upper end. Much of the beauty, however, had been lost to fatigue and worry and the realization that even here they were a target.

Leaving the purloined minivan had required careful thought on Kat's part. The car had to be left in a place where no one would tow it, report it, or even notice it for a week, and a commercial storage yard for recreational vehicles had been perfect.

"There! See the roof at the end of that driveway down there?" Kat said, pointing out their destination and feeling relieved that it was still there.

"Where's Stehekin?" Dallas asked.

"It's an area, not a town, as such," Kat replied. "The ranger station and motel and a few shops are by the boat landing, which is where we're going to dock."

The pilot throttled back the Beaver and turned toward his usual landing spot on the lake adjacent to the diminutive town dock. Kat's 2 A.M. phone call to arrange a 7 A.M. departure had irritated him, but a charter was money, and it was November. Two weeks later he'd have the Beaver hauled out for the winter, anyway. He had met the client a bit gruffly, but was warming up, especially since the morning had turned out to be so beautiful.

Strange group, he thought. They looked bedraggled and scared, carried bags of groceries but almost no luggage, and their clothes were a mess. In addition, one of them had some sort of problem with his eyes and was wearing a bandage. The thought of criminal activity had crossed his mind, but he couldn't fathom what such a disparate collection of exhausted people could be engaged in.

Kat was relieved to find a beat-up car, with its key under the floor mat, parked in a shed near the dock, a sure sign that no one else was occupying the cabin. When all of them had left the plane and squeezed into the car, Kat took the pilot aside and handed him $350 in cash and her FBI credential case.

"What's this?" he asked.

"Open it," she directed.

He flipped it open and read the laminated ID card several times before looking up with a worried expression. "Did I . . . I mean, is there something wrong?"

She put a hand on his shoulder. "No, no, no! But I need your help, and this is very, very critical. This is a federal operation, and the people with me are under the protection of the FBI. They've crossed some very dangerous people who, quite literally, are a threat to national security. Now, no one knows we're anywhere around here except you. If you say anything about this charter to anyone, you could well be responsible for the deaths of all these people. That means to anyone, *including* anyone else who claims to be from the FBI, whether they have an ID like this or not."

"I . . . don't understand," he said, looking nervously from the car to the female agent before him.

"You've heard of the Witness Protection Program?" she asked.

"Yeah," he said, brightening.

"Good. Then you may know that we don't even tell other FBI agents about the people under that program."

"You're relocating them here?"

"No. Merely keeping them out of sight for a while. Now, I can't tell you that your pilot's license depends on your keeping quiet and helping me, but it doesn't hurt to have friends at the FBI who owe you one. Understand?"

He smiled and nodded. "Yes, Ma'am. I'm very glad I didn't see you when I was on this solo training flight I decided to make this morning just because it was such a pretty day."

She smiled back. "That's the idea. Now, I'll call you for pickup in a day or two. Will you be all right with that?"

"Absolutely. Don't worry, no one will know."

"And no paper trail, okay? No logbook entry, invoice, or company record."

He nodded, wondering whether the $350 was supposed to be tax-free.

The key to the cabin was exactly where Kat remembered it: hidden inside a small hatch built into one of the logs that formed the stout cabin. She opened the door gingerly, hoping against new alarm systems, and was relieved to find the place clean and ready for guests.

"The caretaker is obviously doing the same good job of keeping this place ready year-round," Kat said to Dallas, as they turned on lights and fiddled with the thermostat to the floor furnace system. She tried to recall the caretaker's name. He would undoubtedly drop by at some point to make sure the unexpected guests were legitimate. She would have to plan for that.

There were two hide-a-beds in the main room and two bedrooms that could sleep four apiece in the rustic bunk beds. The kitchen was small but well equipped, and a quick round of sandwich-making preceded a general collapse of everyone, except Kat and Robert, into the various bunks for what they all agreed would be a much-needed sleep through the day and upcoming night.

Kat pulled the blackout curtains and replenished the fire

in the main room. She was fighting sleep and trying to stay focused, but was slowly losing the battle. Outside the cabin a beautiful morning was unfolding beneath a clear blue sky, the bright sunshine reflecting off the fifteen-inch layer of early snow covering the peaceful, isolated valley. She had an intense longing to take a walk, but that desire was smothered by a fuzzy blanket of fatigue. The speech in Hong Kong seemed like ancient history. Was it really only a few days ago? It didn't seem possible.

Kat dragged the old bear rug she remembered from childhood closer to the huge river-rock fireplace and sat with her knees pulled up and her arms around her legs, luxuriating in the warmth of the fire. There were three floor furnaces blazing away in the cabin, but the hearth was the most comfortable spot, and she wondered how many times over the years her aunt and uncle had been able to get away to use the place.

Not enough, she figured, though she knew they loved it. Her aunt was a lusty woman with an equally lusty spouse, as Kat had discovered one summer when she'd come back from a trail ride a half day early and surprised them au naturel and passionately engaged on the same rug. She smiled at the memory, though it had been shocking at the time: Aunt Janine in the full-throated cries of a glass-shattering climax as Kat opened the door, causing her uncle's head to pop up from an unexpected and intriguing location. Kat had backed out fast and stayed away for an hour before returning, stomping on the porch and making as much noise as possible. When she opened the door, her aunt was busy in the kitchen and her uncle was writing at the table, both of them smiling and looking smugly satisfied.

Robert MacCabe's footsteps were approaching from the kitchen, and Kat tried to suppress the long-ago memory with a flash of embarrassment, as if he could see the titillating image in her mind. She looked up and smiled at him somewhat sheepishly as he settled onto the rug beside her, carrying two steaming mugs in his hands.

"Kat, I figured it out!"

"What? How to make coffee?"

"No, where Walter hid the information."

Kat brightened instantly. "Where?"

"I also found enough dark chocolate in there to make real hot chocolate," he said, handing her a mug.

"Great, but where'd he hide it?"

"Aren't you going to ask me about the chocolate?" Robert asked.

She shook her head in confusion. "What?"

"The hot chocolate you're holding. Try it. Then I'll tell you."

She looked at the mug in her hand and finally took a sip. "That's wonderful! Where'd you learn to do that?"

"From a little old chef in Lima, Peru, at the Crillon Hotel. I used to get down there on assignment and order tomato-and-egg sandwiches and a pot of this type of hot chocolate. *Chocolate caliente, en español.* Nirvana, in any other language."

"Okay. I'm dutifully impressed. Now, where'd he hide it?"

"His favorite haunt in Washington wasn't a restaurant. I'd almost forgotten. The 'LOC' he mentioned? Library of Congress."

"What? That would be a needle in a haystack, Robert. The place is gigantic."

"Not the library itself. The computer. It has probably the most secure library-related computer in the nation, one that's backed up so many times that short of the complete destruction of the United States, whatever's on the database will remain in some form."

Kat shook her head. "You're telling me Walter Carnegie stored his files on the master computer of the Library of Congress?"

"That's what I'm telling you, although I won't know until I can get into the database and look for a file with the file name he gave us."

"Good grief! Can we do that by phone?"

"I doubt it," Robert replied. "With that sort of master program, you probably have to be on-site and at the right terminal with the right access code to get into the deep files. So we're going to have to go to D.C. before the wrong people figure this out as well."

She sighed and drank some more of the hot chocolate. "Okay. But we also need to find Dr. Thomas, if he's still in Vegas. Question is, which comes first?"

Robert shrugged. "Hell, since we don't know what Walter knew, and we don't know what this Thomas character knows, it's a toss-up."

"We do know where Walter's file is, though. So I think D.C.'s the best start."

"Okay, but not until tonight," he said. "We need sleep."

She shook her head. "I feel almost guilty about this."

"What? Drinking pure chocolate or sleeping?"

She shook her head as she maneuvered herself to a sitting position. "No. I mean, considering all that's happened . . . and here we are in this beautiful place . . ."

"I know," he said, staring at the fire.

Kat looked at him in silence, waiting until he felt her gaze and turned to look in her eyes.

"Dollar for your thoughts," he said, a bit off balance.

"A dollar?" she said, her eyebrows fluttering up.

"Inflation, you know," he added.

She laughed softly, watching the glow of the fire play off his face, and thought how the perpetual smile around his eyes matched his personality. Kat forced herself to look away. "Robert," she said, rotating the cup slowly in her hands, "they're going to shoot down another airliner somewhere. You know that, don't you?"

He was silent for a long time before nodding. "I do now, Kat. Walter Carnegie understood that, too, and someone killed him for it."

"The fact that there have been no demands has to mean that they haven't completed their opening act." She threw her free hand up in frustration. "So who's next? Are we going to get a seven-forty-seven impacting the World Trade Center in New York because the two pilots were neutralized on takeoff from Newark or Kennedy? What if they decide to zap the pilots aboard Air Force One as it lifts off from Andrews? What hurts so," Kat continued, "is that whoever gets hit, the weapon may well be the very one we had in our hands." She shook her head and sighed, registering only mild surprise when she felt Robert's left hand on her forearm, massaging gently. "I'm sure it was a weapon."

"Kat, there's no sense beating yourself up about what happened in Honolulu. I'm certain that wasn't the only one like it."

"I'm not beating myself up," she said, with an edge in her voice that she immediately softened. "I'm trying to figure this out before it's too late for another two hundred people. I mean, I'm not trying to be the Lone Ranger, all right? But the fact is, I can't call Jake, and I really can't call anyone. I'm trained to be a good team player, and half the time I end up with no team and forced to operate autonomously, which is a trait the boys in the Bureau *really* love in a female!"

"You're under some gender-based pressure, I take it?"

Kat widened her eyes. "Whoa. You wouldn't believe. It amazes me how many otherwise levelheaded, intelligent men are threatened by a woman who refuses to fold up and play the helpless female."

"And if you do play the helpless female," he added, "they say you aren't fit to do a man's job."

"Straight from the book *Catch 22*. But this catch needs its own number," Kat said.

"How about ninety-nine? Remember Agent Ninety-nine from *Get Smart*?"

Kat nodded. "Yeah. You're right. Catch ninety-nine. But it's also the name of a great women's pilot organization I belong to, the Ninety-Nines."

"Even more reason to call it catch ninety-nine."

"Very well. So named."

"Kat, a team can consist of two. We're a team."

Kat rolled her eyes. "Yeah, well, I can't deputize you. I'm going to have to go to D.C. alone."

"What? No, Kat!"

"I need you here to keep everyone safe. I'll leave you the sat phone. I'll call if I need help with the details. You need me to call anyone? Your wife, for instance?"

He smiled. "There are probably hundreds of Mrs. Mac-

Cabes around the East Coast, but I'm not legally attached to any of them."

She cocked her head. "What a strange way of telling me you're not married, not to mention a clever way of obscuring whether you're divorced."

He smiled again. "Merely trying to hide the fact that only my housekeeper and my editor care if I'm dead or alive, and I'm not so sure about my editor. Kat, look, I really think I ought to go with you."

"Not a chance. I need you here."

Robert sighed. "Well, you may get me fired. I was supposed to be back at work at the *Post* yesterday."

"And you can bet the other side knows that, too. No, I'm not very recognizable. But you are."

"It's not me I'm worried about, Kat," he said softly, triggering an unwanted blush. Kat looked away and put down her cup, fishing out the number of the float-plane service. She punched it into the satellite phone before lifting it to her ear, looking for something logical and casual to do with her hands and eyes to avoid looking at Robert. She had no time to deal with the sudden ripple of warmth that was radiating through her body. *We're not alone in some idyllic mountain hideaway as lovers, for God's sake,* Kat chided herself. *We're running for our lives. Get a grip, woman!*

The phone was ringing on the other end, and she began to wonder if the pilot had made it back. She could hear Robert's breathing, and she could feel his eyes on her, which kindled deeper reactions.

The float-plane service answered at last, and the same pilot agreed to a morning pickup. "Another solo training flight's a good idea," he joked. "But it'll have to be tomorrow morning. I'm booked this afternoon."

"Look, we need to get out of here now."

"I'm sorry, Ma'am. I've got a business to run, too."

"I'll pay you double."

"It's not about the money, okay? I've got a personal obligation and my marriage probably depends on it. The answer is no. I can't do it. Couldn't you take the afternoon boat back?"

Robert was gently pulling her sleeve and she turned and mouthed the question "What?"

"You need to sleep! Go tomorrow."

She sighed, thought, and nodded, rolling her eyes. "All right. Tomorrow morning. Another good day to pick up absolutely no one at the dock and get paid for it."

"I'll be dockside at eight," the pilot replied.

She confirmed the deal, thanked him, and punched off the phone, placing it down at her side with exaggerated care before breathing deeply and turning to Robert, determined to put things back on a business footing. They spoke simultaneously.

"I, ah . . ." he began.

"The pickup will be . . ."

He nodded too energetically. "Yeah. At eight."

"Right," she confirmed.

"I heard."

"Okay," she said, her eyes locked on his.

"I just wish that . . . you know . . ."

"This was all over?"

"In a way, yes, Kat, but in a way, no."

"I know," she said, smiling too broadly. "It's such a beautiful place. Be nice to be up here when we weren't, you know, *running* for our lives."

He laughed a bit stiffly. "Not to mention trailing a phalanx of others."

"Right," she said. "Our entourage."

"It'd just be nice to be up here . . . just the two of us."

She met his gaze again, and felt the spreading warmth as she fought the temptations running through her mind. For a split second, they moved almost imperceptibly toward each other, then stopped, their eyes still locked together.

Kat mustered the willpower to force her eyes away. "Um, I guess we should . . . you know, find our respective beds and go sleep for eighteen hours," she said, forcing the words out, but remaining in place.

"If we must," he agreed, reluctantly, and slowly got to his feet. He leaned over and extended his hand. She took it, holding on long enough to get to her feet, then pulled her hand away, avoiding his eyes.

"So I'll see you in the morning," he said.

"Yep," Kat said, pretending to study the ceiling, the mantle, and the room. "I'll wake you before going. I need to brief everyone on the care and feeding of the cabin." She turned toward the bedroom Dallas had labeled the girl's room.

"Kat?" he said, his voice low and intense, causing her to turn back and look at him, almost transfixed. She cleared her throat. "Yes, Robert?"

He smiled. "Good night."

She smiled back. "You, too."

chapter
36

Deep shadows still clothed the eastern side of the fjord as the DeHavilland Beaver flew down the right side of Lake Chelan at 500 feet above the water. Kat sat in the copilot's seat and watched the beauty of the landscape as it passed, changing from alpine slopes to arid hills toward the south end. Her thoughts reverted to the cabin, and the unexpectedly emotional departure.

She had decided to approach it as a matter-of-fact exercise of logic under fire: They were all targets who should remain hidden, while she went off trying to find the answers that could make them safe.

But as she briefed them in front of the fire at 7 A.M., the grim and apprehensive looks on every face set off a crushing flash of hopelessness, as if she were kidding herself to think she could guarantee their safety.

"Look, a few days of safe haven can make all the difference," she said.

"Could they track us here, Kat?" Dan asked. "Tell us the truth."

She sighed and pursed her lips. "It's unlikely. It would take an incredible amount of digging to even connect me to this place, let alone assume we're here. I'm going to use a cash machine in Seattle today on the way out, and that will further confuse the speculation on where I'm hiding you."

"But they could still get a lucky break. That pilot could talk. They could find the van," Dan continued.

She fought the urge to spout unrealistic assurances. The five people before her had been through too much to be fed anything but the unvarnished truth.

A wisp of fragrant wood smoke from the fire diverted her thoughts for a second as she searched for a way to spare them the realities of the dangers they still faced.

"Yes, they could get lucky and find you, or me. We know they're murderers with zero remorse or compassion, and we've gotten in the way of some plan. But that's why I want you to stay in the cabin and out of sight. Dallas, I want you to drive me to the dock, and I'm going to leave a note for the caretaker so he won't come by. I've shown you the guns and ammunition here, so you're not defenseless."

"What if someone comes claiming to be an FBI agent, Kat?" Steve asked.

She shook her head. "I . . . can't give you a guarantee. I mean, you can't just shoot anyone who shows up, but . . . first rule is to keep the shades and curtains drawn and do not answer the door under any circumstances. If someone does come poking around, split up. Someone go for the phone down by the dock and call me on the satellite phone. Steve, that's you. Dallas, you greet them if they come in, and Graham and Robert can cover you from the back rooms with the guns."

"We'll work out a plan," Dallas said, her demeanor subdued.

"But," Kat continued, "if they flash FBI credentials, get names, ask them to come back in an hour, and meantime get to the dock phone and call me."

"That's pretty weak, Kat," Dan said.

"I know it, but it's the best we can do."

"I called my mother," Steve said without warning.

There was stunned silence in the room.

"When, Steve?" Kat asked quietly.

"I'm sorry if I messed up, but I couldn't stand her crying over me and all."

"When and where did you call, Steve, and what did you tell her?" Kat asked, working hard to control the panic she felt.

"From that grocery store in Seattle. While you all were buying food."

"Damn, boy!" Dallas said, rolling her eyes. "What'd you tell her?"

"Nothing about where we were going. Honest. I said I was okay and with an FBI woman, but I couldn't come home for a while because people were chasing us."

"Did you give names, Steve?" Kat asked.

"Yeah. Yours. I'm sorry."

"But you did not say anything about heading for a lake, or a mountain cabin, or Chelan, or Stehekin? You've got to level with us, Steve."

He was shaking his head vigorously. "No. I didn't say anything about that. She wanted me to tell her, but I said I couldn't."

Kat sat frozen for a few seconds before nodding. "Probably no harm done. But please, whatever you do, all of you, do *not* try to phone any friends or relatives from that phone near the dock. It will be traced back here in a heartbeat."

"We all have lives, Kat," Dallas said. "I've got a few people to reassure, too."

"I don't," Graham said with no expression in his voice.

Kat raised her hand. "I know we—*you've* got friends and family who may think you're dead. If you're really worried, give me names and phone numbers and I'll call them from a safe distance."

"Do you really think you can solve all this?" Dan asked quietly.

"Maybe," she said. "Depending on what Walter Carnegie left us. At least I can arrange to bring all of us in safely where those goons can't touch us."

"Provided they don't get you."

"There's always that chance." She took another deep breath as she studied her shoes and listened to the crackling of the freshly stoked fire. "Look, if I don't come back within five days"—she raised her head and looked at them one by one—"take the ferry to Chelan together, rent a car or take a bus to Spokane, go to the FBI office there, and tell them everything you know."

Dan had hugged her unexpectedly at the door, the hug becoming a clench as he broke down and cried. His broad shoulders shook as he tried to speak. "Thank you . . . for all you've done to end this nightmare, Kat. I'm sorry. I didn't mean to start bawling like a kid."

Kat hugged him back, patting his arm as Dallas massaged his shoulder. "It's okay, Dan. You've been through a lot."

"Yeah," he acknowledged, the tears still flowing from under the bandages on his eyes. He pulled away at last, though reluctantly.

Graham Tash had tried to shake her hand, but that evolved into tears and another clinging hug, followed by a tentative hug from Steve Delaney.

Robert was waiting by the door, afraid to hug her but determined not to part with the cold detachment of a handshake. Kat put her arms around him for a quick hug, feeling as awkward as he.

"So," she said with a forced smile as she zipped one of the parkas she'd found in the closet. "Ready, Dallas?"

The DeHavilland Beaver had just arrived when Kat stepped out of the beat-up old Dodge and waved a quick good-bye to Dallas, who got out to give her a sisterly hug. "Stay safe, girl, and get back here," Dallas said.

Kat greeted the pilot and handed him her ubiquitous roll-on bag before negotiating the small ladder. The lines were cast off and the engine started when something landed on the rear of the right pontoon.

"What the hell?" the pilot muttered, trying to look out to the right. "See anything back there?" he asked Kat.

"Someone's on the float. I can't see . . ."

The right rear passenger door was flung open, and the interloper threw a small duffel bag on the seat before hauling himself in and turning with a grin toward Kat.

"Robert! What . . . ?"

"Remember what we talked about last night? Teamwork?"

"You're supposed to stay back there and watch the others," Kat said, consternation competing with surprise in her voice.

"Dallas is a force of nature. She can handle it alone. I think she could take Saddam and the Republican Guard single-handedly."

The pilot had throttled back to idle, but the Beaver still drifted slowly toward the middle of the upper bay. The fragrance of the lake mixed with the scent of pine trees as the water lapped gently at the floats. He looked over his shoulder, waiting for the two of them to resolve it.

"Robert, dammit . . ."

"Want me to leave?"

"I work alone."

"Not what you indicated yesterday."

"This could be dangerous, for God's sake!"

"I'm the one who ended up in a crash and running through the jungle, evading cutthroats. Besides, I need to get shot at at least once a year to reclaim my combat reporting credentials. It's a currency requirement."

Kat was shaking her head. "No. I'm responsible for—"

"Not for me, you're not! We may decide to be responsible for each other as a team, but don't forget, I'm a damn good investigative reporter. I know how to look under rugs, I've got extensive contacts, too, and you're going to need all that kind of help you can get. And this is too good a story, and I'm in the middle of it. It's unreasonable to ask a reporter to sit on his tail in a beautiful setting where he might actually enjoy himself, thus pissing off his editor and imperiling his job. Now. Still want me to go back and baby-sit?"

She looked at the floorboards and shook her head again before meeting his eyes. "Yes . . . no. All right. You're deputized."

"*Now* you have that power?" he asked.

"Not really," Kat said and looked at the pilot. "Let's get out of here."

"Yes, Ma'am."

chapter

37

By noon Snoqualmie Pass was twenty miles behind them and the Seattle area was visible in the distance. Kat glanced over at Robert as she drove. He had been deep in thought, but stirred suddenly and turned toward her.

"I have an idea," he said. "Let's find a motel."

She gave him a startled look. "Excuse me? I'm not that kind of FBI agent."

Robert was smiling. "I thought that would get your attention. No, I'm serious. If we can hole up and have time to work the phones, maybe I can save us a trip to D.C."

"How so?"

"I've got a friend at the Library of Congress. If he can get me modem access to the computer, there's no need to go there in person."

Kat smiled energetically. "Great! That's worth a try. Maybe we can get a line on Dr. Thomas as well. We don't have much time."

"Let's get two connecting rooms, and thus two phones."

"Appropriately conservative, Mr. MacCabe. Any hotel preferences?"

He shook his head. "Something between a Ritz Carlton and a Motel Six."

She nibbled her lip for a few seconds. "Robert, about SeaAir, I—"

He raised his hand. "Kat, please. We've been talking about this and racking our brains for hours, and what did we solve? Nothing. All we have is speculation. We know there's a group out there, we know they've got at least one exotic eye-killing weapon, we know that somehow our government is frightened of them, we suspect a mole at the FBI, and other than that, we're chasing our tails."

"There's a pattern here, Robert, and Carnegie's message reinforces it."

He sighed. "Okay, I'll bite. What pattern?"

"Official misconduct."

"Say again?" he asked.

"Somehow, this involves something an agency of the U.S. government has done or become involved in that is so wrong, they're scared to death of exposure."

Robert fell silent for a few seconds. "You . . . aren't suggesting we're being chased by an arm of the U.S. government?"

"Oh, Lord no!" Kat said quickly. "But whoever these vermin are, when we uncover the full story, this administration is going to be terribly embarrassed."

"That's a sobering thought, Kat, but let's stop talking about it until we get into Walter's file. My brain is spinning." Robert reached over and turned on the radio as they continued on I-90 across Lake Washington, tuning across a variety of stations before settling on a newscast reporting the initial response to a major airline accident in Chicago.

"Turn that up!" Kat said.

. . . came down in a residential area approximately four miles from Chicago O'Hare Airport. A massive rescue effort is under way at this moment, but there are no initial reports on how many people may have survived. There are numerous eyewitness reports that the Airbus A-three-twenty was about a thousand feet

*off the ground after takeoff when it did a slow roll
upside down and came down nose-first. Witnesses
reported a tremendous noise and an immediate plume
of smoke from the site. We talked a few minutes ago
with an FAA air traffic control supervisor who confirmed that there were no distress calls or any other
indication of trouble before the crash. We'll continue
to . . .*

Kat turned the radio off and looked at Robert MacCabe,
whose face was as pasty-white as hers. She swallowed hard.
"Undoubtedly . . ." Kat began.

"Yeah. I'm thinking the same thing."

"Could be something else, of course. Flight control failure, some sort of massive aerodynamic failure of flaps,
or . . . or a speed brake on one side. Could even be an
encounter with the wingtip vortex of another large aircraft."

Robert was nodding slowly. "But it probably isn't. Accidents don't happen much anymore. Here's the third inside
six weeks. We know now two were from the same cause.
You said last night it was going to happen again."

Kat hit the dashboard with the heel of her hand, startling
Robert. He looked over to see her jaw set, her lips pressed
tightly together in anger.

"Damn! DAMN! Damn, damn, damn, damn!"

"Kat?"

"SHIT!" she cried out.

"You okay?"

She snapped her head around to look at him. "NO, I am
not 'okay.' I hate being asked if I'm okay when I'm obviously not."

"I'm sorry."

"No, don't be sorry. This is *my* agony. God! I can't
believe I let you get on that flight in Hong Kong when I
should have known you'd be a target, and then I let the evidence, the weapon, and one of the felons slip away in Honolulu because—"

"Because you fell victim to a very professional, very
well-done charade that would have fooled anyone."

"Robert, please don't try to make me feel better. The one thing my dad drummed into me was personal responsibility. You screw up, you admit it and take the consequences."

"So how did you screw up, Agent Bronsky? By not being clairvoyant?"

"Precisely," she snapped.

"Look," he said, "personal responsibility is appropriate when there's been a real lapse, but here . . ."

Kat let out a long sigh and signaled for a right turn. She braked the minivan hard and steered onto the shoulder of the freeway, coming to a lurching halt in a cloud of dust and rearranged gravel.

"What are you doing?" Robert asked in alarm.

"Look at me, Robert."

"I'm looking."

"I'm thankful you see me clearly as a female, and I know your male instincts are to protect me, but you're dealing with someone who is as professional and responsible as you are. Do NOT try to protect me from the consequences of being in the profession I've chosen." She hesitated. "This is why I was going to come alone."

"Kat, I wasn't trying to protect you."

"Yes, you were! You were trying to protect the little girl from feeling bad because she screwed up big-time. I can handle my own self-recrimination."

"So, if I understand this, I can't say *anything* to you that's supportive?"

"I didn't say that. I just don't need you chasing away my faults."

"Oh, okay. You want only faults? Very well, I'll give you a fault. You're too focused on the job to pay attention to the underlying feelings of those around you."

"What? That's bull! I'm a psychologist."

He hesitated, then waved his hand as if to dismiss the subject. "Let's drop it."

"Oh, no you don't. You opened the door. Give me an example." Robert had shifted his gaze to the road ahead, but Kat leaned around to catch his eye. "You can't, can you? You know very well I'm sensitive to the feelings of those around me."

Robert's eyebrows flared as he turned to meet her gaze. "Really? Then how come you didn't know how much I wanted to kiss you yesterday?"

A stunned silence followed, Robert as surprised as she by what he had blurted out. His hand went up instantly as he looked away. "I'm sorry, Kat, I didn't mean . . . I mean, that just slipped out."

She reached over and turned his face back to hers. "I'm glad. And I did know, because I was feeling precisely the same way. It was just the wrong place and the wrong time."

"Wrong time, maybe. Definitely not the wrong place." He looked at her for several seconds, and a smile slowly spread across his face. "What rotten timing," he said. "I find a woman who really turns me on, but it's in the middle of a terrorist crusade."

"Was that why you came this morning?" she asked quietly.

He shook his head no. "That was part of it, but the major reason was precisely what I told you: the story, the chase, and the need for two minds on the same problem."

There was a faint electronic warble in the background.

"Is that your beeper?" Robert asked.

Kat reached down to her purse and flipped it open, intensifying the warble. "Yes. I guess I was trying to ignore it." She adjusted the screen and pressed the button, her expression darkening as she read. "It's Jake, ordering me one last time to contact him and make arrangements to surrender you and the others as material witnesses."

"To what?"

She sighed and shook her head. "An act of mass murder, to start with. He's right. What I'm doing could be viewed as obstruction of justice."

"Oh, bullshit!" Robert snapped.

Kat was pulling out her satellite phone with a freshly charged battery.

"You're sure they can't trace that?" he asked.

"Yes, I'm sure. They can trace it when it uses a ground-based cellular network, but I'm going to program it to stay on the satellite system."

The phone rang suddenly and she automatically punched the Send button to answer it, realizing her mistake as she did so.

Robert was speaking at the same moment: "Maybe it isn't such a good idea . . ."

Kat punched the Off button as fast as possible, hoping whoever was on the other end hadn't heard anything.

The phone began ringing again, making her jump slightly, and she quickly punched the Off button.

The ringing stopped.

"Could they . . . track us with that?" Robert asked.

She glanced over, her face betraying deep alarm. "I . . . don't know. But let's get out of here and find that motel. We've got a lot of digging to do, and we need to keep on being a moving target."

LAS VEGAS, NEVADA

The level of tension in the room was almost explosive as several ashen-faced men milled around while one pressed a telephone receiver more tightly to his ear, his face reflecting sudden intense concentration.

"Hold it," he said, raising an index finger to quiet the others. The temporary office had been set up in an industrial park near Nellis Air Force Base, and the sudden passage of a pair of F-15 Eagles overhead caused him to frown and glance up.

He toggled the phone to get a new line, dialing the number again. "Someone answered Bronsky's phone . . . and there was a guy's voice in the background for just a second. It was like she punched it on and off rapidly. I'm calling back." He waited a full thirty seconds. "Now she's not answering." Suddenly a look of happy surprise crossed the man's face as he turned to his compatriots. "I don't believe this!"

"*What?*" another of them said, crossing toward the first.

"That was the domestic eight-hundred-number for her

satellite phone—the one that tries to connect through the cellular system—and it rang."

"Yeah?" was the response.

"Meaning that when she refused to answer, the system played a message with a little identification tag line. She's still in Seattle, Larry! We've found the bitch."

"You say there was a male in the background?"

"Yeah," he said, excited.

One of the men put a cassette in a small recorder and punched the button. Robert MacCabe's voice from a recent television appearance filled the room. The man stopped it after thirty seconds.

"*That* voice?"

The other man smiled and nodded. "Sure sounded like it."

"Then, gentlemen," the leader said, "we have a double benefit. We know MacCabe is also with Bronsky, and they're somewhere in Seattle."

"How about the other four?"

"Who knows. They could have stashed them, or they could be dragging them along."

There was a moment's hesitation before all five men in the room dove for various phones. There was a jet waiting at Las Vegas's McCarren Airport that could have them airborne in twenty minutes.

"What do we take?"

"All the firepower we can drag along. She's making mistakes. This time we're gonna nail her cute little ass."

Two rooms under assumed names in a nondescript hotel in the south Seattle town of Renton took only a little cash from the proceeds of a quick stop at a cash machine. They settled in to their respective chambers for a few minutes before opening the double doors between them. Kat stuck her head inside Robert's room, made a snide comment about famous motel art on the wall, and glanced at the phone. "Why don't you start the search for a way in to the Library of Congress computer, Robert. I'm going to use the satellite phone to call Jake."

He nodded and plopped on the bed as he reached for the phone and looked up. "First, I'm going to try to scare up my Library of Congress contact."

She partially closed the door and turned on the satellite phone, carefully switching to the satellite system before it had time to connect with a land-based cellular network. She dialed the number of FBI headquarters in Washington, unsurprised to hear the tension and anger in Jake Rhoades's voice.

"Kat! Thank God! What the hell do you think you're doing?"

"Keeping us all safe. There's a leak back there, Jake. I think you know that. Every time I told you something yesterday, the other side heard it."

"What are you saying? Are you accusing *me*?"

"Of course not! Don't be ridiculous. You did your best trying to protect us in Seattle last night, but look what happened."

"So what *did* happen, Kat?" Jake asked. "All I got was a cryptic pager message from you about going underground, then a frustrated team finds you and the others have jumped out of the airplane and run into the night without a trace. I've beeped you every hour on the hour since, but you didn't see fit to call me, though you know a dozen safe ways to do so."

"I have reasons," she said, choosing her words carefully. "I can't go into it right now." Any excuses about remote areas and no radio contact could point to a place like Stehekin and endanger the rest of them. She told him, instead, of the last-minute diversion of the DC-10 to a south gate.

"Yeah," he said, "we heard, once our team shifted to the South Satellite terminal and found out someone else had been flashing false ID around."

"You didn't collar the bogus group, I assume?" she asked.

Jake hesitated. "They were one step ahead of us. They murdered one of our Seattle field agents when we tried to apprehend them. Jimmy Causland was his name. Wife, two kids. Five bullets, three to the head, we think with a silencer. Thanks to that encounter, we *know* these people are real, and we *know* they're using fake FBI credentials, but we don't know who or where they are."

"Which is exactly why we've dropped out of sight for a few days."

"Kat, the Bureau can't protect you *or* those survivors if you go solo."

"You can't protect us anyway. Not as long as we have an unplugged leak. Remember what happened last night at Sea-Tac?"

"Regardless, you've got to bring them in immediately. That's an order."

"I need some time, Jake, and I'm not sure how much. Otherwise, if there's another slipup, we're history. That group of cutthroats has to be frantic by now, and I'm sure the orders have escalated to 'shoot on sight.'"

"At least we now have a name for them."

"A name?" she asked.

"This organization, for want of a better term, is calling itself Nuremberg, as in the Nuremberg War Crimes Trials."

"What on earth? Do we know where they are?"

"Not a clue, though the speculation is it's an organization fronting for Middle Eastern interests such as Libya, Iraq, Iran, you name it. All our dear friends."

"That name," Kat said, "could also mean this is some sort of retaliatory blood feud with the United States over . . . *something* related to war crimes, or the U.S. reaction to someone else's war crimes. Perhaps Serbia."

"We don't know, but a hand-delivered letter was plopped on CNN's desk this morning, devoid of fingerprints or usable identification, and reciting enough unreleased facts to convince us it's valid."

"Thank God! So they've announced their demands?"

"No. They've announced their existence. The essence of the communiqué is simply that they will continue to establish their ability to destroy any aircraft anywhere in the world at any time without telling us how, until we are ready—in other words softened up enough—to listen to their demands."

"Oh, Lord. And this was right after the Chicago crash?"

"Yes. Mentioned it specifically. Kat, the media's shifting to a new level of hysteria, the White House is putting incredible pressure on us for answers, and your name is being prominently mentioned without much love. Now listen to me carefully. I have all but lost control. I can probably protect your tail here in the Bureau for everything that's gone down up to now, but when we disconnect here, if I don't have an arrangement to repatriate you and all of those survivors, the director has ordered us to start hunting you down."

"On what grounds?" Kat asked, her voice subdued.

"Obstruction of justice, possible kidnapping, and perhaps a half-dozen others."

"Those people are with me voluntarily, Jake."

"The teenager, Delaney, is too young to make that decision legally. His father is stirring up a hornet's nest to find him and see you prosecuted."

"His *father*?"

"I don't have the entire story, but the man's gone ballistic. He apparently knows his son is with you and is accusing you, and us, of false arrest and kidnapping, and even hinting at sexual molestation."

"Oh, for God's sake, Jake! Sexual . . . what kind of nonsense is that?"

"I'm merely telling you, Kat, that FBI agents do not have the luxury of sequestering people, especially minors, without due process of law and the sanction of their employer. His father apparently has joint custody. He's within his rights."

"So I'm supposed to give up Steve only to see him cut down by automatic weapon fire as he walks to his father's arms? Now *that's* a plan!"

"We're expected to do things in accordance with the law, Kat. That's your oath. You are, after all, a law enforcement officer."

"Jake, listen to me. All the people involved, with one exception, are hiding of their own free will, and I'm not with them. I am a long way from where the others are holed up, and I've got one of the group with me, and it's not Steve Delaney. We're desperately trying to develop leads. Even if I thought it was safe, which it is not, I'd have no way of just turning the others over to you."

"But you're going to have to tell me where they are, Kat."

"I can't do that."

"DAMMIT! Kat, this is it. This is the last warning. If I hang up without getting what I need, this is your job, and maybe your freedom. You don't *really* want to go from promising FBI agent to convicted felon, do you?"

Kat let out a long sigh. A tense silence on the line hung between them.

"Inside five days, Jake, right or wrong, fired or not, indicted or otherwise, I'll come in. If you can't trust me in the meantime, I'll understand. But these lives are my responsibility. And Jake . . . I'm truly sorry to have to disobey you."

"I'm sorry too, Kat," he began, sighing long and loud. She could tell what was coming: "Because as of this moment . . ."

She disconnected before he could say the word "suspended" and sat there, biting her lip for nearly a minute before looking up. A grim-faced Robert MacCabe had come into the room to stand quietly, watching her.

"Robert, I need to warn you about this." She leaned over the table, trying to keep her voice very low. "I need to make sure you have the option of bailing out."

"What are you talking about?" he asked.

"From this moment forward, anything you do to help me could be viewed as aiding a criminal act, or voluntarily conspiring to commit a criminal act. I have not been formally suspended, as far as I can tell. I didn't hear any words to that effect. But I have no support in Washington, and they're treating me now as a renegade." She told him the details of the phone call. "I hate to say it, but I think you'd better get away from me. Just give me a twelve-hour head start before you call Washington and tell them what you know."

"Cut it out, Kat."

"Robert, I don't want you following me into infamy if this ends up badly."

He leaned down, face-to-face with her, his arms supporting his weight. "I am not abandoning you. You're going to need my help. In fact, you couldn't get rid of me now with a federal court order."

FBI HEADQUARTERS, WASHINGTON, D.C.

Deputy Assistant Director Jake Rhoades looked up from the conference table he had been leaning over, the expression on his face fierce and foreboding.

"Yes?" he snapped.

A male agent in his late twenties held up a piece of paper. "Sorry to bother you, Sir, but I was told . . ."

Jake grabbed it from his hand. "What's this?"

"We've located the area her signal is coming from."

"Good. Where?"

"They . . . can't pinpoint more closely than about fifteen square miles, and it took tremendous pressure to get the communications company to do it—"

"*WHERE*, dammit! Does it look like I'm on vacation here?"

"Seattle. At least, the general area."

"Okay. Thanks. I'm sorry to be grumpy."

"No problem, Sir." The agent turned to go. Jake called after him, causing him to stop and turn back.

"Sir?"

"Look, I've known Kat Bronsky since she joined the Bureau, and I think the world of her, and this is really painful."

"Understood."

"You were trying to tell me how you located the signal."

The agent nodded, moving back toward Jake. "This is an American communications company operating all over the world, and they did *not* want to cooperate at first. But their satellites are at approximately four hundred and fifty miles up, over seventy of them, and their computers can triangulate a signal on the ground. It took pressure from friends at the Federal Communications Commission to get their help."

"Accurate to within fifteen miles?"

"They could do better, but they won't. They have agreed, however, to keep tracking her signal, but they emphasized that's *only* because the FBI owns the phone."

When he had cleared the door, Jake turned to the others in the room. "Okay, everyone. It's deployment time. Kat Bronsky is somewhere in Seattle, and we've got to find her before the boys from Nuremberg do."

RENTON, WASHINGTON

Robert had turned on the TV in his room and left it on low volume as he worked his way through a series of calls,

trying to locate his Library of Congress contact, who was on
vacation. Another line was ringing without an answer when
something on the screen caught his attention. He reached for
the remote when he saw the wreckage of the Chicago plane
crash on screen, but the scene changed to one from Dallas,
and he toggled up the sound. The anchor was saying something about an airport shutdown.

Robert replaced the receiver and moved quickly to the
door to Kat's room, finding her between calls. "You may
want to see this on channel four," he said.

She reached for her remote and clicked to the same channel. Pictures of the huge DFW Airport dissolved to stock
shots of passengers milling back and forth in a terminal
before cutting to a reporter in front of a mob scene at a ticket
counter.

> *Thanks, Bill. The scene here at Dallas/Fort Worth
> International Airport is one of uncertainty and upset
> this afternoon in the aftermath of the apparent cancel-
> lation of all flights, in and out, on the strength of a
> telephoned threat. In the wake of this morning's air-
> line disaster in Chicago, a group calling itself
> "Nuremberg" has claimed responsibility, claiming it
> also is responsible for the crash of an American jumbo
> jet in Vietnam, and another American airliner off
> Cuba last month. Two hours ago, someone claiming to
> be from the same terrorist group announced plans to
> destroy an airliner either arriving or departing from
> DFW this afternoon. The result, as I say, has been
> chaos, with thousands of stranded travelers being
> given too little information.*

There was a sudden scuffling of chair legs as Robert
pulled up the desk chair and sat down, glancing back at Kat,
who was sitting mesmerized. When the report was over, she
snapped off the TV once again and shook her head slowly.

"So we know their next move. Leverage the terror."

"But to what end, Kat?"

"That's the question, isn't it? What do they want?" She

stood suddenly and pointed to the chair he was in. "Up, please. I need the chair. Let's get back to the calls. We need progress. I'm finding no one on planet Earth with the name Dr. Brett Thomas, although I've still got a few tricks to try in a bunch of databases. How about you?"

He filled her in on the vacationing contact.

"Of course! Naturally, he'd be on vacation when you need him!" Kat said in a sarcastic tone. "Murphy never sleeps."

Robert looked puzzled. "Beg your pardon?"

Kat pulled up the chair Robert had vacated and sat at the desk. She laid out a notebook and reached for the phone. "Murphy's Law," she explained, her voice flat.

"Oh, yeah." Robert nodded. "'What can go wrong, will go wrong.'"

"But do you know the prime corollary to Murphy's Law?" Kat asked, watching him slowly shake his head as she continued. "Mr. Murphy was an optimist."

For three hours they worked in the relative obscurity of their respective rooms, both using their laptops plugged into the phones when they weren't using the lines for direct calls. Kat had carefully connected first Robert, then herself, to their respective Internet providers through a series of difficult-to-trace eight-hundred numbers. CNN remained on in both rooms, and the various reports and flashes outlined the rapidly developing crisis of confidence in the commercial aviation system as Atlanta and Salt Lake City joined the list of major American airports temporarily shut down by telephoned threats.

At nearly five in the afternoon Robert entered Kat's room unheard and moved to her side, a smile on his face.

"How's it going?" he asked, his voice causing her to jump slightly.

"Didn't see you come in," she said, turning back to the screen. "So far, still nothing. How about you?"

"Well, for a while all I'd learned is the date and time of Wally's funeral, and the fact that two more threats have been received since we've been here, shutting down Atlanta

Hartsfield and Salt Lake City Airports. This group, Nuremberg, is really flexing its muscles."

"Or it's a field day for kooks with phones," she said,
watching him sit down.

"But I finally located my friend on vacation."

Kat sat forward. "Where?"

"Tahiti."

"Good grief! Will he help?"

"He will, if he can. He should be on a public phone at a
secluded beach right this minute trying to arrange special
research access, while a scantily clad young woman puts
whatever they were doing on hold."

"You just had to get that in, didn't you?" she asked, her
face cradled in her right hand as she leaned on the desk and
rolled her eyes.

"Okay, I'm envious."

"So he'll call you back?" she asked, changing the subject.
"How? Surely you didn't give him this number?"

Robert sat on the bed and frowned at her. "Of course not.
I'll call him back. But I'm worried about those phone card
numbers. Aren't they traceable to you?"

She nodded. "Yes, but not immediately."

"You're sure?"

"I can't be one hundred percent sure, but it's a decent
guess, and we can't use the satellite phone for everything."

The computer chirped. Kat raised a finger and turned
back to the screen, typing in a few keystrokes.

"What's that?" he asked.

"A listing of scientists on a little-used database. I've been
unable—" She sat forward and typed in another command.
"Wait . . . a . . . minute! Wait just a darn minute!"

"What?"

"Just . . . a name I saw . . . triggered an idea. Hold on."
Several seconds elapsed as Robert maneuvered around
behind her, his eyes focusing on the screen at the same
moment a name and short dossier came into view.

"Wait, Kat. That's not Thomas?"

She was shaking her head in excitement. "No, it's not!
Carnegie was fuzzing things up. The guy we're looking

for isn't *Brett* Thomas, it's Dr. Thomas *Maverick*."

"What? Are you sure?" He leaned over her shoulder, following her finger.

"Look at his pedigree, Robert. U.S. government contractor positions in for the last twenty, almost thirty years. Los Alamos; Oak Ridge, Tennessee; NASA; and then Las Vegas."

"Why Vegas, I wonder? What's out there?"

"I'm not sure. Probably a lot of contractors. Nellis Air Force Base is in Vegas, or maybe he's just retired."

"But there's no Thomas?"

She shook her head. "No Ph.D. issued anywhere in the Western world in the past sixty years to anyone even remotely close to that name. But this . . ."

"Bret Maverick. James Garner's character in that classic TV show. Clever way of reversing the names. No address?"

"Don't worry. Now that I know his name, I'll find his address. Get back to work. Call Tahiti. Try not to drool too much."

"We need to eat sometime, Kat."

She shook her head. "Not yet. First we need answers."

In five minutes he was back in her room with a long face.

"What?" she asked.

"He can do it, but not before this evening. There's a window every night in which they update the computer. That's the only time he can add an authorized user."

"So how long?"

Robert looked at his watch. "It's five-thirty now. He said to call him back about nine-thirty tonight, our time."

Kat looked deeply worried. "I wasn't planning for us to stay that long. I don't know who might be closing in on us."

"How, Kat? How could they find us?"

She sighed. "The telephone calls, my mistake with the satellite phone. I don't know, but I'm *very* concerned about staying here a second longer than we have to."

"Gut feeling? Because I trust a professional's intuition."

She nodded. "Another thing I've been thinking." She gestured to the edge of the bed. "Sit, please."

He settled in on the bed next to her chair, and she sat back and looked at him for a few seconds. "Let's go back over this . . . see if we're missing anything obvious."

"Okay."

"First, we lose the MD-eleven over Cuban waters to something that fried the eyes of at least one pilot. We know that for a fact."

"Right."

"Next, Meridian Five is attacked with a similar weapon—some sort of electromagnetic weapon—and you, yourself, live through the crash."

"Yes."

"And now we have a crash in Chicago, with this group claiming responsibility and using the name of the German city of Nuremberg, and now issuing threats to shut down major airports."

"Right. Possibly."

"Okay, but why? These people have gone to a tremendous amount of time, trouble, and expense to kill and frighten. Why are they doing it?"

"Probably money, as we thought before. Maybe power has something to do with it, too, but my first guess is money."

"Why?" she asked, leading him slightly.

"Because . . . they're so well organized and financed?"

Kat nodded enthusiastically. "Precisely. But they've made no demands. Now, maybe they've made no demands because they are just trying to soften us all up, but what if the chaos itself is their objective?"

Robert leaned closer, studying her face. "What do you mean?"

"I was thinking about this a few minutes ago, Robert. How can you make lots of money from seriously undermining the airlines? How about selling their stock short, or softening up the industry for financial takeovers? We've been thinking this is terrorism for political gain, directly or otherwise. But while we're expecting direct extortion or ransom demands, they may already be getting precisely what they want from collapsing airline market prices."

"Are the stock prices down today?" he asked.

She nodded. "Big-time. As much as a ten-percent drop. If this continues, they'll go into free fall."

"Then . . . we should be looking for someone buying a lot of airline stock at the bottom, or selling them short?"

She shrugged. "I don't know, but it's logical. Millions for billions."

He was following her logic. "In other words, this whole thing is built on cash."

"Lots of it, especially when you consider that skilled covert operatives with zero morals and good shooting skills are not plentiful and take large amounts of money to hire." She shook her head and sat back. "No . . . money's behind this in more ways than one. It has to be. Maybe it's just Saddam Hussein or some wild-eyed Middle Eastern country or, God knows, maybe Slobby Milosevic, the butcher, throwing cash around to accomplish what they can't do directly, but somehow this feels more corporate, um . . . more professionally organized and impersonal and nonpolitical."

Kat reached over and turned up the television, using the remote to surf through a dozen other cable channels, and entirely missing her own image as it flicked across the screen.

"Wait!" Robert said suddenly, pointing at the TV. "Go back."

"What?"

"That looked like *you*!" he said.

Kat gave him a puzzled look as she backtracked two channels and stopped.

"There," Robert said. "You're off the screen now, but that's the channel."

The TV news reporter was standing outside FBI headquarters in Washington.

. . . is a current picture of Steven Delaney, age fourteen, who, as I said, is reportedly being held by well-known FBI Special Agent Katherine Bronsky, seen here in a file photo from a year ago when she accepted a national award for her efforts to solve a skyjacking over Colorado. Agent Bronsky is thought

*to be armed and dangerous, and is acting for
unknown reasons. Once again, all attempts tonight to
get the FBI to comment have failed, a fact that angers
Delaney's father.*

The station cut to an interview with the senior Delaney,
who was dripping concern and anger and righteous indignation at the FBI for kidnapping his son without a warrant, following his narrow escape from the carnage of a plane crash
in southeast Asia. He was saying, "I just want my little boy
back safely. I don't know whether this woman has ransom
on her mind, or whether she's a sexual predator, but I want
her prosecuted."

Kat hit the mute button and turned wordlessly to Robert,
her eyes huge, her mind completely stunned. Finally she
managed to get her mouth to work. "Did . . . did . . . you,
good grief, *sexual predator*? Good Lord!"

"I don't believe that!" Robert said, his eyes still on the
screen.

Kat was on her feet, pacing the floor and gesturing wildly
toward the screen. "I'm screwed! Not only did he just call
me a pervert on national television, he just spread my face
over a hundred million households! Or was that cable?"

"No, that was a broadcast channel, but probably more
like fifteen million."

"Holy moley! I can't believe this. Suddenly I can't even
walk outside without running a high risk some guy in an
undershirt swilling a beer will look up from his TV set long
enough to spot me and call in the militia."

She sat down hard beside him on the bed. "I've just been
checkmated."

"Well . . ."

"I mean, unless I adopt a disguise or something . . ."

Kat shot to her feet again before he could reply and paced
to the door, then returned to lean over the desk, where she
began scribbling something.

"Are we a team?" she asked, her head still down as she
wrote. She glanced up at him, sensing his puzzlement.

"Of course. Why?"

"I need you to go find a store and get me some things."

"What do you need?"

She straightened up, her expression deadly serious. "You mind being seen with a blond tart?"

"A . . . *what*?"

"Will it hurt your reputation if a platinum-blond bimbo is hanging on your arm, popping gum?"

"Kat, what on earth are you talking about?"

She handed him a list. "This is what I need."

He took it and began reading. "Leather micro-miniskirt, size six, A-size panty hose, medium-size lacy blouse, either Revlon or L'Oreal platinum-blond hair-color kit, platform shoes . . ." He looked at her with a blank expression.

"You know. High platforms, useless for anything other than advertising for male attention and twisting ankles."

"Oh."

"They should be flashy, but not too much so. You decide. The only hope we have is to change my image so drastically I can hide in plain sight. I've got to look so tarty, no one would believe for a second I even know how to spell 'FBI.' Not flashy enough to draw a crowd, but trash-flash five-and-dime tacky."

"We're talking *Jerry Springer*?"

"Oh, definitely."

Robert was shaking his head. "Believe me, this will do it. I'll never be acceptable in polite society again."

"That assumes you were before," she said, smiling.

"Ouch!"

"Seriously, can you get all that?"

He checked his watch. "If I can find the right store, but I'll have to move fast."

"It may be embarrassing, Robert. That's a lot of girl stuff to buy."

He sighed and smiled thinly as he got to his feet. "You know, Kat, I was just trying to conjure up an image of the FBI Academy course that trained you to do this."

She smiled. "The classes were boring, but the lab work was fun."

"I'll bet."

chapter

39

Dallas Nielson threw open the bedroom door where Graham
Tash and Dan Wade were sleeping in two of the four bunks.

"Guys, is Steve in here?" she asked, her voice urgent.

Graham raised himself up on one elbow. "No," he
replied, rubbing his eyes and looking around the small
room. Dan remained sound asleep.

"Damn!" she said, shutting the door behind her.

Graham got up and followed Dallas into the main room.
"What's wrong?"

She shook her head. "He asked me earlier if I thought it
was safe to go for a walk and I told him not only no, but *hell*
no." Dallas's eyes were focused on the door. "I hate to be
scared of my shadow, Doc, but what if those guys show up
here?"

"If Steve's outside, he shouldn't be," Graham said.

Dallas began pulling on a parka. "I'm planning on whup-
ping his behind when I get my hands on him." She finished
zipping the coat and grabbed a flashlight before opening the
door to a burst of cold night air. Graham held out a loaded
.30-.30 from the stock of rifles. "You need this?"

She turned and smiled. "I'm planning on *finding* the little runt, Doc, not *bagging* him."

"I'll wait right here," he said.

Dallas shut the door behind her and stepped off the porch carefully, listening to the squeak of the borrowed oversized mukluks as she moved through the snow. She thought of yelling for the boy, but changed her mind. Best to look quietly.

She glanced up at the moon, its stark, glowing beauty stunning as it rose radiant and almost full over the eastern ridge of the mountains, bathing the snowy landscape in a soft light that left only the deepest shadows unseen. A small, freshening breeze kicked up again, then died, rustling the branches overhead against a chorus of soft moans as a million pine needles combed the air.

If I wasn't so spooked, I could really enjoy this beauty, Dallas thought. She looked around carefully in all directions, letting her eyes adjust. There were footprints, undoubtedly Steve's, leading away from the porch. They led into a stand of timber, and Dallas moved in the same direction, staying to one side.

This is going to be easier than I thought, she assured herself. A cold chill rippled up her back as a dark shadow loomed ahead, but it was only a tree.

She stopped and stood still for nearly a minute, feeling the cold creep into her body as she listened in silence. She could hear water running somewhere to the west, and the call of a distant bird, but no footfalls or voices. Dallas continued to follow the footprints, wondering whether the deep cold of the mountain valley or her rising apprehension was causing the trembling in her knees.

Another dark shadow appeared to the right and seemed to move. Dallas felt adrenaline squirt into her bloodstream as she momentarily prepared to run.

Oh, Lord! Dallas tried to catch her breath, her hand on her chest. *Another tree.*

She looked down at the footprints once more, wondering why she was seeing double. Something wasn't right about the marks that had been left in the snow. *A second set of footprints!* After Steve had walked by, someone else had emerged from the forest and followed him.

There IS someone else out here! Oh my Lord, what do I do now? Dallas stood stock-still, her heart pounding. The .30-.30 she'd shunned was back in the cabin, but what if Steve were in trouble, or fighting for his life?

She closed her eyes and tried to concentrate on the night sounds, straining to discern anything unusual, such as a struggle in progress.

Steve could be dead. No, that isn't right. They wouldn't kill him. They'd drag him off and question him first. In the distance now, faintly, she began to hear muffled thumping sounds, which grew progressively louder.

Footfalls!

Her eyes strained to see ahead. A shape materialized in the trees in front of her, a figure charging toward her, head down, legs moving like pistons.

"STEVE?" Dallas barked, and saw a head bob up as the frightened face of the fourteen-year-old became starkly visible.

"RUN!" Steve yelled, pointing to the cabin as he passed her. "RUN!"

Dallas turned instantly and broke for the cabin, feeling clumsy in the mukluks, as she turned her head to see what or who was behind them.

"OPEN THE DOOR!" Steve yelled. "BEAR BEHIND!"

"WHAT?" Dallas bellowed back. "YOU HAVE A BARE WHAT?"

"BEAR! BEHIND . . . US . . . a BEAR!"

Dallas looked toward the cabin, seeing a crack of light. Graham was holding the door slightly ajar, waiting for her. "GRAHAM! OPEN IT!" Dallas bellowed.

They were less than twenty feet away when the cabin door swung open, the pool of light from within a welcoming beacon. Dallas could hear Steve's breath coming in ragged gasps. He took the two steps to the porch in one jump and flashed through the door, with Dallas right behind. Steve pivoted and slammed the heavy door in place, turning the dead bolt and motioning Graham and Dallas back to the center of the cabin.

"A bear . . ." he began, panting hard.

A loud, heavy thud reverberated through the door. There was a deep, throaty groan and snuffling outside, and the sound of a heavy body moving along the wooden porch, creaking the timbers.

"Sweet Jesus!" Dallas said, moving to the front window.

"What are you doing, Dallas?" Graham asked.

She didn't answer, but peeked out carefully before turning to the other two. "I heard him, but I don't . . ."

Through the sound of shattering glass a large black paw thrust through the breaking window, inches from Dallas's face. The claws raked in the opposite direction as she threw herself forward and scrambled to the others in the center of the room.

Graham cocked the .30-.30 and raised the gun to his shoulder.

The bear cried out in frustration as he swung a paw at the breaking window frame, shattering the remaining glass and catching the curtains. But when he could see inside, he spotted the humans. The bear stopped, his small eyes scanning the occupants as they stood in the middle of the floor and watched him, one holding the bead of the .30-.30 squarely on his forehead. For several very long seconds the bear weighed his conflicting desires in a basic, instinctive tug-of-war with himself. At last the learned caution about humans in groups won out, and the bear shook his head and backed away, roaming the porch for a few minutes before ambling off into the night, leaving the humans behind to deal with their own pounding hearts.

"I think . . . he's gone," Steve said at last, taking a deep breath.

"For now," Dallas replied, her whole body shaking. "Why isn't he hibernating? Would someone please talk some sense into that dumb bear?"

"Some of them go down late," Dan said. "How big was he?"

"Big enough. A black bear. Probably four hundred

pounds," Graham replied. "We need to figure out how to board up that window in case he decides to return."

Dallas took Steve by the shoulders and turned him to her. "What happened, Steve? Why'd you go outside?"

"I wanted to!" he snapped, squirming out of her grip.

"Where'd you find him? And no, you *can't* keep him just because he followed you home." Dallas motioned toward the front porch.

"Down by the river. He was down there just sitting in the dark by the edge and I walked right into him and scared him. He didn't like it at all."

"Steve, did you see anyone else out there?" Dallas asked.

"No." He shook his head.

"You're sure?"

"Yes, I'm sure," Steve said, looking scared. "Why?"

Dallas looked at Graham before replying, her face grim. "Because I found a second set of fresh footprints out there that followed yours from the forest."

She saw Steve's eyes get big and the blood drain from his face.

"Really? Someone was following me? They were human footprints?"

She nodded.

"Where, Dallas?" Dan asked.

"Less than a hundred yards from the cabin," she replied.

"Then," Dan began, motioning in the general direction of the door, "someone's already here and watching us."

Another thud reverberated through the cabin, this time from the opposite side.

"Oh, wonderful," Dan said. "There are two predictable behaviors for a bear. One, he sees people and he leaves. Two, the promise of food outweighs his natural fear of humans. Did you have any food with you outside, Steve?"

Steve nodded. "I took a roll with some meat in it. See? It's still here in my pocket, wrapped in a napkin."

Dan's mouth tightened. "So now he knows where there's food. Eating is a bear's primary focus in life."

"Which means?" Graham asked, his eyes on the back

windows. The scraping and bumping continued, punctuated by the same cries of irritation.

"Which means we've got a bear problem," Dan replied.

"There are shutters on that broken window," Graham said. "I guess we'd better get them closed." He handed the gun to Dallas and moved to the window, checking both sides before leaning through the destroyed frame and pulling the shutters.

"Without seeing them," Dan said, "I can't tell, but even if those shutters are well made, they're only going to slow him down. When he tries to come through that window—and he will—we'll have to be ready to shoot. You'll get one chance."

"I know it."

"And if you've never heard the old adage about there being nothing as dangerous as a wounded bear, let me tell you, it's the truth."

SEATTLE, WASHINGTON,
RENTON AREA

The shopping foray had taken just over two hours, and Robert made it back to the motel before nine to find Kat in a hopeful but agitated state.

"Robert, I located Dr. Maverick! He lives in Vegas, but he isn't home, and a neighbor I got on the phone said he'd shot out of there two days ago."

"Any idea where he was going?"

She nodded. "An idea, yes. The neighbor gave me some leads. He's got a place in Sun Valley, Idaho, and I'm betting he's headed there."

"Kat, have you considered . . ."

She raised her hand to stop him. "I know. If *we* can find out where he is, so can Nuremberg's goons. But we have no other hard target. I have the address and the phone number, but if he's there, he's holed up and not answering."

"So what do we do?"

Kat pursed her lips. "We slip on a commuter flight in the morning to Sun Valley to look for him."

She took one of the bags Robert was holding and rummaged around for the hair-coloring product, found it, and held it up. "Good. Exactly what I need." She moved quickly into her bathroom and waved as she closed the door behind her and turned on the water.

Robert followed and knocked lightly on the door. "You mind if I talk to you while you're working?"

Kat opened it a few inches and peered out. "Why?"

"Oh, I don't know. Perhaps the idea that we've got a few unresolved issues, like why the hell we're gambling that a frightened man may go to his mountain cabin instead of off the ends of the earth?"

"Call it a hunch, Robert."

"Just a hunch? Or intuition?"

"The same professional intuition you said you trusted."

"Just asking."

Kat peeked out through the crack in the bathroom door. "When a lady goes through this little conversion process, she doesn't like to be visible. So go to your room, close the door, and make that call to Tahiti. We're running out of time."

KING COUNTY MUNICIPAL AIRPORT/BOEING FIELD, SEATTLE, WASHINGTON

A short line of cars was waiting at the curb as a dozen men and women in dark suits spilled out of the lobby of Galvin Flying Service. The special agent-in-charge introduced his team to the arriving force amid a flurry of watch-checking, and waved to the FAA pilots who had flown them in by government jet from D.C. Carry-on bags were loaded and cellular phone numbers exchanged as the FBI team geared up for a rapid trip into the Seattle field office and an intensive all-night effort to find their prodigal sister agent.

As the informal motorcade roared away from the curb, a man with forgettable features sitting in a rented van turned away and lifted a cellular phone to his mouth. "We've got company," he said, reporting the small army of FBI agents.

"Confirms the fact that she's here, doesn't it?" the voice on the other end said. "Get back over to the main airport while we keep the search going from here."

"You having any luck?" the man asked.

"With the help of a little cash, we're narrowing it down."

chapter

40

Kat turned off the hair dryer and used her comb to position a few stray hairs before using the hair spray. She shook her head at the brassy platinum blond in the mirror, suppressing a slight twinge of excitement at the prospect of appearing in public in clothes and makeup that she would never wear as herself.

She left the bathroom, relieved to find the door between the rooms closed. She pulled on the dark panty hose and, piece by piece, wiggled into the rest of the costume before inserting her feet into the high platform shoes. She took a long look at herself in the full-length mirror on the wall, distracted momentarily by noise from some members of a visiting high school basketball team whooping it up in the corridor outside.

Kat looked at the girl in the mirror, worried about overdoing the trash-flash. *All right, Katrina La Femme. It's show time! Let's try it out.*

She opened her side of the double connecting door and stuck her leg into the opening, drawing a wolf whistle from Robert, then applause when she entered and struck a pose with hands on hips and head cocked to one side.

"Incredible!" he said, the telephone cradled on his shoulder.

"Cheap, cheap, cheap!" she replied, pretending to chew gum.

More voices were yelling in the corridor, and the sound of footsteps could be heard running in one direction, then running the other way, accompanied by giggles.

"What on *earth* are they doing out there?" Robert asked.

"Just kids having fun," she said, moving to the peephole on the door and pressing her eye against it. "Any progress?"

"Hang on," he said, turning to talk to someone on the other end. Kat turned around just as Robert replaced the receiver with a large smile on his face.

"Let me fire up the computer, Kat. We've got a clear track to that file for the next thirty minutes."

"Wonderful!"

She sat on the edge of the bed beside him and watched as he programmed the right numbers into the computer and waited for it to make the connection with the Library of Congress. Following his friend's instructions, he found the master file list and keyed a small search routine to find the one hidden file named WCCHRN.

"Okay. This is it. I'm sure no one knew it was there."

"Did you tell your friend what you were doing?" Kat asked.

Robert shook his head. "No. He owed me a big-time favor and I collected. He's trusting me not to destroy anything or leave a trail. But without this access, there's no way we'd be able to get that file. No way."

"Then if we can get this file downloaded, can we erase all evidence of it?"

Robert shook his head. "With the backups they've got? Not a chance. This file will still be around on some computer tape for a hundred years. Maybe forever."

The file name suddenly appeared by itself on the screen. He keyed in the password "Carnegie" and crossed his fingers.

The screen filled with indecipherable symbols and random characters.

"Damn! He wrote the file in some machine code," Robert said. "Could be simple, could be impossible. I'm going to download everything first."

It took twenty-two minutes for the voluminous file from the Library of Congress to transfer through the telephone lines. At last he broke the connection and tried to open what Walter Carnegie had hidden away.

More gobbledygook.

Robert entered more commands, all with the same frustrating result.

"This may not be possible, Kat, without a cryptologist."

"Would you mind if I try something?" she asked.

Kat brought her laptop in and positioned it to face his before taking over the keyboard with a practiced hand. "I'm using our infrared link to download the file to my machine."

"Why?"

"Just . . . a minute. May be easier to do than explain." When the process was completed, she sat back on his bed and put her computer in her lap, calling up a special program from her files. "This will tell me what kind of format, what kind of language or code this thing is written in," she explained.

The results popped up almost instantly, prompting a laugh from Kat.

"What?" Robert asked.

"Clever. Not too sophisticated, but clever. He simply converted the file to a picture. I need to translate it back to a word-processing format." The computer whirred for a few seconds before normal, readable text flashed on the screen.

"Aha!" Kat leaned forward, examining the screen. "This is an index. He's got a long list of items here, and a cover note dated just a week ago."

"Two days before he died," Robert said. "Go on. I've got to make a pit stop."

She began reading, occasionally whistling under her breath. She tore through half a dozen pages before Robert returned.

"Robert, no wonder he was terrified!"

"Meaning?"

"I'm reading his summary. He says that someone in the intelligence community found out he was a terrorist expert with the FAA trying to discover how terrorists could have caused the SeaAir accident. That person came to Carnegie to get his help in blowing the whistle on a major governmental cover-up."

"That would be our Dr. Maverick?"

She shook her head. "No. Someone else. Someone who lives in the Beltway." She glanced at the screen and toggled the document back a few pages before looking at Robert again. "According to this, there was a classified presidential executive order several years back that prohibited any U.S. involvement in researching or building laser weapons designed to destroy human eyesight."

"I didn't know about that. So we *are* dealing with a powerful laser."

"Apparently. He says it was a top-secret project. There are references to it, but he says here he hasn't discovered the name of the project."

"Did he say the presidential order was violated?" Robert asked.

She read over the page again and shook her head. "No. You need to read all this, too, but Carnegie says his deep throat told him there *had* been a major black project run by the Defense Department, which had been doing just such research, and it produced some eye-killing portable lasers. After the President's order, the weapons were stored, instead of destroyed. But he says they weren't buried deeply enough."

"Don't tell me. They were stolen."

Kat nodded. "That's what he says, and that's apparently the nexus of his panic. The whole stockpile went missing, he says, and because of the potential for havoc and the intense worry about public reaction, as well as the potential backlash against the contractor and the Pentagon, Carnegie's source told him a huge effort got under way to hide the fact that we'd ever been fooling around with the idea, let alone actually building devices to destroy human eyeballs. He claims here that according to his source, DOD, CIA, NSA,

DIA, and NRO were all deeply involved in trying to recover the lost prototypes, and that they were gambling they could recover the weapons and protect the technology before some terrorist group started using them."

"And," Robert continued, "they promised that a SeaAir or Meridian–type accident would never occur, right?"

She nodded. "That's implied here but not stated. Also, he says that the FAA has a radar tape of the Key West area when SeaAir's MD-eleven went down, and there was an F-one-oh-six Air Force test drone, but no other targets except a shadowy intermittent one they never identified." Kat looked up at Robert. "Obviously, when SeaAir was shot out of the sky, whoever was begging for quiet had to have known it would all hit the fan if any of those stolen weapons were involved, and that does set the stage. That kind of cover-up would be devastating if exposed."

"Which is," Robert said, "precisely what Walter was threatening to do by merely looking into the allegations."

"As are we," Kat said, feeling a cold chill ripple down her back.

Robert looked toward the hall where more noise from the teen crowd was filtering through the door. "Lord, Kat. I almost said, 'when the press finds out about this,' completely forgetting I *am* the press. No wonder they went ape when Walter contacted me, even if he never gave me anything."

"Whoever 'they' is," Kat added. "I mean, we're coming to these conclusions based on Walter Carnegie's information and his conclusions, but whatever happened to him, somebody's been after you, and now us. That's corroboration of at least some of this."

"My God, do you realize the implications?" he asked, his eyes getting larger. "If this is half the cover-up he's postulating, it's just a matter of time before the truth comes out, whether I break the story or someone else does. Our government knew the potential and did nothing to stop it."

"And there was time, Robert. According to all this"—she gestured to the computer screen—"there was time to sound the alarm and somehow protect commercial aviation."

"But how long ago did the theft occur?" he asked. "A

couple of months? That could be defensible caution."

"Try four years ago, according to Carnegie's source. Since then, there's been false congressional testimony, possible White House involvement, everything. An initial lie compounded by more lies until the entire administration sits in a tangled web of potentially explosive revelation."

Robert sat back in deep thought for more than a minute before leaning forward again, his eyes finding hers. "Did he say anything about the group that obtained the weapons? Who they might be? Whether they bought them on the black market or whether they stole the laser weapons themselves?"

She shook her head. "I've only read his summary, but he was already obsessed with that question. Was it a Middle Eastern, religious-based group, an organization out to extort huge amounts of money, or what? Maybe, as I suspect, one out to profiteer from disrupting the airline stocks? There's one thing I can't quite figure out at first glance, though. Where *were* those weapons for the last four years?"

Robert looked at her in silence. She cocked her head as she watched the progression of worry. "What's wrong?"

"Kat, who's chasing us?"

"Beg your pardon?"

"The alphabet-soup agencies. CIA, DIA, NRO. Did you omit one?"

She shook her head as if to clear it. "I'm not following . . ."

"Did you omit the FBI?"

Kat's eyebrows climbed, and she sat back suddenly with a disgusted look on her face. "Forget that nonsense!"

He lowered his head and rubbed his temples. "Kat, I'm sorry, but *someone* killed Walter, and someone's been trying their best to get us." He looked up at her again. "Someone who consistently shows up with what you yourself called impeccable FBI credentials."

She shook her head energetically, her voice terse and low. "Don't go there, Robert."

"Look, I—"

"The FBI is not capable as an agency of giving or carrying out such an order."

"There could always be renegades," he said quietly. "Perhaps they're taking their dedication a bit too far."

"NO!" she snapped. She put her laptop computer on the bed and got to her feet to pace with her arms folded, staying within a few feet and looking down at him only fleetingly as her agitation grew. She leaned over him again. "No! Dammit, I cannot and will not believe that. *Maybe* the Company, or rogue members within CIA. But not the Bureau."

"Loyalty talking, Kat? Or logic? Think how many times your messages and calls to Jake Rhoades have backfired."

"I admit my first response is based on loyalty. But the FBI could not, and would not, do such a thing, Robert. We're talking about mass murder in cold blood. You don't know these people. I do. There are some of the world's most unapologetic Neanderthals in our ranks when it comes to accepting women, but these are good, solid professional people who live to serve their country and the law. Most of them have doctorates. Juris Doctors, sometimes Ph.D.'s. All well-educated, solid people. They can make mistakes, like Ruby Ridge or Waco, but they—*we*—could not do the things this murderous bunch has been doing."

"Well, if not your agency, then who? You and I both know the Defense Intelligence people, DIA, are definitely not capable of such field operations. Nor is National Reconnaissance Office, or National Security Agency. That leaves only Central Intelligence, and I know CIA isn't a candidate."

"Oh, wonderful! My main media man can't believe the spooks at Langley could go out of control, but he believes the FBI could turn renegade."

"I just know a lot of people at CIA, okay? And I refuse to believe—I *hope* I don't believe the CIA could commit such atrocities. "

"Robert, listen to yourself. You *hope* you don't believe? That tells me you *do* believe they're capable of murder."

He shook his head and looked away, but she maneuvered into his line of vision, drawing him back. "Robert, remember I said this feels more corporate than governmental?"

"Yes."

"I hate to say it, but neither my own Bureau nor Langley would be sophisticated or coordinated enough for such an operation. We couldn't set up and pull off what these people have accomplished, whatever their purpose. There are simply too many managers, too many rules, too many constraints on money, and too many approvals to get, even for covert operations."

"In other words?" he prompted, his arms folded.

"You asked who's chasing us? Not government or military, that's for certain."

"And that's raw speculation," he countered.

"So, what else do we have to work with?"

SEATTLE, WASHINGTON
11:45 P.M. LOCAL/0745 ZULU

The head of the team dispatched from Vegas to Seattle hung up the phone and smiled. A single line of computer code had solved the mystery. The hours of connection with Kat Bronsky's Internet provider had gone through some clever filtering, but it had all originated from the Holiday Inn in the south Seattle community of Renton.

Getting the others to the Holiday Inn parking lot took another fifteen minutes, but creating the unquestioning reaction that four deadly serious FBI agents would trigger in a couple of hotel desk clerks justified the coordination. The frightened, wide-eyed night manager and his one assistant led the way to the back office instantly.

"What do you guys want us to do?" the young man asked.

"First, has either of you seen any of these people?" The pictures of Kat and Robert were laid on the desk, then one of Steve Delaney. The two employees studied them before shaking their heads.

"No, Sir. But we only came on duty at ten P.M."

"Who was on the desk before?"

They passed over the names, addresses, and phone numbers of the off-duty desk crew, with the caution that two of them were headed out of town.

"We need a printout of every guest you have tonight, and

every scrap of information on them, along with all the registration cards."

The two jumped to comply, standing aside quietly while the pseudo–FBI agents methodically combed the list. One stood at last and motioned the leader over.

"Three possible couples. All three registered this afternoon, paid cash, and indicated a one-night stay. This is my prime candidate. Room four-fifteen. John and June Smith, for Chrissake."

The leader shook his head. "Smith? You'd think she'd be more creative. Okay, let's go," he said, motioning to the others before turning to the night manager. "Say nothing to anyone of this operation. Stay in the office, and do *not* involve the local police, no matter what happens. This is a federal matter. You help us like you've been doing, you're heroes. You fail to follow instructions, you could be obstructing justice."

"No problem, Sir!" The manager said.

Two more teens raced down the hall outside of Robert Mac-Cabe's door. Inside the room, Kat paced around, trying to get used to the platform shoes. She moved to the peephole and looked out, wondering if there was any adult supervision of the group. She saw two of the teens stop suddenly at the ninety-degree bend at the end after running into several dark-suited figures who were striding around the corner. The two groups sorted themselves out and the men continued walking in the direction of Robert's door, swimming into view in the tiny fish-eye lens. They stopped two doors down across the hall.

"What's going on?" Robert was asking from behind her, but Kat held her left hand out to quiet him. A cold feeling crept into her stomach as the men positioned themselves on each side of room 415. She pushed her eye closer. The men were pulling guns now, and one of them inserted a card key in the door. He turned the knob, shoved the door inward, and all of them charged inside amid shouted commands.

Kat turned and motioned Robert toward her, then put her eye back to the peephole and whispered frantically out of the side of her mouth. "Go to my door! Put on the chain and the double lock and watch this."

"What?" he asked.

She explained what she'd just witnessed, noticing when she looked back that a small crowd of teens had gathered at the far end of the hall to watch the show. There were shouts from within the assaulted room and one of the men appeared, dragging a protesting woman in a skimpy nightgown into the corridor. A naked man followed, held between two of the intruders. The fourth one looked at papers in his hand and then at their faces.

"They're not the ones," Kat thought she heard him say.

Suddenly the man and woman were pushed back into their room, and the door closed in their faces. All four men regained the corridor and marched in Kat and Robert's direction. They reached the door and continued without breaking stride, passing the peepholes at full speed and disappearing down the opposite hallway.

Kat turned her back to the door, breathing hard. Her eyes betrayed a rising panic as Robert rounded the corner from the adjacent room in a similar state of upset. "Jeez, Kat," he began.

"They've found us. God knows how, but they've found us."

"They've found the hotel, but . . ."

Kat looked at him for a second. "Get packed. Quickly. We've got to find a safe way out of here."

He nodded and turned, but Kat stopped him suddenly.

"Wait, Robert. That was one couple in one room. They're looking for the wrong combination. We may have a few minutes before they figure out the possibility that we'd be in two rooms."

There were loud voices in the corridor again and she looked back through the peephole, unsurprised to see several of the teens talking animatedly about what they had just witnessed. Two of them were almost alongside her door. Kat licked her lips and turned to Robert to whisper, "Quickly, get in the other room." He complied as she threw open the security lock and opened the door.

"Boys, excuse me," she said, in as relaxed and sexy a voice as she could manage. Her appearance stopped the young men in their tracks as they looked at a beautiful young woman in a micro-miniskirt, with incredible cleavage, actually beckoning them into a motel room.

"Yes, Ma'am?"

"Could you two strong young gentlemen step in here just a second?"

They gave each other a lottery-winning look and popped through the door, jostling each other in the process. She closed it behind them. Both stood in the alcove and turned to her, the tallest one keeping his eyes focused on her breasts.

Kat reached out and cupped his chin, raising his eyes.

"I'm up here, Darlin'."

The boy blushed, and his companion snickered; his eyes were equally engaged in mentally recording Kat's feminine features in intricate detail. "Sorry, Ma'am."

"Well, I'm flattered you like them, but the rest of the lady needs your help."

Their eyes grew wider. The chance to help a gorgeous, sexy female in distress, with unknown rewards on the other side, was impossible to resist. "Sure! What do you need?"

"Well, those men who just embarrassed that couple? Did you see that?"

"Yes, Ma'am," they said in unison.

"They're looking for me."

"Why? What'd you do?" the shorter one asked.

"I couldn't pay all my federal taxes on our farm down in Ellensberg. Lost my husband last year. I'm gonna pay, but I need more time and they want to arrest me."

"They can do that?"

"Sure can. Look. All I need is a diversion to give me enough time to get out of here. Think you two could divert their attention without letting anyone know?"

The taller of the two grinned. "Yeah, I guess we could do that."

"What's your name, Sugar?"

"Ah, I, ah . . . Billy Matheson . . . of Yakima."

"And you, Babe?"

"I'm Bobby Nash. I'm from Yakima, too."

"Billy and Bobby from Yakima. Matheson and Nash. Your families listed in the phone book? Can I find you that way to thank you later?"

Two heads nodded enthusiastically.

"Okay," she said, putting an arm around each of them and walking them farther into the room in a huddle. "Here's what I need you to do."

The leader of the group of four checked off one of the names on the printout in his hand and leaned against the interior corridor wall, well aware that time was running out. The assaulted couple in 415 would undoubtedly call the police. Perhaps thirty minutes, maybe an hour, but it would happen.

"Sir?"

He looked up and into the pimply face of a tall teenager. Another teen stood nearby. The tall boy was wide-eyed and upset, his eyes darting back and forth as he looked back at the parking lot.

"The desk clerk? He said you guys were really FBI. Is that right?"

"Why?" the leader asked.

"My—my *truck* . . . they stole it . . . right outside!"

"Son," he interrupted, "you'll have to call—" He stopped himself. "Wait a minute. When and where?"

The teen was practically hyperventilating. *Lord,* the leader thought, *he's going to start crying any second.* He glanced at the other boy, who looked scared, but wasn't saying anything.

"Out . . . there . . . we just pulled up in my father's pickup—it's a blue Toyota—and . . . and this man and woman pulled me out of the seat and yelled something about commandeering my truck for the FBI, and took off. I never saw a badge. I don't think they really were FBI. *Were* they?"

It was the leader's turn for raised eyebrows. He glanced at his three men and back at the kid. "What did they look like?"

The teen recited the description he'd been prompted to give of Robert MacCabe, and of Kat Bronsky with chestnut-brown hair and a pantsuit.

"Show me the direction they went!" the leader commanded, and propelled the teens toward the door.

"How many do you see?" Robert asked, as Kat peered through the partially opened curtain.

"Four. All piling into a van of some sort. Young Billy must be doing an Academy Award job."

"That was grace under fire, Kat."

"It was sex under fire, helped by raging hormones ignited by this outfit." She turned back into the room. "Okay. Make the call. We have to make sure there were only four of them."

Robert phoned the front desk. "Those FBI agents who were here. I need to speak with one of them."

"They've gone, Sir."

"All four of them?"

"Yes, Sir."

Robert nodded to Kat, who was already in motion toward the door. "Thanks," he said, putting the phone in its cradle and following her out.

They slipped out a side door and Robert unlocked the car as Kat spotted the two boys, still standing in the parking lot.

"Thanks, fellows. I owe you one."

"No problem, Ma'am," said the taller of the two. "They went down the street that way, southbound." He pointed to the right. "You'd better get going."

"You, too. Stay in your rooms tonight."

She plopped into the driver's seat and waved good-bye, accelerating onto the main avenue in the opposite direction, passing an oncoming black sedan with U.S. Government tags as it pulled into the drive and headed for the motel office.

When it became apparent that they weren't going to catch the blue pickup, one of the four men called 911 to report its theft and its license number, identifying himself as FBI and asking for the local radio dispatch frequencies used by the police. With a handheld scanner programmed to the appropriate channels, they headed back to the motel, maintaining a fruitless vigil and almost missing the three cars that had gathered near the office, each of them dark-colored sedans with black sidewalls that screamed government.

"Jeez Louise! We can't go in there!"

"Turn around. TURN AROUND!"

The driver wheeled back onto the street as a city squad car turned in the drive.

"So now what?"

"Back to the jet while we try to figure their next move," the leader said, his face a study in frustration and anger.

chapter
41

"I thought it was the cellular call I accidentally answered," Kat said as they watched the headlights on the road ahead and tried to keep each other awake. "But now I think they traced back the series of numbers we were using for Internet access, and that boggles my mind. That should have taken days, at best."

"They're crafty, Kat, but not infallible, or we wouldn't still be here."

She shook her head. "This must be Supermob. I've never even heard of such technological and logistical capabilities in any known terrorist group, so it's obvious we're not dealing with a bunch of rednecks trying to blow up the government."

"You're reinforcing my worst fears, Kat—that we're somehow dealing with an arm of the U.S. government."

The Centralia city-limit sign appeared in the headlights just before 2 A.M. They had already made the decision to drive straight to the Portland, Oregon, airport and sleep in the minivan. There was a Horizon Airlines departure to Sun Valley, Idaho, around noon, and Kat had made reservations from a pay phone along the way, using purposefully misspelled variations of their real names.

The temperature outside was in the upper forties, somewhat mild for a mid-November night. Sleep without the van's heater was all but impossible, but keeping the engine on would make them far too visible on an otherwise empty airport parking lot. Robert suggested a truck stop, and before crossing the Columbia River into Oregon, they nestled the car anonymously into a vast parking lot of idling eighteen-wheelers.

"Kat?" Robert asked at one point, when she felt she was just about to drift off.

"Yes?"

"Are you numb?"

"No, I'm warm enough. How about you?"

"I don't mean temperature. I mean emotionally. I'm approaching the 'whatever' zone."

"You have even more of a right to feel that way, considering the crash and all."

He took a deep breath. "You think they're okay up in—where is it?"

"Stehekin?"

"Yeah," he said. "I have a hard time remembering that name."

"Yes. I have to believe they're okay. But I'm . . ."

"Scared?"

She looked over at him and smiled thinly before nodding. "Yeah. Unbelievably." She sat up and rested her head on her hand. "Robert, I don't know how this is going to end."

"Beg your pardon?" he said softly.

"I mean"—she readjusted herself in the seat to sit completely upright—"what I normally investigate, it's simple. We identify the crooks and go out and find the crooks and catch the crooks and turn them over for prosecution. Everything's clear. No shades of gray. Well, for the lawyers, of course, but for the FBI it's really simple. This . . . this is a trackless jungle of unknown conflicting interests and loyalties."

"You haven't lived in the Beltway, have you?"

She shook her head no.

"Well, life in Washington is like this. Nothing but shades of gray. No one sure from day to day who's on what side, what faction is going to turn around and sabotage someone else's hard-won issue."

"You're talking politics."

"And this isn't? Kat, if Carnegie's only half right, the forces we're facing may not even be associated with the terrorist group that shot down my flight. They may be doing nothing more than trying to protect the political interests of whatever branch of government, or the Pentagon, they're representing."

"With murder and kidnapping and . . ."

"I know. It's bizarre. Where does one group end and the other begin, if it's compound."

"Robert, are you suggesting that an arm of government is protecting the terrorists that stole government lasers and used them for mass murder?"

"I'm not sure what I'm suggesting, aside from the fact that we represent a threat to the interests of at least a couple of scary organizations."

"You think this Dr. Maverick can help? I mean, what if it turns out he wasn't even Walter's deep throat?"

Robert shook his head. "What choice do we have? Even with Walter's file, all we've got is speculation and hearsay. If we can't find Maverick, or get hard information from him, I don't know. Who can we trust in D.C.?"

"Jordan James is the only one I know," Kat replied.

STEHEKIN, WASHINGTON

"That's enough," Dallas muttered to herself. "I'm certifiably awake."

She looked at her watch, which said 6:30 A.M., then slid out from beneath the covers of the lower bunk bed and pulled on an oversized sweater she'd found in the closet—one that fell with sufficient modesty below her hips to be worn alone. Hugging herself against the chill of the room, she moved over the cold pine-plank flooring to the bedroom door and walked to the kitchen.

Freezing-cold air was flowing through the unsealed shutters on the bear-ravaged window, and she stopped for a second to look in that direction, wondering precisely what she'd do if the bear picked that moment to reappear.

Graham had been holding on to the .30-.30 many hours earlier when she went to bed, and she moved quietly now to look in the large easy chair where he'd been. She found the physician asleep at his post, his legs covered with a quilt, the .30-.30 resting across his lap as he snored softly.

Dallas tiptoed back to the kitchen and began assembling the necessary tools for making coffee, making enough small noises to mask the sound of creaking boards on the porch of the cabin.

One loud creak, however, riveted her undivided attention.

Dallas carefully put down the coffeemaker and glanced up at the small light she'd turned on under the Vent-A-Hood. It was still dark outside, and the sudden dousing of a light would be obvious.

Best to leave it on, she decided.

She dropped to the floor and crawled rapidly and silently around the counter and across the throw rug to the big chair.

Another loud, sustained creaking of boards from the porch confirmed that someone, or something, was moving just beyond the wall.

Dallas slid alongside the chair and put a hand over Graham's mouth as she shook his arm with her other hand. Predictably, he came awake with a wide-eyed start and a muffled yelp. She leaned over him with a finger over her mouth for quiet, and pointed at the door as another set of creaking footsteps moved from left to right. The intruder was moving cautiously but steadily toward the door. Graham checked the .30-.30 and carefully got out of the chair, moving behind it with Dallas.

The door handle rattled suddenly, and whoever was on the other side pulled at it a few times before accepting the fact that it was securely locked.

So it's not the bear! Dallas almost wished it were.

A beam of light was being played around outside. A flashlight. The reflections of the beam were coming through the cracks in the shutters that had been pulled in place over the window.

Suddenly, the intruder rattled the shutters, and boots crunched on the broken glass outside. The shutter opened abruptly and a bright beam of light stabbed inside the cabin as Graham and Dallas ducked behind the big chair.

The beam was directed toward the kitchen, then to the bear rug in front of the fireplace, stopping at various points to illuminate the backpack, the computer case, and several other items foreign to the cabin.

Graham and Dallas waited, unsure what to do, until the unmistakable sound of a handgun being cocked filled the room. Dallas felt Graham tense and readjust his hands on the stock and barrel of the .30-.30.

The intruder pulled the other shutter open and kicked at the remaining shards of glass with his boot before climbing carefully into the cabin. Dallas saw he was wearing a heavy jacket and a hat with earflaps pulled down. As soon as he was inside, he turned his back to the interior to examine the broken window.

Graham moved silently, with the speed of a striking snake, from the back of the chair, placing the muzzle of the .30-.30 on the back of the man's neck.

"FREEZE! Don't move a muscle!" Graham commanded. "Raise your hands in the air, holding that gun by the barrel."

The man complied. Dallas plucked the revolver from his right hand and the flashlight from his left.

"Whatever you say," the man mumbled. "Just don't hurt me."

"How many more of you are there?"

"Pardon?"

"Anyone else out there?" Graham asked.

The man shook his head as he stood still, facing the window. "No. Just me."

"Then what are you doing here?"

"That's what I need to ask you," the man said. "I'm the caretaker for this place. Have been for thirty years."

Graham looked at Dallas, who was holding up an index finger. "And what's your name, Sir?"

"Don. Don Donohue."

Dallas shrugged and nodded. "That's the right name, Graham."

"Is it?" Graham asked, looking back over his shoulder at Dallas.

She turned on the ceiling light, and Graham lowered the .30-.30's barrel and asked Donohue to turn around and show some identification. When they were satisfied, Dallas returned his wallet and motioned him to sit down.

"Didn't you get Kat Bronsky's note?" Dallas asked.

Donohue shook his head. "I didn't get any—*Kat's* here?"

"Well, she's been gone now for a few days, but she said she left a note at the dock for you. We're her guests here."

He was shaking his head no and rolling his eyes. "Good grief. I stopped looking for notes at the dock last year when we got in our satellite phone. I guess she didn't get the word. I'm sure sorry about that. I didn't know anyone was here."

"We thought you'd gotten the note, and that you'd see the smoke from the chimney."

"Naw. The central heater's on in this cabin all winter, and it kicks out one hell of a plume of steam, so I wouldn't have noticed. How long are you folks staying?"

Dallas glanced at Graham to make sure he knew that she was planning to answer the question. "About five days, maybe six. There are four of us, plus Kat and another man." She pointed to the broken window and related the bear story.

"Yep," Donohue said, looking at the window. "We've been having trouble with that bear for the last few months, which is one reason I came by to check the cabin. Sorry about the hour. I get up early."

"You know that bear?" Dallas asked.

"Unfortunately, we *all* know that critter. I'm afraid the rangers are going to have to relocate it." He paused and looked carefully at Graham. "Uh, was one of you folks outside late last night, down by the river?"

"Why do you ask?" Dallas replied, hoping to hear the right response.

"Well, I came down to check on our little hydroelectric mill in the river, and I found some footprints in the snow. They looked lighter than you, though," Donohue said, gesturing to Graham.

Dallas shook her head and sighed loudly. "Thank heavens! That was one of us. I found *your* footprints over his and thought someone was stalking us. "

Don Donohue laughed. "No, not much stalking going on around here, although we got a group in last night I'm not too sure about." He turned toward the window. "Say, let me get a hammer and some plastic from the shed, and I'll seal that pneumonia hole for you."

"Ah, what do you mean about a group last night?" Graham asked, sitting down with a tired thunk in a smaller chair.

"Oh, down at the dock. Four men came in on a rented cabin cruiser from Chelan, asking a bunch of odd questions about who was up here and who wasn't this time of year, pretending to know nothing about the area."

"Pretending?" Dallas asked.

He nodded. "Yeah. See, we get these fellows from the government coming every now and then disguised as mild-mannered civilians trying to catch us locals violating Park Service rules."

"I'm not following you," Dallas said.

"Back in the late seventies, a bunch of hunting buddies of Senator Jackson wanted to run us locals out of here so they could have it as their private hunting preserve. Some of us, like the Cavanaughs, been here since the late eighteen hundreds. We fought 'em and compromised on a brand-new animal called a National Recreation Area, sort of a national park with squatters. Ever since, we and the Park Service have had a love-hate relationship."

"So, you think the men you saw are plainclothes Park Service?"

"Well, they don't fit the mold. Cold eyes, you know? Really bothered me."

"We're . . ." Dallas began, ". . . uh . . . did you talk to them?"

"Oh, don't worry," Donohue said quickly. "I said nothing

about this place, and I didn't know anyone was here any-way."

"They weren't armed, were they?"

"I didn't see any guns, but you never know. They looked more like FBI agents than anything else."

FBI HEADQUARTERS, WASHINGTON, D.C.

Jake Rhoades thanked the agents in the conference room and hurried out into the hall and back to his office. He shut the door behind him and stood for a moment, trying to imagine what was going through Kat Bronsky's mind.

There was a tapping on the door and Jake turned to yank it open, irritated that someone was failing to honor his request for a few minutes of uninterrupted quiet.

"Yes?" he said, pulling it open, somewhat taken aback to find the director of the FBI standing on the other side.

"Jake, got a minute?"

"Sure. Come in."

The director moved to a plush leather chair on the other side of Jake's desk and sat down. "Give me a quick update, Jake."

"On the Bronsky situation?"

The director nodded and listened intently as Jake explained the latest developments, and the near brush with capture by the other group at the Seattle-area motel.

The director leaned forward. "The political pressure on this has passed critical mass. The FAA administrator and I, plus the Secretary of Transportation, think it's only a matter of days before we have enough terrorist warnings shutting down enough airports to cause a general explosion of public opinion that we can't do our job and that airline flying is tan-tamount to suicide. The economic damage to the airline industry is already incredible, and the fact—as you know—that we have no formal ransom or extortion demand from this group means they're going to zap someone else out of the sky before they communicate again."

Jake sighed. "Director, I don't know what else we can do but what we're doing."

"How close is she, Jake?"

Jake Rhoades cocked his head and came forward slightly in his chair. "I'm sorry?"

"Kat Bronsky. She's gone autonomous, we're trying to capture her before the other side does and all that, but she's out there trying to solve this riddle. You relayed that yourself."

"Yes, Sir."

"So how close is she?"

Jake shook his head slowly. "I honestly don't know."

"Well, she believes she's chasing down a solid lead, and frankly—unless you can tell me otherwise—that's about the best this entire Bureau has at this point, right?"

"Well, Sir, we've tasked a large part of the Bureau and the investigation is roaring away on numerous fronts—"

"But," the director interrupted, "the only one who *thinks* he or she's got a lead is Bronsky, am I right?"

"As far as I know, yes."

"All right. So my orders are changing. When you find her, form up the entire Bureau around her to help, but don't get in her way. Give her every resource we have and, in essence, put her in charge of a special team effort. But if she wants to work solo, let her."

Jake's jaw had dropped. "Ah, very well. But first we have to find her."

"The prime directive here is don't crowd her, don't suspend her, don't threaten her, just support her."

The director got up to leave and Jake stopped him with a question. "May I ask what precipitated this rather abrupt change, Sir?"

The director turned. "Sure. You can ask, and I probably shouldn't answer, but I will, since this is the opposite of my wishes yesterday."

"Yes, it is."

"With the understanding that this doesn't get passed to anyone, including her."

"Certainly."

"I received a very unusual call a while ago from the acting Secretary of State, Jordan James, who's known Agent Bronsky all her life. He was CIA director for a long time, you may recall, so he knows his way around the intelligence community, and I'm half convinced he's still on their payroll."

"Really?" Jake interrupted. "He called me two days ago saying he suspected we had a leak and that he was setting up a relay through Langley."

The director nodded, unsurprised. "Well, Jordan severely twisted my arm to call off our dogs and leave Bronsky alone. He said we were going to get her killed."

"What?"

"I know. On its face, it makes no sense to me, either, since we're trying to bring her and those survivors in to keep them alive, first, and extract any information they have, second."

Jake was shaking his head. "He wants us to back off from trying to find her? She just missed being killed in Seattle! The next time she may not be as lucky."

"Jake, what James's call tells me, between the lines— since I suspect she's talking to him more than she's talking to us—is that she's working the right leads. I think his network of spooks is still feeding him good information, and I think his loyalty to her is greater than to the Company."

"I'm just not following this, Sir."

"In a nutshell, I believe James's old friends at the Company want us to find and take Agent Bronsky out of this investigation because she's getting too close to something they want to solve. The same old rivalry. But I think, if I'm reading this right, that James wants Bronsky to succeed, and the only way to let that happen is to get us off her back."

"He's selling out the Company to let Kat make the collar?"

"Essentially, yes."

"And if you're wrong?"

The director shrugged. "Then we've lost nothing, as I see it."

"How about Kat herself?"

"As I say, Jake. Find her, offer help, and let *her* decide what she needs. Frankly, I don't give a rat's ass whether the Company solves this one or we do. The stakes are too high for internal gamesmanship. But . . . it would still be nice to see a Bureau win on this."

PORTLAND INTERNATIONAL AIRPORT, OREGON
NOVEMBER 16—DAY FIVE
11:10 A.M. LOCAL/1910 ZULU

With carry-on bags flying and a loud "oomph," a business-
man in his late forties tumbled over another passenger as he
strained to keep his eyes on the miniskirted blond he'd just
passed at the terminal entrance.

Robert rolled his eyes, and Kat suppressed a laugh. Both
of them were approaching security after she waited on the
sidelines for Robert to check her bag and buy the tickets at
the front counter. The 9mm pistol, unloaded and declared,
was inside her checked bag, which left her feeling more
exposed than the costume she was wearing.

The two of them moved through the inspection portal and
walked to the head of the long, carpeted ramp to the Horizon
departure lounge, where Kat came to a halt.

"I can't do this, Robert," she said. She was amused by the
confused look on his face.

"What? Take the flight?"

"NO," she said, lifting her right foot to remove one of the
high platform shoes. "These are too much."

"You wanted trash-flash."

"Oh, you got the right stuff, but . . . I can wear the micro-
mini and the attitude, but these are just over the top. That's

why," she said, struggling to take off the other one and plop them in a cloth carry-on bag, "I brought some standbys."

Robert shook his head disapprovingly as she slipped on the other pair of shoes.

"Sensible. Far too sensible."

"Yeah, but somewhere in this getup I've got to have a little dignity, not to mention the ability to move. I've almost fallen a dozen times."

"Well, I like the rest of the outfit."

"Yeah. I could learn to like this," she whispered. "Watching you boys fall all over yourselves is perverse fun."

He was shaking his head as she resumed walking and he kept pace with her, keeping his voice low enough for her ears only. "Bimbos rule!"

"I heard that. I are not a bimbo."

"Could fool me," he chuckled.

"Cad."

"Cad? *Cad?*" Robert turned slightly toward her, keeping his voice low. "Kat, no one's used that term in thirty years."

"Would you prefer 'male chauvinist piglet'?"

"No."

They emerged in the departure lounge, and Robert pulled the tickets out of his inside jacket pocket. "Who does the honors?" he asked.

"It's a male agent. Me," she said, taking the tickets and inclining her head toward a seat. "I shall return. We want to minimize your facial exposure."

"Okay. I'll wait here," Robert said, "but would you pick up a copy of my paper or the *New York Times* if you can find it?" He indicated a newsstand in the distance and she nodded.

"After I check us in," she said.

The gate agent was a well-groomed male in his thirties whose eyes brightened the second he saw Kat approaching. Predictably, his focus fell about twelve inches below her eyes, then quickly returned as he made a supreme effort to keep from looking at her considerable superbra cleavage.

Good! He's straight. He's putty, Kat thought.

Manipulating him into a cursory check of her driver's

license was simple; Robert's ID check had been easily handled at the front ticket counter. She rewarded the agent with a wink and a bright smile and moved quickly toward the newsstand, carefully scanning the crowd and acutely aware of the stares of interested males and irritated women alike as she sashayed her way across the terrazzo, letting her hips swing a bit more than normal.

Under different circumstances, this could be fun, Kat thought, as she returned to Robert and handed him the tickets and boarding passes before heading for the newsstand. She looked through the newspapers and selected a *Washington Post* containing a banner headline about the airport shutdowns. There would be at least one picture of her inside, she figured, but she was beginning to feel truly invisible, hiding Kat Bronsky beneath the flashy façade.

"Excuse me!" a well-dressed man to her right said, withdrawing his hand from in front of her where he'd been reaching for the same paper.

"No problem," Kat said, smiling at him. She noticed his left arm was in a sling, and his face was bandaged on one side.

"Which way are you heading today?" he asked. His eyes traveled the length of her profile.

"Oh, several places," she replied.

His eyebrows climbed a notch. "Ah, a woman of mystery!"

"No," she countered. "A woman of caution." *Interesting accent,* she thought. *Somewhat Germanic, but not quite.*

Kat tried to turn away, but the man was not ready to abandon his pickup attempt. "Excuse me for being forward, but may I introduce myself to you, so you won't be concerned about talking to a stranger?"

Kat turned back to him, convinced the odds of simply walking away were low. *I'm a heat source in the sights of an infrared tracker and he's not going to break lock easily.* "You may introduce yourself," she said, "but it won't get you anywhere. I'm quite taken."

"As I am with you, dear lady. My name is—"

"Excuse me." Another passenger pushed between them to

grab a newspaper as Kat shrugged and waved, turning to the counter to pay for the paper.

The man with his left arm in a sling materialized beside her within seconds, waiting until she had received her change. "I never finished my introduction," he said.

She took his right hand and shook it in perfunctory fashion. "Hello, so glad to meet you. My husband, the angry and jealous mafia don, will *not* be so happy to meet you, so please go away and have a nice life while you can. Okay? Okay. Bye!"

Kat could see Robert in her peripheral vision, approaching rapidly from the opposite direction, unseen by the man who was now smiling and shrugging.

"As you wish," he said, turning to go as Robert closed to within ten feet.

Kat's attention was on Robert, not the would-be suitor, but she sensed a sudden change as the man froze in place with his back to Kat, his head turned toward the oncoming reporter, his entire demeanor bristling.

Robert came to a sudden stop five feet away with a look of surprise as he recognized one of the goons who'd tried to kidnap him in Hong Kong. Kat followed Robert's startled gaze just as the assailant dropped his newspaper and thrust his right hand inside his coat.

Robert yelled an unidentifiable word and pivoted, shooting off up the ramp toward the main terminal with the man in chase.

Kat pushed through startled passengers to race up the main ramp through security, noting the startled look on the face of a police officer who had made no effort to follow.

Robert disappeared around the end of a ticket counter as his pursuer crashed headlong into a phalanx of passengers, knocking them, and himself, to the floor. Kat was closing, but not fast enough, as the man leapt to his feet and took off again. Robert was racing up a stairway. He reached the top and disappeared to the left with the man in hot pursuit.

Kat saw the man reach the top of the stairs and drop to a shooter's stance as he pulled out his handgun, aiming down the upstairs hallway. She pushed herself as fast as she could, taking the steps two at a time as she closed on the man ahead, her right hand fishing in the cloth bag.

The gunman was taking careful aim, and as she topped the steps, she could see Robert backed against a wall thirty yards away with nowhere to run. She ran straight for the assailant's back, calculating her trajectory as she prepared to launch herself into him, her hand bringing one of the heavy platform shoes from the depth of the cloth bag.

Robert MacCabe could see Kat descending on them at full speed with both hands held high over her head, her approach still unheard by the gunman.

And he could see she wasn't going to make it in time.

Robert dropped to the floor, disappearing from the gunman's sights and spoiling his aim. The barrel of the gun quickly descended toward him once more, but the slight delay had bought the two seconds Kat needed for a precisely timed, maximum-effort swing as she brought the heel of her sturdy platform shoe into the back of the gunman's head with all her strength. The impact sent the gun clattering harmlessly to the terrazzo floor as the gunman crumpled in his tracks. Kat flashed by sideways, falling out of control and tumbling headlong into Robert as he sat on the floor ten feet beyond. He grabbed her as she fell, keeping her head away from the floor and absorbing her remaining speed.

Together they sat in a heap on the cold terrazzo, panting against the river of adrenaline flowing through both their bloodstreams before either could speak.

"Holy . . . mother of . . ."

"Good Lord!" Kat gasped. "Who *is* that?"

Robert told her as he helped her up, retrieving the man's pistol. He checked that it was cocked and loaded before aiming it at the man's head as Kat approached him.

"Robert . . ." She panted. "Look in . . ." She swallowed hard, taking her purse off her shoulder. "Look in here, in the bottom, for my flex cuffs. Cuff him to that pipe over there."

Robert handed Kat the gun and complied, as she kept the gun at the ready.

"Okay. Now frisk him. Look for ID in all his pockets."

The false FBI credentials fell into Robert's hand. "Special Agent Dennis R. Feldman, according to this," Robert said. "The picture matches. There's no other ID."

"And I'll guarantee you, if there's an 'Agent Feldman,' this isn't he."

Kat took the ID and the 9mm from Robert, emptied the bullets from the gun and stuffed them in her purse before placing the gun on the floor and kicking it to the far end of the hallway. She held up the platform shoe she'd used to clobber the gunman.

"Those platforms are lethal!" Robert said.

"Came in handy, didn't they?"

"Forget carrying guns," Robert said. "Platform shoes should be standard FBI equipment."

"Yeah? Then *you* should try wearing them," she teased, still breathing hard and fighting a bloodstream full of adrenaline.

"I saw that clown hustling you," he said. "I had no idea who it was, but I figured you needed a jealous lover to come to your rescue."

They began moving rapidly back to the stairs, then down to the main floor of the terminal, alighting just as two uniformed airport cops came rushing up.

"Hurry!" Kat said, adopting a scared expression and pointing up the stairs. "They were fightin' up there, and one of them guys has a gun."

The two officers raced up the stairs and Kat pulled Robert quietly around the corner to another security entrance. She quietly dumped the 9mm bullets in a trash can before passing through the metal detector.

More police officers passed them, racing back from the concourse toward the gate area as Kat and Robert used an alternate route to return to the gate area just in time to board the flight.

Kat took a window seat, and Robert slipped in beside her.

"Damn," Kat muttered.

"What?"

"I didn't have you check him for a body pouch."

"He didn't have another gun. I patted him down carefully."

"I was thinking of ID," she said. She pulled out the satellite phone and punched in Jake's number at FBI headquarters.

"You need to call the Portland International Airport police immediately, Jake, and confirm that the man they found handcuffed in an upper hallway of the main terminal is a federal fugitive." She filled in the rest of the story.

"Did he see you, Kat?"

"No."

Jake told her quickly of the director's about-face.

"Jake, that's great, but make the call."

"It means we can support you, Kat. We're not out trying to catch you."

"JAKE! Please! Make the call before they spring the guy."

"Okay. Will you call me back?"

"When I can."

She disconnected and sat for a few seconds, trying to absorb Jake's meaning. The cabin door was still open and the flight attendant was still required to allow cellular phone calls until it closed. The attendant was eyeing Kat carefully, obviously irritated by her outfit.

"Will he do it?" Robert asked.

Kat nodded. "Yeah, but they're trying a new tack to suck me in. Now it's all roses and light and the whole Bureau to support me."

"Could be true."

"Could be," she said, still thinking, "but I can't chance it."

A small beeping noise began in the depths of her purse, and Kat reached in to extract the nationwide pager. She read the message with a darkening expression.

"What?" Robert asked.

She handed him the pager.

EMERG.MSG: KAT, ROBT.MACCABE NOT WHO HE APPEARS TO BE. GET AWAY ASAP. TELL HIM NOTHING. REPORT YOUR INTENTIONS ON NEW LINE, 8009464646. JAKE RHOADES.

Robert gave her a stunned look. "What's this? Now *I'm* the enemy?"

"That's what Nuremberg wants me to think. This didn't come from Jake."

"You're sure?"

She nodded. "He never signs his last name. That's a standard procedure."

"So what does this mean?"

Kat took a deep breath. "It means they're closing in on my personal information. They've found my beeper and PIN numbers. The location of my uncle's cabin won't be far behind."

The lights began to refocus slowly as Arlin Schoen blinked his eyes, trying to recall where he was and why there was a terrible pain in the back of his head.

He tried to sit up, but found his hands manacled by plastic cuffs. He looked up into the large black face of a scowling airport police officer with his hands on his hips. There were six other officers standing around.

Someone got me from behind, he concluded, after quietly taking inventory of his body parts as best he could with his hands restrained.

"He's coming around," the Portland Airport police lieutenant said, kneeling down to look into Schoen's face. "Who are you?" the lieutenant demanded.

Schoen made a show of taking a deep breath and closing his eyes. "Did he escape?"

"Did who escape?"

"I . . . was trying to apprehend a federal fugitive. I don't know what happened."

"Yeah, sure. You were KO'd by a real federal agent, buster. We just got the call from FBI headquarters."

He shook his head. "Oh, hell! So they already know I lost him?"

The lieutenant grabbed Schoen by the hair and lifted his head. "I'm going to ask you one last time, turkey, and then I'm going to get angry. What's your name!"

"All right. All right. I'm Special Agent Don Duprey, FBI, assigned to the Cincinnati office."

"Sure you are!"

"If you'll check beneath my right pants leg, you'll find a

pouch with my credentials, my passport, and even my shot record. What did you mean, I got KO'd by an FBI agent? I *am* an FBI agent."

The police lieutenant looked at his men and motioned to one of them to perform the search. The ID wallet and passport were precisely where indicated.

"If . . ." Schoen breathed hard. "If you'll take a moment to call the Cincinnati office, or even call Washington back, you'll find I'm legit."

Unsure and off balance now, the officers helped Schoen to his feet as one of them radioed in the request. The dispatcher came back within five minutes with confirmation and a description, which was relayed to the lieutenant. The officers stepped away from the prisoner to talk while keeping a cold eye on him.

"So *now* what do we do?" one of the officers asked under his breath.

The lieutenant frowned and glanced at the prisoner. "We have a valid ID with a matching picture and FBI confirmation. Did anyone see this female agent Washington was talking about?"

There were blank looks among the uniforms.

"What was that name?" one of them asked.

"Special Agent Katherine Bronsky," the lieutenant replied. "That's the agent Washington said cuffed this guy." He surveyed his men. "Jim? Bill? You two were first here. Did you see anyone?"

"Just civilians," Jim replied as his partner nodded. "A girl and a guy were at the foot of the stairs."

"Could the girl have been Agent Bronsky?"

"Hardly. She was a real piece. They don't make FBI agents like that."

"Wait a minute," the other one said. "That name. Wasn't it a Bronsky they had on the news last night? The FBI agent who's kidnapped a little boy?"

"Yeah," the other one answered, "that's the same name, and I saw her picture, but the gal at the foot of the stairs bore no resemblance to that fed."

The police lieutenant sighed and shook his head. "Call

FBI headquarters, get a description of this Bronsky, and see if it fits the woman you saw. If it doesn't, we're releasing this guy. I don't want any hassles with the FBI, and I've got nothing to hold him on."

The answer came back within five minutes. The two officers who had arrived on the scene first listened carefully, then shook their heads simultaneously.

"That definitely wasn't her."

After being released with an apology and melting rapidly into the crowd, Arlin Schoen found a phone and punched in the direct 800-number to his command post.

"I thought you were on the way back here, Arlin."

"I was waiting for the Vegas flight when I spotted Mac-Cabe." He snapped off a quick description of what had occurred.

"Was Bronsky with him?"

"I don't know, but I suspect she was the one who clubbed me from behind. Someone did." He rubbed his head. "I haven't a clue where they're headed."

"I do" was the response.

chapter
43

The sound of his own breathing was a comforting counterpoint to the "schuss" of his skis as Warren Pierce settled into a comfortable pace. The snowfall the night before had been minimal, but the snowpack through the fields on either side of the main road was substantial and satisfying. It was crystal days like this, he thought, that made cross-country skiing so invigorating—crisp air in his lungs and the blur of evergreens on each side making the valley his own special world.

Another of the summer cabins passed by to his left, a familiar sight to any Stehekin resident. *That one is the Caldwells' place,* he thought, absently letting his eyes wander from the snow-covered roof to the contrail of a distant airliner tracing a feathery exclamation point in the sky above Lake Chelan.

He rounded another bend and crossed the road, trending toward the river. The substantial old log house ahead had been there all his life, and it loomed into view on schedule, the usual wisp of steam curling from the heater vent on the roof.

Warren stopped, unsure why, but something about the cabin was wrong.

Why is the door open?

Warren moved closer, keeping himself within the tree line to the north side as he took in a shuttered window to the left of the open door. There was no sign of life.

A breeze moaned through the evergreens overhead, and the front door swung open even farther with a mournful creaking that startled him. He could see an overturned chair inside, but there were no lights visible within.

A cold feeling of apprehension began to move up his spine, an unreasoned desire to turn and go, but he tried to overrule the feeling and will himself to look more closely. Don Donohue was the caretaker. He checked it every day. How could the front door be swinging open?

Warren forced himself to ski in to the front yard, his eyes taking in shards of broken glass and footprints in the muddy snow by the porch—as well as something by the door that looked red, like blood.

Warren turned and skied toward the road as fast as he could, turning toward the ranger station and the dock, propelled by a mindless fear. Someone needed to investigate, and that someone was not going to be him.

ABOARD A HORIZON AIRLINES DASH 8, IN FLIGHT, FORTY MILES EAST OF PORTLAND, OREGON

Kat had watched the south side of Portland International Airport flash past and drop away as the DeHavilland Dash 8 lifted into an overcast sky from Runway 10 Right. Like the instinctive act of a blue heron lifting off a lake and pulling its long legs up behind it, the spindly landing gear of the Dash 8 retracted backward and tucked itself into the underside of the wing-mounted turboprop engines, leaving Kat with a spectacular view. High-wing aircraft were well suited to daydreaming passengers, she thought. Especially smaller ones flying at lower altitudes over the lush Pacific Northwest landscape of manicured golf courses and a carpet of forest.

The verdant hills to the east of Portland were moving sedately past as the Dash 8 climbed through the bottom of an overcast, turning the world outside into an endless field of milky white. Her view diminished to the right engine pod and the faithfully churning jet-driven propeller.

In the forward cabin the lone flight attendant was preparing her tiny rolling bar for the drink service, when the sound of a ringing cellular phone reached her ears. Her attention snapped to the flashy blond in a midcabin window seat. She left the galley immediately and moved swiftly to row eight, reaching out just in time to catch the ringing phone before the excessively blond passenger could raise it to her ear.

"You'll have to turn that off, Miss." she commanded, happy with the authoritative tone in her voice. The surrounding passengers were turning out of curiosity, but that was fine. The woman deserved some communal condemnation.

But the passenger fairly yanked the phone from the flight attendant's hand, placing it to her ear as she fished for something in her handbag.

"I said, TURN THAT THING OFF!" the flight attendant commanded.

The blond's left hand whipped out a leather wallet and flipped open a badge and an ID that the flight attendant recognized as the emblem of the FBI. She nodded and backed up the aisle in confusion, pulled out a key, and entered the cockpit.

Kat replaced the ID and hunched over, straining to hear Jordan James's voice. "Are you sure, Jordan?"

"I need a rendezvous point, Kat. I need to talk to you in person as soon as possible. I have a plane ready to fly me out to the coast tonight, wherever you are."

"I'm . . . not on the coast. I mean, I'm not that far. There's someone I'm trying to find and interview. I'd rather not say who, or where, just in case."

"Kat, you've got to trust me. This line is clear. Where will you be?"

She glanced at Robert and sighed. There was no time to explain to him, and it was her decision anyway. She was confused now about which lines might be leaking and which were secure, if any were secure. With airports being closed by terrorist threats, the confirmation that stolen laser guns were probably involved, and the growing worry that they were facing a couple of entities trying to find and silence them, speaking the name of the destination city seemed reckless but unavoidable. After all, it was Jordan James asking, and if she couldn't trust Jordan, she was in a house of mirrors.

"Kat, *please*. Where do I find you?"

She sighed again, closing her eyes. "I'll be in Sun Valley. Don't ask why." She could feel Robert's startled reaction, but it was too late.

"Good. I'll arrange the flight right now and be out there by . . . tomorrow morning at the latest. Keep your phone on. I'll call you from the airport."

"Okay. But what have you found? If this line is secure enough for me to tell you where I'm going to be . . ." She glanced at Robert with a quick nod to tell him it was all right.

"Then why isn't it secure enough," he interjected, "for me to tell you what I've discovered? Maybe it is, Katherine. But there's a lot to explain. This is a very complex, very frightening situation."

"You know about the weapons, Uncle Jordan?"

"How do you mean?" he asked, trying to mask caution.

"I mean, did you know the ones used in SeaAir and Meridian may be stolen from a U.S. stockpile—weapons specifically prohibited by presidential directive?"

There was a long pause on the other end. "Kat, that's why we have to talk. There's a lot you don't know, although I'm impressed with what you've found out. National security is at stake here. See you tonight, or early in the morning. Keep the phone on."

She disconnected and turned to meet Robert MacCabe's alarmed expression, trying not to think or admit that she might have just made a dangerous mistake.

A gossamer veil of snow had begun to fall as the Dash 8 pilots made a flawless instrument approach to Friedman Memorial Field in Hailey, Idaho, the commercial gateway to Sun Valley. The world swam into view at 600 feet above ground, and they broke out perfectly aligned with the runway, navigating only by the distant signals of a global positioning satellite system in what was known as a GPS approach.

By the time the Dash 8 had stopped at the gate, a minor blizzard was in progress, with heavy snow predicted all afternoon. The extreme tension they were already feeling didn't help on the taxi ride to Dr. Thomas Maverick's address, south of the town of Sun Valley. The scientist's cabin was in the southern end of the area in a heavily forested community of widely spaced homes and poorly marked roads, and after the third wrong turn, the cab driver's short temper wasn't helping matters, either.

Dr. Maverick's small log cabin finally appeared. Kat paid the cabby quickly and sent him away over Robert's whispered protests. "What if Maverick isn't home, Kat? We aren't clothed for this."

"We'll be fine," she said, zipping up the uninsulated windbreaker she'd carried from Stehekin.

"Fine? We're already freezing! Not that we have any choice now."

There was no answer at the door, and no sign of a fire in the fireplace, but there were fresh tire tracks being covered rapidly in the snowy driveway. Kat moved cautiously around the cabin, finding the front and rear doors locked and nothing suspicious visible through the windows, before returning to Robert, who was standing under the eave of the roof and trying to stay out of the wind.

"If he's here, he's hiding," she told Robert.

"So—as Dallas would say, what now, Kemosabe? Your faithful companion is freezing his ass off."

She ignored the attempt at humor. "We wait."

"Out *here*?"

"No, inside. We find the least destructive way to break in."

Normally, Robert thought, *I would protest being asked to aid an essentially criminal act,* but the cold was reaching serious proportions and being inside, almost anywhere, was rapidly becoming an imperative.

They returned to the rear door, and Kat fumbled in her handbag before pulling out a Leatherman's tool.

"You know how to pick locks, too, Kat?" Robert asked through chattering teeth.

"Not a clue," she said. "You?"

He nodded, then shook his head. "Not really. I've fooled around with some, but that's a pretty stout lock."

She straightened up. "It is, isn't it? Okay. Wait." She left the back steps and selected a piece of firewood from a covered pile adjacent to the cabin. She used the end to shatter one of the windowpanes in the door, then reached inside to unlock it.

"Oh, thank God!" Robert said, his shock at Kat's action ameliorated as he moved into the comfort of the heated interior.

"The heat's a good sign," she said, closing the door behind them. "I doubt he'd keep this place heated all winter. Probably only when he's here."

Kat went out the front door to get the bags and immediately fished out the gun, loading it and dropping it into her handbag. Robert's voice reached her through the partially open door.

"I'll see if I can find something to tape over the broken pane." He rummaged around in a closet and came out as she reentered the tiny kitchen. "I've checked the whole place, Kat. He's not here."

"I'm sure he will be. It'll be dark by five P.M. and I'll bet he'll wait for that."

"So . . . we just wait?" Robert asked.

"Yes. Meanwhile, I'm ditching the hooker outfit. It's served its purpose."

"You're still very blond, my lady." Robert grinned. Kat didn't respond, and her face looked grim. He caught her by the shoulders and turned her around. "Kat? I know you're worried, but have you completely lost your sense of humor?"

She looked puzzled. "What?"

"Your sense of humor. Gallows humor, if necessary."

She shook her head and frowned as she gently pulled away from his hands. "I'm sorry, Robert. I'm a bit preoccupied with keeping us alive."

"Well, we've got to keep laughing. Blonds have to have a sense of humor."

Her expression was still unyielding, but she studied him for a few seconds, then bumped a hip in his direction. "How's that? 'Blond' is an attitude."

"Better," he said, and watched her disappear with her bag into the bathroom.

She returned minutes later in a pair of jeans and a pullover sweater to find Robert at the rear window watching the snowfall, which was becoming heavier.

He turned and smiled at her, inclining his head toward the window. "Kat, if this snow continues, I don't know if James is going to make it in."

"He said by morning," she said, without expression. "We wait, regardless."

PORTLAND INTERNATIONAL AIRPORT, OREGON

The Lear 35 private jet that Arlin Schoen had waited for all afternoon taxied rapidly up to the Flightcraft private terminal and shut down the engine on the left side long enough to lower the steps and bring Schoen aboard. He scrambled into the plush interior, pleased to find six of his men. The pilots of the chartered jet restarted the left engine and departed immediately, flying a direct course to the Sun Valley airport at just under 500 miles per hour. The passengers in the back huddled in conversation. There had been several heavy wooden boxes loaded back in Seattle, and both pilots were increasingly nervous about their clients and what they were carrying—as well as concerned about the deteriorating Sun Valley weather ahead.

The leader of the group, a cold-eyed older man who had handed them $8,000 in cash for the charter, had made it clear that they were to land regardless of the weather, but after the third try with no runway in sight, even he agreed that a dash to Boise, Idaho, was the only reasonable backup plan.

The passengers were inside the private terminal at Boise when the two charter pilots made their decision. Whatever was going on, they wanted no part of it, and a peek inside one of the boxes confirmed their fears: a massive amount of sophisticated assault weaponry and ammunition.

The captain calculated the price of the charter, counted out the overpayment in an envelope, and taped it to the top of one of the boxes before unloading the men's belongings on the ramp and firing up the right engine.

"We saw nothing, we heard nothing, we say nothing," the captain said.

"Amen," echoed the copilot.

One of the men came racing from the building at the sound of the engine start, but the captain had pushed up the throttle and raced away on just one power plant while the copilot started the other and called for an emergency takeoff clearance.

"So what now?" one of the men asked Arlin Schoen.

"Very simple," Schoen replied. "The others should be there by now, or very close. They were driving. Get them on the satellite phone and warn them to hold in place until we can charter another aircraft. Preferably one that can handle a snowstorm. We'll rid ourselves of all three at once."

"What were their orders?"

"Stake out Maverick's place and watch for Bronsky and MacCabe as well as our slippery Dr. Maverick. But if Bronsky and MacCabe end up there first, I don't want them taken until the doctor appears and we arrive."

SOUTH OF SUN VALLEY, IDAHO

Robert finished a shower and dressed before returning to the living room of the cabin to find Kat dozing in the one easy chair. The lights were off in the small room, and without a fire there was a distinct chill in the air. Outside, the porch light was on, illuminating the heavy snowfall and emphasizing the feeling of mountain isolation.

Robert sat quietly on a small chair, but Kat snapped awake with a start.

"It's okay," he said, holding out his hand to calm her. "It's just me."

She shook her head to chase away the cobwebs, then rubbed her eyes as she sat up and smiled at him. "Are you hungry?" she asked. "The good doctor's got a well-stocked pantry."

"So, we eat Maverick's food and make ourselves at home?"

She nodded. "FBI business. He'll be compensated."

"By the way, I, ah . . ." Robert began, "hate to tell you, but there's only one bed in this place, and no couch. So, I guess . . ."

Kat left his implied question unanswered as she stood and turned to walk into the bedroom. She surveyed the pine furniture, aware that Robert had followed and was standing in the door.

"Ever hear of a bundling board?" she said as she turned to him.

He nodded suspiciously, his eyes darting between the bed and her. "Yes. Early American thing. If you had to sleep an unmarried couple in the same bed . . ." He stopped, discerning her meaning.

"Very good," she said, walking across the room to park her bag under the window. "The family would put a large board down the middle of the bed, and the two were prohibited from putting arms, legs, or other body parts across the divider."

"So, instead of either of us sleeping in a chair in the living room . . ."

She nodded. "That's right. We can use a bundling board, without the board."

Robert was smiling. *A bit too much,* she concluded. "Cut it out," she said.

"What? What am I doing?"

"You're thinking wanton thoughts."

"I am not. I'm . . . I'm merely grinning."

She sat on the bed beside him, but not touching. They looked at themselves in a wall-mounted mirror. "Okay, ground rules," Kat said, turning to him. "We're still in the middle of this nightmare."

"I know that."

"It's just about dark outside, we don't know when or if Dr.

Maverick is going to show up, nor whether Jordan will make it, and the other side could show up any minute. I slept in the van before we ditched it at the airport, but I'm still exhausted."

"We should sleep first," Robert agreed.

"Raid his refrigerator, then sleep," she said. "I'm having trouble thinking clearly. I have the sick feeling we're sitting ducks, but I'm convinced Dr. Maverick has answers we need desperately, and this is our best chance to find him."

"Agreed."

She was holding up an index finger. "I . . . just want you to understand . . ."

"What, Kat?"

"That in a different place and time, this would be a real temptation."

"Temptation?" he said, feigning puzzlement.

"You know what I'm talking about," she said.

Robert sat back, looking at her, his eyebrows climbing. "You were thinking of . . . fooling around with *me*?"

"Oh, stop it, Robert!" There was a small laugh, and he took it as encouragement.

"Why, that prurient thought never crossed my mind," he said, with no conviction, his eyes and smile betraying him.

"Sure." She smiled for the first time in hours. "I've been running around in a skirt too short for *Baywatch,* and you've only been reminding me all day how sexy I looked."

She jumped up from the bed and turned to him, offering her hand. "Let's go raid Dr. Maverick's pantry, Robert. Then I'm going to see if he has a spare parka."

"To wear outside?"

"No. To wear to bed."

"Why? Are you cold?"

She shook her head slowly, biting her lip with no hint of a smile.

"No. Just the opposite."

ANDREWS AIR FORCE BASE, WASHINGTON, D.C.

"We're ready for an immediate takeoff, Mr. Secretary."

Jordan James glanced behind him at the murky, rainy vis-

age of the 89th Airlift Squadron's presidential ramp at
Andrews. The last-minute call for one of the Gulfstreams to
fly him to a meeting in Sun Valley had been honored with
typical efficiency, but takeoff hadn't been possible, they
said, before 2 A.M. The jet and the crew were ready for the
nearly six-hour flight when Jordan reached the base.

"Thank you, Colonel," Jordan said. "Let's get moving."

The acting Secretary of State climbed the stairs and
handed his briefcase to the steward before heading for one
of the plush swivel seats, his mind consumed with what lay
ahead. The mission was indefensibly personal but unavoidable, with Kat's life hanging in the balance.

SOUTH OF SUN VALLEY, IDAHO

An impromptu dinner finished, Kat got up and moved in
awkward silence toward the bedroom, aware that Robert
was hanging back and pretending to straighten up. There
was a tiny gas-log fireplace in the corner, and she turned it
up before walking to the window to stand and admire the
silent snowfall some more.

"Suppose he might still show up tonight?" Robert asked
from across the room.

"No," she said, shaking her head without looking back.
"It's snowing too heavily and it's too late. He won't get here
before morning. If then."

"Good" was the quiet reply.

Robert came up behind her and gently placed his hands
on her shoulders. She said nothing for a few seconds, then
moved his hands away.

"Out of bounds," she said softly, still facing the window.

"Sorry." He chuckled, unprepared for her taking his
hands and moving them forward to encircle her waist.

"There," she said. "That's where they belong."

Robert held her lightly, almost in disbelief as Kat turned
around in his arms to face him, her hands rising to caress his
face, and draw his mouth to hers.

BOISE AIR TERMINAL, BOISE, IDAHO
NOVEMBER 17—DAY SIX
3:00 A.M. LOCAL/1000 ZULU

Jordan James stirred and came awake slowly as the commander of the Air Force Gulfstream stood beside him.

"Mr. Secretary?"

He was a major, Jordan noted, but he looked too young to hold such a rank, let alone command an aircraft with a cabinet official aboard. Jordan sat up, momentarily puzzled at the aircraft's lack of motion.

"The weather was substantially below minimums at Sun Valley, Sir. We've landed in Boise to wait it out. The weather should come up before sunrise."

"What time is it, Major?"

"Three A.M. local, Sir. We're perfectly snug sitting right here on the ramp, if you'd just like to snooze some more, or we can get you a room somewhere . . ."

"No." Jordan shook his head. "I'll stay aboard. I don't want to press you, but I need to get there as quickly as possible."

"Yes, Sir. I'll let you know when we can leave. I suspect it won't be long."

Jordan thanked the pilot and swiveled around to look out the window at the private aircraft terminal next to the Gulfstream. His attention was drawn to the cold group of men huddled around the base of a large single-engine float plane, a Cessna Caravan.

Now, how can a float plane land on—oh, retractable wheels on the bottom of the floats. But where the devil are they going at this hour? Fishing trip, I suppose.

Arlin Schoen zipped up his parka against the cold and pulled himself up the short ladder from the right float into the cabin of the single-turboprop Caravan nodding to one of his men already aboard.

The man inclined his head toward one of his compatriots still on the ground and looked at Arlin. "You're sure Jerry can handle this aircraft?"

Schoen nodded. "The Learjet was beyond his training, but this one's easy. If we need to, we can dispose of the charter pilot."

SOUTH OF SUN VALLEY, IDAHO

The insistent ringing of the satellite phone finally penetrated the dream she was having about something already forgotten, and Kat's eyes fluttered open to the predawn darkness of the room.

The ringing had stopped. Had she dreamed it?

She moved slightly, wondering what was entangling her, and remembered with a warm rush the previous night, personified by the male whose body was molded to her backside, his arms still around her, his hands cupping her breasts. A digital clock on the bedside table read 6:25 A.M.

Kat slipped away from him slowly, hating the disconnection as she put her feet on the cold floor and padded naked to the bathroom, trying to think of priorities. She turned at the bathroom door and looked outside through the bedroom window. The snow had stopped, and a clear, star-studded sky arched overhead. She wondered if she'd missed a call from Jordan. Obviously he hadn't made it in, but where was he?

Robert was snoring lightly. He turned onto his back, but

remained asleep as she tiptoed around the far side of the bed, enjoying the rich scent of him as she leaned over to kiss his neck and wake him up.

"Wha . . . ?" He woke with a start.

"The bundling board didn't work," Kat said.

"No?"

"No. I was a bad girl."

He smiled, reaching up to touch her face. "The heck you were."

"But we have to get professional now and get dressed," she said, whipping the covers off of him with one sudden motion.

"Hey! Has anyone called?"

"No, but it's inevitable, and I want us to be ready."

Less than 200 yards away, in the back of a rented utility vehicle, a lone figure raised himself cautiously above the window line and examined the images in his night vision binoculars. A light had gone on in the bedroom of the cabin, and now one in the kitchen, and the figure in the SUV turned to his companion huddled in a parka on the floor. "You'd better get your ears on."

The other man groaned and forced himself to sit up and put on a headset, positioning a handheld electronic dish, which he aimed at the cabin's front windows. A tiny beam of invisible laser light shot out to touch the distant window. The host unit recorded the precise distance of the unit to the window and measured every minute variation of that distance as the windowpane vibrated to the sounds from inside. An embedded computer translated the results and fed an audio signal to the headset.

"What are they saying?" the man with the binoculars asked.

"They're talking about eggs and bacon and where everyone is."

"Who, for instance?"

"Us. And someone else."

"Dr. Maverick, I presume."

The man shook his head and hunched over, waving the

first man to silence as he held one of the earphones close and closed his eyes to concentrate, then sat up, muttering under his breath. "Good grief! Schoen is gonna have a cow!" The man looked over at his partner. "Guess who's coming to breakfast?"

"Who?" his companion snapped. *"Who?"*

"Only the Secretary of State."

The headlights of a car appeared at the end of the road behind them and both men ducked out of sight until it passed. The pickup camper was plowing its way slowly down the snow-covered lane, the driver a dark shape in the left front seat. As the men in the SUV watched, it seemed to slow in front of the Maverick cabin, then accelerate again, turning out of sight at the far end of the road to disappear.

For a split second, Kat thought she heard the click of something metallic somewhere in the cabin, but she could see nothing amiss. She looked at Robert across the tiny kitchen table and shrugged.

"What?" he said.

"Not important," she answered. "I thought I heard—"

The sudden noise of the back door slamming open in their faces caught them both unprepared as a stoutly clothed figure burst into the room with a gun in his hand.

"FREEZE!" The voice was male, deep and menacing, but shaking as well.

Kat and Robert sprang to their feet simultaneously, hands in the air, as the figure slammed the door closed behind him and moved to one side of the kitchen, his eyes wide, his gun hand literally shaking.

"Who the hell are you?" he demanded.

Kat looked at him carefully. "Dr. *Maverick*?"

"Who wants to know?" he snapped.

"Agent Kat Bronsky of the FBI. If you'll let me, I'll get my ID."

The man said nothing as he studied her, then glanced at Robert. "Who's he?"

"I'm Robert MacCabe, a reporter for the *Washington Post* and a survivor of the plane crash in Vietnam several days ago."

Dr. Thomas Maverick shuffled sideways toward the living room door and glanced in before waving the gun at Kat. "Where's your ID?"

"In the . . . in your bedroom, Sir."

"Get it," he ordered. She complied quickly, and he studied the badge and laminated card. He tossed it on the kitchen table, still fingering the gun, his eyes darting wildly between the two of them and the front door.

"Okay. I guess I believe you. The *Washington Post* thing is too bizarre to be made up." He motioned them back to the chairs.

"Dr. Maverick, would you please stop waving the gun at us?" Kat asked.

He glanced at the .38 in his hand and nodded, then turned and pulled up another chair. "I'm sorry. I saw you in my house, and . . . didn't know who you were."

"Doctor," Kat said, softening her voice. "You seem spooked. Is someone chasing you?"

He ignored the question. "Tell me why you're in my house, please."

"Did you know Walter Carnegie?" Kat asked, and noticed the instant reaction of fear ripple across the man's face.

"Why?"

"Because he told us to find you."

"Walter is dead," Dr. Maverick said simply.

"We know," Robert said. "He was my friend."

Thomas Maverick sighed and shook his head.

"We need," Kat interjected, "we need to start at the beginning. We have a lot to tell you, but I suspect you have even more to tell us."

"We need to get out of here. We can talk for a few minutes, but then we've got to go. It's not safe."

FRIEDMAN MEMORIAL AIRPORT, HAILEY, IDAHO

The blue and white Air Force Gulfstream taxied clear of the runway and moved gingerly over the snow-packed surface toward the small commercial terminal, where a car waited in the dark, its exhaust curling around the rear and wafting through the gentle snowfall in the snowy scene.

Jordan James gathered his briefcase and overnight bag and wondered if he should order the crew to stay. There was an Air National Guard facility at Boise, and they were going to wait there, a plan Jordan decided was sufficient. Even if he found Kat immediately, it would be a few hours before they were ready.

When the engines were stopped and the forward stairs lowered, one of the crew raced off to verify that the driver was the one retained to take their VIP wherever he needed to go. He returned to the airplane to help the Secretary off.

"Sir, the major says to just call that cell phone number and we'll be here within two hours. We'll be waiting in Boise."

"Understood. See you shortly."

The crewman saluted smartly and raced back into the Gulfstream, raising the stairs as the pilots started the engines.

"Where to, Sir?" the driver asked.

"Hang on a second," Jordan replied. "I have to call and find out." He pulled out the slip of paper with the number of Kat's satellite phone and punched it in, relieved when she answered on the first ring.

As they left the airport road, the Gulfstream roared overhead and turned to the west, its lights marking its progress as it sped away, soaring over the beacon of an inbound aircraft maneuvering for landing.

The Cessna Caravan slowed as the pilot turned on final approach and lowered the small landing wheels beneath the twin floats.

chapter

45

Kat finished speaking and sat back in the kitchen chair, studying Thomas Maverick's features. He was a bear of a man, carrying close to 300 pounds on a six-foot-three frame, his face wreathed in a full beard of reddish brown and his head almost devoid of hair. He was a physicist, he'd told them, with two decades of experience in the world of "black" projects such as the Stealth B-2 bomber and others he still wasn't free to discuss.

Dr. Maverick was rubbing his head, his eyes carefully alternating between Kat and Robert as he considered what to say.

"Okay. First, understand that I will not go to jail for talking about *my* project. However, I'm not muzzled with respect to other projects for which I haven't signed secrecy oaths. And . . ." He held up a finger and stared at Robert. "One ground rule, Mr. MacCabe, is that this is all deep background. You ever use my name or expose me as a source and, truly, I'll find a way to hurt you. Understood?"

Robert MacCabe caught the steely glint of Dr. Maverick's eyes and knew he meant every word he said. He nodded immediately. "You have my word."

Dr. Maverick nodded. "Very well. I think someone official's trying to find me for the same reason you were. They think I know more than I do."

"One thing first," Kat asked. "Assuming you're not Walter Carnegie's deep-throat source, do you have any idea who is?"

"No. None. He wouldn't tell me, but whoever it is, he knew this field."

"You mentioned black projects," Kat began.

"I never worked on lasers or beam weapons. Do I know unofficially of a black project regarding laser weapons? Yes. Did it include vital defense research into pulse beam, particle beam, charged particle, and other electromagnetic weaponry? Absolutely. Has it made several contractors very wealthy? Yes. Has the nation benefitted? Immeasurably. But are the projects sufficiently accountable to anyone but the project managers? In most cases, yes. But exceptions can occur. That's what I believe happened with the antipersonnel laser research."

"What? The managers lost control?"

Dr. Maverick shook his head. "No, the project developed a life of its own beyond congressional or even Defense Department control, thanks to three men in particular at the top who are quite bright, but devoid of a moral sense of what they should be doing for their country. I've seen a project go out of control only once before, but this one folded into another dimension, effectively disappearing from government oversight."

"I'm not sure I understand," Kat said, watching him get up to make coffee as he talked and periodically looked out the window.

"First, you need to understand that black projects are inherently vital to our country, and they usually work very well. To develop one, it takes billions of dollars and thousands of people. The majority of the workers are civilians, like myself, willing to work in complete secrecy on narrowly defined components of a whole we do not understand and are prohibited from speculating about, in order to build something like the F-one-seventeen stealth fighter, or the Btwo bomber. In the case of antipersonnel lasers, there was an accident in testing a few years ago that I'm not supposed to know about. It destroyed the eyes of a young technician who was a nephew of the President's chief of staff, who was, and is, a very moral and humane individual. The outraged chief of staff learned the purpose of the research and convinced the President to cancel it and prohibit any such work in the future. But in doing so, the President—who was roundly despised by the defense establishment, as you know— threatened to pull several billion dollars of revenue away from the prime contractor on the black project involved."

"So the contractor, or the black project, defied the ban?"

Dr. Maverick turned and held up an index finger. "No. Nothing that dramatic. The Pentagon rallied around the contractor and then rewrote and redirected the project so that no money or momentum was lost, but they were simply to apply their scientific knowledge and research to other, nonprohibited military applications of laser weapons. In reality, the project managers lied even to the Secretary of Defense. I know, because a good friend of mine was highly disturbed about it and had to confess it to someone. He left the project, had a nervous breakdown, and now teaches physics at a forgettable high school somewhere for a pittance."

"So," Kat asked, "and please forgive the interruption— they kept on with the antipersonnel side?"

He nodded. "Oh, they did new stuff, too, but they shifted the anti-eyeball research into a black hole within a black project, with plans to outlast the President."

The coffeemaker had finished its cycle and, after Kat declined, Dr. Maverick poured a cup for Robert and himself before sitting back down.

"MacCabe, are you familiar with the Sputnik Syndrome?"

"I'm . . . familiar with Sputnik."

"There are many versions of the principle. Pearl Harbor is another. In other words, in order to spark a unified determination to develop a weapon or a military capability, there has to be a substantial threat. If the threat doesn't already exist, and you're the national leader who knows it's needed, you may have to invent it. That's what I'm convinced Franklin Roosevelt did by sacrificing Pearl Harbor to get us in the war in time to win it. That was also what Sputnik did for our space program, and our military abilities in space."

"So you're saying—" Robert continued.

"I'm saying that up until the past few months, there has been no credible threat out there that anyone was developing anti-eyeball guns for use against military or civilian targets, and thus no reason for the new President to overrule the old ban."

Kat had been listening in silence. She sat forward suddenly. "Wait. Are you implying that this black project will benefit from having their stolen prototypes used against civilian airliners?"

Dr. Maverick smiled. "Think about the predictable response when these mysterious crashes are revealed as being caused by such lasers. Publicly, there will be a call for an international ban on research. Privately—secretly—we already have advanced technology and can press forward to dominate the science while pretending to adhere to our own international ban. In addition, we'll also be ahead in developing solid defenses against such weapons. We'll order thousands of weapons produced and stockpiled, and more research done, in order to be ready if someone violates the ban. We did the same thing with biological and chemical weaponry."

"And the contractor survives."

Dr. Maverick nodded. "The contractor survives, in the best interests of the country."

"So this black project may have helped lose those weapons?"

He shook his head. "Not directly. But if antipersonnel laser weapons were stolen and sold on the black market, as Carnegie suspected, the black-project managers would know two things. One, they were early prototypes and quite limited versus what could be developed later. And two, it would only be a matter of time before some military or terrorist group used one and created a new Sputnik Syndrome, thus rescuing them from the shadowy netherworld of project shutdown."

"We think," Kat said, meeting his eyes, "that Walter

Carnegie made a good case that the U.S. government may be engaged in a frantic effort following the SeaAir crash to cover up the theft of those weapons, because they said nothing and did nothing for so long. But you're implying the black-project managers may not have wanted anything done about the theft."

"They may not have even reported the weapons were stolen, Agent Bronsky," Dr. Maverick said. "This may be less a cover-up than an embarrassed nonresponse."

"Then, who do you think," Robert began, his eyes darting between Kat and Dr. Maverick, "is chasing us?"

Dr. Maverick raised his bushy eyebrows and glanced around again, paying particular attention to the living room windows. "The terrorists who stole those weapons would be the most likely candidates, but . . . I don't know. Look, you can't work in the black-project world without getting a bit paranoid about our own security. I mean, who's chasing whom? A bunch of suits have been ricocheting around Vegas looking for me, according to friends. Are they terrorists, or are they our own people?"

"What do you mean, Doctor? Security people? I can tell you they aren't FBI."

He licked his lips and looked out the rear window before answering. "I don't know. But someone was obviously scared enough of Walter Carnegie to kill him."

"You know that for a . . ." Robert began, but Maverick was shaking his head no.

"I only know that Walter would never kill himself. Look, can we get out of here? I don't mean to be inhospitable, but I'd prefer to close this place up and go. I was only coming by for supplies when I spotted the light."

Kat was drumming her fingers on the table. "Dr. Maverick, are you familiar with Jordan James?"

There was no particular reaction other than mild surprise, she noticed. He nodded after thinking for a few seconds. "Yes. CIA director a few years back, right?"

"Yes, but now acting Secretary of State." She filled him in on their relationship before looking at her watch. "He should be arriving here in a few minutes."

Maverick looked startled. "What? *Here?* My house?"

She nodded.

"Why?"   •

The sound of an engine and the crunching sound of tires on snow reached their ears simultaneously, the headlights showing through the window of the living room.

She watched as Jordan left the backseat of the car and walked quickly to the front door, buttoning his heavy overcoat. The car remained in front, its driver leaving the parking lights on and the engine idling as Kat introduced Jordan to Thomas Maverick and Robert MacCabe.

"I need to talk with you in private, Kat," Jordan said, as they stood awkwardly in the tiny hallway. "If you folks will excuse us for a few minutes . . ."

She borrowed one of Dr. Maverick's parkas and motioned Jordan through the back door. The first hint of dawn was lightening the sky to the east, but the woods behind the house were still dark and secluded. The blanket of new snow absorbed their voices. They walked in silence for about a hundred feet to one side of the cabin before Kat turned to him. "What is it, Uncle Jordan?"

He chewed his lip for a moment before responding. "Kat, I know for a fact there's a renegade group within the FBI working for Nuremberg. Whoever they are, they've been seduced with the promise of untold riches."

Kat unconsciously leaned away from Jordan, her eyes wide, remembering her impassioned defense of the Bureau. Robert was just a reporter. But this man was not only like family, he was a high-ranking official of the U.S. government. Loyalty to the Bureau alone couldn't dismiss the force of his words.

Kat shook her head. "But how, Jordan? Why? And for what?"

He patted her arm. "Human nature requires bad apples, Kat, and the old adage that everyone has a price is distressingly true. The Bureau is no exception."

"You're saying—" she began. "Wait a minute. You're saying there's a faction of how many?"

He shook his head. "At least two or three, and they're

probably fairly high up. The cooperation they're providing includes support such as IDs, the creation of agents that don't exist, giving these fake agents the intelligence information they need, and probably communications interception. That's why every call you made to Jake Rhoades was fed immediately to those who were trying to silence all of you. Precisely what this Nuremberg group is going to demand, none of us knows, but they're incredibly well financed, and they've bought their way into the Bureau. I know that's hard to accept, Kat, but you must."

She was breathing rapidly, her mind racing to get a logical grasp of what he was saying and how it could happen.

"As we speak, Nuremberg's agents could be closing in on this place. We've got to get you, and Mr. MacCabe, and Dr. . . . Maverick, was it?"

"Yes."

"All of you back to my Air Force jet. They're waiting in Boise for me to call. As long as you're under my protection aboard that jet, they won't touch you."

"Why not?" The question had popped out of her mouth, bypassing the normal filter of respect and deference she felt for Jordan James.

He hesitated before replying, as if startled by the question. He stopped patting her arm for a moment, then resumed. "Because, Kat, there is a vast difference between attacking a civilian airliner and attacking one of the presidential fleet. The former will get a unified response of governmental and law enforcement determination to capture and prosecute, but the latter will unleash the fury of the U.S. military. Only the certifiably insane among terrorist organizations would engage the latter."

She nodded. The explanation largely made sense.

"I decided there was no one I could fully trust to come get you other than myself," he said. "That's why . . ."

Kat grabbed his sleeve and motioned for silence. She was looking intently toward the road in front of the cabin. In the growing light of dawn, she could just make out the dark shape of the Lincoln sedan that had brought Jordan as it idled in front.

"What?" he asked in a low voice.

"Sh-h-h!" she replied, kneeling down for a second and pulling him with her, her eyes riveted on the car. "Your car," she whispered.

The front door of the car closed and a figure slid behind the wheel.

Maybe the driver got out for a moment, she thought.

But there was movement around the back of the car. Two figures, in fact, dragging something down the road and into the trees. With a start she realized they were dragging a body. Jordan James stiffened beside her as he, too, realized what they were seeing.

"Jordan, stay here. I'll get Robert and the doctor out of there."

"Then what?" he asked.

She shook her head and took off in a crouch toward the rear of the house. He saw her go in, watched several lights go out in the back, and more come on in the front of the house before realizing that the three of them had slipped out the back door and were running toward him, carrying their bags. As they reached James's position, Robert finished fastening the hooks over the zipper of the oversized coat he had borrowed.

"Who are they?" Dr. Maverick asked, panting.

Kat shook her head. "I don't know, but what's behind your place? Any roads or police stations or anything?"

"No. Nothing. About a mile from here there's a small shopping center, but it's too far to walk through the woods."

Another vehicle had turned the far corner of the road and was moving toward the house, slowing as it came. It stopped a hundred yards away, behind another parked vehicle, and killed its lights, but no one got out.

"Reinforcements," Kat whispered. "It may not take them long to figure out we've left." She turned to Dr. Maverick. "Does anyone around here have a car we could appropriate? And is there another way out of here?"

He thought for a few seconds, then pointed to the other side of the cabin. "Through that patch of woods, there's a house with a detached garage that has a small snow tractor—a Sno-Cat, I think they call it. It can seat six people. But I don't know if it'll start, and we'd have to break in."

"Would the owner be around?"

"No. Not this time of year. He spends November and December in France."

"Let's go," Kat replied, letting Dr. Maverick move out first.

The lock on the garage was stout, but the screws on the hinge were weak enough to wrench free with the handle of a rake, and there was enough room for all four in the cab. Kat jumped behind the wheel, relieved to find the ignition didn't require a key.

"How do we get out of here?" she asked as the engine rumbled to life.

"Right turn out of his driveway."

The answer momentarily stopped her. "That would take us past your house!"

"No other way . . . oh! Of course. It's a Sno-Cat. Turn left. We'll crush a few gardens, but there's another road about three hundred yards in that direction."

"I'm going to keep the lights off," Kat said, slipping the machine in gear and moving out of the garage. "It's getting close to sunrise anyway."

The sound of an engine in the predawn quiet caught the immediate attention of Arlin Schoen as he crouched behind one of the rented Suburbans. He lifted a small radio transceiver to his mouth. "What is that?"

"Don't know," the answer came back. "It's a block or more away. Sounds like a road grader or snowplow."

Schoen thought for a second, studying the bright lights in the living room of the Maverick cabin. He lifted the radio again. "How many do you see inside the house now?"

"Ah, at the moment, maybe one. Hard to tell. I see no movement."

"Anyone talking?"

"No. They're probably whispering."

"Anyone watching the back?" Schoen snapped, standing bolt upright.

"No. We can see the back door through the front windows."

"They've left, you idiots!" Schoen growled, and turned to the others. "Get in! Head for the sound of that motor." He raised the radio to his mouth again as he climbed in. "Move in on the house. Now! Report back."

The engine of the Suburban roared to life and the lights came on. The driver fishtailed away from the side of the street and accelerated as much as he dared. The headlights were picking up nothing as they crested a small rise on the other side of the cabin and followed the road to the left, braking hard to avoid sliding through a grove of trees at the end.

"This is a damn dead end. Where's that sound coming from?" Arlin Schoen asked, leaping out to stand on the running board and listen. The engine could be heard in the distance ahead, moving away, but also to the right.

He jumped back in and slammed the door. "Turn around! Turn around! There's got to be a road over there."

The radio crackled to life as they roared past the house again. "Ah . . . you were right. There's no one inside."

"Find MacCabe's damned computer and follow us!" Schoen barked.

"There's a larger road just beyond," Thomas Maverick said. "If we get to it and go a couple of hundred yards, we can go across meadows toward the town."

"Which way to the airport?" Kat asked.

"Same way."

"What are you thinking, Kat?" Jordan asked.

She turned partially in his direction as she kept the machine moving steadily forward. "Can you call your Gulfstream back? I've got my phone . . ." she offered.

Jordan pulled out a small digital cell phone. "I've got one." He dialed in the appropriate number and made the necessary arrangements, then disconnected.

"They'll be here in an hour and a half."

Kat glanced at him with a stricken look on her face. "That won't be soon enough."

SOUTH OF SUN VALLEY, IDAHO
NOVEMBER 17—DAY SIX
9:20 A.M. LOCAL/1620 ZULU

The driver of the Suburban was sweating as he turned around at the third snowy dead end and accelerated back toward the one road he was sure of.

"Hurry, dammit!" Schoen barked, as he sat with his nose practically against the windshield, his eyes searching for any sign of the tracked vehicle they were trying to intercept.

"Probably a snowmobile of some sort," the driver said.

There was no response from the right seat.

They rocketed down the feeder road and skidded to a halt just past another turnoff. The driver threw the Suburban into reverse, backed up, and turned onto the road. His headlights caught the glint of something crossing a half mile ahead.

"There they are!" Schoen muttered, his hands opening and closing around the Uzi he was carrying. "Go! GO, GO, GO!"

"I'm *going*! There're limits, you know," the driver replied.

"It's a Sno-Cat," Schoen said, watching the machine move off the right side of the road and accelerate toward a grove of trees, and open fields beyond. The driver skidded to a halt where the tracks crossed the road into the adjacent field.

"Follow him!" Schoen demanded.

"We'll get stuck."

"DO IT!"

The driver cut the wheels to the right and moved into the ditch, where the Suburban sank instantly up to the running boards in snow, its wheels spinning uselessly.

Schoen was already out, leaping into knee-high snow and struggling to run in the direction of the accelerating Sno-Cat. It was obvious he couldn't catch it, but he could stop them with a lucky shot. He made it to the first tree and used it as a platform, taking careful aim with the snub-nosed weapon before squeezing the trigger.

The chilling impact of multiple bullets pinging into the metal in the back of the Sno-Cat was unmistakable. Kat glanced in the rearview mirror, looking for the source of the shots. She jammed the accelerator to the floor and turned to the others. "Stay down!" she yelled, struggling to be heard over the engine. "Everyone okay?"

"Yes," Robert answered, surveying the others and turning to look out the back. "I think they got stuck in the ditch. I see the headlights, but they're not moving."

"Dear Lord," Dr. Maverick was saying to himself. "I've never been shot at."

"The airport's ahead, maybe a mile," Kat said. "I can see the flashers."

"They'll know where we're going, Kat," Jordan said, his face ashen.

She was nodding. "If they're in the ditch, it'll take time to radio for help. Maybe we can scramble the local sheriff."

Jordan was shaking his head. "No. This group will have covered that angle."

Kat glanced at him in alarm. "What? Bought off the sheriff?"

"Neutralized him, somehow."

"Your jet won't be here for another hour, Jordan. We have to do something."

Robert was leaning between them from the backseat. "Kat, we're sitting ducks in this thing. It took those slugs because he was firing low, but this is thin metal around the cab."

"I know it," she said, correcting their direction as the vehicle lurched to the left.

"So what do we do?" Robert asked gently, almost in her ear.

"We can hide—or find another plane. Quickly."

"Hiding won't work," Robert said.

She looked around at him, then at Jordan and Dr. Maverick. "You're right. We commandeer a plane. Hang on. I'm going to run this machine flat-out."

Arlin Schoen held the radio to his lips and kept his voice under control. "We'll leave this car and use yours. Just get here. We've got them now."

He pocketed the radio and safetied the Uzi before wading back through the snowdrifts to wait at the side of the road. It would take the other Suburban less than three minutes to reach him, he figured, and perhaps another ten to drive the circuitous route to the airfield. But there would be no place to hide. With the exception of their chartered Caravan, the airport had been all but deserted. He turned to his driver and motioned him over. "Bring the guns. Hurry."

"Robert, I just remembered something," Kat said as they bounced violently over a patch of rough ground and stabilized. The airport was less than a mile distant.

He leaned forward. "What, Kat?"

"Don't ask me why I just thought of this. But in Walter Carnegie's file that we downloaded?"

"Yes?"

"He said the Air Force had stonewalled his requests for information about a test they were running off Key West with an old F-one-oh-six drone the day and hour the SeaAir MD-eleven went down."

"I read that. What about it? You think it's connected?"

She shook her head while looking back at the rearview mirror, half expecting to see headlights bouncing across the field after them.

The landscape was clear behind them, no vehicles or people in sight.

"I don't know," she replied. "But that business jet we flew wasn't stolen until after the MD-eleven went down, so it wasn't the firing platform. They could have used another airplane, but what's been bothering me is, Carnegie said the air traffic control tapes around Key West showed no other aircraft in the area. That means not one but two airplanes are missing from the radar tracks. The one that fired at the MD-eleven, and whatever Air Force aircraft was working with the F-one-oh-six drone."

"I don't understand," Robert said, aware that both Dr. Maverick and Jordan James were listening intently.

"Well, they don't fly a target drone aircraft unless there's someone up there to shoot at it. So, there should be another radar track from the Air Force craft, and according to Carnegie, there wasn't. Second, there should be a radar track of some sort on the aircraft that shot the laser at the MD-eleven."

"Maybe the Air Force craft was a stealth fighter. An F-one-seventeen, or something new," Robert said.

Kat steered the machine around the end of a gully and accelerated again. "No, I mean—well, yes, that's possible—but . . . what if there was another aircraft up there, not a stealth, and it purposefully wasn't using its transponder? Carnegie said the FAA tapes showed an intermittent target."

"Kat, that's the road we came out on. We'll have to cross it," Robert said.

She nodded. "I know. If there's a fence, we'll just plow through it."

"Okay."

"What is a transponder, Kat?" Dr. Maverick asked.

"A little black box," she said, "that electronically listens for an incoming radar beam from air traffic control. When it senses one, it sends an answering burst radio transmission back to the same radar site with altitude and identification information, so the controller knows who you are and precisely where you are."

"And without it?"

"Without it, or if you purposefully turn it off, all the controller can do is look for what we call a 'skin paint' target. Just the raw radar beam bouncing back to the antenna from the metal of the airplane. That's what military stealth technology prevents. The skin of the aircraft absorbs the radar beam so nothing bounces back, and, without a transponder, they're essentially invisible to radar."

"But a normal airplane without a transponder will still show a skin paint target to the controller?"

She nodded. "Usually. Like a shadowy, intermittent target, which were Carnegie's words. So why would an Air Force test aircraft turn his transponder off?"

Robert tightened his grip on an overhead handrail as they bounced over a small depression. "Kat, what are you thinking? That the F-one-oh-six was involved?"

She glanced at Robert as they neared the road. There were no signs of cars coming in either direction. A barbed wire fence loomed ahead of them, and she gestured to it. "Hang on."

The Sno-Cat plowed easily through the wire, and climbed onto the road and off the other side as she steered across the grounds toward a row of hangars.

"What am I thinking? They use F-one-oh-six drones for target practice. So who was shooting at this one, and why were they trying to stay hidden from radar? We know it wasn't a stealth, because a stealth wouldn't leave an intermittent target."

"Wait," Robert said, shaking his head. "You mean, who was shooting at the drone, or who was shooting at the MD-eleven?"

Kat looked at him. "What if it was one and the same, Robert? What if the test went bad and they got an airliner instead?"

In the growing light of dawn the flight line looked deserted at first. There were rows of light aircraft and a few light twins, all of which had obviously been out all night in the storm. Only a Cessna Caravan on floats at the other end of the field appeared to be free of snow.

"Okay, everyone. Time to borrow a bird."

"How about the float plane?" Robert asked.

"Possibly. Those are easy to fly."

"You don't want to get close to that one," Jordan said in a firm voice.

"Why?" Kat asked.

"It was in Boise when I left. Now it's here, as are a bunch of assassins."

Kat braked to a halt. "Oh, Lord. You think they came in on that?"

Jordan was nodding. "Count on it."

She looked around quickly, spotting a hangar with its doors partially open. She let out the clutch and accelerated toward it, trying to make out the type of aircraft inside. Something large with high wings that were a shadow through the upper windows of the hangar. *An Albatross!*

She stopped and jumped out to peer into the hangar, returning in less than thirty seconds. "This will have to do."

"Can you fly it?" Robert asked, raising his hand suddenly before she responded. "Never mind. I don't want to know."

"We don't have a choice," she said.

Robert and Jordan jumped from the Sno-Cat and hauled at the hangar doors, pushing them open slowly as Kat ran the snowmobile inside and parked it to one side. She grabbed her handbag and motioned to Dr. Maverick to follow, then ran to the right rear side of the huge amphibian. The ladder was down and she scrambled up, racing to the cockpit to turn on the master switch and check the fuel. *Thank God! Almost full tanks.*

The cockpit side window was open. She yelled to Robert and Jordan. "Hurry with the doors and get in. Pull up the ladder behind you."

Checklist. There has to be a checklist. Kat searched rapidly through the papers in a side pocket, and retrieved a laminated checklist. She ran down the Before Starting Engines portion, locating the applicable switches and finding the primer for the two big radial propeller-driven power plants before turning on the switch and checking to make sure all three of the men were aboard.

She engaged the starter, holding her breath as she jockeyed the throttle slightly and waited. Two, three, four times the huge prop on the right rotated. She was considering priming it again when the cylinders began to fire, slowly, then in a smooth sequence. Kat adjusted the fuel mixture and started the left engine.

"Fasten in, everyone. Robert? Come up here with me."

"You're sure about this, Kat?" he said as he launched himself up into the bucket seat and fumbled for the seat belt.

She nodded. "Of course I'm sure. And if you believe that, I've got some swampland in the Mojave I'd like to talk to you about!"

"That's what I was afraid of."

"Find their damned tracks!" Arlin Schoen jabbed a finger in the direction of the north taxiway as the Suburban changed directions and raced over the snow-covered concrete.

"There are the tracks!" one of the men said, pointing ahead.

"They're hiding. Probably inside one of these hangars," Schoen said. "Good. That'll make it easier to—"

He trailed off as they rocketed around the northeast corner of the hangar and saw an Albatross come shooting through the open doors, its ample wings rocking as the pilot steered the craft toward the runway. From their angle, they could see nothing of the pilots or occupants.

The driver braked to a halt in confusion. "What now, Arlin?"

Arlin turned around, looked at the open hangar, and shook his head. "No. They didn't have enough time. Drive into the hangar!"

The Suburban's driver accelerated through the open doors and screeched to a halt by the empty but still-idling Sno-Cat. "Godammit!" Schoen snarled. "Turn around! They're in that aircraft."

The driver fought the wheel as he backed and then shot forward, floorboarding the vehicle to give Schoen a closer firing platform.

"Get on the runway! Get in front of them!"

To reach the end as a pilot would for a normal takeoff, the

Albatross would have had to taxi north several hundred yards. But whoever was steering the amphibian wasn't following the rules. It bounced across the snow-covered ground between taxiway and runway and turned on the runway, its engines coming up to takeoff power. "We're not going to make it, Arlin," the driver said.

"Try! Floor it!"

"I am."

Schoen toggled the right side window down and leaned up and out as he cocked the Uzi and aimed at the plane's tires, firing a burst that went wild when the Suburban lurched off the taxiway in angled pursuit of the accelerating craft. Again he fired, trying to walk the bullets toward the wing to get the fuel tanks, but nothing happened.

The Albatross was accelerating away from them, moving at more than fifty knots as the Suburban's driver tried to match speeds. The roughness of the plowed snowpack on the runway forced Schoen back inside.

"Forget it. Get to the Caravan. We'll get them in the air."

The bone-jarring trip across the snow-covered grass to the runway and then down its washboard surface had been brutal, but the big World War II–vintage amphibian lifted clear of the surface at a sedate ninety knots with the engines screaming at full power. Kat pushed the nose over slightly to gain airspeed before fishing for the landing gear lever and pulling it up. She turned almost due south, checking the round gauge on the front panel called the artificial horizon, as well as the airspeed indicator, making sure she kept it right side up.

Engines. Throttle back, set the prop pitch. I'll have to estimate. I have no idea what settings to use.

"Where do we go, Kat?" Robert asked.

She glanced at him and smiled briefly. "Boise, if I can find it."

"Why?"

"Safety in numbers, I suppose. There's an Air National Guard base at the airport, and Salt Lake is too far south."

She kept the aircraft climbing, looking for a passage

through the mountains to the west in the growing light. She spotted the pass she was looking for and banked toward it, leveling the aircraft just high enough to clear the ridge, then nosing it over and staying close to the mountainous terrain.

Kat pointed to the rear. "I threw my purse down in the back, Robert. See if you can get the satellite phone out and call the police in Boise, and the Air Guard. Get them ready to protect us when we land."

"How long? An hour?"

"At least," she said.

The Hailey Airport manager, alerted to an inbound Air Force Gulfstream, had arrived in time to see the visiting Albatross roar into the air, followed by a Caravan on floats. The occupants of the Caravan had thrown something on the ramp as they left, and the manager drove to it, unprepared to find the crumpled body of a man in a pilot's shirt, lying in a growing pool of red.

chapter
47

"I can see them to the south," Arlin Schoen said to the member of his team who could fly, as the Caravan climbed in pursuit. "Get as high as you can but stay with them."

"We're faster, Arlin, but not that much."

The Albatross's turn to the west was a lucky break. They altered course to intercept the lumbering amphibian and followed it for nearly ten minutes before Schoen tapped the pilot on the shoulder again. "Bring me to his left and stay high so they can't see us."

Kat was breathing easier as she sat back to survey the engine instruments. She gave a small prayer of thanks that the weather was clear. Her eyes had just focused on the airspeed indicator when it suddenly exploded in a hail of bullets.

The slugs were stitching their way through the side window from somewhere above and behind. She rolled the control yoke to the right and kicked the rudder hard in the same direction, wheeling the big aircraft out of the way.

More staccato impacts, this time somewhere on the wing. She rolled out of the turn, looked to her left, and was startled to see the Caravan hanging in the left window. Its right side door was open and two figures with guns crouched there.

She rolled left and pulled up sharply, glancing at the only remaining airspeed indicator on the copilot's side. The Caravan pilot yanked his craft up as well, pulling away just in time, but the shooters still had the Albatross in their sights.

More bullets found their mark on the left engine.

Kat felt the big aircraft yaw dangerously to the left as number-one engine lost power. There was a large red feather button on the overhead for each engine, and she punched at it, hitting it on the second try. She jammed the right rudder pedal forward as the prop streamlined with the wind and the Albatross righted itself. She was searching for the other controls to shut off the fuel when Robert's voice reached her. "Kat! We're on fire on the left!" She could already see the orange light of flames cascading from the left engine and smell the stench of burning fuel and oil.

"See if you can find the engine fire extinguisher button!" she called.

Robert searched the overhead panel as she looked left again, spotting the floats of the attacking aircraft above and to the left. To the right, a narrow mountain valley opened up less than 2,000 feet below, and she wheeled the Albatross in that direction, throttling back the right engine. She spotted a substantial river running through it that she could follow. They were less than 1,000 feet above the ground, and she kept descending, leveling a few hundred feet above the trees. She pushed up the right engine again, fed in corrective right rudder to compensate for the absence of power on the left wing, and checked to her left.

The sky seemed empty.

"Robert. Check the right."

He stopped looking for the fire extinguisher and looked to the right and up. "Nothing there, Kat!"

Bullets stuttered through the fuselage, this time behind them. The plink-plink-plink of the powerful slugs as they punctured the metal skin was unmistakable. She banked sharply left and pulled up, once again exposing the Caravan on the left. But this time the pilot anticipated the maneuver and hung back, close enough to shoot but far enough away to simply follow as she tried unsuccessfully to outmaneuver the more maneuverable aircraft.

The Albatross was heading for the rising terrain on the west side of the valley. She banked sharply to the right to follow the valley again, knowing the Caravan would stay on her tail. More bullets hit them, and a muted cry came from the back. There was no time to look back. As the fire grew, Kat's confidence sank; she knew the Albatross was simply too big, too heavy, and too damaged to outrun the smaller, turbine-powered craft.

Suddenly the right engine began running rough just as Robert, who had been watching out the right side, yelled, "Kat, something's wrong. Look at the engine!"

Kat stole a quick glance, and her stomach froze at the sight of a dark stream of oil covering part of the cowling. A check of the oil pressure gauge told the tale.

She looked ahead in the valley, spotting a small dam and a lake beyond. The dam was moving under the nose, and the far end of the lake looked too close to accommodate a large amphibian.

I've got no choice!

"Hold on! I'm putting it in that lake!" she yelled, turning her head as far as she could to yell the same warning to Jordan and Dr. Maverick.

The right engine had begun to sputter as she jammed the yoke forward in a stomach-turning near-zero-G excursion. She yanked the right throttle to idle and found the flap handle, pulling it full down as she aimed for the water, gauging her altitude above the surface by the shoreline.

Too fast! she thought as she pulled hard just over the surface, stopping the descent and slowing, letting the nose come up as it settled toward the water.

The end of the lake was coming up rapidly. There was no power to climb, a raging fire on the left side, and no way to slow anymore. She thought of the landing gear too late, just as the fuselage touched the surface.

The Albatross kissed the water at first without slowing, and she tried to pull the yoke back to raise the nose and spoil the lift, as she'd seen seaplane pilots do. But the hull wasn't far enough into the water, and the Albatross obediently climbed back into the air twenty feet above the surface.

The end of the lake and the bank were less than 500 yards away and coming up fast. Kat relaxed the back pressure and let the Albatross settle heavily into the water. The hydrodynamic pressure sucked the hull down as she yanked back again, this time achieving a cascade of spray and deceleration as the plane slowed.

But they were still moving far too fast at the end of the lake. Traveling at more than sixty knots, the Albatross slammed into the shoreline with the nose up. The fuselage screeched in protest as it slithered up the shallow embankment and spent its remaining energy on a grove of sturdy fir trees, which, one by one, progressively separated the burning left wing from the fuselage, causing the right wing to dig into the ground and spin the fuselage to the right.

"Come around and land. Quickly!" Schoen ordered his pilot as the Caravan flew over the wreckage of the Albatross.

The pilot wheeled around, extended the flaps, and pushed up the prop RPM, setting the aircraft into the water toward the middle of the lake. He dropped to a sedate speed and aimed for the spot where the Albatross's tail jutted into the forest.

Fed by leaking aviation gasoline, the burning remains of the Albatross's left wing and engine suddenly exploded, but the force of the explosion merely chewed into the ruined tail section of the aircraft.

Schoen motioned to the man in back to check his weapons before turning to the pilot. "Bring me to shore just to the left and beach her until we finish this. Shut it down, secure it, and follow us."

The impact of the collision with the trees had slammed Kat's head into the instrument panel, but not enough to knock her out. She shook her head and looked at Robert as the detached left wing exploded somewhere behind them. He was wiping blood off his face, but seemed okay otherwise.

"We've . . . got to get out of here," she began. "They'll be landing."

Robert unstrapped and stumbled through the cockpit door before turning back to help Kat out. They saw Dr. Maverick kneeling beside a prone Jordan James. "He's been hit!" Dr. Maverick said, his voice an octave higher than normal.

Kat moved to Jordan, finding his eyes open and his chest soaked in blood. "Oh God, Uncle. What happened?"

He took a breath and shook his head. "Not . . . that bad, Kat, I think . . ."

She opened his shirt and saw a major entry wound on the right side of his chest just below the rib cage, the bleeding steady and serious. "Can we move you? We've got to get out of here."

The whine of the Caravan's turbine engine could be heard outside as Kat and Robert and Tom Maverick struggled to lift Jordan James through the main door to the ground. "My pistol's in my handbag," Kat said to Robert.

"I'll get it and a first-aid kit," Robert answered.

They laid Jordan in front of the wreckage, by the nose, and Robert scrambled back into the aircraft. He jumped out again with Kat's handbag and the first-aid kit. Kat grabbed her purse and pulled out her gun as Robert knelt beside James with the kit.

The click of a powerful gun being cocked reached their ears at close quarters, and Kat looked up to see Arlin Schoen step from around the nose.

"Drop it, Bronsky," the slightly accented voice commanded. She looked into the expressionless face of the man who had tried to pick her up in Portland.

"This is an Uzi," he said. "You won't even get one shot off before it rips you to pieces. Put it down." His men, guns at the ready, moved up to stand beside him.

She sighed and laid the gun on the ground.

"Kick it over here," he ordered.

She complied, pointing to Jordan. "Do you realize who this is?"

Arlin Schoen smiled thinly. Two others were at his side,

weapons at the ready. "Our esteemed acting Secretary of State? Of course. How are you, Jordan?"

"What?" Jordan replied as he winced in pain.

"Oh, come on, Mr. Secretary. As one of the directors of Signet Electrosystems, I'd think you would remember me. After all, we've talked many times."

Kat looked from him to Jordan in confusion. "Jordan, you *know* this man?"

Jordan James took a ragged breath and looked at Schoen, ignoring the question. "So what are you planning to do, Schoen, kill us all?"

"Of course" was the reply. "What else can I do now?"

Kat knelt at his side. "Uncle Jordan, what's going on here?"

"MacCabe? Doctor?" Schoen said, gesturing with the gun. "Sit behind Miss Bronsky, please. You people have been an extraordinary pain in the ass. You thought we were trying to kill you, when all we wanted, Mr. MacCabe and Miss Bronsky, was to retrieve a vital piece of classified research stolen from us by a man named Carnegie, whom I believe you knew." He smiled a serpent's smile at Kat and Robert.

No one answered.

"You two gained access to the disk we need. If MacCabe hadn't been so efficient in getting away in Hong Kong, perhaps we wouldn't have had to shoot down his flight."

"So you're admitting to mass murder?" Kat said.

He ignored her and continued. "Oh, by the way, I didn't introduce myself. I'm Arlin Schoen, director of security for Signet Electrosystems Defense Research. I have the responsibility for keeping the vital American secrets away from irresponsible people such as Carnegie and you, Mr. MacCabe. Agent Bronsky's involvement I can more or less understand. She thinks she's catching crooks, and ends up stealing classified material. And Dr. Maverick, over there, has a big mouth."

"What is Signet Electrosystems?" Kat asked, breathing hard.

"You're insane, Schoen," Jordan said suddenly.

"Possibly," he replied. "But my job was to protect this project."

"Uncle, what is he talking about?"

Her heart sank when she saw tears in Jordan's eyes. He was in agony. "I tried to stop him, Kat."

Arlin Schoen turned to the armed men standing beside him. "Go ahead and kill them. I'm not in the mood for confessions." He turned and walked under the huge right wing, now broken and drooping.

"Schoen?" Jordan called out, summoning all his strength. "I've got the whole story on paper . . . and in the hands of . . . third parties, ready to blow up in your face. You hurt or kill any of these people, or me, and the whole thing will be exposed."

Arlin Schoen turned around. "Clever ploy, Jordan, but I know you better than that. You've served ten presidents. You'd rather die with your reputation intact."

"Can you take that chance, Schoen?" James asked with difficulty. "If I'm telling the truth, you'll end up . . . in a gas chamber, and the project . . . as well as the company, are history. All of it's there. The botched test firing, the cover-up of the MD-eleven shootdown, all of it. And there are four others out there . . . who know the details."

"Bullshit. There is no document because you never expected this to happen, James. And we've already taken care of those other four witnesses, despite Miss Bronsky's attempts to hide them."

"What are you talking about?" Kat asked in alarm.

"I wrote fifty pages of details and . . . names and documents, Schoen," Jordan began, and stopped to cough and gasp for breath, ". . . as soon as I realized you were trying to kill Katherine."

"If you did"—Schoen shrugged—"we'll find it."

"Impossible. You'll never be able to stop it."

"Well," Schoen replied, "I suppose we'll just have to take that chance."

"Or . . . you can let all of us live," Jordan continued, "knowing that we'll all keep quiet because you're still out there."

Arlin Schoen sighed and turned away, sidestepping a growing pool of gasoline under the wing. He laughed sarcastically. "I'm beginning to see why you've lasted so long in Washington, old man." He turned back to Jordan. "Okay. Let's see. I refrain from blowing your head off and you won't talk because you go to jail if you do. I let MacCabe walk, and he's going to refrain from blowing the cork on this because you asked him to? Give me a break. He'd have his super-liberal, Pentagon-hating national desk on the line in ten minutes and spill his guts. But how about this, James? I kill the rest of them, spare you, and you *still* have to keep quiet because you're guilty as sin. In fact, let's have some fun with this. You seem very fond of Miss Bronsky, there, so what if we start dismembering that cute little blond piece of ass in front of you? How far would I have to go before you'd tell me just where you hid such a document? Rape her in front of you? Cut off her breasts? Shoot her in the spine?" He glowered at Kat. "Nice hairdo, Bronsky. Had me fooled in Portland."

"If you've killed the others," Kat said quickly, "where were they? Where did I hide them? I think you're bluffing."

Thomas Maverick and Robert MacCabe had both been working to stem Jordan James's bleeding. Ignoring Kat's question, Arlin Schoen looked at them derisively and turned to walk back under the wing, gesturing for his men to join him. When they reached him, Schoen swung around and fastened his eyes on Jordan.

"No, I think you're lying, James. And it's a real shame you and these three were all killed in a plane crash in Idaho and burned beyond recognition. "Fire on my command. READY."

"This is a fatal mistake, Schoen," Jordan said, his voice raspy.

"Fatal for you, of course," Schoen replied. "AIM."

The gunmen drew a bead on the four of them. In her peripheral vision, Kat saw Robert's right arm moving up.

"By the way, Bronsky," Schoen added, "the name of the place is Stehekin."

Kat felt her insides run cold. She opened her mouth to

protest when a loud pop sizzled away from Robert's direction and the phosphorescent streak of an emergency flare shot forward into the pool of fuel beneath the wing, igniting it instantly.

A wall of searing gasoline-fed flames erupted between the gunmen and their targets, surrounding them in seconds. The gunman on the right of Schoen let out a hysterical yelp as the flames ignited his pants. He stepped backward and tripped into a pool of burning gasoline, screaming for help as his body exploded in flames.

Robert scooped James off the ground in one fluid motion and yelled to Kat and Thomas Maverick to follow as he raced for the safety of a grove of trees.

Arlin Schoen heard his man's scream and ignored it. He lunged for a small pathway along the fuselage not yet engulfed in fire, with his other gunman right behind him. Before they could reach safety, the trigger finger of the burning gunman involuntarily tightened, and a fusillade of bullets ripped through the fuel tank above.

The monstrous explosion fragmented the wing, the fuselage, Arlin Schoen, and the remaining gunman, spraying flaming shrapnel in all directions. Some of it whizzed harmlessly over the hollow Robert had found, followed by the staccato sounds of large shards of sheet metal and other assorted parts clanging and clunking their way back to earth. The stench of burned hydrocarbons stained the air.

It seemed like minutes had passed before Kat dared to look. What had been the broken fuselage of an Albatross was now a hulk of burning, smoking wreckage indistinguishable as an aircraft. Through the flames and smoke she could see the Caravan sitting undamaged at the water's edge, its cabin empty.

"Robert?" she called out.

"Right here," he answered slowly.

"What was that? What happened?"

"I found a signal flare pen in the . . . first-aid kit. Looks like a fountain pen. It was all I could think of."

"It was brilliant," she said.

"Agent Bronsky?" Thomas Maverick raised up from

where he'd been examining Jordan James. "The bleeding isn't slowing."

Jordan's eyes were open as he clutched his chest and tried to clear his throat. Kat moved to him, feeling helpless. "Don't try to talk, Uncle Jordan."

James shook his head. "No! I must . . . tell you this. Is he dead? Schoen?"

She nodded.

He nodded in return. "Good. He and Gallagher were crazy. They . . . they decided there was no price too great to pay to protect the project."

"The project?"

"Yes. Project Brilliant Lance. Lasers designed to blind and kill. Deep black project. I invested my life savings in Signet Electrosystems, Kat. When I left CIA, I thought . . . it was the last assignment. I . . . thought they were a good company, and they had this . . . this incredible fast-track black-project . . . contract. It was supposed to be the greatest defense coup yet."

"Before the nephew of the White House chief of staff lost his eyes?"

Jordan nodded, coughing and wincing. "I was on the board. No one formally told me the . . . development was . . . continuing off the books. But I knew it. The arrogance of . . . an old intelligence hand. 'We know better than . . . this stupid President.'"

"Then the weapons *were* stolen?" Kat asked.

He shook his head, looking at Robert and Thomas Maverick, both of whom were kneeling beside him. "There was no theft. I just let you . . . follow that . . . conclusion."

"And . . . no leak in the FBI?"

He shook his head no.

"Who is Gallagher?" Kat asked.

"Signet's CEO," he replied.

She looked at him in silence for a few seconds. "Schoen mentioned a botched test firing, Jordan. Was the SeaAir crash an *accident*?"

"Yes," he said. "They were . . . doing another . . . secret test series with an even more powerful version, and someone in . . . a C-one-forty-one from . . . Wright-Patterson got trigger-happy and fired . . . at the wrong radar target."

"So, the Air Force—"

"Not involved directly. We had the power . . . to order everything sealed." He stopped and gasped for breath a few times. "They pulled the test dummy from the F-one-oh-six later . . . that day, expecting a normal test hit. They knew about SeaAir, but no one . . . on the test team had any suspicion at all they . . . might have been involved, let alone responsible. But they looked at . . . the dummy, and there was no laser hit, even though the cameras showed one. They enlarged the video image . . . of what the laser *had* hit, and . . . two commercial pilots came up, sitting in the crosshairs a microsecond before the laser destroyed their eyes and probably killed them instantly." He looked at Robert. "This is an incredibly . . . powerful weapon to be shoulder-fired. It's . . . it's a fearsome thing. I've always worried . . . one could fall into the wrong hands."

"Such as a terrorist?" Robert prompted.

Jordan nodded.

"But there is no terrorist organization, is there, Mr. Secretary?"

Jordan James looked up at Robert. "Oh, yes, there is. Signet Electrosystems. We . . . became efficient terrorists, even inventing our own name, Nuremberg."

"Schoen's idea?" Kat asked.

Jordan nodded with great difficulty and gasped for breath before continuing. "Under the leadership, if . . . you can call it that, of our . . . CEO . . . Larry Gallagher."

"Mr. Secretary," Robert MacCabe said quietly, "are you saying that Schoen did all the rest of this, the Meridian seven-forty-seven, the airport shutdowns, the Chicago crash, just to cover up that accident?"

Jordan closed his eyes for a second and appeared to drift off, then came to. "I . . . didn't know what he was doing. I only knew from a phone call to him that something was about to happen . . . as a diversion. I tried . . . dear God, I really tried to stop them." He closed his eyes and panted for breath, forcing himself to stay conscious. "Gallagher . . .

wouldn't listen. Schoen . . . wouldn't. I . . . suspected Australia or Hong Kong, or even Tokyo, which . . . is why I had you pulled off that flight, Kat. I knew he was crazy by then. I just didn't . . . I . . . I wanted . . . you not flying . . . a few days. Didn't know . . ."

He drifted off. Kat could see the pool of blood growing beneath him.

"He's bleeding out, Kat, and there's nothing we can do," Robert said.

Jordan opened his eyes again, fixing his gaze on Kat's tear-streaked face. She was sobbing silently as she watched his eyes flutter open again.

"I'm so sorry, Kat. I've destroyed your faith . . . and fifty years . . . of government service. I just . . . didn't know what to do. I'd gone from . . . six hundred thousand net worth to twenty million . . . all in stock, and it would all be gone. But . . . if they had time to clean this up . . . I thought . . . thought . . ." He coughed violently and recovered. "I . . . was too busy being rich and sage. Even had a school . . . named for me."

"Who was Schoen, Jordan?" Kat asked softly.

"Former . . . East German. Defected in the sixties . . . then CIA. Rewarded for service to the U.S. with a . . . naturalized citizenship. I hired him at Langley."

"I'm so sorry, Jordan," Kat said. Tears flowed down her cheeks, but he had already drifted into a coma.

She sat with him for nearly a half hour as his life ebbed away. A Medivac helicopter summoned by satellite phone sat down nearby at last, but too late.

Kat stood shakily as Thomas Maverick climbed into the helicopter that would carry Jordan's body back to Hailey, Idaho. "Robert, we've got to get to Stehekin," she said.

"You think there's any chance he was bluffing?" Robert asked.

She took a deep, ragged breath and looked at him, shaking her head no. "There's no way he could have guessed the name Stehekin if they hadn't found them. I'd like to hope they haven't reached them yet, but I know better. At any rate, we have to find out. And I can handle a Caravan."

With an in-flight phone call, a park ranger was waiting at the dock with a car when they tied up at Stehekin. They jumped in and roared toward the cabin.

There was a wisp of steam coming from the roof vent, but no smoke from the chimney as they approached the front door. The ranger briefed them on the false alarm the day before. "A local had spotted the front door open with no one around. I checked things out, glanced around inside, noted the remains of a hummingbird feeder and its spilled red syrup on the porch, and then reclosed the door. Everything seemed okay to me."

Kat tried the door and found it unlocked. She held her gun at the ready as she opened the latch and swung it inward, greeted instantly by the familiar heavy sweet aroma of burned firewood. It was stale, as if the fire had been out for some time.

"Stay here," she told Robert and the ranger, but Robert stepped inside and stopped, leaving the ranger on the porch.

The door to one of the bedrooms was open. Kat strained to see inside as she moved carefully, calling their names and hearing nothing. "Dallas? Graham?"

The creaking of a floorboard ran cold chills up her spine, but she forced herself to keep moving.

"Anyone here? Steve? Dan?"

There were feet visible through the bedroom door, one pair at the end of a bunk, and an arm hanging lifelessly toward the floor from the side of the bed. Kat felt her heart sink as she moved in that direction, knowing instinctively what she was about to find. They were too late. Schoen had found them after all.

"Who're you, Darlin'?"

Kat whirled around to see the source of the familiar throaty voice, her mind in confusion. Dallas Nielson was standing on the porch, a load of firewood in her arms, questioning the young ranger, as Robert raced back out through the door to grab her in a big hug.

"Whoa! Robert! *Robert,* my man!" Dallas yelped, hugging him back.

Kat glanced back at the bedroom in confusion. The feet

and arm were gone, and in their place a sleepy Steve Delaney was standing in the door, blinking at her as Graham Tash and Dan Wade followed. "Kat?"

She felt the tears welling up and struggled to control them, but it was no use.

Epilogue

The managing editor's secretary leaned into his office and pointed at his computer screen. "MacCabe's teaser is in. He says to tell you he likes the idea of a six-part run for the story, he's ready with final copy for the copyright, and he says to tell you he's been asked to do *Face the Nation* and *Meet the Press* on Sunday as the first installment kicks off, and wants to know which one you'd recommend."

"*Face the Nation.* I've always loved Leslie Stahl."

"Leslie's not doing that show anymore."

"In her honor, then. CBS needs the help."

The editor turned to his terminal and called up the copy Robert MacCabe had written for a teaser introducing a series that everyone expected would put him in the running for another Pulitzer.

THE ANATOMY OF A TOP SECRET DISASTER

Somewhere along the way,
Project Brilliant Lance became a monster worthy
of Mary Shelley's Frankenstein.

Washington, D.C.—*Amid a firestorm of public outrage this week stemming from the Signet Electrosystems scandal, the President announced yesterday that he is making virtually everyone in his administration available, including himself, in the growing investigation of how a United States "black" defense project could metastasize into a terrorist group. "Nuremberg," as the security force-cum-pseudoterrorist* *organization called itself, ultimately caused the deaths of hundreds of airline passengers in two separate crashes (an airline accident in Chicago around the same time was found to be unrelated). The revelation that Nuremberg was the creation of the security forces protecting a black project called Brilliant Lance has triggered the resignation of the Secretary of Defense, who technically controlled such projects; the resignation of the director of Central Intelligence, whose agency may have unwittingly protected the effort; and the discovery that over $2 billion of taxpayer funds were spent in the past four years to sustain a project specifically prohibited by executive order.*

While it will take months, if not years, to sort out the full extent of this seismic scandal, much is known already, including the background of Project Brilliant Lance, up through the terrifying flight and subsequent crash of Meridian Flight 5 in the jungles of Vietnam, an atrocity that killed over two hundred passengers, but somehow spared this reporter's life.

This six-part series (starting in Sunday's edition) comprises reporting both from a personal, participatory point of view, and an overview of the anatomy of an American crisis—a crisis now propelling a further erosion of confidence in government.

The fact that Americans could be murdered, an entire industry imperiled, and the ability of the U.S. to respond to genuine terrorist threats seriously undermined is compounded by the fact that many of those involved—and now indicted—apparently believed they were serving the best interests of their country.

In this case, the alleged criminality of those trying to protect Project Brilliant Lance led to the deaths of innocent civilians, dedicated FBI agents, and a beloved figure in American government, perpetual statesman Jordan James (acting Secretary of State at the time he was killed). But these are merely the black-ink statistics in a crisis whose details begin with a single, horrific idea: A military adversary whose eyes have been destroyed cannot fight effectively. That premise, and the horrors it could spawn in future wars, are earning the U.S. cynical condemnation internationally from many countries frantically working on similar capabilities.

How it started, what happened, and where it will lead are the sinews of a tragic story of murderous misconduct veiled in official secrecy—a story every American needs to know, lest it happen again.

(Robert MacCabe's exclusive six-part series begins on Sunday.)